Unbreakable

Blayne Cooper

Spinsters Ink
2006

Spinsters Ink, Inc.
P.O. Box 242
Midway, FL 32343

First published by Bookends Press

Printed in the United States of America on acid-free paper
First Edition

Editor: Cindy Cresap. Technical editing by KG Mac-Gregor and Karen
         Appleby
Cover designer: LA Callahan

ISBN 1-883523-76-1

For the women who make my life richer

About the Author

Blayne Cooper is the author or co-author of a variety of fiction ranging from mystery/romance to outrageous parody. While she enjoys the challenge of working in multiple genres, it's writing about the humor found in every day life that gives her the most pleasure.

The University of Oklahoma College of Law grad loves travel, reading, and spending long, sleepless nights crouched over her computer in search of the perfect words that will make people laugh or weep uncontrollably. She's still looking, but having a great time on the journey.

A rolling stone at heart, Blayne currently resides in the Midwest with her loving spouse, two young children, and Cairn terrier.

Chapter 1

Present Day
Town & Country, Missouri

Slender hands trembled as fingers bejeweled with several rings and one thick gold band poised over the keyboard, hovering with uncertainty. The woman squeezed her eyes shut briefly, tears filling them as she forced down several gulps of air. With a final burst of willpower, she clicked the printer icon at the top her screen, reluctantly acknowledging that the words would be no more horrible on paper than they were on the screen.

"Honey?" a deep male voice called from outside her closed office door. "I'm leaving now."

She sniffed once, blinking back tears, and snatched the paper from her laser printer just as it hit the receptacle tray. Wiping her eyes with a Kleenex she retrieved from the holder on her desk, she slid the paper into the top drawer and answered her husband. "You can come in, Malcolm. Since when do you stand outside my office door and shout?" But this time she was glad of the privacy.

Malcolm Langtree poked his blond head through the door and gave his wife a boyish smile. "Since I wasn't sure whether you were in here or in the library next door and I was too lazy to check both rooms."

She chuckled and watched fondly as her husband trotted into the room, his chipper attitude and the spring in his step running counter to any claim of laziness. It had been less than six months since he'd been discharged from the hospital, and his recovery from a heart attack was all but complete. He was carrying a tennis racquet and wearing a tasteful, pale yellow Polo shirt and crisp white shorts, both of which showed off his tan. She patted his belly, which had yet to take on the softness of middle age that plagued his peers.

He set his racquet on her desk and surprised her by cupping her cheeks and looking her square in the eye, oblivious to the turmoil she'd been in only moments before. "I'm going to win today." He winked. "I just know it."

She laughed and shook her head. "Tucker always beats you, Mal. It's your punishment for spending all that money on those ridiculously expensive lessons."

Malcolm gave her a gentle kiss on the lips before snatching up his racquet and excitedly heading for the door, his tennis shoes sinking into the plush maroon carpet. "It wasn't a waste of money," he protested mildly. "He's on an athletic scholarship, isn't he?"

She nodded, deciding not to point out that their son's tennis scholarship at Webster University would never come close to reimbursing them for the thousands of dollars they'd spent over the years on lessons and camps. Still, the look on Malcolm's face and the pride in his voice when he talked about Tucker was payment enough. And it always would be.

"Did you remember your sunscreen and a towel?" Early September in St. Louis could still be brutally hot and humid.

Malcolm waved a dismissive hand as he stood in her doorway. "We're playing at the club this time." He tried not to look sheepish. "I reserved an indoor court. I'll be home by dinnertime. Now wish me luck at slaughtering our son."

"May you have no mercy," she dutifully replied, already knowing what the outcome of the match would be. Tucker had been beating Malcolm since he was in high school. Nowadays, if the match lasted more than an hour, Tucker was humoring his old man, something Malcolm had yet to catch onto; but was an example of thoughtfulness that, as a proud mother, she cherished.

"Love you," Malcolm called as he jogged down the hall, leaving her office door open, the clean scent of his aftershave going with him.

A few seconds more and she could hear the door to the formal dining room open and close. "Love you . . . too." The words stuck in her throat, the grief over the e-mail rushing back full force now that Malcolm's reassuring presence was gone. She padded to the door in her stocking feet, her shoes still resting under her desk, and locked it, laying her cheek against the cool cherry-wood surface as she thought about what to do.

The housekeeper wouldn't disturb her for several hours, when the heavy-set black woman would come knocking and inquiring whether Mrs. Langtree wanted a cocktail before dinner. She usually did.

A familiar question reared its ugly head. *How could this be happening? Things weren't supposed to end up this way.*

She retrieved the printed e-mail from the drawer and opened a long, heavy-paned window that overlooked the south lawn. She gazed out onto an expanse of towering sycamore trees, lush green grass, and manicured flowerbeds. Heedless of the air conditioning escaping into the hot afternoon, she continued to stare sightlessly.

As the breeze kissed her cheeks, she sorted through the pages of her memory. It was so easy to dwell on the mistakes and tears, the guilt and regret that haunted her now and had for many years. As with every story, though, there was a beginning. She couldn't help but chuckle when she thought of theirs.

It had been golden.

November 1972
Hazelwood, Missouri

"And the Pilgrims and Indians shared a great feast in honor of the cooperation and friendship they'd shown one another. And it's because of their ability to share and help each other that we have this great nation.

And for that and our other blessings, we give thanks."

"Ha!" Jacie snorted, slouching a little in one of the small chairs that filled Mrs. Applebee's third grade classroom. "It was the beginning of the end for the Indians. They were doomed," she said cryptically, stretching out the last word until several other children gasped. "You're not telling everything, Mrs. Applebee."

Most of the children stared at Jacie in utter disbelief, though a few disobedient snickers could be heard from the corners of the room. Half the class dressed in feathers and war paint, the other half dressed like Pilgrims with tall hats and bonnets and big construction paper buckles taped to the tops of their shoes.

The teacher's eyes narrowed. This was only her second week teaching at Armstrong Elementary, and she'd already heard more out of this little girl than she would have liked. Jacie didn't participate much in class discussion; but when she did, whatever she said was bound to be provocative and, thus, disruptive. "I'm teaching you everything you need to know, Jacie Anne Priest. But if you'd rather discuss this with the principal, I'm certain that he'd be more than happy to see you. Again."

Jacie sank a little lower in her seat, the prospect of the principal calling her mother making her cringe. "No, ma'am," she mumbled, not making eye contact.

Mrs. Applebee gave her a satisfied nod and went to her desk to pick up a stack of handouts that included a Thanksgiving word search, tidbits of information on the Pilgrims, and a recipe for pumpkin pie that the children could make with their mothers.

When the teacher's back was turned, a freckled girl with wavy, sand-colored hair covertly reached across her desk and slid a tiny, many times folded piece of paper under Jacie's David Cassidy three-ring notebook. Jacie cracked open the note with the same caution she would have applied to handling a stink bomb. For all she knew it could be a stink bomb. Instead, it was just an ordinary note with uneven letters that read: "Wow!" Next to the words was a carefully drawn smiley face complete with ears and hair and the name "Nina."

Jacie flashed the normally shy girl a triumphant smile, quickly shoving the note into the small pocket at the top of her brown polyester skirt and doing her best to look completely innocent when Mrs. Applebee walked by her with a raised eyebrow. Nina had been in a different second grade class last year, so even though she lived just down the street from Jacie, somehow they'd never really gotten to know one another.

With a tiny, embarrassed smile, Nina glanced away and started fidgeting with a thick pencil.

Jacie absently lifted the lid of her desk and shoved the packet the teacher had given her inside without looking. It took several seconds for her to push aside the many other crumpled papers before the desk would close properly again.

Mrs. Applebee returned to her normal place in front of the blackboard. "Class, I want you to—" The afternoon recess bell drowned out the rest of the sentence, and the children eagerly sprang to their feet, their little bodies all leaning toward the door, poised to bolt on her command. The teacher smiled. Hazelwood, Missouri, was in the throes of a deliciously late and long Indian summer. She couldn't blame the children for wanting to soak up every moment of it. Knowing that no one would be listening now anyway, she indulgently gestured toward the door. "Enjoy recess."

"Yes!" was the collective shout, and within a matter of seconds the children had cleared the classroom and coatroom and were on the playground laughing and chasing each other in circles. A group of boys dressed like Pilgrims lined up against a group of boys dressed like Indians, ready for a rousing game of Red Rover, various revolting epithets being exchanged as they chose spots and linked arms.

As always, Jacie headed straight for the swing set. This was going to be the year that she swung clear over the top and down the other side in an enormous circle, so long as her nerve and the rusty chain didn't fail her.

"Hey, Jacie, c'mere! Please!"

Jacie reluctantly ground to a halt, grumbling under her breath when a skinny boy who had wet his pants the first day of kindergarten and was forever labeled "Stinky" cut in front of her and stole the last open swing. She turned and pinned Gwen Hopkins with an evil glare. "What?" she demanded, her hands moving to straight hips in a move that she'd seen her mother execute a million times.

Gwen was at least two inches taller than Jacie, and she straightened to her full height, doing her best not to be intimidated by Jacie's narrowed, dark gaze. "I wanna show you something."

Jacie groaned, but walked over to Gwen, who was standing alone and leaning against a cement tunnel. "This had better be good, Gwen. I'm going for the world's record highest swing ever this winter. I need to practice."

"You said that last year."

Jacie looked dismayed. "Breaking my arm took months off my training."

Not the least bit interested in Jacie's attempt at everlasting fame, Gwen shoved a piece of paper in front of her face, causing Jacie's eyes to cross when she tried to read it. The paper was a dull pink and was one of the sheets that Mrs. Applebee had passed out to the class just before recess.

Jacie glanced at it briefly, wondering why Gwen was talking to her at all and not busy skipping rope with her best friend, Amy. "So? It's a bunch a names or something from the"—she paused to sound out the word—"Mayflower."

"That's right," Gwen gushed. "That was the name of the boat the Pilgrims came over on."

An indignant expression overtook Jacie's square-shaped face. "But the Pilgrims—"

Gwen held up an imperious hand. "You shouldn't talk about our founding fathers that way, Jacie."

"My neighbor's son told me all about Thanksgiving. His name is Andy and he's home from college in California and he says—"

"My mom says you can't trust people from California. That they're all fruits and nuts."

Jacie blinked. "Huh? What does that mean?"

Gwen shrugged. "I dunno. Anyway, the Pilgrims were heroes, Jacie. There is an entire holiday just because of them. And we get two whole days off of school. So they couldn't be bad, could they be?"

Jacie chewed her lip. Gwen did have a point, but she felt compelled to give her argument one last try. "Mr. Parker's son said they were the beginning of the end of the Indians."

"Maybe," Gwen allowed. Jacie was one of the smartest girls in the class. "But we still get two days vacation," she repeated, as though that said it all.

And for Jacie, it pretty much did. She let out a discouraged breath. "Is that all you wanted to tell me? You could have told me I was wrong after recess, you know."

"Your name is on the list of people on the Mayflower."

Jacie's eyes widened. "It is not. I wasn't even born then, goof." She peered at the fluttering paper again, tucking behind her ear a blowing strand of long auburn hair that had escaped her ponytail. When one of her Indian feathers got in the way, she tucked it behind her ear, too.

"You weren't born. But maybe your grandpa or somebody else in your family was on the boat. Your last name isn't that common. Not like Smith or Hogg or something. If your family was on that boat, that would make you a real live hero, too."

Jacie wrinkled her nose. "How can I be a hero without doing anything?"

"You just can," Gwen announced with utter certainty. "See?" She pointed again and read Jacie's surname out loud. "Priest."

"My grandpa is not a Pilgrim. He's a shoe salesman from Macon, Georgia," Jacie said impatiently, her gaze drifting to the still full swing set. "I really need to go now, Gwen."

It was clear that she was already plotting a way to get that last swing. Everyone knew that was her favorite.

"That's not all." Gwen's eyes darted sideways to make sure that no one was close enough to overhear them. "I'm there, too. Halfway down the page."

Jacie's brow furrowed as she started reading the list.

But Gwen couldn't wait that long. "I looked at the entire list. There are four of us from this class on the list. Four! All girls!" Her excitement was getting the best of her, and she looked as though she might have an accident. "Isn't that neat?"

"I guess," Jacie said doubtfully.

"Audrey! Nina!" Gwen bellowed, startling Jacie and causing her to jump back a step. "C'mere!"

Audrey Mullins stopped dusting off her lucky hopscotch rock long enough to yell, "No way, Gwen. I'm gonna win, so I'm not moving. You come over here." Then, with the skill of a playground master, she tossed her rock, pumping her fist when it landed.

Katy, Audrey's cousin and latest hopscotch victim, had white-blond hair and the knobbiest knees in the entire third grade. She moaned as Audrey successfully navigated the hopscotch board.

Gwen huffed for a few seconds, grumpy that she was being forced to cross the playground but quickly got over it and grabbed Jacie's sleeve, tugging her along as she made her way to Audrey.

Nina, who had been sitting on the monkey bars quietly watching the game of Red Rover, hurried over to the small group. She was equal parts terrified and thrilled that somebody might ask her to play.

"Hi, Nina. I like your sweater," Audrey said, surprised to see that the girl had given up her spot on the monkey bars. She was almost as attached to that spot as Jacie was to the last swing.

Nina smiled, showing off white teeth and a sizeable hole that had once held the last of her baby teeth. "Th-thanks, Audrey." She tugged a little at her burnt-orange macramé sweater; her mother was taking a class.

Gwen looked around again, glad that no boys were anywhere near them. Her voice dropped to a whisper. "I've got something to show you all. It's super groovy, but let's start walking back to class first. The bell is going to ring soon anyway."

The girls all sighed loudly. The best part of the day always came and went too quickly, but if they started back early they could at least be in the front of the line to get back into class and not get the drinking fountain just inside the doorway after one of the boys licked it just for spite.

The girls had just begun to pad toward the building when Gwen inserted herself between Audrey and Katy. "I'm sorry, Katy, but this is private, *secret* business. You can't come with us." Her voice held a note of true regret.

Katy blinked. "Why not?"

"Yeah." Audrey began to bristle at the insult. "Why can't she come?"

"Because she's not on the list," Gwen said between clenched teeth, glaring at Jacie as though she expected her to offer some sort of moral support for her decision.

"She can come if she wants," Jacie said pointedly. "All we're doing is walking back to class and it's a free country."

"Wh-what list?" Nina ventured tentatively, her heart pounding at her daring. All the other girls in the class had gone to the second grade together, and even if they hung out with different groups, they knew each other well. Only she and a handful of boys had been promoted from a different class. And now, even after several months, she still felt, and was usually treated, like an outsider.

Gwen held out the paper as she explained that all of them except Katy had last names on the passenger list. "This means we're special," she finally declared. "We might be real Pilgrims! We're practically famous."

Jacie snorted. "I told you, I'm not a Pilgrim."

"Is your name Priest?" Gwen asked curtly. "If it is, then read it and weep. You *are* a Pilgrim." She turned to Katy. "Sorry, Katy. Schaub isn't on the list. I looked twice."

Katy looked as though she might cry, but she held it in. Tomboys didn't cry like big babies when they didn't get their way. "But I'm cousins with Audrey and her last name is on the list. If she's a Pilgrim, then I am, too. We're related." With a quick hand Katy scrubbed the green war paint from her cheeks, then plucked the white feather from her hair in a showing of Pilgrim solidarity.

Gwen drew in a thoughtful breath, and then tugged her purple, construction paper bonnet a little tighter on her head so it wouldn't blow off. "I don't think that counts, Katy. I think we should make our own club since we're all on the list. Amy is moving to Toledo over Thanksgiving, so I'll have lots more time to play with you all at recess because I won't have a best friend."

"You don't stop being best friends with someone just because you're apart," Audrey said, frowning. She tugged her skirt a little higher on her thick waist.

"True, but I won't be able to play with Amy ever again." Gwen turned to Nina, who was quietly watching the entire exchange with intelligent, interested eyes. "You never play with anyone, Nina. You just sit and watch." Then she addressed Jacie. "And all you do is swing, swing, swing. Even if there *was* a highest swinging record in *The Guinness Book of World Records*," which she doubted, "the people from the book are never going to come to Hazelwood, Missouri, Jacie."

"If I break a world record, they'd have to," Jacie challenged hotly, kicking a rock that wasn't really bothering anyone.

"But wouldn't a club be way more fun than breaking a record?" Gwen glanced at the building nervously, sure the bell was about to ring any second.

"No," Jacie said flatly. "I hate *Mickey Mouse Club* reruns. They sing too much and act stupid."

Miffed, Katy crossed her arms over her chest. "Talent Round-Up Day isn't so bad."

"C'mon, Jacie, let's do a club," Audrey said, loving the idea of being in something special. "It could be fun." Then she gave Gwen a poke in the chest, causing her to drop the pink passenger list. "But only if Katy can be in it, too."

"No way, Audrey." With a scowl, Gwen pinched Audrey's arm, earning a squeal. Then she picked up the list. "Everyone can't be in the club or it will be too big. No boys and nobody off the list. That has to be the rule. And don't hit or poke me again or I'm telling Mrs. Applebee."

"No fair!" Katy protested, with Jacie nodding her agreement. "I want to be in the club. I would be a good member. Maybe they just forgot my name."

"W-wait." A faint voice interrupted them and all eyes swung to Nina. The girl prayed that her stuttering would magically disappear. But, of course, it didn't. "I th-think . . ." She stopped and forced herself to slow down and think about every word, as her mother had reminded her so many times. "I think K-Katy should be able to j-j-join." She exhaled as though she'd just run a mile and then smiled. Everyone was still paying attention. "See?" She pointed to a name on the list at the very bottom. The last name wasn't Schaub, but the first name was Katherine.

"That's my name!" Katy crowed, nearly choking on her wad of Bazooka bubble gum. "I'm *Katherine* Schaub. My name *is* on the list."

Gwen's mouth dropped open. "But your last name isn't on list. There are lots of Katherines."

Jacie and Audrey grinned. "A rule is a rule, Gwen," Audrey reminded. "Katy's name is right there."

Gwen thrust her chin in the air. "Fine. We should take a vote then. And since it's about Katy she can't vote. And since Audrey is her cousin, she can't vote. That leaves me and Jacie and Nina."

"I vote that we let Katy in," Jacie said instantly, "and that we make *her* president."

Gwen stuck her tongue out at Jacie, but she didn't protest. After all, the vote had been her idea. "I solved the mystery of all of us being Pilgrims, so I vote for myself to be president. And for only people with last names from the list should be in the club. Sorry, Katy." She turned to Nina. "Nina?"

Nina gulped and ran a hand through her wind-tousled hair, feeling the pressure and sheer importance of the moment. It was truly up to her now. She looked at each girl in turn, unintentionally lingering long enough so that they all began to sweat.

Jacie gave her the tiniest smile of encouragement and Nina felt her confidence pick up steam. "K-Katy is in. I vote w-with Jacie."

"Yes!" Katy and Audrey hugged and jumped up and down in each other's embrace, Audrey's mop of curly brown hair flopping up and down as they moved.

Just then, the bell rang and a horde of eight-year-olds began stampeding for the door.

"Can I be president after Katy?" Gwen asked loudly, accepting defeat graciously and fighting the urge to step aside and lose her space near the head of the line, despite the risk of being trampled.

"Sure," the girls said, clustering near the door.

Nina smiled. She'd never been anywhere near the front of the line before. Her smile grew. Because of her height, she'd never even seen the front of the line. It wasn't that she was short for her age; Nina had gone to only the first few days of first grade before being promoted directly into the second grade.

Mrs. Applebee opened the door and then, waving the children in, disappeared back into the classroom.

"So what will we do in this club?" Jacie asked Gwen as they entered the coatroom, not even noticing the familiar scent of dust, must, and sweat. She wasn't sure she wanted to be in a club at all. And no way was she going to sing or be in a talent show. No way.

Before Gwen could answer, Bucky Lee plowed past Nina, elbowing her hard. "Out of the way, N-N-Nina," he mocked with a cruel laugh. Several of his friends joined in the taunt, all stuttering "N-N-Nina."

Nina grimaced, feeling a bruise bloom instantly on her ribs. She whirled around with her fists in the air, eyes blazing, but she didn't have to say a word.

Audrey and Katy, each of whom had three older brothers, descended upon two of the teasing boys with the practiced ease of hyenas on the prowl, pushing them hard against the pegged wall and knocking several pair of old galoshes from the rack above the jackets onto their heads. Audrey's attack was clumsier than her naturally athletic cousin's. But her strength and mass made her devastatingly effective.

Jacie launched all of her seventy-five pounds at Bucky Lee, pinning him to the ground and shaking the life out of him by the collar of his shirt before the boy could even blink. He'd recently teased her about her failed world record attempt and this was the last straw. He had this coming.

Gwen stepped in front of Nina, ready to fend off any further attacks, even though she knew her mother would take a strap to her if she tore her last pair of tights. Her face turned the same shade of red as her flaming hair at the thought of having only panties to wear under her dress, but she stood her ground.

Jacie and Bucky Lee rolled around on the floor for a moment, but Jacie quickly regained control. "With teeth like that"—she bared her front teeth and made a chittering sound like a beaver chewing wood—"how can you tease anyone, *Bucky*?" He began to squirm beneath her again, but this time her grip was solid. "Say you're sorry, dog breath," she demanded.

"Sorry, dog breath," Bucky instantly replied, laughing hysterically at his own wit.

"You rotten—"

"What is going on here?" Mrs. Applebee walked into the coatroom to find Jacie with her fist raised high above her head, ready to pound Bucky, and Audrey using her considerable bulk to keep her prisoner from escaping as she administered a wedgie he wouldn't forget for weeks. And Katy was industriously stuffing her chewing gum in the ear of a screeching girl who had the bad sense to join in with the boys' mean teasing.

The coatroom went deathly silent.

Mrs. Applebee blew her heavy bangs off her forehead and grabbed Jacie by the collar, lifting her off Bucky Lee. As she called out the names of the other fight participants, she pointed toward the door with an authoritative finger. They would all be spending the afternoon in the principal's office.

Nina drew in a breath to protest, but Gwen turned around and clamped her hand over her new friend's mouth. "Shhh! If you say anything then you'll probably get in trouble, too. Mrs. Applebee is already really mad."

"B-but it's not their fault and now they're in t-trouble!" Confusion showed in Nina's blue-green eyes. "Why d-did they do that? I can take care of my-myself."

"Because we're a club, silly. C'mon." She guided Nina through the coatroom and back to her seat, which was across the aisle from her own. "I live by Audrey," she whispered. "I can go to her house tonight after school and tell her mom that the fight wasn't her fault. And her mom will tell Katy's mom. Maybe then they won't get into too much trouble."

Nina nodded, liking that plan. "I live by Ja-Jacie." She'd seen the girl walking to school but had never had the nerve to approach her. "I'll talk to her mom, too, if you think I-I-I should."

"Of course you should! The most important part of being in a club is being best friends and sticking together." Gwen retrieved her pencil from her desk and pulled a wide-lined piece of paper from her tablet, readying herself for Mrs. Applebee's return.

An enormous smile lit Nina's face. She'd never had best friends. "Really?" she asked hopefully.

Gwen was filled with pride at how their club had defended one of its own. "Really."

"Wow. This is going to b-be so fun."

Present Day
Town & Country, Missouri

The chiming of the grandfather clock jerked her from the memory, and she stood up and closed the window. She moved to her desk and lifted a photo in a burnished copper frame. It was of five girls in their earlier teens, their slim arms wrapped around each other's waists. Their faces were wreathed in smiles, two of them grinning wildly despite the railroad tracks that were wrapped around their teeth. It had been early summer, she recalled, and the attire was cut-off blue jeans and white muslin shirts embroidered with bright flowers and cut with an empire waist, or peasant blouses made of gauzy cotton.

The mysteries of the world were still theirs to explore and their happiness and innocence showed.

Tears stung her eyes as she slid the photo from its frame, careful not to crease it. She pulled her PDA from her desk drawer and laid the photo in her scanner as she searched for a phone number and e-mail address. When she found them, she moved to her computer and spent a few moments composing an e-mail before picking up the phone.

"Gramercy Investigations," a man answered. "This is Ted Gramercy speaking."

"Hello, Mr. Gramercy, this is—"

"Mrs. Langtree, I'd recognize your voice anywhere." She'd called him the day before, but had rushed off the phone when Malcolm came home unexpectedly.

She cringed, reminded once again of the distinctive, if gentle, Southern twang that she never had been quite able to lose completely and that clearly denoted a lower-class bloodline to St. Louis society.

"I'm glad you called the agency," Ted continued. "It's my pleasure to have the opportunity to work for you. What can I do for you, ma'am?"

She rubbed her temple with one hand, feeling a headache coming on fast. "I just e-mailed you a photograph, Mr. Gramercy."

"I'm printing it now."

She nodded even though he couldn't see the gesture, appreciating his efficiency.

"It's finished printing. Nice photo."

A tiny smile tugged at the edge of her lips. "Yes. It is." She picked up the photo again and studied it, knowing he was doing the same thing. "There is a list of names in the e-mail. They're in the same order that the girls appear in the photograph from left to right. I've also included as much other information about each girl as I could. I'm afraid it's not much."

"And what do you want me to do when I find them?"

She smiled at his use of "when" and not "if." "I don't want you to do anything . . . at least not yet. Just contact me with their addresses and then I'll give you some additional instructions." Pausing, she gently cleared her throat. "I trust that you understand your complete discretion is required, Mr. Gramercy."

"Of course. As far as anyone but you is concerned, I don't exist. I'll e-mail my standard contract back to the same address and be in touch soon."

"That's fine. I'll overnight your retainer in cash. Good—"

"Wait! Mrs. Langtree, you only have four names listed here and there are five girls."

She ran the tip of her finger over each girl's smiling face. "You only need to find four girls . . . I should say women, they're all nearly forty now." A pause. "The fifth girl in the photograph is me . . . in another life. Gwen Hopkins."

Chapter 2
Present Day
St. Louis, Missouri

The phone rang and Katherine Schaub swiveled sideways in her office chair, shifting her unlit cigarette to the corner of her mouth. "Damn communist 'No Smoking' buildings are killing me," she murmured. She glanced at her caller ID box before answering, mindful of the hounds from her credit card companies who had already called work three times that week. Pressing the receiver to her ear, she dropped a manila folder into her outbox and said, "Hey, sweetheart, I was wondering if you were ever going to get back to me." Unconsciously, her hand moved through her white-blond hair, and she straightened the short spikes as she spoke.

"How could I resist? In fact—"

Her lips curled into a slow, coy smile when the words coming from the man on the other end of the phone began to get steamy enough to get her pulse racing. "Yes, you're forgiven," she said gently. "Tonight then?" Her smile broadened and her face took on a dreamy expression. "I can't wait either. Love you, too. Bye." Long after the line was dead she hung up, unable to focus on anything but the vision of a sexy pair of brown eyes. She and her beau had been a couple for more than a year and she still felt like a lovestruck teenager. That was a very good sign.

Finally, she grabbed another file from her inbox and opened it, plucking a pen from the plastic holder that was overflowing with them.

The phone rang again and she grinned.

Without looking, she reached behind her and picked it up, her voice melting into a sexy purr. "Couldn't wait 'til tonight, huh, lover?"

A burst of laughter from the other end of the line caused her to scramble back and look at the phone display. "Toby, you bastard."

"Me?" Toby laughed again. "What did I do, lover?"

"Funny."

"I thought it was."

"What do you want, Toby?" Her tone was a cross between impatience and teasing, heavy on the impatience. "If I want to get out of here before six, I need to get busy."

"Well!" Toby let out an indignant snort. "I'll bet you weren't this grumpy with lover boy."

"Toby."

"Fine. Since you're in such a great mood, I'll cut right to the chase."

Katherine gave a mental groan. "I'm sorry." She reached down and took off her shoes, tucking them under the desk before leaning back in her chair. It had already been a long day and she still had hours to go. "You know what early September is like for me. I'm swamped."

"And don't forget that you're mean because you're giving up cigarettes."

"How could I forget?" Katherine removed the cigarette from her mouth and sniffed the end, taking in the pungent scent of tobacco with a look of unadulterated bliss. "Those bad, bad things," she murmured insincerely. For a fleeting moment she wondered if she couldn't just eat the tobacco and get her nicotine buzz that way. How many calories could tobacco really have? "I just hate them." With the tip of her tongue she tasted the end.

"Uh-huh." Toby's voice was doubtful. "You hate them the way I hate hot dogs and cheesecake."

"Oh, God." Katherine's eyes rolled back in her head. "If I could have all the cheesecake and cigarettes I wanted, sex would be irrelevant because I'd be so satisfied." Then she thought about that for a moment. "Well," she conceded, "I might get horny when the high from both wore off. But only then."

"You'd be too fat and cancer-ridden to even reach your horny parts."

"Ugh." With a look of disgust, Katherine tossed the cigarette on her desk. "Now I know why I stopped dating you. Was there a reason you called? You usually don't call me at work."

"Well, I thought you'd be interested that my nerdiness has finally paid off for you. I hit on the finger."

"In English, Toby, please. We can't all be senior information consultants, aka uber-nerds, for Fortune 500 companies."

"Wow, when you say it that way I sound really important. Will you describe my job like that to my mother?"

"Toby," Katherine warned.

"Fine. Fine. In laymen's terms, after we spoke last month and you told me about your trouble with the credit reporting agencies, I did a little creative account accessing—"

"Hacking, you mean."

Toby continued to speak as though he hadn't heard Katherine's comment. "I put a tracer on your file so that I could peek in on anybody who was peeking in at you. With me so far?"

A nod. "Still with you."

"Earlier in the week you had an interesting hit. I didn't have the time to check it out then, but it stuck in the back of my mind, and so today I did a little digging. Someone has been checking you out, Katherine . . . thoroughly."

Katherine tensed in her chair. "Somebody who?" Her voice rose a notch. "You mean those damned VISA people? God, a little bad luck and a few late payments and they're all over me like stink on shit. I paid my full payment this month!"

"No, not them. That's what caught my eye. It was a smaller company. One I'd never heard of."

Katherine could hear Toby lean forward in his chair.

"Here's where things get interesting. It took me some major digging—this guy is good—but I found that whoever was poking around was logging on from a small local company. And they were using a bogus name and office address to do it." All traces of good humor left Toby's voice. "What kind of trouble are you in?"

Katherine blinked slowly, too surprised to speak. Who would be checking her out? And more importantly, why? Something came to mind instantly, but she dismissed the notion as paranoid and the product of an inflated sense of guilt. "I got a little over-extended. When my meager investments went tits-up last spring, I tried to cover them with cash. And soon the cash was gone too. Things have been rough for a while, you know that, but I'm trying to work my way back."

"On your salary?"

One of Katherine's eyebrows quirked. "Yes, even on my pitiful little office manager's salary."

"I'm sorry, Katherine." Toby winced. "I didn't mean it like that."

"I know." Katherine picked up her cigarette and put it back in her mouth, this time not bothering to fight her urge to chew on the end. "So why is someone checking me out?" She audibly gulped. "What the hell do they want?"

"You sound a little worried for someone who's not in trouble."

She shifted uncomfortably in her chair. "Don't go there, Toby. If you don't believe what I've told you then that's your problem."

Toby knew a "back off" when he heard one. There was something his friend wasn't telling him, but it would have to wait. "Listen, I gotta go. I have a meeting in five. The name of the company doing the digging, and I mean digging, we're talking credit report, tax returns, DMV, bank records, everything, is a local detective agency called Gramercy Investigations."

Anxiously, Katherine searched her mind for even the slightest hint of recognition. "But"—she shook her head a little—"I've never heard of them."

"Well, Katherine, all I can say is that they've sure as hell heard of you."

Present Day
St. Louis, Missouri

"What are you doing here at five?" Jacie's lips thinned as she un-latched the chain on her door, but she pointedly didn't offer an invitation to come inside. She schooled herself in patience as she spoke. "What happened to seven thirty?"

She had just walked in the door from an unexpected trip to the office when her doorbell rang. Her briefcase was still in one hand, a scuffed yellow hardhat in the other.

"Nothing happened to seven thirty. I'm just a little early to pick up Emily."

"Two and a half hours isn't a little early. Listen." Jacie tossed her hardhat and briefcase onto the floor next to the closet, causing the hat to bounce several times on the ceramic tiled floor. She stepped out into the hallway and quietly closed the door behind her. "I don't give a good God damn what you're ready for." Her jaw bunched and released as she tried to control her temper. "It's my weekend with Emily, and that doesn't end until seven thirty tonight. That's our court-ordered arrangement."

Nervously, she peered over her shoulder at her front door and ran a hand through auburn hair that tickled her collar as she consciously lowered her voice. "Don't fuck with me over this." She let her hand drop tiredly, wondering why, after more than two years apart, they were still having the same old arguments. "I've changed my plans twice this month just so you could accommodate your girlfriend's schedule. I'm not changing today. We haven't even eaten dinner yet." Her voice went a little cold. "Deal with it."

"You bitch."

Jacie crossed her arms over her chest. "Takes one to know one."

"I never—"

"Yes, yes, I know," Jacie interrupted, knowing this particular rejoinder like the back of her hand. "Let me save us both some time, shall I? You should have never allowed me to adopt *your* child. What a horrible mistake that was on your part . . . Asshole," she added as her temper flared. "Never mind the fact that we planned having her and went through the months of you trying to get pregnant together. And never mind that I've been loving, raising, and supporting her since the day she was born. The judge clearly made a huge mistake by awarding me joint custody of *our* daughter."

"Don't take that tone with me. This is your fault, Jacie. If you hadn't left us—"

Jacie's eyes flashed. "I left you because you are impossible and we were all miserable. I never left Emily. Don't you dare even say that." Her words were met with a stony silence. "Come back to get our daughter at seven thirty. We're going out for dinner, so don't bother showing up early." And with that, she marched back inside her condo and slammed the door behind her, hearing muffled cursing traveling down the hall. "Goodbye, Alison. You have a great evening, too," she said under her breath, feeling the knots in her stomach beginning to ease now that she was out of her ex-lover's presence. For the millionth time she wondered how one of the worst mistakes of her life could have also produced the best thing in it.

She stepped over to a chair and angrily threw herself down. Her condo was cluttered, but not really dirty, and filled with low, whitewashed furniture and littered with marble coasters. Pale chairs and a large sofa sat atop colorful woven rugs and several watercolors graced the walls. It was the kind of atmosphere where Jacie could sink into the sofa, close her eyes, and put her feet up after a hard day's work. She'd found a home in this small, eclectic building near Forest Park.

Just then a dark-haired seven-year-old bounded out of the kitchen with two cans of RC in tow. "Who were you talking to, Mom?"

Jacie smiled, her soft brown eyes now glittering with affection rather than anger. "Were you eavesdropping again, young lady?" Slender eyebrows lifted as she waited.

"No." Emily scowled, knowing she was caught. "I just heard people in the hall," she explained in a weak voice.

An unexpected chuckle erupted from Jacie as she began unbuttoning her lightweight, denim blouse and made her way toward her bedroom. "Don't worry, sweetheart. I told her that you're staying the whole visit this time. She's coming back in a couple of hours."

"Yes!" Emily pumped her fist, a little dizzy with relief.

Jacie grimaced and laid a hand on her stomach when it growled loudly. "We need food."

The girl nodded eagerly. They'd spent most of the afternoon on one of Jacie's jobsites and then at her office. Lunch had consisted of cheese and crackers from the vending machine and sodas. "I'm starved."

"Thanks for being a good sport about my needing to stop by the site for a while today." Jacie sat on her bed as she unlaced her well-worn work boots before peeling off sweaty socks.

"No problem." In truth, Emily loved to accompany her mom to Priest

Tile & Marble whenever she could. The workmen treated her like one of the guys, teasing her and buying her candy bars when her mom wasn't looking. And Jacie always explained the details of her newest project. Once, her mom had even allowed her to pick tile designs for the hallway of a fancy apartment building on Brentwood Drive. "You can make it up to me by getting us pizza for dinner."

Jacie laughed as she entered her bathroom, leaving the door open so that she could hear Emily over the shower. "Do we ever eat anything besides milk and pizza for dinner on the weekends?"

"Is there anything yummier than cheese pizza?"

"Good point." Jacie shook her head knowingly and opened the shower doors, already dreading the lonely, seemingly endless days between now and their next weekend together.

Present Day
Salt Lake City, Utah

"What do you mean she's getting married?" Audrey Mullins-Chavez grabbed both sides of her own head, fearing it would explode.

Her husband, Rick, looked down at his hands, his eyes wide and uncomprehending. Quietly, he set the phone back on the cradle and dropped down to the bed to bleakly stare at their white popcorn ceiling. "That's what she said. She said, 'I love him, Papa. I'm not pregnant, and we've run off to get married.' They're in Las Vegas and coming home in a couple of days."

"Jesus Christ!" Audrey believed in spontaneous combustion and was sure she was going to be starring in tonight's evening newscast as nothing more than a smoldering pile of ashes on a Berber carpet. "She's gone insane!"

Rick's head bobbed mechanically. "I want to call the police." He whimpered. "But she's eighteen. We can't stop her." His eyes turned to slits. "I want to kill that boy."

Audrey threw her hands in the air and started pacing around the bedroom. At the moment, the room's neutral blue and crème décor wasn't having its intended soothing effect. "I knew we should never have let Tina live until she turned eighteen! Now look what's happened. This is your fault." She pointed an accusing finger at her husband. "I wanted to kill her when she was five and drew that huge picture of a horse in permanent marker on the living room wall. And you talked me out of murder! Bet you're sorry now." She knew she was being irrational, but she couldn't help it.

His brow creased. "I thought it was a pig."

Audrey just waited, tapping her foot.

Rick closed his eyes. "What happened to my baby? I'll tell you what's happened. She's run off with a boy who only two years ago was called 'Stubby' by the entire varsity basketball team." If the students knew how much gossip their principal was privy to, most of them wouldn't be able to meet his eyes in the hallway.

"What the hell sort of nickname is that?" Audrey's brow creased again. "He's six feet four. Doesn't he have all his fingers?"

"Yeeeeees," Rick said slowly. "Uh . . . that's not it . . . exactly."

"Well? Don't play Twenty Questions with me, Rick. I'm not responsible for my actions right now. You might not live through me asking you again."

A slow blush traveled up Rick's neck.

"What's wrong? I—" When realization hit Audrey between the eyes, her face twisted in revulsion. "Oh my God. That's gross! I don't want to know things like that. Ick. Ick Ick! I'm the mother-in-law!"

The corner of Rick's mouth twitched upward. "I know."

Then their eyes met, and they couldn't help but burst out laughing. After a few moments, Audrey's shoulders slumped. "What are we going to do, Enrique?"

At the plaintive use of his real name, he sighed and patted the bed next to him. "What can we do, querida?" He wrapped his arms around his wife's sturdy body and pulled her close, kissing the top of her head. The twenty pounds she'd needed to lose in college had turned into thirty-five over the years. But she was still active and vivacious and, to Rick's eyes, gorgeous.

"We could go to Vegas?" Audrey offered hopefully.

Rick thought about that for a moment. "We could. But who would watch Ricky Jr.?" Their thirteen-year-old was outside playing soccer.

"Your mother could watch him." She began to massage his temples, smoothing back the kinky gray hair there with gentle fingers.

He shook his head. "They were just about to go into the chapel, honey. We can't stop them. We won't make it in time."

Audrey closed her eyes and let out a long sigh. "But they're just babies."

Rick nodded. "Stupid babies . . . who are going to need a place to live. Their dorms are not for married couples."

Audrey's face darkened momentarily. Her head was spinning and she felt sick. "I don't want to take any chances on either of them dropping out of school. You'd think straight-A students would be too smart for something like this. I must have dropped her on her head when she was a baby and just blocked it out." She rolled over until her chin was resting on Rick's chest. "We could turn the attic above the garage into a little apartment and they could live there."

"Can we afford to do any remodeling on top of Tina's tuition?"

Audrey's stomach clenched at the thought of discussing their finances. "I can work some overtime if we can't get a good deal on a loan."

"Mmm . . . ." Unhappily, he began to chew his dark mustache.

Audrey felt a lump develop in her throat. "Did she sound happy?"

Rick blinked at the change in his wife's voice and pressed his lips to her soft curls once again. "She's on Cloud Nine."

Audrey was at a loss. "I don't understand," she groaned. "No one was keeping them apart. They both love school. They see each other all the time anyway. What's the hurry to get married?"

Rick shook his head. "You're asking me? I'm sorry I let her start dating." He took a deep breath, catching a whiff of Audrey's shampoo. "They don't make any sense," he mumbled.

Audrey sighed. "They're in love."

He took a moment to think about what she'd said, then commented. "They're like us. Except you were not a freshman, and I had a real job. God, my poor mama." He slapped his forehead. "I'm going to call her this afternoon and beg her forgiveness." He felt Audrey chuckle, and he knew she was reliving the moment they'd broken the news of their own elopement to his mother.

Audrey shifted in his arms. "Maybe we shouldn't have made our midnight run to Reno sound so romantic." Problem was, their elopement *had* been romantic and whether it was amazing luck or fate, that night had turned out to be one of the best decisions of her life. She had no regrets.

As if reading her mind, Rick said, "Maybe they'll be as lucky as we were."

It took a few seconds, but finally, a dreamy grin split her cheeks. "Maybe." She scooted up and brushed her lips against his.

They lingered that way for several long seconds, sinking into the contact and finding comfort and affection exactly where they knew they would . . . in each other. When they finally parted, they both looked a little less frazzled.

With a groan, Audrey moved off the bed and offered him a hand up. "Why did we have children again?"

"*Jack Daniels?*"

She snorted at his valiant attempt at humor. "Don't be silly. I'm partial to the dark handsome types." She winked at him. "It was Jose Cuervo."

Despite himself, Rick laughed and rolled his eyes.

"C'mon. Let's go take a look at the garage attic."

He puffed out his lower lip as he swung his feet over the bed. But before he stood he reached out and hugged his wife to him, pressing his face into her soft chest and sighing contentedly; he decided not to move from this wonderful spot for a very long time. "Can I still kill Stubby?" he murmured.

Lovingly, Audrey petted his head, returning the embrace. "Not if I get there first."

Present Day
Clayton, Missouri

"Is that the last box, dear?"

"The very last one." Nina held her iced tea to her forehead and allowed the condensation that had collected on her glass to drip down a pink cheek, mingling with a tendril of perspiration. "Remind me never to move again, will you, Mom?"

Mrs. Chilton laughed. "That would be my pleasure."

Nina reached out for her mother's wrinkled hand, stroking the thin, soft skin with her thumb. She gave a gentle tug and scooted over so that the older woman could drop down beside her on the front steps of the old, but well-kept Colonial home. They both sighed and gazed out into a yard filled with poplars as they caught their breath.

Nina's grandmother's death hadn't been unexpected and as per the old woman's wishes, the family home had been passed down not to her widowed daughter, who would never leave her house in Hazelwood anyway, but to her unmarried granddaughter, Nina.

Nights of soul searching and some cajoling from her own very persistent mother, and Nina's resolve never to move back to Missouri had wavered. Then, when her blanketing of the area museums with résumés just to appease her mother had resulted in an offer from the Missouri Historical Society, a large history museum in Forest Park, Nina had bowed to fate and come home. Finally, she admitted privately, it felt like the right time.

The afternoon sky was a bright, pristine blue, and she shielded her eyes from the sun as she glanced around the large yard. "Where's Robbie?"

"The last time I saw him he was in his bedroom unpacking."

Nina frowned. Her nine-year-old son was boisterous, fearless, and rarely quiet. She'd gone far too long without hearing a peep out of him and was only mildly placated by the fact that she hadn't heard a loud crash or smelled smoke yet. "Robbie," she called out as she glanced back toward the house. "Where are you?"

"I'm up here, Mom," a proud voice called from about midway up one of the trees in the yard.

Nina blinked, her eyes widening when she saw the height of the tree. "Shit."

Mrs. Chilton gaped. "Nina!"

"Sorry, Mom." She jumped off the porch and jogged over to the tall tree, her heart beating a little faster as she craned her head and struggled to see through the thick branches and masses of leaves. She heard a creak and her eyes flicked to his slender form, which was about fifteen feet off the ground. "Robbie?"

"Yeah?" This time his response was much quieter as he sensed he was in trouble.

"What are you doing in a tree?"

There were a few seconds of silence as Robbie considered his answer before he said the only thing he could think of. "Climbing it."

Nina rolled her eyes, realizing her question had been a stupid one. "I can see that, Son. But you're going to get hurt." Real worry threaded her voice and her mind flashed to a similar scene and a fall. "Come down."

"Aww . . . C'mon, Mom. I'm not so high. See?" He bobbed up and down on the branch, sending a shower of loose bark down on his mother's head.

"Now, Robbie." She fought the urge to stamp her foot. "I don't want to be taking a trip to the emergency room with you today." *Or ever.*

A few moments later, two sneaker-clad feet hit the ground next to Nina. Robbie wasn't quite up to her five feet six inches, and she figured she had a good couple of years left where she'd still be able to glare down at the boy. She decided to put that fleeting ability to good use. "Do I have to even say it?" She gazed at him expectantly.

He trained his eyes on the ground and sighed. "I guess not."

Suddenly, Nina felt like an ogre. He'd been excited about moving from a condo into a "real" house and finally having a place to play that didn't require a trip to the park. They'd only been here a day and she was already ruining that.

She ruffled his short fair hair and wrapped an arm around him, guiding him back toward the steps and his waiting grandmother. "Maybe we could build a tree house," she offered finally, unable to take Robbie's uncharacteristic silence. "But one that's not too high off the ground," she added quickly.

His head shot up, his eyes sparking with delight. "Really?"

"The neighbors won't like that, Nina," her mother warned gently, knowing full well it wouldn't do any good.

Nina's face suddenly broke into an unrepentant grin, and Mrs. Chilton saw a glimmer of the headstrong girl she remembered. Her museum technician daughter usually kept her rebellious side well under wraps, but it was there all the same, simmering, and something she clearly shared with her grandson.

"They'll live, Mom. And if not they can bite my butt."

"Tsk." Mrs. Chilton gave her a stern look. "I didn't teach you to talk that way, young lady."

Nina and Robbie, who was about to burst from excitement, sat down on the steps. She handed him her glass of tea, and he took a grateful gulp, fishing a few lemon seeds from his mouth after he chugged down the remainder of the glass.

"Piggy," Nina chided indignantly, taking back the glass that now held only a few chunks of ice and a soggy wedge of lemon. "I know I didn't teach you to do that, young man." Nina mimicked her mother's Missouri accent to a T.

Mrs. Chilton narrowed her eyes at her daughter's good-natured impudence.

"Sorry." He smiled impishly, wiping his lips with the back of a dirty hand. "Can I go online and look at pictures of tree houses?"

Nina nodded slowly. "After you wash your hands and as soon as I call and get us hooked back up to the Internet."

He groaned a little. He'd forgotten about that.

"Aren't you going to tell him about your tree climbing fiasco, dear?" Mrs. Chilton reminded her daughter helpfully, ignoring the high-wattage glare she got for her troubles.

"No," Nina ground out, dusting off her hands on her jeans. "As a matter of fact, I wasn't."

Robbie's jaw dropped. "Mom climbed a tree?"

"Don't make it sound like a physical impossibility." Nina gave him a mock sneer. "I'm still in pretty good shape, you know."

"Yeah," he snorted. "Right, Mom."

Nina reached out to tickle Robbie but only felt a wisp of contact as he bolted from the steps. Not to be outdone, she was hot on his heels, and the chase was on. They ran around the yard, circling the streets, and skirting a large hedge for nearly ten minutes before Nina was forced to admit that her days of running like the wind were long gone.

Chest heaving, she stopped in front of her laughing mother and bent at the waist, her dark blond hair, laced with the barest hint of gray, falling into her eyes and sticking on her wet cheeks and neck. "Stop looking at my hair, Mom," she said in a flat voice, not needing to see her mother to know what she was thinking. "I don't want to start coloring it."

Mrs. Chilton unconsciously ran a hand through her own, permanently light brown hair. "You'll be sorry. Remember Bob Barker when he let his real hair color come in? He looked like he'd seen a horrible ghost and aged twenty years overnight. You're a young woman. You don't want to look old, do you?"

Nina sucked in an enormous gulp of air. "Too late. I'm pathetically old."

"Men don't like gray hair."

Nina bit her tongue then addressed Robbie. She was still out of breath. "How do you like my hair, champ?"

He shrugged. "It's pretty."

Nina grinned. "Well, there you go, Mom. *All* the men in my life are happy with my hair."

Mrs. Chilton grumbled something Nina was quite glad she couldn't make out.

Nina motioned her son closer. "I surrender, Robbie."

The boy stopped dancing just out of her reach and stepped forward to pat her on the back, feeling the heat through her thin tank top.

With disgust, she noted that he wasn't even breathing hard and his faced was wreathed in an enormous smile.

"That's okay, Mom. You're pretty fast for an old lady. You nearly caught me." Impossibly, his smile grew. "Not." He began to giggle.

Nina groaned, forcing herself upright to wipe the sweat from her eyes.

Robbie flopped down next to his grandmother on the steps and fished a mostly-melted ice cube from his mom's glass. He stuffed it into his mouth. "Tell me about Mom climbing a tree, Grandma." He leaned forward so he wouldn't miss a single word.

"Mom," Nina whimpered. "Shouldn't you be too senile to remember things like that by now?"

"Hush." Mrs. Chilton reached out and swatted her daughter twice and Robbie squealed in delight at the sight of his mother not only being bossed around, but punished.

"Thanks a lot." Nina winked at Robbie and then rubbed her recently molested thigh before joining her son and mother on the steps. She leaned back on her elbows and crossed her ankles as she readied herself for what she was certain would be a distorted version of her childhood.

"Well, it all started . . ." Mrs. Chilton paused and turned twinkling eyes on Nina. "On second thought," she said, smoothing the fabric of her crisply pressed cotton slacks, "why don't you tell the story? I'm sure your perspective would be far more exciting than mine."

"Fine. Fine." Nina sighed good-naturedly, knowing when she'd been beaten.

Robbie moved to the edge of the step he was perched on and settled in to listen to his mother's clear, melodic voice.

As Nina thought back, she chuckled and then blushed.

Summer 1973
Hazelwood, Missouri

The summer heat was scorching and even in shorts, shoes without socks, and T-shirts, the girls were miserably hot, their clothing sticking to irritatingly moist skin.

Nina looked up into the tree with wide eyes. "Nuh-uh." She shook her head violently. "Sorry, but n-no way."

Katy threw her arms down. "Come on, Nina! You're the lookout. The smallest member of the group is always the lookout. They're lightest and so they can climb the highest. You can tell us if you see Stinky or any other boys."

Usually the girls played in the field behind Jacie's house or in Katy's basement, because her house was the most central to them all. But today the Mayflower Club had gathered at Nina's. They were about to begin their daily meeting when Katy noticed Stinky, a boy from last year's class, going into a house only three doors down. Wanting to ensure the privacy and sanctity of their club, which had an inviolate "No Boys" rule, she had devised a plan under the protective branches of a sycamore tree in Nina's backyard.

Nina glanced at Audrey, who for once was looking quite pleased about being chubby. She scowled. Then she looked at Gwen, who was looking back at her expectantly. Finally her attention turned to Jacie. The slim girl had her hands on her hips again, a sign that would forever mean she was running out of patience and about to blow. Nina sighed internally.

"Why don't I do it?" Jacie said, already reaching for the tree's trunk. "Then we can get on with this meeting. I wanna watch TV later."

Nina rocked back and forth as she considered her current predicament. She could let Jacie go up the tree for her. That would mean, though, that she was nothing more than a puny chicken who would never get any respect from anyone. "No. I think I c-can do it."

Jacie pinned her with a serious, though not unkind look. "You don't have to, Nina."

Nina's insides were quaking, but she did her best to push that feeling aside. "I know," she told Jacie. "But I-I want—" *To be brave like you and Katy.*

Audrey threw herself down on the ground at the tree's base and quickly moved onto her hands and knees. "You can use my back for a ladder. And don't look down or you'll get scared."

Nina swallowed hard. "Okay." She stood on Audrey's back and then Katy and Gwen put their hands on her butt and pushed her up to the first branch as Jacie looked on worriedly.

"Be careful," said Jacie, regretting that she hadn't simply climbed up the tree herself. She enjoyed high places and the euphoric feeling of freedom that went along with seeing the world laid out beneath her. It was far more nerve-wracking watching one of her friends do any of the stunts she regularly engaged in.

Audrey scrambled to her feet and looked up the tree and watched Nina go. "Far out, Nina!"

Katy nodded her agreement with her cousin. "She can really climb. I knew she'd make a good lookout."

Nina grinned recklessly as she continued her path up the tree, the branches getting thinner and thinner as she went. She cleared her mind of every thought except for putting one foot higher than the next. The smell of the damp grass and dirt from below was replaced by the pungent odor of sap.

"What do you see?" Gwen asked in a raised voice. "Any B-O-Y- S, or can we start the meeting?"

Nina's fair eyebrows drew together so tightly they nearly touched. "See? I thought I wasn't sup-sup-sup-posed to look down. All I see is the t-tree," she yelled.

Jacie rolled her eyes. "You have to look down sometime, Nina. Or what's the point of climbing?"

Nina licked her lips. She was as high as she could go. Her calves and arms were burning from the exertion and the sensitive skin on her palms felt raw and itchy. Reluctantly, she tore her eyes from the tree trunk and peered across the neighbors' yards. Instantly, her knees went weak and her stomach lurched. "Uh-oh." She closed her eyes again. "I don't feel s-so good." Whimpering, she wrapped both arms around the tree trunk, and held on for dear life.

The girls on the ground all looked at each other and shrugged, unsure of what was taking so long.

"What did you say, Nina?" Gwen called up. "We can't hear you."

Tears filled Nina's eyes. "I-I-I-Arghhh!

Four sets of eyes went round. "Is a boy coming?" Katy whirled around and lifted her fists, ready to defend their territory.

Jacie adjusted her ponytail and continued to peer up at Nina. "I don't think that's it." She chewed her bottom lip. "I think she's stuck."

"Only cats get stuck up trees," Gwen decided. "Nina's not a cat and she can just come down the same way she went up."

Audrey circled the tree for a better view of the top. "I dunno, Gwen. Somethin's not right."

Jacie's anxiety rose. "Nina, come down now, okay?" She and Katy were confirmed tomboys and climbed trees nearly everyday. But watching her openly-frightened friend try the same thing was making her a little sick to her stomach.

"Yeah, Nina," Audrey and Gwen agreed. "Just come down."

Nina heard their voices, but she couldn't seem to make her mouth work. A sharp branch was digging into her side, and without letting go of the trunk, she adjusted her position, causing her to sway dangerously.

Nina and Gwen screamed bloody murder at the exact same time.

"Shut up, Gwen!" Katy hissed, covering her now ringing ears.

Audrey began to fidget and circled the tree several more times, reminding Jacie of a puppy who needed to pee and couldn't find a good spot. "What do we do?"

The girls looked at Jacie, who was surprisingly pale. "Jacie?" they chorused.

The auburn-haired girl scrubbed her tanned cheeks. "We have to help her."

Gwen gave her an exasperated look. "We know that! What should we do?" She threw a nervous glance toward Nina's back porch. "I could go tell her mom?"

"Right," Jacie grunted, her eyes still glued to the top of the tree. "Then she'll just get a spanking or be grounded for sure."

"That's better than falling and twisting your ankle or something," Katy said.

"Or landing on your back and becoming a cripple."

The girls all stared at Audrey, uncomfortably reminded that her oldest brother, Willy, had come back from Vietnam in a wheelchair.

A gust of wind caused the tree branches at the very top of the tree to sway, and Nina cried out, pressing her cheek against the rough bark of the trunk until her face hurt.

"I'm going for help!" Gwen took off running toward Nina's back door.

"I'm going for Nina," Jacie said grimly, her eyes quickly traveling up the tree for the best route to the top. Without another word, she leapt for the first branch and struggled to pull herself up. A second later, Audrey and Katy were grunting with the effort as they pushed her up from below.

"I'm coming, Nina. Hang on." Jacie tested a branch with her foot, hoping that it would hold her weight.

Nina pried her eyes open. "Jacie?"

"That's me," she heard from somewhere below her.

"You can't fit up here," Nina told her quickly, hoping she wouldn't try to come up the same way she had. "You're too big, Jacie. You'll fall." Katy had been exactly right about the smallest person being the best person to be the lookout.

Jacie frowned, squinting as she peered through the branches. Nina was right. She'd never make it. "I'll come up a different way." She altered her course where the tree trunk split into two and continued to climb.

Katy rocked back and forth below her. "I can't stand it!" she said finally, unable to take the sense of helplessness that had crept over her. "I'm gonna rescue Nina, too."

"What?" Audrey punched her cousin on the bicep. "Are you a retard? Jacie is already gonna save her, and Gwen went to get Nina's mom."

Katy lifted her chin a little. "What if Jacie needs my help?"

Audrey stood motionless for a moment, unable to think of a good answer to that question. "Okay, but I wanna help too."

"You're not good at climbing, Audrey!"

"I don't care. I'm not a klutz!"

Katy just stared at her.

Audrey sighed. "Fine, but I'm not too big of one."

Katy was forced to nod.

"I want to help. You can push me up and then I'll stick my arm down and help you, 'kay? You could never lift me."

"Deal!"

And within minutes, Katy and Audrey were weaving their way up the tree, no more than a branch behind Jacie.

Gwen banged on the Chiltons' back door. When no one immediately answered, she began dancing around the back porch in a panic. "What do I do? What do I do?" she asked herself, her pulse racing. Gathering her courage, she opened the back door, which led into the kitchen and barged into the small home. "Mrs. Chilton?" she called out. "Mrs. Chilton?"

Upstairs, Agnes Chilton's head was inside a large, turquoise-colored hair dryer. Hot air pounded her curlers, setting the utterly natural-looking style that would, with a hefty dose of Miss Breck, last for no less than four days. "Oh, tie a yellow ribbon da da da da daaaaaaaaaa," she sang softly. "It's been three long years."

"Mrs. Chilton?" Gwen poked her head into the dining room. "Rats."

Agnes flipped the page of the magazine she was reading. "Da da da da meeee?"

"Mrs. Chilton?" Panting, Gwen surveyed the empty living room. "No!" In desperation, she bolted back through the kitchen and out the door, leaving the screen wide open.

The wind ruffled the long layers of her red hair as Gwen sped back to the tree. Under its boughs, she abruptly skidded to a halt, her eyes widening as she looked around. She was alone. "Where is everyone?" she wailed. Just then she heard crying and looked up.

Nina was still near the top of the tree, clinging to the trunk, her fingers locked together. But what had Gwen's mouth hanging open was the sight of Jacie, who was nearly as high as Nina but on a different set of branches and unable to reach Nina, with Audrey and Katy directly below Jacie.

"What are all you guys doing up there?" No one was moving.

"We're stuck," Katy cried pitifully, her skinny arms wrapped so tightly around the tree trunk that her hands were turning white from lack of circulation.

"No," Audrey and Jacie said in unison. "Katy is stuck!" Audrey kicked at Katy's head, but the girl refused to budge, issuing a curse that Gwen had never heard from a girl before.

"Move it, Katy!" Jacie roared in frustration. "My arms are getting tired and I want to get down." This wasn't quite the heroic ending to the rescue that Jacie had pictured in her mind.

Gwen wrinkled her nose as she saw Audrey begin to slip. "You'd better go fast, Katy! If Audrey lands on you, you're dead for sure."

"Hey!" Audrey screamed indignantly. "Shut up, Gwen. What if I land on you?"

Gwen's mouth snapped closed, and she took two large steps backward.

Nina sniffed and bent her head to wipe tear-stained, freckled cheeks on her T-shirt. Her guts were churning and bile burned the back of her throat, but she forced herself to take a step down. A trembling foot found purchase on a lower branch and then she made herself do it again and again, not looking anywhere but at the trunk of the tree.

"That's it, Nina!" Jacie cheered her on. She sent a far more impatient look Katy's way. "Now you do that, too, you big stupid chicken!"

"You didn't call Nina a chicken," Katy complained, still refusing to move.

"That's because she wasn't stuck right below me and keeping me from getting down! Plus, I know you can climb trees. We climbed a bigger one than this last week, dummy."

"C'mon, Katy." Even though her arms and legs were wrapped around the trunk of the tree, Audrey was losing her grip. "You'd better move!" Knowing she was about to fall and crush her cousin to death, she began to cry, the sounds of her whimpers mixing with Katy's.

"I'm as b-b-brave as Evel Kneivel. I'm as brave as Evel K-Kneivel," Nina chanted as she made her way to the bottom branch.

"Here, Nina." Gwen got down on her hands and knees so Nina could use her back as a step on the way down.

Maybe it was the fact that the rest of the way wasn't very far and she was elated that she'd conquered her fear. Or maybe it was that she really, really had to use the bathroom. Nina never knew what possessed her to jump the rest of the way down. But jump she did. "G-g-g . . ." She never finished the word "Geronimo" as her shorts snagged on a small protruding branch and ripped clean off her body as she sailed over Gwen's back, landing unevenly in the grass and falling to her knees.

"Uh-oh." Nina tried to cover herself, but nothing could keep her bright pink panties from making their presence known.

Gwen looked at Nina and started to giggle. "It's not even Tuesday, Nina!" She pointed to the word that was stitched into the cotton in fancy cursive letters and Nina flushed a scarlet red.

"I see London, I see France—" Jacie began before choking on her own laughter and having to grapple for a branch to keep from toppling over.

"What in the world?" Mrs. Chilton, who was miffed over finding her screen door hanging wide open, towered over Nina. She stared down at her and then up into the tree where Katy and Audrey were now sobbing and Jacie was laughing so hard she looked as though she was having a seizure. "Is there a good reason you're in your underpants, Nina?" she asked as she hurried over to the nearby garage and emerged with a short stepladder. "Well?" She set the ladder up at the base of the tree.

"No, ma'am," Nina answered, her fingers twisting her underwear.

Mrs. Chilton quickly grabbed Katy, who weighed next to nothing, and set her on the ground. With a deep breath and a bit more elbow grease, she helped Audrey off the tree next. "I don't understand you children," she said. "Why can't you play dolls like normal girls?" Her brow creased. "I can't reach you, Jacie Ann. You're going to have to get down on—" She was still talking when Jacie scampered down the tree and dropped onto the grass next to Nina.

Mrs. Chilton blinked. "Well, then." She took in the sight of two tear-stained faces. Then her eyes flicked to Jacie, who had several bleeding nicks on her from her hasty descent, her humiliated daughter, who was trying to stretch her T-shirt over her bottom, and Gwen, who looked more frazzled than all the rest combined, and sighed. In a chipper voice she asked, "Who wants Kool-Aid?"

An hour later and safely tucked into the Chiltons' garage, the girls sat in a tight circle recounting their adventure with enthusiasm. Nina's back was to her father's black Chevrolet and sore from where the branches had poked her.

Jacie finished off her Kool-Aid, not bothering to wipe away her purple moustache. "Your mom thinks we're crazy, Nina."

Nina just shrugged. "I-I don't care. We can still play together." Her eyes got a little intense. "Sh-she said so. Even though she doesn't think t-t-tomboys are p-proper."

"Cool," Katy interjected.

Gwen's face took on a thoughtful expression. "I think grownups just don't understand our club."

"I don't think they understand anything," Jacie added, picking at a scab from an old mosquito bite on her leg.

Katy set down her glass. "We won't be like that when we grow up."

"No way," Gwen agreed. "Hey, I know! Let's make a pact."

Katy's face scrunched up and her white-blond hair fell into her eyes. "What's that?"

Gwen had only learned the word the week before, though she did her best to act as though she'd been born with the knowledge. "It's a promise. Let's promise to never get old and stupid."

"If you don't get old, then that means you're dead, Gwen," Jacie reminded her reasonably, still paying more attention to her leg than anything else.

Gwen frowned. She hated it when Jacie was right. Which she usually was. "Then let's promise that when we get old we'll still be friends."

"What if w-we don't l-live near each other anymore?" Nina asked, lifting the pitcher her mother had left in the garage and refilling her glass. She set it down carefully and wiped her wet fingers on Jacie's shorts.

Jacie either didn't notice or didn't care.

Gwen thought for a moment. "Then no matter where we live we'll come back for a sleepover. It's the only way."

Audrey scratched her jaw. "Grownups don't have sleepovers unless they're married."

"That just shows how stupid they are," Gwen shot back. "Remember the one we had last month at Katy's house where Jacie ate too much popcorn and barfed in Nina's shoes?"

Jacie lunged for Gwen, but a laughing Nina and Katy held her back.

Gwen lifted her nose in the air and ignored Jacie, trying not to look afraid. "Let's promise then. When we're old, we'll have a sleepover."

"How old?" Katy asked, settling back into her spot after letting go of a grousing Jacie.

"Really amazingly incredibly old."

"Twenty-five?" Audrey suggested.

"Older."

The girls gasped.

"Forty?" Jacie ventured, the thought of being that shriveled up and decrepit making her wince.

"Wow," Nina murmured. "Now that's old. That's even older than my mom."

"Okay." Gwen nodded, satisfied. "Forty. Let's swear."

Katy and Jacie's gazes met and they shrugged. Instantly, they hurled large gobs of spit onto their hands and held out their palms while Nina and Gwen looked on in horror.

Audrey followed her cousin's lead, but not without cringing first.

"H-how 'bout we pinky swear?" Nina asked hopefully, her eyes pleading with Gwen.

The redhead looked so relieved Nina thought she might faint. "Good idea!" She thrust out her little finger into the air and waited until Katy, Audrey, and Jacie had wiped off their hands before crooking the digit. Then Nina added her pinky to the mix and the girls solemnly intoned "I swear," and gave their pinkies a shake.

The deed was done.

"So, Nina," Jacie started, her eyes sparking with humor. "What color are Sunday's panties?"

Nina blushed again and the other girls snickered and hooted, starting the "underpants" song all over again.

Present Day
Town & Country, Missouri

"Mrs. Langtree?" A large hand waved in front of her face. "Where'd you go?"

Gwen's eyes snapped up and she shook her head a little as she handed the manila folder back to Ted Gramercy. He looked a little guilty for jolting her out of her thoughts.

"I'm sorry. I drifted off there for a moment." The late afternoon sun peeked through the thin white blinds in the main office of Gramercy Investigations, painting stripes across Gwen's yellow silk pantsuit. She moved a little in the chair, her backside numb from sitting there so long. She handed back the folder and the reports she'd spent the past hour reading. She felt like a voyeur for looking in on her old friends' lives this way. But one of them, at least, had left her little choice. "I can't believe you found them all so quickly."

The tall man sat back in his chair and his lips curled into a pleased smile. "It's always someone close."

"I didn't want to believe it could be one of them," Gwen broke in emphatically. Then she drew in a measured breath to calm herself. "It's not easy to accept that one of the people I loved so as a child is now blackmailing me." Her grip on the e-mail in her hands tightened.

He gently cleared his throat and gave his client what he hoped was a suitably sympathetic look. It was one he'd cultivated over the years after having to tell many a wife and husband that their spouses were indeed cheating. "I'm sure it isn't, Mrs. Langtree. Should . . . umm . . . I understand that you want to keep this quiet, but the best way to deal with blackmail is the police. They're the best—"

"No."

He reached out to comfort her. "I'm sorry I—"

Gwen gave him a wan smile. "I have another plan in mind. One that doesn't risk my life going up in flames quite the way going to the police would."

He removed his hand, noting the determined eyes looking back at him. "And does Gramercy Investigations fit into this plan?" His investigation hadn't turned up any likely suspects and if Mrs. Langtree hadn't given him a list of people to investigate, he would still be at square one. He was eager to be of some use in this case, and very eager to continue getting paid for as long as possible.

For an answer Gwen reached into her Louis Vuitton purse and extracted four blindingly white envelopes, each one closed by a gold seal. "I want you to hand deliver these to each of the women you located, including Audrey in Utah. I need to know with absolute certainty that they received what's inside these envelopes. And I don't want them being returned to the house if something goes wrong with the post office or a courier."

He nodded, turning the square envelopes over in his hands. "You're inviting your blackmailer to a wedding?" he ventured, unable to curb his curiosity.

Gwen rubbed the bridge of her nose. "Not to a wedding. Though those are invitations. I need to find out who is doing this and put a stop to it before it's too late. They'll all come . . . ." Her voice gentled and nearly dropped to whisper. "No matter what happened, they promised." She swallowed thickly but quickly regained her composure. "You see I'm the oldest of the bunch and I'm having a birthday next month."

Ted Gramercy blinked slowly, still clearly bewildered.

The corner of her mouth quirked. "In a few weeks I'll be really, incredibly, amazingly old."

He whistled through his teeth. If Gwen Langtree were what old ladies looked like nowadays, he was missing the boat by dating younger women.

She stood to leave. "I'm going to be forty."

Chapter 3

Present Day
St. Louis, Missouri

Katherine emerged from her kitchen, licking chocolate icing from her index finger. There was another loud rap at her door. "Hang on a sec. I'm coming." Absently, she padded across the room, her mind focused more on her upcoming date and the brownies she'd broken down and bought at the supermarket that afternoon than on who could be knocking.

She peered through the peephole to find a tall, but nondescript man in a ubiquitous blue blazer, white shirt, and wrinkled, beige Dockers standing in the hall. He smiled brightly, knowing she was looking at him, and she found herself smiling back, despite the fact that she figured he was here to sell her something she didn't want and couldn't afford even if she did want it. She unhooked the chain and opened the door, stepping out into the hallway.

"Katherine Schaub?" he asked hopefully, producing an envelope from the breast pocket of his jacket.

Automatically, she extended her hand to take it. Then, abruptly, the smile disappeared and the blood drained from her face. She yanked her hand back as though the envelope was on fire. "I'm being served?" she shrieked, her hand coming to her throat. "No fucking way! I am not Katherine Schaub. Never heard of her."

"Bu—"

She jumped back into her apartment and jerked the door closed, only to come up short when the man inserted his foot in the doorway.

"Ouch! Shit!" he hissed as the wood collided with this shoe, and his face turned red from pain. "Jesus."

Katherine hesitated, instantly feeling guilty for hurting him, but then thought better of it and began to kick his shoe. "Get out! I paid my credit card bill." Her kicks moved to his ankle. "Don't you people ever give up?"

"Wait!" His face contorted in pain. "God almighty!" He stuck his arm out to hold the door and snatched his foot away, shaking it wildly and wincing. "I'm not a process server. I swear." His eyes begged her to believe him.

"Who are you then?" she asked, her eyes narrowed warily. Suddenly she wished she hadn't spent so many late nights watching all those A&E shows about serial killers.

When she appeared to calm a bit, he took a step back into the hall and put what he desperately hoped would be a safe distance between them.

Katherine audibly exhaled.

"I'm Ted," when he saw her eyes widen he quickly added, "not Bundy, by the way. He got the electric chair years ago."

She didn't appear convinced.

"Uh . . . Okay. I've been hired to give you this envelope." When her mouth flew open and she shot him a glare that had him worried she was going to kick him right in the balls, he held up a hand to forestall her. "I promise it's not a summons."

"Really?" She couldn't help but be skeptical after he'd refused to let her shut her door. "You're just a delivery guy?"

"I'm just here to deliver an invitation, honest to God."

Against her better judgment she took the envelope, smirking when she heard him let out a relieved breath. "Sorry about your foot." She shrugged as though the entire incident had been completely out of her control. "Let me get my purse. I—"

"No need for a tip," he said quickly, not giving her a chance to do or say anything further before he disappeared back down the hall.

Katherine flipped over the envelope in her hands, examining it curiously as she shut the door and made her way back to her sofa. It was addressed to "Katy," letting her know that whoever had sent it had to be someone who knew her very, very well or someone who didn't know her at all and had inadvertently used the diminutive from her childhood.

She tore open the envelope and removed a heavy-stock, white card. Her eyes scanned to the bottom of the page and then widened almost comically and her heart began to pound. A small piece of paper fell out of the note and onto her lap. She promptly ignored it. "I'll be goddamned," she whispered to herself as she focused on the small neat script that covered every inch of available surface.

Katy,

It's been forever. But I guess you know that. For me, forever has been filled with regret over the way our friendship ended. The way the Mayflower Club ended. My fault, I know, but I'm hoping that time hasn't run out on my chance to heal old wounds and renew the friendships that were more important than I had the sense to understand way back when.

It finally happened. One of us, me, to be precise, is about to hit the ancient number we all laughed about as children. With my birthday comes a promise that I'm going to selfishly hold you to. I know it was given from the heart then . . . please don't break it now.

The Langtrees own a small B&B just outside the city named Charlotte's Web. I hope to see you there. Oct. 24-26.

Gwen

Katherine found it hard to swallow. "Christ." She dropped the card onto the cushion next to her and mechanically made her way to the freezer, where she was hiding a pack of cigarettes from herself. With a groan, she let her head rest against the freezer door for a moment as she thought. Finally, she pushed aside a stack of Lean Cuisines and fished out the cold pack of Salem Lights, tapping one free from the pack as she wove her way around her small kitchen table and back to her sofa. Placing the cigarette in her mouth, she felt the chill against her lips as the paper stuck.

Her conversation with Toby earlier in the week came rushing back to her. Was it a coincidence that someone was checking her out and then she'd received a letter from a long-lost friend? *No way.*

A wave of guilt crashed over Katherine, making her sick to her stomach. She sat down on the sofa and leaned over, putting her head between her legs until she felt better. Her first thought was to call her boyfriend for emotional support. But before she could reach for the phone, she caught sight of the small piece of paper that she'd disregarded earlier, now sitting on the floor. She was almost afraid to look.

She lit her cigarette and exhaled a long stream of smoke, her hand trembling a little as she held up the paper and read.

In soft cotton shorts and a slightly oversized T-shirt, Jacie sat at her dining room table scanning a set of architectural plans for a restaurant's dining area. She would visit the work site tomorrow, but she'd already had several phone conversations with the owner, who, like many of her clients, gave her vague instructions as to color preference, specific restrictions with price and quality, and left the design details up to her.

Which was just the way she liked it.

She'd been back in St. Louis for nearly five years, and during that time, Jacie had developed a reputation as not only a craftsman and good businesswoman, but as an artist. Her tile and marble designs graced the floors and walls of some of the most spectacular historical and contemporary rooms in the South. And though her small company would take on standard commercial and exceptional domestic projects, she was finally in a financial position where she could restrict herself to the projects that sparked her creative interest. It had been a long time in coming.

Tiles of every color imaginable were stacked along the edges of the restaurant plans and she pushed aside a large pile of unopened mail to make room for another stack of hand-painted squares, purchased in New Mexico last spring. She was so engrossed in what she was doing that when the phone rang, she jumped.

She answered it absently, her eyes still fixed on the tiles, one hand sketching out an idea on a large notepad. "Jacie Priest."

"Hello, Ugly."

Jacie dropped her pencil. "Holy shit," she exclaimed, a disbelieving smile lighting her face. "Katy?"

Katherine laughed. "That would be me. Damn, it's good to hear your voice, Jacie."

Dark eyes went glassy. "Yours, too. I can't believe you're calling me after all these years. How did you get my number?" she asked quickly, knowing her home phone to be unlisted. "Where are you?"

"I'm here in St. Louis just like the paper says." There was a long pause. "Didn't you get an invitation?"

Jacie's brow crinkled. "What invitation?"

"An invitation from Gwen."

Jacie's smiled vanished and her grip on the phone tightened. Katherine could hear a few muffled curse words. "Why would I get an invitation from her?"

"Aww . . . shit, Jacie."

Jacie picked up her pencil again and began tapping it on her kitchen table. "Look, I have no idea what you're talking about. I was never very good at guessing games. I know I haven't gotten anything from Gwen." Her voice took on a dark edge. "And if I did, it would go in the circular file. If that's what you called me for, then you're wasting your time."

Unseen by Jacie, Katherine crossed her eyes in frustration. "Just check your mail. The invitation might be there. I got mine today."

"I don't—"

"God!" Katherine exploded. "You were always a pain in the ass. How could I have forgotten that?"

At that, Jacie couldn't help but chuckle. "And you're not?"

"Of course I am. We all were. Nobody could stand us but each other. Check your mail."

Jacie groaned and reached across the table to grab a stack of unopened mail that had been piling up for several days. "Fine. Here we go: Credit Card Bill—"

"Ruthless bastards!"

Jacie smiled. "Junk mail shoe catalog." She tossed that one over her shoulder, not caring that it landed in the sink. "More junk mail about the gazillion dollar low-interest loan I qualify for."

"I wish I'd get that one."

"Huh?"

"Nothing. Keep looking."

She tossed the loan envelope over her shoulder. "Junk mail flyer about how to meet sexy, busty women online." She set that on the table to check out the photos later. "That's it. Now, enough about a stupid invitation. What have you been—?"

"Wait. It might have been a special delivery. Mine was."

Jacie sighed loudly. "There hasn't been—" Then her eyes widened with recognition and she went over to her sofa and started digging through her briefcase, her phone still pressed to her ear. "Some guy came by the office this morning. Of course he happened to be there at the same time as the UPS guy and my postman, so I just stuck his envelope on my desk at work. I figured it was another one of those charity dinner invitations where I should be grateful to be invited to a $250-a-plate rubber chicken dinner."

Her satchel-style briefcase was so full that she finally resorted to dumping it upside-down and shaking things out of the pockets. When she saw a crumpled white envelope fall out, she grabbed it and went back to the table.

The return address was from Gwen Langtree in Town & Country, Missouri, a ritzy suburb about twelve miles outside of St. Louis. "Well, I'll be goddamned," Jacie breathed.

"That's what I said."

"What does she want?"

"Open it and see."

Jacie jumped up from the table and stuffed the invitation into the trashcan. "No. Gwen can go fuck herself."

"Jesus, Jacie. Fine. I'll tell you what it says. She's apologizing and wants us all to get together. She put all of our addresses and phone numbers there. That's how I found you. I didn't even know you were back in town."

Jacie stalked back to her chair but continued to shoot daggers at her trashcan. "I've been back in St. Louis for years. I got tired of all that fresh air and clean living in Santa Fe," she said dryly.

"Audrey's in Utah. I wonder if she's a Mormon or one of the Osmonds by now. She always did want a dozen kids."

Jacie leaned back in her chair. "Wouldn't you know? You're in the same family, for Christ's sake."

"I haven't seen or spoken to her for years. Back in college my dad hated one of my boyfriends, and after I moved in with him, dad and I had a falling out. I stopped going home." She sighed. "Over the years even the phone calls from my mom trickled off and we pretty much fell out of touch. Audrey and I drifted apart after . . . Well, things were never the same once we all split. Seems like funerals are the only thing that get the whole family together anymore. And most of the older generation is gone already."

"Umm . . ." Jacie did her best to sound casual. "What about Nina?" The name tasted funny on her lips after having gone so many years without saying it out loud.

Katherine let out a knowing grunt. "She's here."

Jacie licked her lips as butterflies began to dance in her belly. "In St. Louis? You're kidding." Visions of running into Nina at some gas station or the post office filled her with a combination of dread and ever-present longing.

"Well, yeah, but not in the city. In a suburb. I guess we all find our way home eventually." Impatient as ever, Katherine got right to the point and asked, "So are you going to accept Gwen's invitation?"

Was she? Could she risk it and try to be mature, letting bygones be bygones after all these years? "Fuck no."

"Why not?"

Jacie felt an explosion of burning anger that extended from her heart to the tip of her tocs, and she fought to keep from growling out her words. "How can you ask me that?"

"Do you think I want to go? I don't want to see her either, but I can ask you that because I love you . . . moron. I've been thinking about this all day. And I've come to the realization that I miss you. I miss all of us."

Jacie sat there, stunned. "I . . . I don't know what to say, Katy. I miss you too. Just the other day Emily did something goofy that reminded me of Audrey. I about fell over laughing."

"Is Emily your dog? Audrey always could lick her own nose."

Jacie smiled. "She's my daughter."

"You have a kid?" Katherine screeched, her voice rising several octaves. "How freaky! I heard you were allergic to penises. You could have told me, you know."

Jacie rolled her eyes. "Oh, Christ."

"Poor Emily."

She laughed as she put her elbow on the table and rested her chin in her palm. "How have I gone all these years without talking to you, Katy?"

"Good question. I wanna see you, Jacie, and I know if we get off this phone and say we'll set something up that real life will get in the way and we won't end up doing it. That's why I want to know if you're going to come to this thing Gwen is having. I don't particularly want to go, but if everyone else is going then I'll bite the bullet."

Jacie fell quiet. "You don't know what you're asking," she said after a moment of soul searching, all traces of good humor gone.

"Yes, I do. I'm asking you to let go of the past and step into the future with your friends."

"I can't," Jacie said through gritted teeth. "There's more to it than you realize."

"If I can, you can, too," Katherine insisted with all the stubbornness of a two-year-old.

And with that, both women dug in their heels.

Katherine waited a half a moment before speaking, hoping in vain that Jacie would back down first. They had both been strong-willed girls and were now even stronger-willed women, their obstinacy surpassed only by that of Nina, who was practically unbeatable in that department. "Just so you know, I'm going to go. I'll call in sick on Friday if I have to."

"Have fun."

"I'll bet anything Audrey will come."

"Say hello for me."

Katherine cocked a challenging eyebrow. "And Nina."

Shit.

"And you promised you'd come. We all did."

Double shit. "Ugh. I have to go now, Katy." Jacie's gaze darted around the room desperately, as though an excuse might suddenly jump out from behind the sofa. She wouldn't have bothered to give an excuse to most people. But this was Katy. "I'm ahh . . ."

"You don't have jack crap to do and you know it. You're just going to go and sulk and think about what I said and come up with some more excuses."

Jacie bared her teeth at the phone. "You're trying to quit smoking again, aren't you?" Katherine had been in the process of quitting since she was seventeen.

Arctic blue eyes turned to slits. "Are you implying that I'm irritable?"

"I'm not implying anything. The norm with you is irritable. When you're trying to give up smokes you're irritable and irrational."

The women fell back into the easy banter, each hearing the smile in the other's words. They always had been too much alike for their own good. They talked for a few moments, exchanging nothing but the bare bones of their current lives, before another awkward silence fell.

"Well, I guess I'll talk to you later," Katherine said.

"I," Jacie paused, a million emotions swirling through her head. She sighed, abandoning what was she going to say. "Take care, Katy."

Present Day
Clayton, Missouri

Robbie slurped down the rest of his milk and happily licked away the remnants of his milk mustache. "Can I be finished now, Mom?"

Nina smiled indulgently, knowing the boy was anxious to try out their newly installed Internet connection and e-mail a friend or two back in Detroit. "Sure."

"Oh, thanks, Mom," he said quickly, jumping out of his seat and placing a quick peck on her cheek and then his grandmother's.

They were eating dinner at a small oak table in the kitchen. The dining room, which was lit by an enormous gold and glass chandelier and still held her grandmother's shiny, cherry-wood dining set, was too far from the refrigerator, not to mention overly formal for Nina's taste.

"Don't run," Nina called after him, rolling her eyes at the sound of Robbie's footsteps pounding up the wooden staircase.

Nina's mother set her napkin on the table, chuckling. "I'd forgotten what a joy and handful a child can be. He's such a sweet boy."

Nina beamed. "He is."

"I can't believe how well he's turning out. And all without a father."

Nina's smile dissolved and Agnes was quick to clarify herself. "Not that I disapprove of your choice, dear." She forced a cheerful look on her face. "I know there are a lot of single women today. Still, I can't believe most of them are single because they want to be. There's no reason on earth for a pretty, smart girl like you to be home on Saturday nights."

Nina sighed, not wanting to have this discussion for the thousandth time. What Nina said never changed, but somehow her mother managed to appear suitably shocked by what she heard every single time. Nina's lips thinned with residual anger over feeling that she needed to explain herself one more time. "I don't want a man, period. You know that I'm interested in women, not men. You've known that for years. Must you pretend like it's not true?"

"It wasn't always true," Agnes answered sharply. Then she visibly took hold of her emotions. "And who's pretending? I was talking about another parent for Robbie. One parent, no matter how much they want to, can't be everything to a child. It's impossible."

"I have always preferred women and you have always acted like you didn't hear me when I made it crystal clear that I never intended to find or settle down with Mr. Right."

"Well." Agnes scoffed. "Not with that attitude."

Nina tilted her face skyward. "Why am I being punished?" She lifted her hands in supplication. "I'm a good person. Honest, I am."

Mrs. Chilton ignored her daughter's theatrics. "It's not as though you've ever taken the time to explain how all in one day you went from dating that nice boy Lucas to moving in with that Carol person."

"There were years, not days, between those two events, Mom. And I just—" Nina sighed and pushed her plate away, her appetite gone. How could she explain the uncertainty and anxiety that went along with her heart telling her one thing while everyone else she cared about was insisting on another? *Do I even want to try?* Then she thought of Robbie and the life she wanted to build here. "I didn't talk more about it because I was confused myself. Things were never bad with men. They could even satisfy me in bed."

Agnes paled slightly, hoping the conversation wouldn't drift into specifics.

"But something was missing. Always." Her hands flailed in a vague gesture. "Some sort of connection that I found I more than wanted. I needed it. And by the time I really figured out what was right for me . . . I dunno." Her gaze dropped to the table. "It didn't seem like it was worth the effort to convince you of something you were always going to be opposed to." She licked her lips and dared a glance up, realizing her mother had remained unusually silent. "Aren't you going to say anything?"

"No," Agnes told her gently. "I think this time I need to do the listening."

A little surprised, Nina gave a quick nod. "I needed some time and space to understand myself. I guess I was a slow learner, Mom, and I'm sorry if that somehow gave you an impression that it just wasn't true." She refused to call her brief sexual liaison with Robbie's father a "mistake," because it had yielded the light of her life. "It took me a long time to be happy with myself and who I am. But I am happy." *And don't forget lonely*, her mind whispered, much to her dismay. "Can't you be happy for me?"

Agnes lifted her chin. "I don't want you happy."

Nina's eyes widened and the older woman shocked her daughter by reaching out and gently cupping her chin. Then she gave her an intense, direct stare. "I know I haven't acted like it, but I want you more than happy. I want you blissfully happy. So . . ." She gathered her courage and sent a request for Divine forgiveness in case this wasn't the right thing to do. "My friend Joan has a great niece who is a lesbian. Joan assures me she's a lovely girl, no unsightly piercings. I asked about that. Anyway, she's single and—"

Nina's jaw dropped and her hand shot up to forestall her mother's rambling. "Who are you and what have you done with my mother?" she demanded. "Now you're trying to set me up with a *woman*? Sweet Jesus, I'm in the Twilight Zone!" But an incredulous smile was tugging at her coral lips.

Agnes crossed her arms over her ample chest. "Don't act so shocked. It might have taken me fifteen years to work up to this, but now that I'm here, you're in big trouble, young lady. We should have had this talk years ago, but your visits were so short and every time I broached the subject . . . Well, things never seemed to go very well."

Nina gave her a pointed look that said "not my fault." And Agnes nodded, accepting the gentle rebuke graciously. Then her hazel eyes twinkled. "The phone just never seemed like a good place for me to hatch my devious plan."

"Oh, my God." Nina blinked slowly as the full force of what her mother was saying hit home. "You're going to check out every woman with jeans and a short haircut in the supermarket and ask them if they're gainfully employed and single, aren't you?"

Agnes leaned forward, her interest piqued. "Is short hair and jeans a secret code for being gay? I've always wondered how you all knew."

Nina continued to stare at her mother as though she'd grown a second head.

Agnes's brow creased. "But you don't have particularly short—" Her gaze suddenly darted downward and her eyes shaped twin moons. One hand moved to her own head while the other went to the neatly pressed denim covering her thigh. "Oh, my. No wonder the checkout girl with the skull tattoo from Lane 3 is always so nice to me!"

Nina's head swung toward the back of the room and waited for the Candid Camera crew to come bursting through her pantry door. "You can come out now," she demanded, her eyes narrowing. "I know you're in there."

Agnes looked toward the back of the room, too. But, of course, there was no one there. Then she focused on Nina's glass. While Nina's attention was on the pantry door, she covertly lifted her daughter's glass and delicately sniffed it. "What are you drinking, dear?" She sniffed again, her nose wrinkling. "Alcohol, by any chance?"

Nina turned back and scrubbed her face. "No, but that's not a bad idea," she murmured into her hands, her mind still reeling.

"Are you all right?" Agnes stood and took her daughter's hand, squeezing it gently.

Nina sucked in a breath and took stock of herself. "I am." She squeezed back, feeling the unparalleled reassurance of her mother's love that came in the form of a small but strong hand wrapped around hers. "I'm just confused. I . . . I don't understand why you haven't acknowledged the fact that I was a lesbian for all these years and now all of a sudden you're playing matchmaker. How am I supposed to react to something like that?"

Every ounce of confusion Nina felt showed on her face and in her voice and her mother's heart clenched in response. Nina groaned, "I feel like my head is going to explode!"

Agnes sighed, her eyes conveying true regret. "I needed some time and space to understand you, too. I guess I was a slow learner."

Nina made a face at her mother as her own words were lightly tossed back at her. "God, I hate it when you do that."

Agnes allowed a small smile to appear. They were going to be all right. "It's a gift." She leaned over and pressed her lips into her daughter's soft hair, kissing the dark blond head several times before resting her cheek there. "I can see life hasn't given you everything you want from it, Nina. Granted, I don't understand the way you feel you have to live. But whatever it is that you so desperately want . . . I want that for you, too."

A lump grew in Nina's throat and as she blinked, the room began to blur.

"Time for me to go home. You know how I hate driving past dark. We'll talk more when you get over the shock of my being reasonable." Another kiss. "Give Robbie a hug for me."

Nina stood and pulled her mother into a tight embrace. "Thanks, Mom," she whispered, hearing a note of hoarseness in her own voice.

Agnes closed her eyes. "Even if we disagree or I don't understand your choices, I love you no matter what. I know I hurt you, but I want things to be better between us. I'm so sorry, Nina." She sucked a deep breath and let it out slowly, struggling to express herself and still maintain her composure. "Moms make mistakes, too," she finally murmured. "You know that, right?"

Silently, Nina nodded. She did know that. One of the many blessings of her becoming a parent herself was the realization that, as impossible as it was to really believe, parents were just people, too, full of imperfections and good and bad choices waiting to be made. "Good night, Mom."

On her way to the door, Agnes tossed her paper napkin into the trash and caught sight of a white card and envelope that had been delivered earlier in the day. "What did that turn out to be?" She carefully extracted the crumpled card from the trash, shaking off several sticky spaghetti noodles as she examined it.

"Hey!" Despite, or perhaps because of, the emotional moment they'd just shared, Nina's temper flared. She marched across the room and stood toe-to-toe with her mother. "I think I'm entitled to a little privacy."

Agnes's eyes widened and she had the good manners to look embarrassed. "I'm sorry. I didn't mean—"

"No, no." Nina winced. "It's okay." She groaned inwardly, knowing she'd overreacted. "It's nothing secret. I apologize for being such a bitch. I don't know what's wrong with me today."

Agnes picked up her purse from the kitchen counter and adjusted the strap. "You're never a"—she lowered her voice, her lips thinning in disgust—"the 'b' word."

Nina couldn't help but laugh and wonder how well her mother really knew her after all. "Aww, Mom, I wish that were true."

"You're not yourself today," Agnes allowed thoughtfully, suspecting that whatever was bothering Nina was contained on the mysterious white card. She waited for a moment, hoping that Nina would tell her what was wrong and forcing herself not to read what was in her hand.

The younger woman was well aware of her mother's struggle and she didn't make her wait long. "The card is an invitation from an old . . . a former friend. You probably remember her. Gwen Hopkins? She wants me and some other girls from Hazelwood to get together for a long weekend next month." Nina shook her head, her gaze going a little unfocused. "She's crazy," she whispered, not realizing she'd spoken the words out loud.

"I could come here and watch Robbie so that you could go." An enormous smile exploded onto Agnes's cheeks. "I'd love to, in fact. You don't start work until early November."

"Mom, please . . . ."

"Are all the girls from that club of yours going to be there?"

"Mmm," she hummed softly. That was the real question. Would they all show up? "I doubt it."

"Still, how sweet of Gwen." Agnes nodded her approval. "She always did have good manners, not that those overbearing parents of hers didn't pound them into her." After a bit of one-handed searching, she extracted her keys from her purse. "It would be wonderful for you to have some friends here your own age."

"It would." Nina swallowed thickly and then kicked herself for feeling the mixture of anxiety and anticipation that flooded her belly at the thought of the Mayflower Club reuniting, but mostly at the thought of laying eyes on Jacie again. "But it doesn't matter, because I'm not going."

Agnes's thin eyebrows lifted. "Why ever not? These are your friends." She shook her head in confusion. "You were inseparable as children. Especially you and that Jacie Ann."

A flash of pain swept across Nina's expressive face at the mention of her friend's name, but Agnes plowed ahead, oblivious. "At one point your father and I considered clearing out your bedroom and adding another bed. You had so many sleepovers I felt a little guilty about those girls spending all those nights in their raggedy sleeping bags."

Nina's jaw set as she quickly turned away from her mother, busying herself by turning on the faucet, then hunting below the sink for the dish soap. "You can't go home again, Mom. I haven't seen any of those women in twenty years. If we'd wanted to get in touch before now, we would have." Not quite true. She'd searched for Jacie for several years before giving up completely. "What could we possibly have in common now?"

Agnes made a clucking noise. "What more could you have in common? A shared past is a powerful thing, Nina. Those girls were like sisters to you. Not that Janet wasn't a good sister, but there was such an age gap between you . . . you never really played together as children."

Nina stood and leaned against the sink, her mind easily skipping past the sounds of running water and Robbie's footsteps upstairs to the soft-spoken sister she'd lost so many years ago . . . and the friend who had held her so tenderly when she cried.

Halloween 1973
Hazelwood, Missouri

Nina pressed her face against the glass of Jacie's kitchen window and peered inside the modest split-level home. She had to stand on Audrey and Gwen's shoulders in order to see inside the high window and even then she had to stretch up on her tippy-toes.

With her arms crossed petulantly over her chest, Katy leaned against the house in a cave woman costume, complete with a bone in her hair and a large brown club made from papier-mâché. The day had been sunny and warm enough for shorts, but as the sun disappeared the air took on a typical autumn chill. Katy's mother, in a move so evil that Katy could barely contemplate it, had ruined her outfit by forcing her to wear a zip-up-the-front sweatshirt over her fake fur clothing. She'd tried to take the sweatshirt off as soon as she went outside, but Mrs. Schaub had been peeking through the window in anticipation of her daughter's deception. Ten minutes of threats later, a thoroughly chastised and partially grounded Katy was still allowed to go trick-or-treating, but to the girl's disgust, the sweatshirt was zipped clear up to her chin and safety-pinned closed.

Nina took the rare chance to just look at Jacie unobserved. The group of girls was together so often that it was easy to almost envision them as a pack and forget the strong, individual personalities that populated the club. Jacie was, Nina decided, different looking . . . pretty even, with thick wine-red hair so dark that it almost appeared black except in the direct sunlight and large brown eyes whose corners curled upward mischievously when she smiled. She was tall, but not as tall as Gwen and she always fiddled with her long ponytail when she was nervous.

"Well?" Audrey said impatiently, trying to straighten the colossal purple clown wig that was falling onto her face. She had tripped over her big clown shoes on the way over and her enormous pants were now torn at the knee. "What do you see?"

"Ja-ja-jacie eatin' d-dinner. Alone. She won't eat them a-again, I think."

Jacie sat at the kitchen table, dressed in her pirate costume. The slightly grungy plaster cast on her left arm, gotten when she'd failed at her most recent world record attempt, detracted from her tattered leggings, sword, and black eye-patch. She glared evilly at the large serving of vegetables that was still on her otherwise empty plate, taking the time to occasionally poke at it with her fork.

This was a common battle at the Priest house. Jacie couldn't leave the table until she'd cleaned her plate. If she didn't like what was for dinner she would steadfastly refuse to eat it.

Sometimes Mrs. Priest would give in and sometimes Jacie, but to-night her mother had held strong, knowing that Jacie wanted to be turned loose to go trick-or-treating with her friends.

Nina tapped on the window. Jacie's scowling face softened into a smile as she got up and with a grunt opened the window. She shivered a little when a blast of cool air poured into the room. "Hi."

Nina grinned. "Hi!"

"Hurry up, Jacie!" Katy called from the hedges below. "It's almost dark!"

Jacie sighed and stuck her head out the window to observe her friends. "It's brussels sprouts night."

A chorus of sympathetic groans and retching noises met her words.

"Can't you just eat 'em real fast?" Gwen suggested, thinking that her shoulder would break from Nina's weight.

"No way," Jacie said. "I'll barf."

Katy pushed off from the house. "Pitch 'em out the window then."

Jacie shook her head. "Last time I did that, my dad found them the next day when he was trimming the bushes and I had to go pick my own switch from the back yard. My butt was striped for a week!"

Nina frowned. Jacie wasn't exaggerating about that. "I could do it," she offered bravely, wobbling a little on the bigger girls' shoulders.

Jacie's eyes went round. "You could?"

"Y-yes," Nina answered firmly, her knees cold against the bricks. "I like 'em."

Gwen and Audrey both went, "Ewwwww."

"Neato," Katy said, clapping her hands, her mood swinging from one end of the spectrum to the other as it often did. "Hurry up and do it then or all the best candy's gonna be gone. I've already seen Bucky Lee in front of Old Man Kressler's house dressed like Frankenstein and eating a big bag of Sugar Babies."

Jacie digested this information with a dour look. There was no way that Bucky should be getting candy while she was stuck in her kitchen. She regarded Nina seriously. "You really like brussels sprouts, Nina? Because I am not eating them," she said stubbornly. "You guys can go on without me."

"Aww . . . Jacie," Gwen moaned.

"No," Nina answered quickly. "I me-mean yes. I like 'em. R-really."

Jacie stared at her for several seconds before grinning broadly and dashing back for her plate. She snatched it off the table and then poked her head out of the kitchen to make sure one of her parents wasn't on the way back for a cup of coffee or another slice of pie. "Here ya go." She held out the plate.

Nina lifted a hand but began to sway dangerously. "Whoooa. I c-can't reach them."

"She needs to hold onto the trellis or she'll fall," Gwen panted, trying to save time by explaining things on Nina's behalf.

A look of indecision flickered across Jacie's face.

"Just put 'em in my m-mouth." Nina opened wide and waggled a pink tongue.

Jacie nodded quickly and picked up a large, soggy brussels sprout between two fingers. "Uck!" She turned the same gray/green color as the mushy vegetable when Nina happily chomped it to pieces, gulped, and then opened her mouth for another bite.

Gwen, Audrey, and Katy wholeheartedly cheered her on, forgetting that they were supposed to be quiet as they hid in the shadows of Jacie's house.

When she'd swallowed the last bite, Nina licked her lips and signaled for Audrey and Gwen to let her down. Katy moved quickly behind her to help her to the ground.

Jacie let out a triumphant whoop and climbed out of the kitchen window and down the trellis like a one-armed monkey, hampered, but still agile. "Thanks, Nina!"

"No p-problem," Nina said shyly, her face heating. She was so proud of herself that she was about ready to bust.

Gwen pointed upward. "What about the window, Jacie?" The wind changed directions and she caught the strong whiff of coffee and what she thought was chipped beef on toast.

Jacie peered back toward her house and the window she'd forgotten to close on her way out. She shrugged. "Doesn't matter. It was too hot in there anyway and this will get out the smell of green mush."

The girls laughed and half-walked, half-skipped down the sidewalk. Porch lights were just being flipped on around the neighborhood and the eerie, glowing smile of jack-o-lanterns lit most front steps. Leaves chased each other in driveways and the cool wind gusted fitfully, rustling them and rattling branches.

Jacie pulled out a large pillowcase that she'd stuffed into the waist of her pants, fluffing it out the best she could with one hand as she walked.

"You think that'll hold enough?" Katy teased, eyeing the pink pillowcase with interest.

"You're just jealous." Jacie grinned. "Heh." Then Gwen caught her eye. "What are you supposed to be dressed as?"

Gwen gave her friend an indignant snort and fingered the satin sash that was draped across her shoulder. She was wearing an ill-fitting puffy dress and a rhinestone tiara. "Miss Missouri, of course."

Jacie stepped closer and squinted.

Gwen held out the sash that actually read "Miss Missouri."

"Figures," Jacie murmured with a smirk.

"Let's start here," Audrey suggested, readying her bag. "Last year Mrs. Foster gave out popcorn balls."

"Big ones!" Katy agreed, humming her approval.

All the girls but Nina trotted up the sidewalk to the first house. Gwen rang the doorbell.

Jacie noticed that Nina wasn't with them; she turned toward the tattered hobo, who was staring down the street. Curious, she trotted back to her and looked in the same direction, pale eyes were riveted. "Wow!"

A police car, red lights flashing, sat in the driveway of a house about a block down the street.

Jacie turned to Nina. "Is that coming from your house?"

"I-I don't think so." Her chin began to quiver. "B-but maybe. I dunno."

Even in the dim light, Jacie could see Nina's heart beating in her throat. "C'mon, guys!" Jacie motioned for Gwen, Katy, and Audrey to join them, and the girls took off sprinting down the sidewalk with Gwen lagging behind in her fancy dress.

Nina skidded to a stop in her yard, her breath coming in soft pants. Her eyes were wide and glassy, and Audrey instantly wrapped a comforting arm around her. They could hear voices inside the house, but the girls were frozen in the face of what they might find if they went inside.

They stared warily at the cruiser in the driveway.

Nina looked as though she would burst into tears long before she made it to her front door. Police captured crooks and bad guys. And there were none of those in her family, so there was no good reason for the police to be at her house.

Jacie swallowed and took Nina's hand, leading her up the sidewalk. "C'mon, Nina. Maybe your dad caught a bank robber or something?"

Nina turned hopeful pale eyes in her friend's direction. "Ya think?"

Jacie hummed as she thought. "Could be. A regular guy helped catch a criminal on *MacMillan and Wife* just last week."

Katy, Gwen, and Audrey exchanged worried glances as they trailed after their friends.

When they reached the front steps, Nina could hear a police officer speaking in low, soothing tones. The front door was wide open and through the screen door she caught sight of her mother sobbing hysterically and a group of people gathering around her in comfort. Nina's stomach lurched.

Even under Nina's dirty hobo makeup, Jacie could see that she had gone pale as a sheet.

The smaller girl's feet froze. "No! I-I—" Nina shook her head wildly. She dropped the broomstick with a kerchief tied on the end that made her hobo pack in order to grasp the porch railing with both hands. "I don't wanna g-go inside!"

The other girls soaked in her fear like little sponges, the flashing lights illuminating their frightened faces. It wasn't long before the sound of sniffles filled the air.

Nina whimpered.

"I'll go see what it is," Jacie offered, not knowing what else to do. "Is that okay?" She searched Nina's face and received a wary but pathetically grateful nod in response.

Jacie gulped down her fear and reached for the screen door with a shaky hand. Once inside, all adult eyes turned her way. There were several seconds of utter silence where she felt as though she might melt into a puddle. Then she said, "Ni—" she had to stop and clear her throat so that her voice wouldn't shake. Whatever this was, it was bad. Very bad.

"Nina's outside." She glanced around the room and the mournful faces looking back at her caused her stomach to twist painfully.

At her words, the noise in the room resumed as quickly as it had stopped. A horrible keening noise was coming from Nina's mother, who was bent at the waist and jerkily swaying back and forth like a screen door in the wind. Nina's father had a large hand resting lightly on his wife's back. He was staring off into space and standing so stiffly that he looked as though he might crumble into dust with the slightest breeze. Several neighbors that Jacie recognized stood around looking uncomfortable and talking quietly to each other and the officer. She heard the words "party" and "balcony" several times but couldn't make out much more than that.

Two older policemen entered the front door and a heavy-set man with several yellow stripes on his sleeve growled at the younger cop for attracting the attention of the entire neighborhood. The red-faced young man quickly apologized to Mr. and Mrs. Chilton and ran past Jacie on his way to turn off the squad car's flashing lights. Jacie began to tug nervously on her ponytail while she waited for something to happen. She was about to go back outside when several milling neighbors stepped aside and the room parted to allow a slim woman with a pointy chin and salt and pepper hair worn in a bun to make her way through the crowded living room.

As the woman drew closer, Jacie could see that her cheeks were wet and her eyes bloodshot. "I'm Imogene Chilton, Nina's grandmother," she said gently, trying to give Jacie a comforting smile and failing miserably. "Is Nina outside, dear?"

Dumbly, Jacie nodded and Imogene patted her cheek with a bony hand as she moved past her. She followed Imogene into the damp night air and stood by silently as the old woman knelt down on the sidewalk and explained in a soft, quivering voice that Janet, Nina's college-aged sister, had fallen from the fourth floor balcony of a friend's apartment earlier that evening. The young woman had died on the way to the hospital.

Nina burst into tears and flew into her grandmother's waiting arms.

It wasn't long before Audrey was crying almost as loudly as Nina. Gwen and Katy, with tears in their eyes, shifted nervously from one foot to the other, wishing they were any place else on earth but here. Jacie stood there behind Nina's grandmother, unable to tear her eyes off her friend, her heart hurting like it never had before, a sick feeling burning in her guts. She'd never known anyone who had died. Not that she'd ever done much more than say hi to Janet, but Nina was one of her best friends, and that was close enough for her. She reached for her ponytail again and tugged on it nervously.

After a moment, Imogene drew her face up from Nina's tear-dampened neck and focused on Katy, Gwen, and Audrey. A touch of wistfulness entered world-weary eyes before rapidly being replaced by sorrow. "Why don't you girls go on trick-or-treating," she said kindly, patting Nina's slender back as she spoke. "Nina will be fine."

The girls gave her a doubtful look, their gazes flickering back and forth between Nina and the old woman.

"Go on," Imogene prodded, the movement of her hand shifting from a pat to a soothing circular motion. "It's a sin for young people to waste special nights like this one, especially since there isn't much that you can do here."

Katy and Gwen nodded, more than happy for the reprieve. Audrey looked guilty for wanting to bolt, but she wasn't burdened with the feeling for long, and she quickly gave Nina a sad wave as she hurried to catch up with her friends. In her haste, she bumped into Katy. Katy let it go without even a gentle tease about being clumsy. This wasn't the time or place for a familial tussle. The girls made their way down the sidewalk, their step devoid of the liveliness it had had only moments before.

A group of goblins and witches stood at the end of the driveway trying to decide if there would be candy amidst all the chaos. But the police cars spooked them enough so that they hurried past the house and ran to catch up to the girls who were now crossing the street.

Tired eyes swung in Jacie's direction. "Aren't you going?" Imogene asked quietly, straightening to her full height and letting out a soft groan as her spine popped into place.

Stubbornly, Jacie lifted her jaw. "No, ma'am."

A fresh wave of tears spilled onto wrinkled cheeks and Imogene's lips twitched into something resembling a smile. "Good." She petted Nina's head, and then a gentle hand moved down to lift the girl's chin. She gazed into lost, red-rimmed eyes. "Why don't we go inside, dear?"

"No!" Nina clutched at her desperately, burrowing her face in her dress and looking as though she'd crawl under her grandmother's skin if she could.

"Shh . . . . Don't worry. You can go straight to your room and your friend can come, too. Your mother and father will need to go to the hospital soon."

Nina pulled away, her cheeks glistening in the amber porch light. Her befuddlement was clear. The hospital was for sick, but alive people. "But—"

Imogene instantly recognized the source of Nina's confusion. "The ambulance drivers tried their best to save Janet, honey. They couldn't, but they took her to the hospital anyway. Your parents can go see her there and then take her to Parson's Funeral Home. Do you remember it? You went there for your Great Uncle Eugene's funeral."

It had been more than three years since Nina's Uncle Eugene had died and the details surrounding his death were fuzzy at best. What stuck out most in her mind was that it was the first time she'd seen grownups cry. She thought hard, then grasped hold of a faint memory she could share. "The p-place with all the flowers and the or-organ? Where we said prayers?"

Imogene nodded her approval at Nina. "That's the place. I'll stay here to look after you so your parents can leave." Tenderly, she wiped the little girl's cheeks. "Your mother and father are very upset, Nina. If they don't take time to be with you tonight, it isn't because they don't love you. You need to understand that."

Nina's mind wailed that she was upset too. But outwardly she remained silent in the face of her grandmother's words.

"Do you understand?"

Jacie's eyes flickered to Nina, and she wondered what she'd say. She'd seen her friend glance longingly at her mother through the door and knew Nina had only barely kept herself from rushing to the woman's side, despite the fact that she was afraid to go inside.

Nina didn't understand at all, but she swallowed hard and mumbled a soft "y-yes" because she could tell that was what her grandmother wanted to hear.

Imogene smiled gently. "That's my brave girl."

It took them only a few moments to be shuffled through the gathered people and into Nina's dark bedroom. They both sat down on the bed, not knowing what to say. Barely a handful of heartbeats had passed when the bedroom door opened slowly and Agnes Chilton came inside.

"Nina?" she whispered brokenly, her throat raw from crying.

"Oh, Mommy," Nina jumped off her bed and propelled herself into her mother's legs, wrapping her entire body around her much the way she'd done with her grandmother. "I knew you wouldn't l-l-leave without say-saying goodbye!"

Jacie smiled in relief, but was embarrassed that she was a little jealous of Nina even under these terrible circumstances. She wasn't at all sure her mother or father would have come to her if the situations were reversed. Her father forever had his face in the newspaper and her mother seemed to be more concerned with her social life within their church than anything else.

Jacie could see Nina's father standing in the doorway, watching his wife and daughter with hollow eyes. But the man made no move to be part of the physical comfort or to join in the softly spoken words of love and compassion. His tear-filled gaze lifted to meet Jacie's and he gave her a curt nod. Jacie took it to mean she had permission to stay the night.

Finally, Mr. Chilton whispered something into Agnes's ear and, with a tender pat on Nina's head, the adults were gone, leaving the girls alone in the room where no one had bothered to turn on the light.

The dark wasn't so scary when they were together and the window provided enough light to see into the shadows.

"Are . . . are you okay, Nina?" It seemed like a stupid question and Jacie kicked herself for not being able to think of anything better to say.

"I-I don't think so."

"Oh." Jacie felt like she was floundering. "Do you wanna take off your makeup?" Nina's tears had painted stripes through the black makeup and the haphazard effect actually made Nina look more like a real hobo than she had before, but Jacie knew its cause and hated it. The white streaks of pale skin nearly glowed in the blue-tinted moonlight and she thought idly that Nina's freckles had somehow disappeared.

Nina nodded and accepted Jacie's pillowcase/would-be trick-or-treat bag. Without water the cloth only served to smear the makeup around her cheeks, but neither girl particularly cared and the attempt to get clean was half-hearted at best.

Silently, Nina pulled her nightgown from her top drawer while Jacie shrugged out of her Halloween costume. She let Jacie pick from her pajamas; the auburn-haired girl selected a baby-blue nightshirt with a picture of Mickey Mouse on the front. She didn't particularly like Mickey, so she turned the shirt inside out.

They crawled into Nina's twin bed together, and Nina snuggled close, wanting and receiving unconditional comfort from her friend. Jacie, she realized, acted tough, but when it came down to it, she was kind and gentle and it was a shame that no one knew that but her and maybe the other girls in their club.

"Will your m-mom get mad?" Nina whispered into the dark, holding Jacie close and trying not to think of her sister in a coffin like Dracula, or whether it hurt to die, or if something extra creepy happened to a person who died on Halloween.

Jacie pulled up the bed sheet, mindful of its incredible power; knowing that nothing could hurt them if it was pulled all the way up to their eyes. "When we were on our way to your room I told your granny my phone number." Her breath caused the sheet to billow in front of her mouth. "She said she'd call my mom for me. My folks won't care if I stay." It would be, Jacie realized, the first time she'd ever stayed the night here without Katy or Gwen or Audrey being here, too.

"I'll n-never see Ja-Janet again."

There was a long pause before Jacie tried to be convincing and said, "Maybe in heaven you will."

Nina hitched herself on one elbow, worried eyes boring into Jacie. "You don-don't think there is one."

"There could be, I guess," Jacie allowed slowly, not wanting to dash Nina's obvious hopes. She figured she was going to be worm food, just like animals were when they died. Plus, she'd stopped believing anything her preacher said when she'd caught her mother having to slap the old man's hand away when they were supposed to be in the church office counting the weekly donations.

"Hmm . . ." Jacie's answer wasn't all she'd hoped for, but it was better than an outright no. Nina's heart began to pound as she considered the possibility of truly never seeing her sister again. And someday her parents would die, too. And all her friends. It was too much and her chest jerked with a sob, startling Jacie with her sudden outburst. "I'm sorry I wrecked Hal-Hal-Halloween!"

Helplessly, she started to cry again and Jacie felt the salty tears dampen her nightshirt. Unbidden, Jacie's own tears came, but it was dark and Nina was crying so hard herself that she didn't feel embarrassment. "It's okay, Nina." Her chest felt heavy and she adjusted her casted arm, moving it in case that was the problem. It didn't help and she tried to think of something to make Nina feel better. Anything. "It's not your fault."

"I know," Nina sobbed out. "But I-I'm still s-sad."

Jacie didn't tell her not to cry. If she'd had a sister who died, she figured she'd be sad, too. So instead, she cried with her friend for a very long time.

The moon hung higher in the sky by the time the last of the snuffles had turned into soft hiccups and then even those melted into quiet breaths as an exhausted sleep began to steal over them. "I'm sorry about your sister," Jacie finally whispered, realizing she hadn't said it yet, though she'd been thinking it all night. Her voice was a little raspy and her dark eyes trained themselves on the window as she spoke. "She was really cool, right?"

Nina nodded a little and this time when her eyes slid closed they stayed that way. She felt safe with her head resting on Jacie's shoulder and the stomachache she'd had since she'd seen the police car in her driveway was beginning to ease. Her whispered voice was slurred with sleep. "Almost as cool as you, Jacie."

Present Day
Clayton, Missouri

In Nina's mind her sister would forever be a teenager and Jacie, no matter what, would always be her hero.

The silence in the room stretched out for a few moments as Agnes and Nina stayed lost in their own thoughts.

It was Agnes who was first to pull herself from the past. "Well . . ." She exhaled slowly and let the memories fade firmly back into the recesses of her mind. "I hope you reconsider meeting with your old friends." She jingled her keys lightly. "But it's your social life, honey. Well, at least that part of it is yours. The romantic part I'm meddling in—whether you want me to or not."

Nina gave her a rueful, lopsided grin. "My good luck just never stops."

Unrepentant, Agnes grinned back. "Too true."

Nina retrieved the last dinner plate from the table and shook her head over the pile of brussels sprouts still sitting there.

"Why do you bother fixing them? You've hated brussels sprouts since you were a baby."

"I do hate them. But Robbie loves the nasty things so I always put a little on my plate too and try to stomach one or two." Nina smiled to herself. "It's a small price to pay for someone I love." Moving a glass aside, she placed the plate on the counter and approached her mother. "Good night, Mom."

The phone rang just as she was kissing her mother's cheek.

Agnes waved her off. "Shoo . . . Go get that before they hang up. I'll stop by tomorrow afternoon."

Nina nodded and offered a final wave before turning off the faucet and running for the phone in the hallway. Even after unpacking every box, she was still missing two phones, a planter, her ice cube trays, and all her white socks. The mysteries of moving never ceased to amaze her.

She leaned against the wall and wiped her wet hands on her T-shirt, wishing her grandmother had believed in dishwashers as she pressed the receiver to her ear. "Hello?"

Nothing.

"Helloooo?"

She was met with a long silence. Having run out of patience, Nina was about to hang up when she heard a throat being gently cleared and then what sounded like a dry swallow. "Hello?" she tried one last time, now listening intently out of pure curiosity.

"Nina?"

Blue-green eyes slammed shut as the achingly familiar burr traveled through her ear to pierce her heart. Her knees gave way, and she slid down the wall to the floor, her bottom thumping loudly against the cool wood.

"Nina, is that you?"

She had to swallow a few times before she could speak. "Yeah, Jace," she finally said softly, her world turned upside down. Again. "It's me."

"Nina—"

A surge of panic struck Nina so hard she wasn't even aware of what she was doing. "I can't talk now." She slammed the phone down, panting. It took her only a few seconds for her to regret what she'd done. She moaned. "Brilliant, Nina."

The phone rang again, causing her to jump. She held her breath and with a trembling hand, placed it to her ear, a million unanswered questions roaring in her head. "H-Hello?"

"Hi. Nina?"

Nina exhaled heavily, not sure whether to cry from frustration or relief. The voice on the other end of the line wasn't Jacie's, but it was still as familiar as her own shadow. "Katy Schaub?"

"Are you surprised?"

Nina swallowed thickly. "Yeah. You could say that."

Present Day
Salt Lake City, Utah

"Come to bed."

Audrey frowned as she ran a brush through medium-length brown curls. She sat down on a low padded bench, her back to the bed, and stared off into space. The room was dimly lit, and the sounds of crickets and buzzing insects drifted in through the open window. "In a minute, Enrique."

The man sighed and flopped back on his pillow, his longish dark hair falling into his face. "Not in a minute," he said, but there was no heat in his words. "It's late."

Audrey's brushstrokes were short and frustrated, and she grunted as she encountered a small snarl near her left ear. "I don't know where she gets off. Who does she think she is?"

Enrique closed his eyes and yawned. He was wearing a pair of black silk boxers and the bedding was cool and soft against his skin. "Who gets off?"

"Gwen." Frowning, she set her brush on the table in front of her and turned around to face her husband. Her eyes were flashing. "Who else?"

"Why are you still thinking about her and her invitation?" He threw his arm over his face to block out the weak light spilling from the bedside lamp on his wife's side of the bed.

"Humph." Raising an eyebrow at Enrique, Audrey turned back around and faced the mirror in silence. She picked up the brush again, then changed her mind and set it down in favor of a tin of rose-scented powder.

The man cringed, not needing to see his wife's face to know that the silence that had met his last words was not a good sign. "You know what I think?" he murmured.

"Most of the time." She sprinkled some powder into her upturned hand and tugged on the string that held closed the front of her nightgown, partially exposing her chest.

"Funny." He sat up and looked at the mirror, catching her gaze in the reflection. "I think you want to go." The rest of what he was going to say completely fled his mind as he realized where Audrey intended to apply her powder. His eyes darkened a shade.

Audrey's mouth dropped open and the hand that had been on the way to her neck and chest froze.

Enrique frowned.

"I do not!"

"Sure you do," he insisted absently, still avidly watching his wife's unintentional but surprisingly erotic display. "I love you so much and you are so beautiful."

"Err . . . thanks, honey." She was a little surprised by his sudden declaration of devotion, but still pleased. With a delicate touch, she applied a small bit of powder to her neck, then her hand drifted slightly lower and Enrique stifled a groan.

"Here," he scrambled down the bed and jumped off, tripping over his own feet as he stood. "Let me help you."

Audrey's eyebrows lifted and she glanced up at Enrique who was already at her side. "Are you okay? God, I haven't you seen you move that fast in ages." She gave him a confused look. "I don't really need any more pow—"

"A little more is always okay, right?" he asked eagerly, nodding in answer to his own question. "It can't hurt."

"Well, I guess it can't—"

Deciding he'd been granted permission, he snatched up the tin. What he didn't realize was the lid was already off. Powder flew everywhere, but mostly over Audrey. "Oops."

"Enrique!" She waved her hand through the thick cloud of powder that now hovered around her head. And she began to cough.

"Sorry, sorry. Here, let me rub that in." He reached out for her with both hands, his fingers spread wide apart and a sexy smile curling sensual lips.

"Enrique, you pervert!"

"Whaaaat?" he complained, trying to look innocent. "I'm helping."

She started to laugh, but soon that shifted into violent coughing. Then a split second before his hands reached their prize, she slapped them away.

"Oh, come on." His voice was pleading. "I'm a good helper!" He blew a stream of air in Audrey's face, trying to disperse the powder, but only managed to send more of it up her nose and into her lungs.

"I don't need anymore"—a cough—"of your"—another cough—"help." Then her face twisted. "Aaaaaaaaaaachu!"

"Bless you," he said quickly, his hand moving to pat her back.

She glared up him. "Do not—Aaa—aaaa—aachu!"

"Bless you again, sweetheart."

"Shut-up, En—" She shook her head wildly. "Aaaaaaaaachu!"

"Gesundheit."

In a lightning fast move, she wrapped her arms around his bare legs and propelled them both back onto the bed, sending several pillows and a quilt tumbling to the floor in the process.

Enrique landed with a grunt but quickly turned the tables on Audrey. He straddled her and pinned her arms over her head. "Oh, no, you don't!"

She grinned unrepentantly. "Oh, yes, I do!" Then her eyes widened and her nose twitched. "I—aaa—aaa—"

"Here." With one hand, he grabbed a pillow and pressed it over Audrey's face as she sneezed and then thrashed around, her muffled squeals of laughter still loud enough to make Enrique cringe.

Then they heard a loud knock on their bedroom wall. "Hey!" Ricky Jr.'s voice caused them to freeze and Enrique lifted up the pillow so a red-faced, disheveled Audrey could hear, too. "Could you keep it down in there, Mama and Papa? I have school in the morning, ya know."

"We'll be good, mijito," Audrey sang out, her words laced with humor. "We promise."

"Don't make me come in there," Ricky Jr. called out playfully, giving the wall a final knock.

Enrique and Audrey stuck their tongues out at each other. "It's your fault," they both whispered at the same time, each dissolving into muffled laughter at the other's words.

"Whew." Enrique settled next to Audrey and held out his arm, waiting until she turned off the bedroom light and tugged up the wrinkled quilt before wrapping a strong arm around her and sighing. "You do smell good," he said in a low voice, smiling into the darkness.

She chuckled. "I should." She sat up a little and stripped out of her nightgown, tossing it onto the floor before snuggling back into her place with a happy grunt. "Mm . . . Better."

"Much." He ran his fingers up her bare back, lightly rubbing her spine as he went. "Now, tell me why you're not going to Missouri when I know you want to."

Audrey felt a big portion of her good mood vanish and she let out an unhappy breath. "Why should I go, Enrique? I'd rather stay here."

He nodded a little. "Good."

She blinked. "Really? You don't think I should go?"

"Not really." He made a dismissive motion with one hand. "I never want you to go away because I miss you when you're gone. But that's not the point. Gwen didn't give enough notice to plan for such a big trip. That was presumptuous of her to think you'd want to go or that we could afford something so large at the last minute."

"Inside Gwen's invitation was a first class plane ticket. She didn't have to do that," she murmured into his shoulder, her hand finding its way to his chest where her fingers played with the dark, curly hair there. "But it's not like she can't afford it either." The anger and hurt she felt toward Gwen reared its head with little provocation.

"Can we afford for you to go, even with a free ticket? Remodeling the garage wasn't cheap and we weren't expecting that expense."

Audrey shifted uncomfortably. Finances had always been a bone of contention between them. She had a savings account that was in her name only that her husband didn't know about and she could afford to go to Missouri if she wanted. Now, however, wasn't the time to bring that up. "This is about my putting out a big effort to see someone who makes my blood boil. I could find a way to go if I really wanted to."

Audrey was starting to get grumpy and so, cringing, he backed off a little. "I know."

Audrey immediately sensed his discomfort. "Aww . . . Ricky." She tugged on his hair affectionately. "I'm not mad at you. This invitation has just thrown me."

He smiled a little, relieved. "If you go to Missouri, you'll have to rent a car right? Or maybe you can use one of your parents' cars. And what about work?" he reminded, his body relaxing under her familiar touch. "You'd have to take a few work days off. Could you even do that? You know I want us to visit my uncle in Oaxaca this Christmas."

"I could," she admitted, biting her lower lip as she thought. She'd been a recreational specialist at the local YMCA for going on fifteen years. "I have more vacation built up than I can even use this year. And none of it will carry over to next year."

"But you'd want to spend your vacation with her?" He scrunched up his face. "I remember how she made you crazy and how rotten she was. Why would you want to see her again?" He knew the answer already, but he also knew that Audrey needed to come to her own conclusions in her own time. And talking always helped.

"She wasn't always that way," Audrey heard herself saying. "Dammit, Ricky, why am I defending her? It's not like we're even friends anymore."

"No, but you were once."

"And she blew it."

"You're right," he agreed softly. "She blew it. And nobody changes that much over time."

Audrey's brow furrowed and she shifted in bed, resting her chin on his chest and peering up to try to find the dark eyes she knew would be looking back at her. "Some people do, don't they?"

He smiled a little. "I have faith that they can. And it won't be just her there," he prompted, knowing Audrey would love to see her other childhood friends.

"I'm crazy to even think about it," she whispered, wishing he'd talk her out of what she was about to decide. "But just hearing from Katy was so wonderful. Even if it was just her voice on our answering machine. I've missed the brat." Then she thought of Nina and Jacie and all the things they had to talk about and, despite herself, even some things that she found herself wanting to share with Gwen.

"You might be crazy, but you're crazy with me. And that's all I need." He leaned forward and captured her mouth in a soft, heartfelt kiss. "C'mere." He tugged her higher onto his body and wrapped his arms around her back, his lips moving to her neck where the powder tasted slightly bitter but the skin underneath was so salty sweet that he didn't care.

She moaned softly when his mouth found a particularly sensitive spot and his hand moved down to the soft skin of her bottom. "I'll think about how to lose forty pounds in a few weeks . . . later . . ." she decided on a slightly uneven breath, her hips moving forward of their own accord.

"Mmm . . . You do that, querida," he breathed against her skin. "In the meantime, I'll enjoy every luscious inch of you."

She felt more than heard his rumbling chuckle and she gladly returned his loving touch, all thoughts of trips, diets, and the past banished in the wake of a vibrant and happy present.

Chapter 4
Present Day
Town & Country, Missouri

"No!" The sound of exploding glass echoed throughout the house. Gwen closed her eyes for a moment, hearing nothing but her own panting breaths and the wild thumping of her heart. "Christ." She was alone in her bedroom and half-dressed for a dinner out that night when she foolishly decided to get directions to the new restaurant from her laptop. While online, she checked her e-mail. And there it was. Another blackmail demand. After venting her anger, though, she did as the private detective had instructed and printed out a hardcopy for her private file.

Tears leapt to her eyes and she wiped at them with a shaking hand. She dropped the printout of the latest blackmail threat on her bed and slowly walked across the room to pick up the remains of her shattered crystal brandy snifter. She hadn't meant to throw it.

"Gwen?" A voice sounded from outside the room. "Honey? Are you all right?"

When she heard her husband's voice, she jerked in reaction and a sliver of glass cut deeply into her index finger. She hissed in pain as crimson drops splashed onto the pale carpet, leaving a spotted trail as she moved. "Just a minute, Malcolm." She clenched her hand to her chest and dashed back to the bed to pick up the e-mail before he could see it.

She didn't make it.

Malcolm strode in, his worried eyes scanning the room as he tried to figure out where the crashing noise had come from. "Are you okay?"

Gwen plastered on a tight smile and retracted the hand that had been reaching for the paper. "I thought we were meeting at the restaurant," she said, a red stain blossoming on her bra where she held her injured hand.

"I forgot my wallet so I—Jesus, Gwen, you're hurt!" The tall man rushed across the room and grabbed his wife by the biceps. "Let me see." His hands ran lightly over her body as he searched for other injuries.

"It's nothing." She tried not to look at the e-mail that was lying in plain view on the bed. She decided it would be best to put as much space between her and it as possible. Roughly, she tried to pull out of his grasp. "Just a little cut. I'll go to the bathroom and—"

"Let me look." His heavy brow furrowed in confusion over his wife's strange behavior.

"It's nothing," she insisted, shocked when she looked down and saw blood spilling between her clenched fingers and running down her naked torso to pool at the top of her nylons.

"I'm the doctor in the family." Frustration leaked into his voice. "Why don't you let me tell you if it's nothing?"

"You're a damned dermatologist, not Marcus Welby, M.D.!"

Malcolm blinked a few times and released his grip on Gwen's arms and took a step backward. "What in the hell is wrong with you?"

When she finally focused on the bewilderment and concern showing so plainly on his face, her features instantly softened. "I don't know. I'm sorry." Helplessly, she began to cry, the thought that she could be seconds away from fracturing the relationship with the man she loved so dearly too much to take.

Malcolm pulled her into a tight embrace, heedless of the blood. "Shh." He whispered into her hair, pressing his lips into its fiery strands. "It'll be okay. I'll take you to the hospital. Here . . ." He gently disengaged from her embrace and stripped out of his stained shirt. He held it beneath her hand to catch the droplets. "Can I see it now?" His gaze dropped to her hand and when she awkwardly uncurled her fist he let out a low hiss of sympathy. "That's a bad one." His gaze lifted and he gave her a serious look. "It's going to need stitches."

She sniffed and cursed her own stupidity. "Are you sure?"

He nodded. "Even dermatologists go to medical school, Gwen, remember?"

Gwen suddenly felt very ashamed and a memory of Malcolm studying for his med school exams with a very young Tucker lying asleep in his lap flashed behind her eyes. "I know that. I . . . I was just scared, I guess." Her voice conveyed true regret and a healthy dose of fear. "I don't like hospitals."

"I have a feeling you'll like the scar you'll get even less than the emergency room. I could sew it up here, but—"

The blood suddenly drained from Gwen's face and a million tiny black spots invaded her peripheral vision.

"Whoa!" He grasped hold of her firmly and guided her to the bed just as she began to sway. "You'd better sit down."

Her eyes widened as the thought of where he was heading jerked her back to alertness. "No! I—" But before she could stop him, Malcolm picked up the paper containing the latest blackmail request so that she wouldn't sit on it.

"What?"

Gwen swore at that moment her heart stopped beating completely. "I . . . I—" She floundered for something to say, praying he wouldn't look at what was in his hand. "I don't want to drip on the comforter."

He waved his hand in the air. "I don't give a damn about the comforter. Stay put. I'm going to set this over here." He waved the e-mail and then quickly set it on her dresser, not bothering to read a word of it. "My bag's in the closet. Hold my shirt to the cut. I'll be right back."

Gwen let out a shaky breath and ran for the dresser as soon as he disappeared into his walk-in closet. She stuffed the e-mail inside her top drawer and barely made it back to the bed before Malcolm returned with a black leather medical bag and his gym bag.

"I can give you a shot for the pain, sweetheart." He stroked the back of her wet cheek with his knuckles.

She shook her head. "I don't need that. I just want to go and get this over with and have a nice dinner with you." She smiled weakly. "I was looking forward to that new restaurant in the city."

He brushed his lips against her cheek. "Me, too. But I think we'd better save that for another night. Let me at least start taking care of this." Gwen didn't notice when he used tweezers to remove a large sliver of glass from her finger. She didn't even feel the bandage being wrapped around the cut or the clean T-shirt Malcolm extracted from his gym bag and gently slipped over her head.

She stared across the room with unseeing eyes as her husband worked, thinking only of one thing. And how she would do anything to keep from losing it.

Present Day
Rural Missouri

A black Mercedes CLK500 convertible roared up the long, oak-lined driveway. Seeing the speeding car through the front window of the parlor, a stout woman with friendly eyes framed by bushy silver eyebrows strode out of Charlotte's Web Bed & Breakfast with a purposeful gait. She was headed for an old but immaculately kept carriage house, which now served as a garage for guests. The woman straightened an imaginary crease out of her cargo pants and shoved her hands into her fishing vest as she leaned back on her heels and waited for her guest to emerge from her car.

Gwen pulled into the carriage house and killed the engine, checking the tape on the white bandage that covered her finger before she exited the car.

"You must be Mrs. Langtree." The woman extended a large hand. "I'm Frances Artiste. We spoke on the phone last week. Welcome to Charlotte's Web Bed & Breakfast."

Gwen smiled and grasped the woman's hand, her eyebrows rising slightly at the brisk, enthusiastic shake. She was dressed casually in a pair of tan linen slacks and a pale blue, sleeveless silk top. She had goosebumps all along her arms. She would have to put the top up for the ride home. "Thank you." She hummed a little in admiration. "It's lovely here. The house looks like something right off of Lafayette Square." Gwen knew several families who lived in the exclusive, thirty-acre residential district that was well known for its immaculate nineteenth century architecture.

Stepping out into the breeze, they left the garage and began the short trek to the house.

"She is a beauty," Frances agreed, gazing at the house with pride. "There's not much Federalist architecture left in these parts."

The three-story B&B was narrow, but tall, with a dark wood, six-paneled front door that contrasted nicely with the pale blue walls. The trim, shutters, and latticework were freshly painted a crisp white and two red brick chimneys stretched high into the bright morning sky. Each floor sported its own walkout porch, each of which was surrounded by a white railing and held two small wrought-iron chairs with a circular table between them. It looked to be the perfect place to have a quiet conversation as the sun went down or to sit and watch the squirrels play over morning coffee. It was refined and light in its presentation and Gwen found herself admiring the simplistic, homey feel it exuded.

Rocks crunched under their feet as they walked. "But I was grateful to sell the place and let someone else deal with the financial side of things. I'm more suited to spending my retirement years thinking about what type of suet is best to keep my favorite woodpecker fat and happy than picking one crooked contractor from the next every time a branch hits the house. I'm pretty handy myself"—she patted her own rather hefty bicep proudly—"but this body is too old for climbing up on the roof and other foolish things like that. My Norman always did the cooking and I did the home repairs, but luckily for the guests I did manage to learn my way around the kitchen in the fifty-five years we were married."

Frances didn't elaborate on Norman, and Gwen assumed that he'd passed away. "You're being modest, Mrs. Artiste. I hear that you're an excellent cook." It was the truth. Gwen had spent several days investigating potential locations for the gathering. The Langtrees had modest property holdings, but they included a small luxury hotel and two other B&Bs, all in the St. Louis area. "I wouldn't be spending my time someplace that served beans and weenies or Dinty Moore Beef Stew for dinner."

The older woman blushed at the compliment, her short, paper-white hair standing out even more vividly against her ruddy skin. "I'll make a note not to serve either of those things while you're here," she promised, a little surprised that Gwen Langtree even knew what Dinty Moore was.

Gwen chuckled as they ascended the front steps. "Thanks."

Frances opened the front door and gestured for Gwen to go in ahead of her. "How many guests should I be expecting?"

Gwen stepped inside and onto a large gray drop cloth that covered the entryway floor. A smile swept across her face as she took in the lovely décor. *Nice.* "Myself and four others." She hadn't asked anyone to RSVP, but she felt sure all the women would come. And whoever was blackmailing her couldn't afford to stay away and cast suspicion on herself. At least she hoped that's the way things would work. Lastly, Gwen was relying on the fact that even if Jacie, Nina, Audrey, and Katherine didn't particularly want to see her, they'd at least want to see each other. It was hardly a foolproof plan. But it was all she had.

As it always did, the thought of one of her friends doing something so utterly hateful as blackmail caused anger and hurt to well within her. She quickly turned her attention to something else. "How are the renovations coming, Mrs. Artiste?"

"Call me Frances, please." She pursed her lips as she thought. "Faster than I expected. We should be back open for business in a week or so after your visit. We're refinishing all the floors next week." She shook her head. "I can't understand why you'd want to use this place before it's completely ready. If you'd only wait a little longer, you'd see her at her best, which is pretty darned good if I do say so myself."

"What is it they say in the real estate business?" The women continued to move through house. "Location, location, location?" Gwen gazed out a large window at the expansive back lawn and the several stone paths that crisscrossed there before disappearing into the trees beyond. Other than a small servants' quarters that sat just to the west of the property, which Mrs. Artiste used as her personal residence, there wasn't another house for miles around. Through the open window, Gwen could hear the whispering wind, the jangling of the tree branches, and the occasional birdsong. It was, above all things, private. Which made it perfect. "So long as the place is mostly ready, and we have beds, bathrooms, and a functioning kitchen we'll be just fine."

Frances shrugged. "Whatever you say. Would you like to see the rooms? Each one is decorated differently and filled with gorgeous antiques. Norman was a collector and a stickler about the details, too. There are only five rooms and they're all in different stages of renovation."

"Lead the way." Gwen hesitated, but with a deep breath, bravely pushed forward with her plans. "Umm . . . I don't think there's an easy way to ask this, but I have a special bedding request that I'm hoping you'll be able to accommodate."

Frances laughed. "This is your place, Mrs. Langtree. You can sleep in the hammock by the river if you want to. Lord knows I won't stop you."

Gwen scratched her nose and hid a wry smile. "I hope that won't be necessary. But I have a feeling that my little gathering of friends could turn out to be . . . interesting. When the Mayflower Club gets together, Mrs. Artiste, anything can happen."

Frances swallowed at the serious look on Gwen's face. "Anything?"

"You have no idea."

Late Spring 1975
Hazelwood, Missouri

It was an unseasonably warm day and four fifth-grade girls lay in the deep, fragrant grass, of Audrey's backyard. Having come home from school and changed out of their school clothes, they were now in various types of shorts and T-shirts, tennis shoes or sandals, and gazing up into a brilliant blue sky dotted with fluffy clouds. They were slightly sweaty and dirty from a game of tag that had ended up in a ticklefest.

Katy rolled over onto her belly, plucked a blade of grass from the lawn and popped the end in her mouth. "You can't just be that, Audrey. You should be that plus something else."

Audrey frowned at her cousin and gazed unhappily over at Nina and Gwen to give Katy a nasty look. "Why? My mom is just a mom. So what's wrong with me wantin' to be one when I grow up?"

Katy's gaze dropped to the grass and she shrugged. "I dunno. It seems so boring. Don't you want to be an astronaut or rock star or anything? I'm gonna be a race car driver."

"There are no girl race car drivers," Gwen said. "Maybe you can be the first."

Nina's head bobbed. "Yeah, you can b-be the first and I'll go to-to all your races."

"Me, too," Gwen and Audrey chorused in unison.

"Groovy." Katy wriggled with delight. "What about you, Audrey? You could be a race car driver with me."

"No, thanks," she replied quickly. "I want to have six children. I've got my dolls at home lined up just like my babies will be. Three boys and three girls. And I'm going to name them William, David, Peter, Heather, Misty, and Tina. And we'll have a dog named Jack."

"Don't you already have that dog?" Gwen crossed her feet at the ankles and pointed to the fat pit bull who was sleeping with its head hanging off of Audrey's back porch.

"No."

Gwen's forehead creased. "But I heard—"

"My brother has 'A Dog Named Jack.' That's his name, 'A Dog Named Jack.' If anyone but him calls him by his nickname, Jack, then he pounds them."

Katy hummed her agreement. "It's true."

Nina had rolled over on her side to face Audrey, bracing the side of her head with her grass-stained palm. "You have all the na-na-names picked out for your kids already, Audrey?"

Audrey looked a little confused. "Doesn't everyone?"

Katy stuck out her tongue. "No, stupid. Just you. And you're getting weirder by the day." Lately, Audrey had started to seem a little more like Gwen and Nina than her and Jacie.

"Well, I do," Gwen stated boldly as she sat up on her elbows. "After I become either Miss Missouri or a doctor, I'm going to get married and have a baby boy named Tucker and a baby girl named Wendy. And they'll both have red hair like me, freckles like Nina's"—she paused when Nina crowed in delight—"and dreamy brown eyes like Freddy Prinze."

"Ooo, yeah!" Audrey squealed enthusiastically, the other girls joining in her giggles. "I just luuv him." Then she stuck her tongue out at Katy, vindicated. "Good names, Gwen."

Gwen beamed. "Thanks."

"How about you, Nina? What do you want to be when you grow up?"

They all flopped back down and gazed back up at the clouds, wishing that summer would hurry up and come.

"Well," Nina began, "I think I-I'd like to b-be a vet. I like cats and dogs."

The girls nodded their approval, instantly deciding that a vet would be a perfect job for their tenderhearted friend.

"You can be my Jack's vet," Audrey told her. "I'll need someone I trust to give him shots and stuff."

"I'll be ex-extra careful," Nina swore. "He won't f-f-feel a thing. I always win when we play Operation."

The girls all nodded. Nina had the steadiest hand in the bunch.

"Audrey," Katy started. "Will you bring your kids to my races?"

It was as close as she was going to get to an apology for Katy making fun of her career choice and she knew it. "Of course, dog breath. But only if you win."

Katy snorted. "Well, duh. I've got it all figured out. Girls weigh less than boys, right?"

Audrey looked down at herself and frowned.

"Well, most of the time, right?" Katy said quickly.

They all murmured their agreement.

"So since I'll be lighter, my car will have less to pull and I'll win."

"Nuh-uh." Gwen said. "If that were true then all the best racers would be midgets. They'd weigh the least of all."

"Wrong," Katy stated smugly. "Their feet can't touch the pedals. They couldn't be good drivers."

"Oh yeah." Gwen felt foolish for not realizing that herself. "Sorry."

They'd laid for a long time, talking about nothing at all and everything important—where they would live when they grew up, what popular girls had snubbed or befriended them, and whether Bucky Lee's cowlick would ever lay flat . . . . They watched the clouds change shapes, pointing as they saw faces and objects form and dissolve in the swirling billows. Gwen even swore for a split second, when two clouds collided, that she saw a perfect vision of President Ford peeking down at them.

But someone was missing from the scene, and when her voice interrupted their conversation, each girl smiled, a little happier that their circle was now complete.

"Whatcha doin', guys?" Jacie strode up, still wearing her red, white and blue bell-bottoms school pants, her book bag slung over her shoulder. Her hair was in her usual long ponytail and her longish T-shirt fluttered in the late afternoon breeze.

"Waitin' f-for you," Nina answered, her face wreathed in a happy grin.

"Yeah, where've you been?" Katy wondered out loud. She peered at the mostly hidden sun, noting it was noticeably lower than when they'd all arrived at Audrey's backyard. "We've already been here for nearly forty-five minutes."

Jacie bit her lower lip, trying to decide whether she should lie and confused that she felt the urge to do so in the first place. "I stayed after school for a little while."

"What?" Gwen scooted over so Jacie could lie down between her and Nina. "Again?"

Jacie let her bag fall to the ground and looked up at the sky, wondering what her friends had been pointing at when she'd arrived. She didn't see a thing. "Yeah. S'okay though, I didn't mind."

In a quicksilver move, Audrey stole the blade of grass that Katy was chewing and laughed as she addressed Jacie. "Did you get detention, Jacie? That hasn't happened since last year. I thought you were reformed or something."

Four sets of eyes swung up to stare at the dark-haired girl and she squirmed a little under their weight. "No . . . err . . . Yes . . . errr . . . I just stayed after to give Mrs. Toliver a little help cleaning the blackboard and pushing in the chairs. Stuff like that." She rocked back on her heels. "She's pretty cool," she said, hoping to sound casual. In truth, she knew she'd use any excuse to spend a little extra time with her favorite teacher. The woman was young and vivacious and unlike any teacher Jacie had ever had or even seen before. And most of all, Mrs. Toliver listened intently to whatever Jacie said and smiled at her in a way that thrilled her to the core, causing her stomach to flutter wildly.

Katy's eyes went wide. "You helped clean?"

"Yeah." Jacie lifted her chin indignantly. "So?"

Audrey snorted. "We've seen your messy room. Your mother is always trying to get you to clean, but you're a pig, Jacie."

Every fiber of Nina's being wanted to jump to Jacie's defense. Unfortunately, she'd seen Jacie's room, too, and Audrey was actually being kind by calling it messy.

Gwen couldn't help herself. "Oink. Oink." She wiggled her nose. "Oink."

That's all it took to send Nina and Audrey into fits of helpless giggles.

Jacie put her hands on her hips and stamped one foot. "I am not a pig!"

"She's right, guys." Everyone turned to gape at Katy, shocked at her words because she and Jacie had been antagonizing each other for weeks. "She's not a pig . . ." she paused for effect, "but she's some sort of animal because she's teacher's pet."

Once again, all except Jacie dissolved into laughter.

Jacie's cheeks flushed a bright red, contrasting sharply against her white T-shirt. "Shut up, Katy," she warned darkly.

Nina recovered quickly and forced herself to smother her smile. "S-sorry, Jacie." She caught sight of Jacie's flashing eyes and winced internally, feeling a little guilty for teasing her friend.

"Me, too," Gwen added sincerely with Audrey quickly joining in the apology and patting Jacie's sneaker-covered foot with her outstretched hand.

"And what if I don't shut up?" Katy shot back to Jacie, ignoring Nina and the other girls and directly challenging Jacie, the group's natural, if reluctant, leader for control. It was a common struggle.

"If you don't shut your hole, I—" Jacie stopped and stared at Katy. She squinted, looking closely at the blonde's shorts. "Isn't that a spider crawling up your leg?"

Screeching like a banshee, Katy jumped to her feet and began frantically swatting at her own legs. "Did I get it?" She danced wildly. "Did I get it?"

Jacie sniggered and dropped down on the grass as the other girls roared with laughter, and it took only a second before Katy knew she'd been had. Her face turned beet red with embarrassment and she stomped off in the direction of the playground, muttering under her breath words that all the girls were forbidden to speak.

"Th-that was mean," Nina said, still laughing a little. But no one else bothered to comment on Katy's departure. A least once every week or two, she or Jacie would get mad at the other and stalk off in a huff. But by the next time they all saw each other, the fuss had been long forgotten and everything was back to normal.

"It really was." Audrey high-fived Jacie. "Way to go!"

Gwen's gaze sharpened when something about Audrey caught her eye. "Oh. My. God. You're wearing one, aren't you?"

Audrey's cheeks flushed as dark as Katy's had and she nodded, correctly guessing what Gwen was referring to.

"Wow," Gwen breathed, trying to decide if she was brave enough to ask to see it.

"Wearing what?" Jacie glanced at her friend, and saw the same old Donny Osmond T-shirt she'd seen a million times and a pair of cut-off jeans for shorts.

Gwen gave Jacie's leg a smack. "You're so dense, Jacie! Just look."

Jacie looked again, and Audrey thrust out her chest. "Is that a new hair barrette?" she ventured, clueless.

Gwen's hands flailed in frustration. "She's wearing a bra!"

Jacie screwed up her face. "Gross."

"Shh!" Audrey gasped. "Not so loud, Gwen." She looked around to see if anyone else could have heard. "That's private!"

"No, it's not," Gwen insisted stubbornly. "I can see the straps through your shirt. How can it be private if I can see it?"

"It just is," Audrey said hotly. Then her expression cleared and she smiled as she crossed her arms over her budding breasts. "We went shopping for it special last week. Just Mom and me. We left my brothers at home."

Jacie looked over at Nina's board-flat chest, then down at her own equally unimpressive boobies. "I don't need a bra and I don't want one. Yuck." She let out an aggrieved sigh and turned pleading eyes on the other girls. "Can we talk about something else, please?"

Nina chewed the inside of her cheek. "Well, I-I sort of want one. They're really pretty, Jacie. They come in white and pi-pink and my mom says we'll all have one sooner or later, so we might as well p-pick a cute one."

Jacie stared at Nina as though she was insane.

"Outta sight!" Gwen enthused, looking a little smug. "I not only want one, but my mom is taking me to the store to buy one next Saturday."

"Cool!" Audrey crooned. Suddenly, she felt a new connection with her friend. She had always had more in common with Katy, Jacie, or even Nina than she'd had with Gwen, who was such a girly girl and who had worked hard to get one or two popular friends outside the Mayflower Club. But lately, she and Gwen had spent more time together and she'd discovered that they both liked looking at *Tiger Beat* and talking about a lot of the same things.

A secret part of Audrey longed to be accepted by that other group of girls the way Gwen was. They were a sometimes-mysterious gaggle that boldly hung out in the very center of the playground and in the bathroom at school. They had only the coolest hairstyles and a different pair of shoes for each outfit, and most of all, the boys noticed them in ways they never did Jacie or Katy.

"Did you try it on at the store?" Nina asked, wondering if they came in extra-extra small.

Jacie shut her eyes and groaned as if she was in pain.

"Yup. I had to try on a few to find one that fit. Oooo . . . I almost forgot. They have the most far-out skateboard you can imagine right next to the baseball bats."

Jacie's ears perked up. "Really? What store?"

"Kmart. Right next to the—"

Gwen gasped. "Kmart!" Her face showed her distaste.

Audrey's eyebrows jumped. "Yeah. What's wrong with Kmart?"

Jacie and Nina listened avidly. They both shopped there.

Gwen sniffed and repeated the words she'd heard her mother say. "It's cheap and tacky."

"It is not!" Audrey defended angrily. "You're just being a snot." She fought the urge to remind Gwen that her family was the poorest of the group and that she didn't have any cause to be uppity.

"Yeah," Jacie agreed. "There's nothing wrong with that store. I bought my bike there and it's got a boss banana seat and super tall flag. And when I jump over things the tires don't go flat like they did with my last one."

Nina frowned when Jacie mentioned jumping her bike. The dark-haired girl had set up two wooden ramps at the edge of a local park and had taken to jumping over anything she could get her hands on. She'd even talked Audrey and Gwen into laying on the ground as she sky-rocketed over them. Jacie rarely went a day without crashing, which Nina hated. "You just got your l-last cast off."

"Yup." Jacie happily wiggled the cast-free fingers of her left hand in response.

"You gotta b-be careful, ya know. You'd b-b-better not jump for a while," Nina reminded her friend, knowing that Jacie's mom had recently forbade her from the activity, though that wasn't likely to deter Jacie. Then she turned back to Gwen. "My-my dad bought a hose f-for the garden last week at Kmart. The s-store is okay to me."

"But those are bikes and hoses." Gwen waited for her friends to catch on, but they just looked at her, clearly confused as to what she meant. She sighed. "That stuff's not the same as clothes."

"I think you're a retard, Gwen," Jacie mumbled. "Uff. Hey!" She rubbed the ribs Nina had just elbowed.

"So where am I supposed to get my clothes?" Audrey said, starting to get upset. "My mom likes Kmart!"

"Well," Gwen began, considering the question carefully, "I think it's fine to get them at Kmart, so long as nobody knows you got them there. And this is a bra we're talking about." Jacie made a series of gagging noises that Gwen promptly ignored. "So if you don't tell anyone, they won't know."

"Oh." Audrey thought about that. She didn't particularly care where her clothes were from so long as she liked them.

Gwen leaned forward a little. "Does it have a pink or blue bow right here?" She touched a spot between her own non-existent breasts.

Audrey beamed. Apparently, the style was right even if it was from the dreaded Kmart. "Uh-huh! Blue!"

Gwen grinned her approval.

"Wanna see it?" Audrey asked, glancing over to Nina and Jacie a little self-consciously.

"Yes!" Gwen jumped to her feet and offered a hand to the chubby girl, grunting a little as she helped her up. Her gaze flicked to Nina and Jacie. "You guys coming?"

Jacie snorted. "I don't want to see Audrey naked." A single dark brown eyeball appeared and she added, "No offense, Audrey."

Audrey plucked a piece of grass from her curly hair. "S'okay. It's not like I want to see you naked either." Both girls laughed. "How 'bout you, Nina, you wanna see it?"

"Nah." Nina yawned. "I saw 'em at the s-s-store. And I gotta go h-home soon anyway."

"Okay then." Audrey and Gwen started walking for Audrey's back door. "Catch ya on the flip side."

"Bye." Nina and Jacie waved from their positions flat on their backs, their faces already pointing toward the sky.

"Well," Nina started after a moment or two of comfortable silence. She paused as an exceptionally pretty cloud caught her eye. "I guess I-I should go home."

Jacie sighed. She didn't particularly want to go yet. The new grass was cool against her back and the sun was still strong enough to warm the soft cotton of her shirt. Nina didn't jabber on and on like Audrey and Gwen tended to do and it was still at least an hour until supper. "I guess I should go home and do homework too." She made a face as though she smelled something incredibly stinky.

Nina sat up and tugged over Jacie's book bag. She unzipped it and peered inside. "How far are you on r-r-reading?" She moved aside Jacie's math book and three-ring binder and pulled out a copy of *Where the Red Fern Grows* and Jacie's social studies book.

"Finished up to Chapter 21 in social studies. Haven't even started the book about plants."

Nina's eyes bugged. "Ch-chapter 21 already! Bu-but we were only assigned Chapter 21 t-two days ago."

Jacie turned just her head to face Nina and this time it was her turn to stutter. "Well, I-I—"

"You're the s-smartest of us all," Nina pronounced, knowing full well that Jacie didn't like it when anyone pointed out how intelligent she was.

But they were alone now, which meant Nina could say pretty much anything she liked.

"Am not," Jacie said stubbornly, crossing her arms over her chest. "You get all A's and B's and I nearly failed Mr. Richards' bogus science class last fall."

Nina playfully swatted Jacie's belly. "That's because I-I-I did all my homework and half the time you forget to-to turn yours in."

Jacie gave her friend a lopsided grin. "I only forget when it's extra boring."

Nina let out a long breath. "I haven't even st-started social studies but I'm halfway th-through *Where the R-Red Fern Grows*." She held up the book they'd recently been assigned in their advanced reading group. "It's really good and it's not about p-plants at all."

Jacie glanced at the book dismissively. "Looks old and boring."

"It's not!" Nina opened the book. "I'll sh-show you." And then she began to read aloud.

Jacie just closed her eyes and listened. She couldn't recall the last time anyone had read to her, and Nina's voice was soft and clear and it lulled her into a completely peaceful state. Nina read for a long time and Jacie was completely absorbed by the story until—"Hey!"

Nina nearly jumped out of her skin. She dropped the book and rose to her hands and knees. "What?" Frantically, she began looking around, trying figure out what caused Jacie to yell.

"You're not stuttering any more."

Nina's expression grew dark. The Mayflower Club never, *never* made fun of her stuttering. "What are you talking a-about?" She heard herself stutter and her chest clenched. She hated the way she sounded.

"When you were reading, you weren't stuttering," Jacie insisted. She grabbed the book and forced it back into Nina's hands. "Read some more." She gave her a little shove. "Go on."

Nina sighed and set the book down on the grass. "I-I always stutter, Jacie. Mama said I'd g-g-grow out of it. And it's better then w-when I was little. But not that m-much better. Mama even made an a-a-appointment with a speech therapist."

"Just try it," Jacie begged. "Please?"

When those dark pleading eyes were turned Nina's way, the girl found herself helpless to refuse. "Okay," she said hesitantly, picking up the book and finding her place. "But it w-won't work."

"Just try."

Nina took a deep breath. She read the first line and stuttered several words. Angrily, she slammed the book closed and felt tears sting her eyes. "See!"

"Try again." Jacie's voice was soothing and filled with confidence. "You weren't stuttering before, Nina. Honest." She handed her back the book. "One last time. And this time just think about the story. It is good, just like you said. My favorite part was where . . ."

Nina tucked a strand of dark blond hair behind her ear as she listened to Jacie, a little surprised at how intently she'd been listening. When she found the right page, she glanced over to Jacie, who was lying in the grass peacefully, her eyes closed as the sun painted her face. Nina gathered her courage and began to read again. She stuttered at first, but Jacie didn't interrupt her, and before she knew it, she was lost in the story. It was a full ten minutes later when Jacie rolled over on her side to face Nina, her mouth shaping a triumphant grin. "Toldja."

Nina froze mid-sentence and looked at Jacie and found the courage to try again. She swallowed hard, then read a few more lines and realized that the words were coming out in a steady stream. Nina blinked. "Jinkies!"

Jacie let out a loud whoop of victory. "You did it!"

"How did I-I-?" She pounded the ground with one fist. "Argh!" She was stuttering again.

Jacie frowned. "You don't do it when you read. Maybe you just need practice. You can read to me after school."

"But what about your p-piano lessons? You have to practice three da-days a week."

Jacie groaned. She'd forgotten about those. "If I tell my mom I'm reading with you, she might let me quit. Can't you save me from them?"

"I c-can try." Nina paused and then bravely plowed ahead. "After all, wh-what are best friends for?" She searched Jacie's face for a reaction, well aware that she'd never called Jacie her best friend before, though she'd felt it was true for so long, she couldn't remember when it wasn't true.

A thrill chased its way up and down Jacie's spine and she shot her a toothy grin. "Exactly. Best friends help each other through thick and thin."

Nina released a nervous breath just as Gwen and Audrey emerged from Audrey's house and trotted over to their friends.

"How come you're still here?" Audrey asked. "Jacie, don't you have to eat dinner by now?"

"Damn!" Jacie roared, jumping to her feet. "I gotta go." She snatched up her book bag and took both of the books from Nina, who also stood. Then she did something she'd never done to anyone outside of her family. She pulled Nina into a heartfelt hug, which Nina giddily returned.

"You shouldn't swear, Jacie," Gwen admonished, still shocked that Jacie had hugged anyone. "It's not ladylike." She scratched her head. "Hey, what's up with you two?"

Jacie gave them a brief rundown of what had happened, and Gwen and Audrey squealed with delight, jumping up and down and hugging Nina.

"You can read to me on Mondays after school, Nina," Gwen offered, eager to help.

"And me on Tuesdays and Katy on Wednesday," Audrey piped up, sure that her cousin would want to help too. "Would a magazine be okay?" All eyes turned to Jacie, the newly anointed expert on the subject.

Jacie flipped her ponytail off her shoulder and brushed some grass from her shirt. "How should I know?" But she gave the question its due. "I don't see why it wouldn't work. Reading is reading. Even if it is about foxy, dorky boys."

Audrey smiled. "Then I'm picking a magazine. 'kay, Nina?"

"Okay." Nina felt like she might cry and her chin began to quiver. "Th-thanks, guys."

The moment was thick with emotion and Jacie shifted uncomfortably. "I really gotta go now."

Nina sniffed and nodded. "I'll walk b-back with you part way." And then they were off in the direction of their street, turning their heads after a couple dozen paces when Gwen called their names.

The tall girl cupped her hands around her mouth so that her voice would carry. "Jacie, you oughta be a doctor when you grow up."

Jacie waved at them but didn't answer. "So," she glanced down at

Nina as they walked. "Do you think I should be a doctor?"

Nina scrunched up her face. "Of course n-not. You're going to be too b-busy breaking world records to be a doctor."

Jacie's smile was so wide it was a wonder her face didn't crack in two. Nobody knew her like Nina.

Present Day
Clayton, Missouri

"Who are we going to see again, Mom?"

Jacie steered the truck onto the quiet residential street where Nina now lived. "We're going to see an old friend of mine." *I can't believe I'm doing this after she hung up on me.* When she realized that her palms were actually sweating, she wiped them on her T-shirt, wondering if Emily could tell how nervous she was.

The girl rolled down the window and stuck her head out like a dog on a truck ride and grinned wildly, the wind whipping back her dark hair. "Why are you scared then?" she asked loudly.

Jacie sighed. "Get your head back in the truck, crazy, and I'm not scared. I'm . . . Well, I'm just . . ." *What am I?* She let out a frustrated breath and decided to change the subject. There had to be some benefit to being the adult in the relationship. "My friend doesn't know we're coming today, and I hope it's going to be a nice surprise."

"Can you at least roll down your window?"

Jacie sighed, knowing it was too cool to need the windows rolled down, but doing it anyway because it made Emily happy.

The little girl was quiet for a moment, watching the trees and houses with an interested eye. "I was surprised when you came to pick me up from school today." She turned toward Jacie. "We don't usually see each other during the week."

Jacie felt a lump form in her throat, and she had to swallow around it to speak. "I know. But I thought you might like to come with me today." She was still amazed that Alison, the evil whore-bitch, had allowed the impromptu visit at all and Jacie figured that her ex must have had plans for the night anyway and that Emily was simply destined for an evening with a babysitter.

An enormous smile met her mom's words. "I always want to come with you."

Jacie nodded and grinned back. "Same here, kiddo." She eased through an unmarked intersection. "My friend's name is Nina Chilt— Uhh," she realized she didn't know whether Nina was married or if she even had the same last name. "Anyway, I guess you can just call her Nina unless she introduces herself differently." *I have lost my mind. I know it.*

"Okay." Emily shrugged. She didn't much care what they did, so long as they did it together. "Is it her birthday?" She reached back to the back-seat and retrieved a small wrapped box.

"Uh . . . No. I just . . . I had something that I wanted to give her." She licked her lips nervously. "I figured now was as good a time as any."

A few more minutes passed and Jacie pulled up in front of the gray Colonial. "Wow," she murmured. "It's just the same as I remember it."

"You've been here before?" Emily asked as she unbuckled her seat-belt.

"Sure." Jacie didn't move except to peer out of her daughter's window. "I stayed the night here several times when I was a kid when my friend was here to visit her grandparents."

"That long ago?"

Jacie snorted. "Way back in the 1970s if you can imagine that."

Emily's eyes went round. "Cool!"

Jacie chuckled at the awe in her daughter's voice, though her stomach was in knots.

Emily exited the truck and stood on the curb to wait for her mother, taking the opportunity to look around. The neighborhood was nice, she decided. Pretty houses sat back far from the street and were separated by thick sets of bushes or trees. Then she spied something near the back of the house. "A treehouse!"

Jacie craned her head as she stared out the window but couldn't see what Emily was looking at.

"C'mon, Mom," the girl rapped on the window excitedly. "Aren't you coming out?"

Jacie sucked in a deep breath, a little unsure of the answer. She hadn't wanted to know Nina's address or phone number, and yet, here she was. She'd picked up Emily and driven over here on impulse, taking only the time necessary to wrap a small gift for Nina. Now that she thought about it, she felt incredibly stupid for showing up unannounced. "Get back inside the truck, Emily. I think this was a bad—" She stopped when a tow-headed boy exploded out of the front door of Nina's house and ran down the walk at full speed.

Jacie was afraid he was going to smash headlong into the truck, but he stopped just short of Emily, sticking both of his hands in his jeans pockets as he curiously regarded the younger girl. He was a sturdy-looking boy, whose face was covered with freckles. His hair was tousled despite being cut short and spiked on top and the thick locks were a lighter shade of blond than Jacie ever remembered seeing Nina's. There was, however, not a doubt in her mind that she was looking at Nina's son.

"Hi, I'm Robbie," he said to Emily, glancing warily at the grownup in the truck.

Tentatively, Emily gave him a friendly smile, pleased that an older boy was talking to her at all. Then she cast her gaze to the ground, suddenly shy. "Hi. My name is Emily."

Unconsciously, Robbie puffed out his chest and stood a little taller.

Jacie's eyebrows lifted at the natural interplay. "Gimme a break," she mumbled.

"How come you're parked in front of my house?" he asked in a clear but gentle voice. "If you're lost, I might be able to help you."

Jacie smiled at his kindness.

"We're here to see your mom." Emily pointed through the open window to Jacie, who was still rooted in place. "That's my mom." She crossed her eyes. "She's afraid to get out of the truck."

Jacie shot Emily an evil look.

Robbie jumped off the curb as though he was competing in the broad jump at the Olympics and then ran around the side of the truck, stopping just short of poking his head into the window.

Jacie was glad she was sitting down, because when his blue-green eyes met her gaze it was Nina looking at her all over again, and her knees felt like jelly. "H—" She swallowed a few times. "Hi." She tried to smile reassuringly. "I'm Jacie."

"Nice to meet you," Robbie said politely. "My mom's not home." Already bored with Jacie, he glanced back at Emily.

With a reprieve from those eyes, Jacie's gaze strayed to the house and she wondered if she should fish for a little information. *Oh, what the hell.* "What about your dad? Is he home?"

The boy shook his head. "No dad, just us and Grandma, who's watchin' me tonight."

Just then Agnes Chilton stepped out onto the front porch, still drying her hands on a yellow kitchen towel. "Robbie?" Her brow furrowed. "Who are you talking to?"

"A friend of Mom's," he bellowed back, loud enough for the entire neighborhood to take notice.

Jacie winced and rubbed her now-ringing ear. She sighed inwardly, knowing that she couldn't change her mind now and that she'd have to at least say hello to Nina's mother. *At least it's not my mother.* The thought left her cold.

Under her breath, Jacie cursed herself for not sneaking away while she had the chance. Then she cursed herself some more for being a hopeless chicken. The older woman slowly made her way down the front walkway as Jacie, who felt like she was eleven years old again, emerged from the truck. "Hello, Mrs. Chilton," she said, trying not to look as surprised as she felt at the sight of Nina's mom. *God, how did she get so old?*

Agnes smiled warmly. "If it isn't that scamp Jacie Ann Priest, all grown up and as beautiful as ever." She held out her arms. "Come and give me a hug. I haven't seen you in ages."

Jacie let out a relieved breath. Clearly, Nina had never told her mother what had transpired between them. She closed the remaining steps to Agnes and gave her a gentle hug, laughing when the older woman increased the pressure just to hear Jacie squawk.

"I'm not so old I'm going to break, Jacie Ann. Don't you dare coddle me!" But the smile on her face took any sting from the words.

After a long moment, Jacie stepped back and reached for Emily, taking her hand. "Can Nina come out and play?" she asked mischievously, earning a chuckle from Agnes.

Agnes repeated what Robbie had said, adding that Nina had had to go into her office for some paperwork for her new job and that she probably wouldn't be home until late. Jacie wasn't sure whether to be relieved about Nina being gone or not.

"Is that going to be a tree house?" Emily pointed to the pile of wood at the base of a tree that was just visible around the side of the house. Several boards had already been nailed into place.

"Yup," Robbie said proudly. "Wanna see?"

"Yeah!" Emily took a large step forward and then remembered she was supposed to ask permission. She turned and opened her mouth, but Jacie got there first.

"Go on." Jacie waved toward the side of the house. "Just stay with Robbie and no touching anything sharp." She lifted her eyebrows meaningfully. "Got me?"

Emily rolled her eyes. "Gotcha, Mom. Thanks!"

The children took off running toward the tree with Robbie slowing down just enough so that Emily could keep up. Jacie shook her head. "Remember when you were young enough to run everywhere you went?"

Agnes sighed. "No."

Jacie started to laugh. "Neither do I."

The two women sat on the porch and chatted for a few minutes with Agnes doing most of the talking and Jacie giving the occasional nod or adding a scant detail about her own life. It was hard to stop Agnes when she was on a roll.

"So," Agnes began casually, "you are going to that gathering of your old friends this weekend, aren't you?"

The smile that Jacie had been wearing since she arrived slipped from her face. The more she thought about it, the less convinced she was that she'd be comfortable being in the same room with Nina, much less Gwen, whom she might strangle just for the fun of it. Perhaps missing Nina tonight was a sign that the past was best left dead and buried. "Umm . . . No." She looked away. "I have plans this weekend."

"Oh, I see." Agnes's tone was thoughtful. "Nina will be so upset."

Jacie's jaw sagged. "She will?"

"Of course! The main reason she decided to attend was because you were going to be there. She's all packed."

Jacie looked skeptical. "She actually said that?"

"She wants to see all you girls." Agnes's gaze softened. "But you most of all, Jacie Ann."

Jacie chewed on that for a moment, not knowing what to say.

Agnes sighed. "Well, I hope you change your mind. You will change your mind, won't you?"

Jacie had to admire the other woman's persistence. "As I said, I have plans. And"—she slapped her thighs—"it's getting time for supper."

"You're welcome to join us for dinner," Agnes said quickly, hoping that Jacie would stay. "Since Nina's not home, we're having all of Robbie's favorites, a kid-friendly meal that's all white and consists of macaroni and cheese, cottage cheese, and french fries."

The women shared knowing, chagrined looks. "Emily would be in heaven, but as tempting as that is . . ." Jacie stood from her spot on the stairs and jumped the two stairs to the bottom as Agnes rose from her nearby chair. "I'll have to say no thank you, Mrs. Chilton. Emily and I already have a date with a pizza parlor."

"If you're sure?"

Jacie nodded.

"All right then." She patted Jacie's forearm. "She's a beautiful girl, Jacie Ann. How proud you must be."

Jacie's face broke into a dazzling smile. "I really am." And as she said the words, she realized that she'd been looking forward to showing off her daughter to Nina. She wasn't close to any of her family and the thought of someone she cared about meeting her Emily was very, very appealing.

"Time to go, Emily!" Jacie called out, not surprised when both children came racing around the corner in a matter of seconds. But before they left, she asked Emily to fetch Nina's gift from the truck.

Jacie looked at the box for several long seconds, deciding whether she was going to part with it or not. With a deep breath she said, "Can you give this to Nina for me?"

Agnes took the slender box. "Are you sure you wouldn't rather give it to her this weekend?"

Jacie smiled sadly. "No. I think this way is best. She'll understand."

Robbie patted Emily on the back. "Thanks for coming over to play. Can you come back when the tree house is done? It's gonna be really cool."

Emily looked hopefully at her mother, but Jacie didn't answer, un-willing to commit to something only to have to break her word later. "Maybe," Emily finally ventured.

"Goodbye," Jacie said warmly, directing the words to Nina's son. Then her gaze lifted to Agnes, who was still standing on the porch. "And thanks."

Agnes and Robbie waved as the pickup pulled away and disappeared down the street.

Robbie sighed as he took the wrapped box from his grandmother and gave it a little shake, trying to determine what was inside. "Emily was pretty cool for a girl. And her mom, too," he said absently.

Agnes slung the dishrag over her shoulder and wrapped an arm around Robbie's waist to lead him inside, the wheels in her head spin-ning at a furious rate. "Mm. They certainly were."

It was nearly nine o'clock by the time Nina pulled into the driveway. Agnes was waiting on the porch with a pitcher of lemonade and an extra sweater for Nina to ward off the evening chill. She was big into constant hydration and warmth. A few sluggish bugs buzzed around the amber porch light and the smell of damp leaves filled the air. For the first time all year, it felt like autumn.

"I'm sorry it's so late, Mom." Nina ran a hand through her hair. "Tonight was so hectic. They're trying to get a new exhibit up for this weekend and I decided to stay and help." Her gaze strayed to the second floor. "Is Robbie already in bed?"

"Bathed and snoring away."

Nina let out defeated groan. "You're a miracle worker. I usually have to all but threaten his life to get him to bed by nine. Especially on Friday nights."

"I do my best." Actually, Agnes had threatened his life. But Nina didn't need to know that. It was best to keep the all-knowing mother thing going for as long as possible. "Here," she gestured to an empty chair. "Sit and put this on."

Nina flopped down the seat and took the thin sweater, wrapping it around her shoulders. "I'm so tired," she moaned, already looking forward to sleeping in. She reached for the pitcher of lemonade as she stretched out her legs. "Anything interesting happen today?"

"Your friend Jacie Ann and her daughter Emily stopped by tonight."

Nina nearly dropped the pitcher. "Jesus Christ." With wide eyes, she fumbled with it for a few seconds before getting a good grip on the damp glass. "What? Jacie came by here? And she has a daughter?"

"That's what I said."

In shock, Nina shook her head a little. "Wow. I can't believe . . . How did she seem? Jacie, I mean."

Agnes tilted her head to the side. "Witty. Smart. Pretty. Same as always."

Nina wasn't sure whether that was good news or not. Jacie was a mom? Wow.

"Are you going to Gwen's gathering this weekend?" Agnes asked suddenly.

Nina shook her head. "I already told you I decided not to go."

"But Jacie Ann is going to be so disappointed."

Nina blinked. "Since when!"

"Since I spoke to her tonight. She said the entire reason she was going was to see you." Agnes gave Nina a woeful look to complete the effect.

"But . . ." Nina was still shell-shocked.

"She even brought you a gift." Agnes reached down behind her chair and handed Nina a small box wrapped in brown Kraft paper.

"What's this for?" Nina turned the box over in her hands and shook it, exactly the way Robbie had done.

"I have no earthly idea, but she said that you'd understand."

Nina licked her lips and wiped her damp palms on her jeans before tearing open the paper and lifting the lid. When she saw what was inside, her eyes slammed closed, a glistening tear escaping one corner.

Agnes gaped. "I didn't know it would make you cry." She peered through the dim light to see what sort of gift could elicit such a strong reaction. "Well, what is it? What does it mean?"

Nina pulled the gift from the box and pressed it against her heart before handing it to her mother. She wiped her eyes and when she spoke. Her voice was heavy with emotion. "It means I need to go upstairs and pack. Can you still look after Robbie if I go to this gathering?"

Agnes's eyebrows jumped. "Of course. But I—"

"Thanks, Mom." Nina pressed a quick kiss to her mother's cheek and then hurried inside, leaving the older woman alone with the chirping crickets.

"Huh." Agnes held the gift up to the light to get a better look.

It was an old, tattered copy of *Where the Red Fern Grows*.

As she traced the letters on its cover, she wondered why a book about plants would bring anyone to tears. But, she decided, it really didn't matter. What mattered was Nina's ultimate happiness and toward that end she lifted her glass in a toast. "To friends and reunions"—she paused to nibble her lip, and then added—"and to as many chances as it takes to get things right."

Chapter 5
Present Day
Town & Country, Missouri

"Here you go, Mrs. Langtree." A diminutive housekeeper with skin so black it held a tint of blue handed Gwen a stainless steel traveling mug full of steaming cappuccino. "Can I get you anything else?"

The morning air was cool, and Gwen could see her breath as she leaned against her convertible and accepted the warm mug. Her red hair was swept up in a clip that held it just off her neck and she was wearing a sleeveless white sweater, deck shoes, and soft jeans she hadn't had occasion to put on in several years. She smiled weakly, more nervous about reuniting with the Mayflower Club than she thought she'd be. "No, thank you, Ruby." She brought the mug to her lips and peered over the rim. "Did you remember to add the whiskey?"

Ruby's eyes widened and her gaze flicked to the car. "But—"

Gwen chuckled and took a sip. "Just kidding." She sighed. "Mostly."

Ruby pointed to the passenger seat that held a small travel bag, and her normally rich voice rose to a squeak. "Is that all you're bringing?"

A sassy eyebrow lifted. "Would you be surprised if I said yes?"

Ruby just snorted.

Gwen shook her head. "Fine. I have more. Tucker came by to have breakfast with Mr. Langtree and I sent him inside to get my other bags."

Ruby hummed a little and spoke under her breath. "Thank Jesus, I'm too old to carry them myself."

"I heard that, Ruby."

Malcolm, dressed, but with a dab of shaving cream still on his cheek, trotted out of the house. He dismissed Ruby with a quick wave of his hand and the small woman shuffled back into the house.

Gwen frowned. Malcolm wasn't usually so rude.

He stopped in front of her, a curious expression on his face. "There was a phone call for you just now."

"Really?" Gwen answered absently, fishing through her purse for her driving glasses with one hand. "Who was it?"

Malcolm's normally mild-mannered expression went a little hard. "He didn't say."

Something odd in his voice made Gwen look up from her rummaging. "Malcolm?"

"That's happened a couple of times this week."

"Has it?"

"You know it has. I've asked you about them."

"Do you want me to call the phone company?" she asked tentatively, unsure of where the conversation was headed.

Their gazes locked and Gwen felt the bottom drop out of her stomach.

A pained, lost expression swept over his face and tears filled his eyes. "Are you having an affair, Gwen?"

The unexpected question stole the breath from her lungs as surely as a punch to the gut would have. She actually had to grab hold of the car to steady herself. "Wh-What?" *Oh, my God.*

He sniffed and lifted his chin, not caring that he was having this discussion in his driveway. "Are you?"

She stared at him for a moment, flabbergasted that he actually appeared to be serious. She reached out to touch his forearm, and he flinched before her bandage-covered hand could graze him. "How could you even ask me such a thing?" she asked harshly, her voice a loud whisper.

"How could I not!" He threw his hands in the air. The phone call this morning had been the last straw. "You're acting so strange. I keep asking you about it and you won't talk to me!" He gently grasped her arm and held her bandaged hand in front of her face as proof of her erratic behavior. "Someone is calling here but won't leave his name. If I go near your computer, you act as though you're going to have a heart attack." He let her hand drop. "What's going on, Gwen?"

Her heart began to thump wildly in her chest and she looked around self-consciously, despite the fact that the nearest neighbor was several hundred yards away and behind a privacy fence. "Nothing."

"It's not nothing," he growled. "Jill saw you!"

"What could your secretary have seen? Jesus Christ, Malcolm. Are you insane? I'm not having an affair!"

"You told me you were visiting your mother yesterday."

"I was!"

"Then why did Jill see you coming out of the Werner Building downtown at lunch?"

Dead silence.

Gwen closed her eyes. *Shit. I never should have gone to Gramercy's office in person.* Too close. Everything was closing in on her. "Malcolm—"

"Do you deny it?"

Her gaze was heartsick. Lying to him tore at her insides, but the truth was even more unbearable. "Of course, I don't deny it, sweetheart. I went to Mother's after I stopped by the new gallery on the third floor of the Werner Building. It just opened last week." She dug around in her purse and pulled out a creased brochure from the gallery, holding it up for him to see and privately thanking God that she'd picked it up on a whim as she'd exited the building. "I must have forgotten to mention it because I was there for such a short time. You know how I feel about impressionists and that was the entire display."

Uncertainty colored Malcolm's features and he swallowed hard.

This time when she reached out he accepted her touch, and she felt her racing pulse began to calm. Gwen could tell by his eyes that he desperately wanted to believe her, and she knew the very second when painful uncertainty shifted into belief. She vowed on the spot to fire Gramercy Investigations and never contact them again. She couldn't risk it. "I don't know who's been calling here; it's only been two calls, but we'll contact the phone company and have it blocked or traced." She gently rubbed her fingertips through the hair on his arm. "It's probably some teenager playing a stupid prank."

She sounded so reasonable, so calm, that his wild accusation appeared rash and foolish. With an unsteady breath, he took the brochure from her hand and felt his cheeks began to heat. "I—I don't know what I was thinking." His jaw worked and shook his head. "I—"

Suddenly, she kissed him hard, feeling a strong arm wrap around her and pull her body tighter to his, the embrace so tight it hurt. When she pulled away, she spoke against his lips and his mustache tickled her mouth. "I love you, Malcolm. You believe that, don't you?"

"Yes," he whispered, but his brow was deeply furrowed. "But there's still something wrong." He chewed his lip as he thought. "Something you're not—"

"No buts," she interrupted quickly, hoping the tremors she was feeling on the inside weren't noticeable. "It's true, I've been out of sorts thinking about this reunion." She lowered herself from her tiptoes, but maintained firm eye contact as she offered up a wan smile. "I'm a little spooked about coming face-to-face with my childhood again."

"That's all it is?" he asked skeptically. "You haven't been sleeping." He trailed his fingers down her arm and circled her slender wrist, holding it up for inspection. "I'm worried about you, Gwen. You've lost weight." He licked his lips, hating to press the point but unwilling to let it go without a fight. "All because you're seeing your friends again?"

No, her mind screamed. *Because I can't stand the thought of losing you and Tucker!*

"I can tell there's more." He cupped her chin with a firm but gentle hand and tilted her face upward. "And—"

"Hi." Tucker jogged up to the couple and looked questioningly between his parents, who both plastered on welcoming, though visibly uncomfortable smiles.

In Tucker's hands were two large leather suitcases. "Did I interrupt something?" His voice lacked its usual warmth and Gwen instantly wondered what he'd heard, but a second later he flashed his father his usual smile and her concern was cast aside.

Tucker was several inches shorter than his father's 6 feet 2 inches, with a slim waist and dark brown hair that curled around his ears and just above his collar. He was handsome in a brooding sort of way, with soulful eyes that held a perpetually vulnerable look that drew women the way blossoms drew bees.

Malcolm took the bags from his son and with a lingering look at Gwen, moved to the trunk, which was already open. "You know your mother," he teased gently. "She always decides it's a good time to talk as she's walking out the door."

Gwen stepped around Tucker to address Malcolm, affectionately patting her son on the back as she moved. "We'll talk when I get home, Mal?"

"Count on it." Malcolm's eyes conveyed his apology, and Gwen couldn't help but give him a hug, feeling his heart still beating fast from their discussion. "It's going to be okay," she whispered in his ear, her voice so low that only he could hear it, and was rewarded with a tightening of his embrace. "I know you want to talk, but I need to go."

Malcolm brushed his lips against the top of her head, torn between insisting she stay and not wanting to make a bigger fool of himself. "Have fun," he finally said, reluctantly admitting what he hoped was only a temporary defeat.

Gwen breathed a sigh of relief, her breath creating a fog in the early morning air. Worry still gnawed at her guts, but she did her best to ignore it. She needed to get out of here before she did something foolish. Something she couldn't undo, like telling Malcolm everything and begging his forgiveness. With a sigh, she gently disentangled herself from her husband to give Tucker a goodbye kiss, but the young man was already seated in his blood-red Mini Cooper, which was parked a few yards from Gwen's car. A little disappointed, she picked up her travel mug as Malcolm closed the trunk. "Bye, Tuck." She gave him a quick wave.

He was very aware of the awkward interaction between his parents, and his forehead wrinkled as he waved back. They usually got along quite well, and he could always tell when they were arguing. But this, somehow, was different. "Bye, Mom." He let a grin overtake his face when he turned to Malcolm. "C'mon, Dad!"

Malcolm closed Gwen's car door after she climbed in, giving the roof a pat when he was finished. He opened his mouth to say something else when Tucker playfully honked his horn.

The college student gave his father a woebegone look. "I'm starving, ya know."

Malcolm held up his hands in surrender and chuckled weakly. "All right, I'm coming." He gave Gwen a warm, apologetic smile, not quite able to look her in the eye. "I love you," he mouthed silently.

Gwen's heart clenched and for a long moment she was once again tempted to tell him everything. Instead, she said, "I love you, too," and started the ignition.

Tucker's horn sounded again and Malcolm shot his son a slightly an-noyed look. "Hold your horses, chow hound. I'm sure the club won't run out of eggs and orange juice," he mumbled.

She watched her husband fold himself into the tiny car, wishing that Tucker drove something safer, like a Volvo. Or a Sherman tank. When they were well out of sight, Gwen rested her forehead against the steering wheel, her fingers gripping the leather until her knuckles showed white. "What am I gonna do? What am I gonna do?" she chanted. This visit was important. Things were beginning to unravel at home. She'd handled this badly so far, and she'd worked too hard to have her life fall apart.

As she pulled out of her driveway, she thought bitterly of the women she had loved and how one among them was driving a knife into her heart . . . and twisting it.

Present Day
Rural Missouri

Dressed in jeans and a soft, red fleece shirt, Audrey sat with her el-bows on her knees on the front porch of Charlotte's Web B&B. The mid-morning fog had yet to completely clear, and the vibrant autumn colors were just starting to peek through the mist. She smiled and took another sip of the rich Kona coffee Frances Artiste had graciously greeted her with when she'd arrived at the B&B only moments before.

She lifted her head, a tiny smile edging its way across her face. The Missouri countryside smelled just as she remembered and no place else could quite replicate the combination of wet, bruised plants, fertilizer, and fragrant wood smoke that tickled her senses. It felt very much like home, and despite the fact that she loved her life in Salt Lake City, she felt a pang of homesickness that she hadn't experienced since her earliest days on her own.

The sound of a far-off car engine caused her head to turn and the butterflies in her stomach to flutter.

Audrey stood as a rusty, mint green Karmann Ghia clanked down the long driveway. Through the lightly tinted windows she could see a shock of pale hair and could feel the vibration of the pounding music as "Jessie's Girl" blasted out of the car's amazingly loud stereo. *Katy.* Her excitement began to build, and she had to force herself not to run over to the carriage house-turned-garage to greet her cousin.

It took Audrey a second to realize that there was no reason in the world to tamp down her impulse. She was excited, dammit, and she couldn't bring herself to be ashamed of that. Grinning wildly, she set off toward the old garage.

"Katy!" Audrey hollered as she walked, hearing the vehicle door squeak loudly as it was opened and then slammed shut. "Only you would be driving such a butt-ugly car, but manage to have a state-of-the-art stereo system."

"Audrey?" came the disembodied voice from inside the carriage house.

She stopped dead in her tracks, listening to a rusty trunk open and close. "Yes?"

"Are you still short and round?"

Audrey snorted, taking the insult in stride. She tapped her chin thoughtfully. "Depends. Are you still a trashy slut?"

There was a few seconds' pause before both women shouted, "Yes!" and began to laugh.

Smiling broadly, Katherine emerged from the garage dragging a dinged suitcase behind her. "Hiya, cuz," she drawled.

Audrey's excitement bubbled over. "Hiya, cuz. Now that the pleasantries are over, hurry up and get over here!"

The women threw their arms around each other and held on tight for a long time, rocking with the slight breeze.

"You look beautiful," Katherine whispered emotionally.

Audrey's eyes closed and she let her insecurity over her appearance fade into the recesses of her mind, though after a lifetime of being self-conscious, it was something she'd never truly get over. "You too." She pulled away and affectionately ran her hands over the very tips of Katherine's short, spiked hair, giving it a critical once over. She nodded decisively. "I think it looks just like Grandpa's did."

"Hey!" Katherine gasped and slapped Audrey's fingers away from the stiff peaks. "I'll have you know that I paid good money for this. It is a platinum blond spike. Not a white, jar-head crewcut!"

Audrey affected a serious pose. "Oh, yes," she said slowly, making a show of examining the locks again. "Now I see the difference." She plucked at Katherine's lightweight jacket and blouse and peeked down inside. "So where's the *Semper Fi* tattoo? Grandma said Grandpa's was right on his—"

"Don't you dare go there, Audrey." Katherine wrinkled her nose. "And I'll have you know, since it took you all of three seconds to mention it, that I'm not nearly the slut I used to be. I'm too tired to stay out all night nowadays." A twinkle entered her glacier-blue eyes. "I have a steady boyfriend who I'm crazy about. I think I might be off the market for a good long time."

"Ooo . . . Will I get to hear all the torrid details?"

"Torrid details mixed with lies. The usual."

"Heh. Good." Her face suddenly sobered as she took a good look at the woman standing so close to her. Katherine was several inches taller than her own five feet three inches and had stayed slim over the years; a slight softening around her jaw line was the only clue as to the onset of middle age. She looked healthy and happy. Audrey's voice took on a serious tone that was rarely used with her mischievous cousin. "My God, Katy, I feel like Aunt Gladys is looking back at me."

The women shared sad, slightly watery smiles. Katherine's mother Gladys had died unexpectedly five years before.

"Thanks," Katherine rasped, her heart swelling from the sincere compliment.

Audrey stuffed her hands into her pocket. Her gaze dropped and shame colored her voice. "I'm sorry I didn't make it back for the funeral." She kicked at a pebble and it skittered into the leaf-strewn grass. "Tina was sick that week and—"

Katherine made a dismissive motion with her hand. "I don't need a reason, Audrey. It's okay."

Audrey glanced up doubtfully.

"Really," Katherine assured her, wondering how they got talking about something so serious so fast. "We didn't have a formal service anyway. Mama hated funerals. Dad just had a reception for the local family and friends and we toasted her all night long." She shrugged. "It's what she would have wanted."

"Still, I could have called you." Audrey hesitated, and then said, "But I was too embarrassed to make contact after we'd been so out of touch for so many years."

Katherine sighed. That summer had been one of the lowest points in her life and a simple phone call, just one to make sure she was okay so that she'd have known Audrey cared, would have gone a long way. She was about to say as much, when the look in Audrey's eyes told her she already knew. Katherine arched an eyebrow for emphasis. "Next time I need a friend, you'll call me." It wasn't a question.

Audrey let out a breath, immeasurably grateful at being so easily forgiven. Her stomach had been in knots over this very subject and she had promised herself on the plane ride from Salt Lake City that she wouldn't put it off. "I will," she confirmed quietly, deciding a shift to lighter subjects would be welcomed. They had three days to rehash old mistakes and make promises for the future. "C'mon." Her face visibly lightened, erasing a handful of years. "You have to see this place." She turned toward Charlotte's Web and opened her arms wide. "It's gorgeous inside, though it looks like they're doing a little bit of renovating."

Katherine wrapped her arm around Audrey's waist as they strode toward the house. Tilting her head toward her cousin, she conspiratorially asked, "Did ya steal any ashtrays or pretentious paintings?"

Audrey snickered. "I've only been here for a half hour. Give me time," she teased, a smile firmly reaffixed on her face. Their footsteps were loud as they crunched through the rocks on the stone-filled path. "We're the only ones here so far, except for the woman who runs the B&B." She drew in a deep, satisfying breath of scented air. "I've spent the last half hour enjoying the morning and beautiful fall colors."

Katherine's gaze flicked to the expanse of forest behind the B&B. It was so easy to forget to appreciate what was all around you, the little things and not so little things that surround you on a daily basis. Complacency, she decided, was its own sort of disease, stealthily diminishing the importance of things that truly make life special. Things you don't notice until they're gone.

Near the door of the home was a sign that bore the B&B's name and the year of establishment. "Langtree Enterprises" was written in smaller letters below Charlotte's Web.

"Looks like Gwen wanted home field advantage." Katherine separated from Audrey and huffed a little as she began toting the suitcase up the porch steps. "Not that I can blame her. Damn, cheap wheels," she grumbled petulantly. "If she expects anyone to speak to her this week, she's got a lot of fences to mend." Though Katherine knew she herself was going to go out of her way to do that as well.

Audrey nodded. "I'm here for you, Nina, and Jacie. We'll see about Gwen later."

Katherine paused at the front door and studied the contemplative look on Audrey's face. "You haven't forgiven her, have you?"

Audrey let out a slow breath and gave the question its due. Her gaze darkened. "I'm not sure, Katy. I want to. But when I think of everything that happened to us all, I get so mad and hurt. Sure, she didn't do to me what she did to Jacie, but she still cut me too, ya know?" She shook her head, at a loss to express exactly how she felt. "I guess I'll know what and how much I can forgive when I see her."

"I don't know," Katherine admitted honestly, opening the front door and being greeted by a blast of warm air that smelled like caramel rolls. She thought she might swoon.

Audrey flashed her a wicked smile. "Are you thinking we should raid the kitchen for whatever smells like heaven?"

"Yes."

"Good." Something caught Katherine's eye. "Hey, you forgot your coffee." She trotted across the porch and picked up the cup, taking a drink from the cup without giving it a second thought. "Mmm . . . sweet."

Audrey smiled and grabbed Katherine's suitcase to carry it inside. "Holy Mother of God, what do you have in here? A dead body?"

A low, downright evil chuckle emerged from Katherine, causing Audrey to cringe. "Do you remember the summer we were obsessed with being tanned and spent all our time at that pond on Jacie's uncle's farm?"

"Yesssss," Audrey answered slowly, wondering what that had to do with anything.

Katherine only smiled.

"Oh! My! God!!" Audrey screeched, a bright red flush working its way up from her chest to her round cheeks. "You swore you threw those pictures away!" She dropped Katherine's suitcase and fumbled with the zipper, but it was locked.

Katherine sniggered.

Audrey pressed her hands against the soft cloth of the suitcase and felt the sharp corners of several bulky objects. Her eyes widened to a nearly comical degree. "You framed the photos of me topless that you swore to God you burned?"

Katherine's sniggers turned into snorts that sounded as though they came from something more porcine than human, and she had to clamp her hand over her mouth. She chortled through her fingers, "I wouldn't do a thing like that," and stepped inside Charlotte's Web. From just inside the doorway, she glanced over her shoulder and smiled unrepentantly. "I'm an atheist, Audrey. And what you're feeling are books. The pictures of you are pages sixteen and twenty in one of a set of photo albums that I keep on my coffee table for guests to browse thr—"

"Argh!" Audrey lunged for her cousin, but Katherine was too quick and began running through the house with Audrey hot on her heels.

At the sound of squeals of laughter and shouting, Frances made her way out of the kitchen, her fingers covered with sticky bread dough. "What in the world . . . ?"

"Hi," Katherine panted, skirting around a table so that Audrey couldn't reach her. "You must be Charlotte."

"You'd think that, wouldn't you?" Audrey answered for the older woman. She jumped forward, then whirled around and headed around the opposite side of the table, the surprisingly agile move catching Katherine completely off guard.

"Uff!" All the air left Katherine's lungs when Audrey tackled her and they both went smashing onto the floor.

Frances's eyes widened and her hand went to her mouth. "But—"

"The key," Audrey demanded, wrestling Katherine into a position of submission and pinning her slender arms to the hardwood floor.

"Never!" Katherine cried, laughing so hard she thought she might wet herself. She began wiggling, but Audrey had her firmly trapped.

"God dammit, Katherine Schaub, don't you make me rifle your pockets!" She did her best not to, but a tiny smile flashed across Audrey's face before it was covered up by a suitably outraged look. "Cough it up."

Katherine's body suddenly went totally limp and tears filled her eyes. "I can't believe you're manhandling me like this. We're grown women, for God's sake. What's the matter with you? You're hurting me!"

Audrey's jaw dropped and her heart began to hammer. "I—I—I'm sorry. I—" She instantly let go of Katherine, only to find herself flipped onto her back with Katherine straddling her chest.

"Sucker!"

"Argh!" Audrey struggled wildly. "Asshole."

"I've been pulling that one on you since kindergarten." She paused, nearly being bucked off. "Whoa! Hehe. You'd think you'd have learned by—wah!"

Audrey succeeded in throwing Katherine off her and scrambled to grab the woman who was desperately trying to crawl away.

Frances continued to watch them with wide eyes.

"Gotcha." Audrey used her greater mass to hold Katherine down, her knees pinning her by the chest, her arms holding Katherine's wrists to the floor. Her chest was heaving and her dark curls were hanging in her face, sticking to skin now glistening with perspiration.

"Lemme go, you cow," Katherine sputtered, straining against Audrey's grip and thinking this beat the hell out of Pilates any day.

"Yeah, right." Ebony-colored eyes narrowed. "You're in for it now."

Katherine froze. She'd heard that tone of voice many times before. "I am?" she squeaked.

"Oh, yeah. I have a thirteen-year-old boy. I've seen, heard, and smelled things so disgusting my toes curl just thinking about them."

Katherine's eyes bugged. "Uh-oh."

Remembering one of Katherine's favorite and totally repulsive childhood tricks, Audrey gathered a large glob of spit in her mouth and began to slowly push it forward.

"Shit!" Katherine screamed, redoubling her efforts to escape.

Frances was transfixed by the unlikely scene playing out before her. "Sweet Jesus," she muttered, now quite glad she'd never had any children. Even forty-year-old ones.

Audrey nearly choked to death on her own spit when she began to laugh, and no one in the room heard the front door open over the sounds of her gagging.

"Stop, stop!" Katherine's head thrashed back and forth. "I'll do anything!"

"Wasn't that your reputation in high school, Katy?" Nina, gripping her bag a little tighter, calmly stepped over both women. She turned to Frances. "Rooms are upstairs?"

The stunned woman nodded mutely.

"Save me, Nina," Katherine begged. "Puhleez!"

Nina's body shook with laughter, and she forced herself not to turn around as she ascended the first few stairs. "My son told me that if you spit up just as the other person is spitting down, you can fling their own spit back on them along with yours."

Frances looked horrified and began wringing her hands at the inevitable.

Audrey slurped back the tail of saliva that was beginning to dangle from her mouth. "Oh, my God! Gross!" She jumped off Katherine, not willing to have such a disgusting event occur. "No fair telling her that, Nina. For once I had her right where I wanted her."

"You've been wanting to spit on me?" Katherine squealed, eyes dancing with naughtiness. Despite everything, she was going to have fun this weekend.

Nina turned around and grinned impishly at her friends. "Hi, guys."

Katherine and Audrey ran up the stairs and threw their arms around her in a group bear hug that threatened to crush the air out of all their lungs. Just being in the same room together was a little uncomfortable, like something was out of place and yet familiar. And Nina decided that being reunited with people who knew so much about her past, knew so many intimate details about what shaped her from the girl she was into the woman of today, was a little scary and a lot wonderful.

Nina felt a lump grow in her throat, emotion welling within her. She looked at them both, love showing clearly in her eyes. "It's so great to see you both."

Katherine and Audrey could only nod their agreement. When Katherine sniffed a few times as though she was actually going to break down and cry, Audrey rode to the rescue, knowing how much that display of emotion would bother her cousin. "You said you have a son, Nina?"

Nina beamed. "Robbie. He's nine."

A million other questions danced on the tip of her tongue, but Audrey settled for saying, "That's so great. I always thought you'd be a wonderful mom."

Frances breathed a sigh of relief that things appeared to be getting back to normal.

A few other words were exchanged before Katherine wondered out loud. "What did you get Gwen for her birthday?"

"Hemlock," Nina answered immediately, resituating her bag.

Katherine whistled through her teeth and then let out a low-pitched, "Damn." She was glad she wasn't Gwen.

"That sucks." Audrey sighed aggrievedly, pushing her thick hair out of her face and straightening her shirt. "Now I'm going to have to take mine back."

All three women shared grim smiles and trotted up the stairs, Katherine taking a few extra seconds to retrieve her own mammoth suitcase before trailing after Audrey, the wheels of her case thumping loudly on each wooden step. Seeing her friends brought back the memory of one of her favorites 80s songs. The one that always reminded her of the car windows rolled down, sun glasses, and the radio blasting. She began to hum it as she walked.

Nina and Audrey couldn't help but sing along. After all, the words were burned into their brains.

Late Spring 1981
Hazelwood, Missouri

"Jessie's girl!" Katy crooned loudly, the stereo of her brown, dented, '72 Chevy Impala blasting at full volume. She pulled up in front of Jacie's house, the summer wind ruffling her freshly permed bob. She tapped the horn, the only thing besides the radio that was in good condition on the car she'd gotten a few weeks before.

Jacie ran out of the house with her sneakers unlaced, a towel in one hand, and a bottle of bug juice in the other. "Hi!" She smiled and wedged into the backseat, crawling over Gwen to slide in between her and Nina.

"Hi, Jacie," Nina greeted brightly, bracing her hand against the door-frame as Katy pressed hard on the gas and they all were flung backward.

Jacie frowned. "Watch it!"

" 'Cos she's watching him with those thighs." Audrey screeched off key.

"Eyes!" the girls corrected in unison.

The car jerked and this time they were all rocked forward.

"Jesus Christ!" Nina gasped. "I think we ran over something."

"That was just a pothole and Audrey's singing voice," Katy cheerfully informed them as she pulled onto Charbonier Road.

Audrey turned to face Nina, her massive hoop-earrings clanging against her neck as she moved. "Do you think I sound like a wounded animal when I sing, Nina?"

Katy, Gwen, and Jacie promptly answered, "Yes."

Audrey made a face at her cousin. "I wasn't asking you, tin grin." She'd had her braces removed last week, while Katy was still sporting hers. And she gleefully rubbed it in whenever possible. "I'm asking Nina."

Nina's eyes widened. She was trapped. "Well . . . Uh . . . I-I-I—"

"You haven't stuttered in years, Nina," Katy reminded her drolly.

Nina sighed. "Well, maybe you don't sound exactly like a wounded animal."

"Like one in heat then?" Jacie supplied, lighting a cigarette and waving out the match.

Katy began to wail like a bloodhound as she reached over to poach a cigarette from her friend. "Jessie's grrrrrrri—arhroooooooo!"

"Shut-up, Katy!" Audrey gave Katy a vicious pinch right on the boob.

"Ouch! Fuck!"

"Ahh!" Gwen and Nina screamed as the Impala swerved into the ditch, kicking up an enormous cloud of dust and spraying gravel in all directions.

It took a full seven seconds for Katy to regain control of the car and ease it back onto the road. "Don't do that, Audrey!" she spat, rubbing her boob with one hand, her cigarette hanging limply between her teeth.

Audrey's skin was pasty and she nodded her agreement. Boob pinches at fifty miles per hour were definitely out.

Jacie breathed an enormous sigh of relief that was echoed by the entire back seat. With slightly trembling hands, she lit another cigarette and exhaled slowly. Acrid smoke wafted into Nina's face and she waved her hand around furiously, trying to help it make its way out the back window. "I wish you wouldn't smoke," she said, wrinkling her nose in disgust.

"Why?"

"What do you mean, why?"

Jacie shrugged. "I mean, why do you hate it when I smoke? I only smoke every once in a while, so I'm probably not hurting myself physically. And Katy bogarts most of the pack, anyway. Surely a little smoke can't be that bad?"

"Gag me with a spoon, Jacie, it's totally grody! It is bad for you and you smell like an ashtray. And . . . and . . ." Nina's hands flailed as she tried to think of another reason.

"And Jerry won't want to kiss you," Gwen broke in, her teeth still rattling from their latest near-death experience with Katy driving.

"Oh, Jerry can kiss me all right. He can kiss my ass!" Jacie plucked her cigarette from her mouth and glared at it, irritated that she was considering throwing it away just because Nina had said she didn't like it. But it didn't take much self-convincing that it was easier to talk without one in her mouth anyway. She passed it up to Katy, who murmured her thanks and unrepentantly slid it into place next to its twin.

Dying to know more, Audrey turned to face the backseat again and leaned forward. This almost qualified as something juicy and she couldn't believe that it was coming from Jacie. "What happened? You guys have been dating since Christmas. I thought things were going just fine."

Scowling, Jacie crossed her arms over her chest. "Things were fine, I guess. Until he made it his life's mission to get into my pants."

Nina gaped. "What?"

"Well, duh, he is your boyfriend," Gwen laughed.

Nina's face began to flush, but she bit her tongue to keep from blurting out what she was thinking.

"Yeah," Katy piped up. "Jerry's cute and he's a guy. What do you expect?"

"I expected him to keep his paws to himself," Jacie shot back. "I had to wrestle my way out of his Mustang last night and I broke up with him on the spot." She brushed her hands together as though she was wiping off something repugnant. "No more Jerry."

"That bastard," Nina seethed, losing her battle with her temper as her gaze darkened. "Wait till I see him in homeroom on Monday." She began plotting his demise.

"Noooooo!" Gwen cried, startling everyone. "I thought you and Jerry were going to go to Prom together. Peter told me he was sure that Jerry was going to ask you . . . eventually."

Jacie snorted. "Eventually? After I put out, you mean." *I never should have agreed to go out with him.* "And not that I'd bother to go to something that lame anyway, but the prom isn't till next spring. So get a grip, Gwen. I'm sure you'll try to set me up with a half dozen losers before then." *And this time I'll use my brain and say no.*

"But Jerry has his own car."

"Katy has her own car." Jacie spread her arms wide and tried not to burst out laughing. The car smelled like a combination of smoke, cheap perfume, and mildew and the seats were so torn up that occasionally a spring popped out and nailed you right in the rear.

"Jerry's car is not a piece of crap," Gwen pointed out.

"Watch it, Gwen." Peeved, Katy pointed at the redhead. "You can always walk home." Then she thought about the last time she'd actually filled up the gas tank and hoped they all wouldn't be walking home.

"Sorry, Katy, but it's true. Besides"—Gwen couldn't help but try again with Jacie—"Jerry's on the football team. He's going to be a starter in September," she whined, not understanding how Jacie could just give up on her boyfriend because he had dared to try to kiss her. She enjoyed kissing her boyfriend and last weekend he'd even, at her insistence, worn a tie to dinner at her house. Boys could be trained, at the very least.

"I'm sorry about Jerry," Nina said sincerely, resting her hand atop Jacie's. She licked her lips and softly admitted, "I never liked him much anyway. You can do way better."

For a reason completely beyond her own understanding, Nina had taken a dislike to the boy who wanted to spend so much time with Jacie. It wasn't that there was anything wrong with him . . . exactly. He seemed to genuinely like Jacie, but that still didn't change the fact that he wasn't good enough for her.

Nina let relief wash over her. Even though she was livid at what he'd done in his Mustang, she was thrilled to have an actual reason to think that he was a dick. After all, that meant she wasn't just being irrational.

Jacie looked down at their hands and swallowed hard. She felt more in that simple, loving touch from her best friend than she had in the dozens of sloppy kisses she'd endured trying to be a "real" girlfriend, as Jerry had put it. But things weren't supposed to be that way, were they? It was all so confusing that it was starting to give her a bellyache. But even amidst her inner turmoil, she couldn't help but hope that Nina decided to leave her hand there for the rest of the short trip. "Thanks, Nina."

Their eyes met and each smiled, well aware of the emotions thrumming between them.

"Almost there," Katy announced, making a final turn down the dirt road that would take them to their secret spot alongside the Missouri River. They whiled away many a summer afternoon at that spot, and they all had bronzed bodies and sun-lightened hair to show for their effort.

At Katy's words, the girls began stripping off their T-shirts and wiggling out of their shorts to reveal their swimsuits beneath.

Audrey threw her shirt behind her, hitting Gwen squarely in the face, and the tall girl responded by tossing the shirt out the window of the moving car.

"Gwen!" Audrey moaned, looking longingly after the bright orange garment. "I loved that shirt."

"We'll get it on the way back," Katy promised, slowing down and turning off the main road as she headed for a thick stand of trees.

Nina stowed her shirt and shorts at her feet and readjusted her flip-flops.

The car pulled to a stop just as Jacie finished stripping down to her suit. When she turned to say something to Nina, her mind went absolutely blank and she forgot how to breathe.

Nina saw where Jacie was looking and cringed. "You don't like it?" Her face showed her disappointment. "I bought it yesterday. I've never owned a bikini but I thought . . . Well . . . I thought . . ." Last year she'd lettered in track as a sophomore and her body showed the time she spent putting herself through a year of stringent workouts.

"It looks great!" Audrey said, envious that her friend had a figure cute enough to pull off the hot pink number. Audrey was wearing the least revealing one-piece suit in the history of mankind. She only lamented that none of those skinny-assed designers had taken the time to invent a long sleeved, turtleneck version yet.

"You think it's okay?" Nina's gaze shifted off of her chest and toward the front seat.

"Absolutely," Katy confirmed, throwing her T-shirt onto the dashboard and running her hands through her hair to feather her bangs. She could see Nina in the rear view mirror. "You're going to have to beat the boys away with a stick." She smirked. "By the way, I hear Jerry is available."

"Very funny," Nina answered curtly, the mention of Jerry's name reminding her that she was going to strangle him at school on Monday.

Gwen checked out Nina's suit with a critical eye. "Very pretty," she finally pronounced, giving Nina a brief, encouraging smile and vowing to never let her boyfriend within five miles of Nina in that suit. Then she exited the car. Daylight was burning.

Audrey and Katy stepped outside, their doors creaking loudly as they closed them. Katy then popped her arm inside the car to turn up the tunes.

"You're awfully quiet, Jace," Nina said once they were alone, worry coloring her words. "Is it Jerry you're upset about?"

Who? Jacie's eyes shot to Nina's face and she suddenly realized that she was supposed to be able to speak under these impossible circumstances. "Err . . . No," she muttered dismissively. "I'm fine about Jerry."

"Is it what I'm wearing then?" Nina tugged at the fabric self-consciously. Her cheeks began to heat. "There isn't much to it. My dad's probably going to freak and—"

"It's sexy as hell," Jacie breathed, hearing the husky note in her voice. She blinked furiously. Had she said that out loud?

Nina's face suddenly brightened. "It is?"

Jacie hoped her friend couldn't hear her racing heart. She no longer trusted her voice, so she just nodded like a demented bobble-head doll. Then, to her mortification, she did something she couldn't ever recall doing. She blushed. Badly.

"Whew!" Nina wiped mock sweat from her brow, secretly overjoyed that Jacie thought she looked good. Her best friend was the most attractive person she knew, and a good word from Jacie left a warm fuzzy feeling swirling inside her.

Jacie wasn't sure whether Nina had noticed her red face or was simply too kind to point it out. She figured it was the latter and mentally thanked Nina's parents for their stellar childrearing efforts.

"Aren't you coming?" Nina tilted her head toward the river, scattering her fair hair around her shoulders. "I know how much you like to swim and the water's bound to be extra warm today." It was nearly a hundred degrees outside.

"In a minute." Jacie wrapped her arms around her own middle, feeling her guts clench every time her eyes strayed below Nina's face. She glanced up, and then when she looked into Nina's eyes, it happened again anyway. "I don't feel so good."

Concerned, Nina scooted closer and laid her hand on Jacie's clammy forehead, which only served to intensify Jacie's stomachache. "What's wrong?"

You! "Nothing." Jacie did her best to put on a weak smile. "It was probably that last cigarette that did me in."

"Promise you'll quit then?" Nina said seriously, giving Jacie her sternest look. Then she gentled her voice and watched curiously as Jacie's expression softened in return. "I can't stand the thought of you being sick all the time. Katy's lungs probably already look like a used oil filter and she's not even eighteen." Unconsciously, Nina began to stroke Jacie's forehead with her thumb.

"I promise." At that moment, she realized, she would have promised anything to get Nina, her thumb, and her teeny bikini out of the car. "Go on. I'll be there in a minute."

But Nina didn't move. "Maybe I should stay, I—"

"No!"

Nina's eyes widened.

Dammit. "I mean . . . go ahead," Jacie said more gently. "I'll be right out." She peeled Nina's hand from her forehead and laid it to rest in her friend's lap, trying not to touch any golden skin so close to her fingers. "I think I just need to rest." *And throw up.*

It was clear that Jacie wanted her to go, but for the life of her, Nina didn't know why. Then something occurred to her. Maybe her staying would only keep Jacie from resting. "You're sure?"

Thank God. "I'm sure. Don't forget these." She reached down and passed Nina a bottle of sun tan oil and a can of bug spray.

"Scream if you need anything, okay?" Reluctantly, Nina took the items and waited for Jacie's confirmation nod before heading toward the riverbank, where her friends were already spread out, sunning like a trio of lazy lizards on a hot rock.

Jacie couldn't help but notice the gentle sway of Nina's hips as she strolled away. And in that instant she couldn't stop herself from feeling the rush of raw emotion that she'd held at bay for so long. Jerry Brewster never had a chance. Not only did she want Nina to hold her hand, she wanted more than anything to brush her mouth against Nina's and see if her lips were as soft and luscious as they looked. She dreamt of running her fingers along the curve of her breast and down the line of her thin waist. She craved melting into that beautiful, naked skin as Nina's body was pressed intimately against hers.

Realization hit her like a hammer between the eyes. "God," she groaned, truly in pain as she lay down in the backseat and curled into the fetal position. *Oh, God. Oh, God. Now what am I going to do?*

"Hey, Jacie!" Audrey's voice drifted into the beat-up Impala. "Crank that tune, will ya? This is my favorite song."

Jacie leaned forward and snaked her hand between the front seats to turn the knob. It only took a second for her head and stomach to begin pounding in time with the raspy strains of "Bette Davis Eyes."

Present Day
Rural Missouri

Gwen Langtree sat in her Mercedes with the engine off, staring at the back wall of the Charlotte's Web garage. Her foot was nervously tapping the carpeted floor. She'd been in this exact position for nearly twenty minutes.

Three other cars were parked neatly next to hers; a compact rental that she assumed belonged to Audrey, a sedate Toyota Camry that she would have bet money was Nina's, and a ratty-looking, ancient Ghia, which could only be Katy's. Jacie, despite, her blue-collar job title, had earned over two hundred and fifty thousand dollars last year and Gwen couldn't see that she'd have a cheap rental, a rust bucket, or the best-selling, most boring car in America.

Which meant Jacie wasn't here yet. A surge of dread welled within her.

Calm down, she reminded herself. *She's probably just late. The invitation just said the date. Not an exact time. She could still be coming.*

Gwen rubbed her hands together, trying to increase her circulation and ward off the sudden chill that had overtaken her. She longed for this weekend to be about nothing more than rekindling old friendships, not finding a blackmailer. But it wasn't and whatever happened she couldn't let herself forget that. She wanted to make amends, but more than that, she wanted her life back. If she had learned anything through painful years of trial and error, it was that lying to yourself yielded nothing but pain. She knew she deserved most of the Mayflower Club's rancor. But she didn't deserve this.

"I've got to keep my guard up every second," she murmured, closing her eyes. "Search for clues in every glance, every word. And not let anyone know what I'm doing. I can't tip my hand too early." She nodded a little to herself, resolving to simply gather the entire group in a room at the end of the weekend and ask them all flat out, if she couldn't figure things out sooner. It would be humiliating. Not to mention as ridiculous as an Agatha Christie novel. But her blackmailer was using something more important than her pride against her. "Then, once I find out who is doing this and convince them to stop"—she wasn't sure exactly how she was going to do that—"I can make up for lost time with the rest of them." She paused. *At least I hope I can.*

She let out a shaky breath, gathered her courage, and decided to leave her bags for later. When she left the garage, she was surprised to see Nina, Katherine, and Audrey exiting the B&B and taking seats around a small table on the porch. Their occasional laughter wafted over the yard, causing a stab of envy in her chest.

She nearly made it to the front stairs unnoticed when Katherine spotted her and the hum of conversation melted into a cold silence.

Gwen could feel her hands trembling and clasped them behind her back as she came to stand before the other women. "Hi," she said quietly, surprised that her voice wavered on that single word. There was a moment of shock as she looked at these middle-aged women, all of whom looked great, but none of whom exactly matched the young college girls who'd taken up residence in her memory.

Nina blinked. Had she not known who she was looking at . . . well, she still wasn't quite sure she knew.

"Gwen?" Katherine breathed. "Wow." Gwen had always been attractive in an ordinary sort of way. She'd used her striking hair color and creamy complexion to its best purpose, and even as a teenager how she looked had been of utmost importance to her. Some things, Katy acknowledged privately, never change.

A look of uncertainty swept across Gwen's face. She'd wondered countless times what her old friends would think when they saw her and now that the moment was here, it was surprisingly underwhelming. Unwilling to stand the silence for another second, she blurted, "You'd be surprised at what a nose job, a boob lift, caps for my teeth, and a touch of Botox can do."

"No kidding," Audrey breathed, not sure why Gwen had changed her nose or needed a boob job, but forced to admit the overall look, the hair, the designer duds, was one of sophistication and style. Even her voice was different, the severe twang now replaced by a gentler but still distinctive tone.

Nina wasn't particularly interested in Gwen's Botox treatment. "Hello, Gwen."

"Yeah," Audrey shifted uncomfortably. "Hi. You really look . . ." She reminded herself that she was a grownup. "You look really nice."

Gwen managed a smile as the wheels in her mind cranked furiously. "Thanks." Katy's greeting appeared to be the most genuine. But was that a ruse? *She's got the least motive, but she's practically broke and in debt up to her eyeballs.* "Thank you. Did everyone get settled in this morning?" *Audrey looks so serious, like she's studying me under a microscope.* Even though Gwen didn't really believe that Audrey was capable of blackmail, she couldn't rule her out. Not yet, and especially not after Audrey so recently spent the exact amount of her last blackmail payment. Her gaze shifted to Nina, who seemed a little sad.

"They're doing a few repairs, but they shouldn't get in our way," Gwen said conversationally. *I wonder if Nina's diamond stud earrings are real? They're at least a half carat each.* She leaned against the porch railing and tried to pretend her next question was a nonchalant one. "I . . . uh don't suppose anyone knows whether Jacie is going to make it?"

"Bored with us already, Gwen?" Nina said. She didn't mean for her words to come out as harshly as they did.

Gwen blinked. "No! I uh . . . ."

"I know whether Jacie is coming," Audrey said, rising to her feet.

Nina suddenly became very interested in the conversation. "You do?"

"Unless that's somebody else driving up in that pickup truck." She pointed to the truck that was just turning onto the driveway.

Nina's heart leapt at the same time her stomach dropped. She thought she might throw up.

Gwen's reaction was nothing but relief. "Thank God," she whispered to herself.

Jacie stopped the truck when she saw the small pack of women quickly making their way over the sloping lawn, wet leaves and blades of grass sticking to their shoes. But as she climbed out of the tall truck, feeling the tingle of anticipation laced with worry, she only had eyes for one of them.

"Holy Christ," Audrey murmured as they approached the driveway. "She cut her hair. She's friggin' gorgeous. Even better than before."

Katherine sighed, but was smiling. "That stinkin' bitch."

Audrey chuckled low in her throat as she stepped over a log. "If I ever jump the fence, I wanna land on her. Well," she scrunched up her face. Jacie was like a sibling. "Maybe not exactly her. But her hot-as-hell twin."

Katherine hooted and high-fived her cousin, delighted by her unexpected statement.

Nina snorted softly.

Gwen tried not to look as shocked as she was. Had men somehow gone completely out of style without her knowing it?

"Jacie!" Katherine crowed, running the last few steps to stand in front of her friend.

Jacie dragged her gaze away from Nina, who couldn't seem to meet her eyes directly, and smiled. "Katy!" It was clear that they were both excited, but they didn't embrace, instead they awkwardly patted each other on the arm and grinned like idiots.

"Hiya, Jacie," Audrey said, looking up into dark eyes that glittered with enough affection to make her feel warm all over. "I wasn't sure you were going to make it."

"Hi, Audrey." A flash of white teeth. "I wasn't going to come," Jacie admitted, "but then I got to thinking that I might never have this chance again." She shrugged, not wanting to discuss the hours of soul searching it had taken just to get her this far. "So here I am."

Next, it was Gwen's turn to step up to the plate. She took a deep breath and steeled herself, knowing full well it was time to face the first of what was likely to be a series of awkward moments. "Hello, Jacie. Thank you for coming."

Jacie's smile faltered and the temperature of the yard dropped several degrees. "Gwen," she acknowledged calmly, pinning her with an indifferent gaze before effectively dismissing her by focusing on the only Mayflower Club member who had yet to greet her.

Nina's pulse raced and was visible against her pale neck.

For the first time that Jacie could recall, Nina's expression was totally unreadable to her. And that hurt.

Frozen, the women silently looked at each other for so long that Katherine, Audrey, and Gwen shared nervous looks and began fidgeting in the wake of the palpable tension. Then something behind Nina's eyes seemed to spark, and she closed the space between her and Jacie with surprising speed. Invading her personal space in a way the other women hadn't dared do, Nina grabbed hold of Jacie's thin, cable knit sweater with both hands, pulled her close, and gave her a soft, chaste kiss on the mouth. It lasted only a second and when she pulled away, she looked directly into Jacie's eyes. Seeing the confusion there, she bared a tiny piece of her soul. "That's because I love you, Jacie."

Four mouths dropped open and Jacie began to stammer. "Nina, I . . . I—"

Smack!

The sharp crack of Nina's open hand striking Jacie on the cheek made everyone flinch, and it sounded unnaturally loud against the whispering breeze. Glistening tears pooled in her soft, blue-green eyes, before several spilled down wind-chilled cheeks. "And that's for letting me wonder for the past twenty years whether you were alive or dead!"

"Jesus," Nina said under her breath. She couldn't believe she'd just done that. Her hands were shaking. Without another word, she spun around, tucked her hands under her armpits, and marched back toward the house, leaving a stunned silence behind her.

"Holy shit!" Katherine finally sputtered. "I thought if anyone was gonna get clocked this weekend"—she jerked her thumb sideways—"it would be Gwen."

"Hey!" Gwen protested, completely missing Katherine's mostly-teasing smile and Audrey's muffled chuckles.

Jacie's temper flared and for a few charged seconds she was on the verge of racing after Nina, wrestling her to the ground . . . and kissing her senseless? "Oh, Christ." Jacie's eyes fluttered closed and she reached up to her lips. They were tingling, but she wasn't sure whether it was from the kiss or having the snot slapped out of her.

A large red handprint had already blossomed on her cheek, and she winced as she rubbed the abused flesh. She was familiar enough with this type of injury from her childhood to know that a black eye would likely follow. Furious with Nina and herself, she stalked back to her truck, trying to decide whether or not to simply drive away from this entire mess. Her life was complicated enough without borrowing trouble. But when she reached the cab, she couldn't help but glance back at the compact form fleeing the yard and kicking the leaves and twigs out of her way as she moved.

Then Jacie's heart overruled her head with such startling ease that she was forced to roll her eyes at herself for even thinking she might have the wherewithal to leave. What she wanted was clearly right here. Making her decision, she grabbed her carry-on from the passenger seat and rejoined her friends, who were murmuring among themselves and casting worried glances in Jacie's direction.

Katherine gave Jacie a wishing look. "I guess you're not taking off then?"

Gwen mentally crossed every extremity she had and prayed that she hadn't misinterpreted what Jacie was doing. If her number one of prime suspects fled before they'd gotten a chance to talk, her plan would be ruined.

"I'm staying," Jacie confirmed and began to walk back toward the house, her pride and her cheek still stinging. "So long as you guys protect me from the dishwater blond tornado in there." She lifted her chin toward the B&B. "Deal?"

Gwen suddenly paled.

Jacie saw it happen and took an abrupt step closer, putting her nearly nose to nose with the taller woman. "What?"

Gwen licked her lips and took a step backward. "Now, Jacie, I thought you'd both like it." She lifted her arms to forestall Jacie, gulping at the look on Jacie's face. "I swear!"

"What. Did. You. Do?" Jacie ground out harshly, her hands clenched in half fists.

The words spilled out of Gwen like water rushing through a broken dam. "They're renovating, honest! There were only three rooms available and Katy and Audrey took one and I took the other."

Jacie's eyes turned to slits.

"Mine only has a twin bed!" Gwen protested. "The king-sized is having its frame stripped and the mattress has been removed to be replaced.

I didn't think we'd need it."

Katherine scratched her jaw. She didn't particularly want to give up her spot in a room with Audrey, and there was no way she was sleeping on the floor in the same room as Gwen, the snorer from hell. "Looks like you're bunking with slugger, Jacie."

Jacie's stomach fluttered, and she looked skyward in appeal. However, there would be no mercy for her this weekend. She could just tell. Trying not to be too hopeful, she squared her shoulders and set her sights on the blue house, wondering if she was the one going to be caught in Charlotte's Web this weekend.

From the window and the warmth of the parlor, Nina's gaze softened as she watched her childhood hero determinedly walk back into her life . . . and her heart.

Chapter 6
Present Day
Rural Missouri

The Charlotte's Web Bed & Breakfast smelled like chicken soup and fresh cut vegetables as the Mayflower Club sat eating their late lunch. The mood of the meal was, to say the least, subdued. And Frances Artiste had to be reassured several times that it wasn't the cuisine that had soured everyone's mood.

Nina sighed and set down her spoon. She kicked herself for the way she'd behaved with Jacie. She'd always had issues controlling her anger when it came to things she was passionate about, but there had only been one other time in her life that her actions had devolved into violence. And the recipient of that particular act just so happened to be this weekend's host.

Nina's gaze strayed across the table to Jacie, who was industriously digging into her salad. She winced. Her hand hurt and she could only imagine how Jacie's cheek felt. In truth, however, there wasn't much left to the imagination. Her old friend had a lurid red handprint on her face and the skin below one of those beautiful brown eyes had grown puffy and turned a disgusting shade of purple. Fuck.

Katherine had worked herself into a private tizzy wondering if Gwen was really investigating her and how she could find out for certain without directly asking her and looking ridiculously paranoid. Audrey sat and stewed, her residual resentment toward Gwen showing on her face despite her best intentions. Worst of all, the silence in the cheerfully decorated room was so loud that every clank of a spoon against a bowl was deafening, and Audrey swore she could hear the steam rising from her soup.

As the *X-Files* wisely advised, Gwen trusted no one. Ignoring the soup, whose thick, evil noodles were undoubtedly packed with calories and carbohydrates, she restlessly picked at her salad.

Jacie, who didn't give a damn about calories, finished her soup in record time and then pulled the bread bowl squarely in front of her plate. She was a big fan of easy access. "Pass the butter, please," she asked Gwen, who shot her an envious look as she handed over the round dish.

"So."

Everyone stopped mid-bite and glanced up at Gwen.

"I was the only one married when we all . . . ." awkwardly, she paused. "Err . . . So, are any of you married?" She knew the answer of course, but it was going to be hell to figure out what was going on if she couldn't get everyone talking.

Nina gave her a grateful look for getting the conversation going. If this weekend was going to be tolerable, she was going to have to at least try to play nice with Gwen. "I'm single. But as I mentioned before, I have a son."

"Never married?" Katherine asked, her appetite returning along with the conversation. "C'mon," she smiled, "you have to have had a crack at plenty of Mr. Rights over the years. You're a great catch."

An enigmatic smile twitched at the corner of Nina's mouth, and she gave her head a tiny shake. "No, no Mr. Right for me. In fact, I gave up looking for him a long time ago."

Audrey bumped shoulders with her. "Don't worry, it'll happen. I'm married." Her cheeks began to heat, and she nearly lost her nerve. But in a rush she added, "In fact, I married Enrique Diaz."

Katherine just kept eating. Her grandmother had said that Audrey had gone and run off with Ricky Ricardo. Of course, this was the same woman who had believed that Richard Nixon was really an alien sent to earth to facilitate an extraterrestrial take over. So Katherine hadn't paid much attention at the time.

Everyone else gave Audrey blank looks.

Audrey groaned inwardly, and with a deep breath she clarified, "Our Mr. Diaz."

Jacie leaned back in her chair and set her napkin on the table. "Our Mr. Diaz who?"

Katherine's head suddenly lifted as a light bulb illuminated in her head. "No goddamned way!" she shrieked.

Everyone jumped.

"Not that Mr. Diaz!"

"What are you talking about?" Nina asked, totally adrift. "I don't re-member anyone named Diaz. Well . . ." Her brow furrowed as something occurred to her. "I guess except for Vice Principal Diaz. And Audrey couldn't have married him. He—" Then she got a good look at Audrey's face, she stopped cold. "Oh my God." A laugh bubbled to the surface. "When you said he had a cute butt in the eleventh grade, you really meant it!"

"Rick the Prick?" Katherine scrubbed her eyes as though to wash away the mental image. "You married 'Rick the Prick?' You actually have sex with Vice Principal Diaz?" Marrying their former vice principal, the one who used to gleefully assign them detention when they ditched home-room seemed . . . well, it seemed . . . "That is so totally gross!"

"It is not!" Audrey defended hotly. "He's wonderful."

"I thought it was 'Rick the Dick,' not 'Rick the Prick,' " Jacie com-mented casually as she reached for her coffee mug.

Audrey gasped, looking appropriately outraged and just a little amused. "No one called him that."

Katherine snorted. "Oh, yes they did, Audrey."

"They did not."

"I'm quite sure I never said either of those horrible things," Gwen protested haughtily, all the while searching her memory to find out if what she'd just said was actually true.

"I did," Nina admitted with a rueful smile. "Rick the Prick sounded so mean, I could never bring myself to use it. Somehow 'Dick' had a much nicer ring to it."

Katherine burst out laughing. "Thinking of you two together is like envisioning my parents having sex." She affected a full body shiver. "Bah!"

"Feel free not to envision it then," Audrey ground out. "It's not gross. He's only ten years older than we are."

Katherine suddenly stopped. "It's not the age thing at all. Trust me. It's the principal thing." She waggled her eyebrows. "Does he punish you at home?"

"Is he a psychotic, heartless shrew, hell-bent on destroying your life and the lives of those around you?" Jacie asked nonchalantly.

Audrey's blinked slowly. "Buh . . . Of course not!"

Jacie grinned. "Then you beat me as far as finding a mate goes. Way to go."

The smile Nina had been wearing slid from her face, and she felt a familiar gnawing in her guts that had always signaled her worry for Jacie's happiness and well-being. What sort of nutcase had Jacie partnered with?

"I think it's great that you're still together, Audrey," Gwen said seriously, her suspicion of Audrey waning. She seemed too much like the sweet, but spirited girl next door to be a blackmailer. "I'm so happy for you."

Audrey's gaze bore into Gwen's, and for once she didn't see a self-serving motive lurking beneath the surface. "You really mean that, don't you?" she asked, hearing a note of surprise in her own voice.

Gwen's gaze softened. "With all my heart."

Audrey's face relaxed into a smile. "Thanks. I really am happy." A bit awkwardly, she decided to share a tiny part of her recent personal history. "Things have been trying lately. A co-worker quit just before our busiest time of the year and I had the chance to work some serious overtime and took it." She didn't mention that her working more in order to save some extra money had seriously tweaked Ricky's pride and caused more than a few arguments. "Anyway, I socked away the money"—there was real pride in her voice now—"and we used it to turned our garage into an apartment for our oldest last month. But things are more back to normal now, and I'll get to spend more time at home with our family." Her smile grew. "We have two beautiful kids. Well, a teenaged son and my daughter, Tina, is a young woman now—eighteen."

Overtime. Gwen wasn't sure whether to be relieved or disappointed. Audrey was always a horrible liar and now that she had a reasonable explanation for the money, Gwen's suspicion of her as her blackmailer ebbed even further.

"I have a daughter, too," Jacie said, watching in amusement as Audrey tried to cover her shock.

The chubby woman squirmed in her chair as she tried to recover. "But I thought—"

"I'm still a lesbian, Audrey," Jacie quipped, but not unkindly. "I adopted my former partner's birth daughter right after she was born. She's seven and we share custody now."

"Former partner?" Nina asked, her eyes on her soup.

Jacie nodded and her voice took on a deeper timbre. "Very former. For years now."

"Mmm." Nina thought about that. Years were much too long to go without love. She would know. She glanced up and caught Jacie's gaze, trying not to linger on the vivid discoloring around Jacie's eye. "Do you ever miss her?"

"All the time," came the immediate answer.

Nina's stomach dropped.

Then Jacie winked her good eye. "But my aim is bound to improve eventually."

Gwen shook her head and smiled. "Well, you all know about Tucker. I never had any more children and I'm still with Malcolm." She cocked her head to the side. "How about you, Katy? Thank you," she murmured to Frances as the older woman quietly entered the room and set a plate of frosted pumpkin bars on the table along with a fresh pot of coffee.

"How about me what?" Katherine had been dreading this moment.

"You know what she's asking," Audrey said, dark eyes dancing. "Tell everyone how many times you've been married. Go on."

Katherine threw Audrey an evil look. Clearly her cousin had stayed tuned in to family gossip over the years, while she herself had remained in the dark. "How many do you know about?"

Jacie laughed and let out a low whistle. "This has gotta be good."

Nina smiled. This was more the way she remembered things being between them.

"C'mon, Katy," Audrey crooned, trying to pretend she didn't see the appetizing dessert sitting squarely in the middle of the table.

Jacie elbowed Katherine. "Spill it."

Katherine hung her head, and her friend caught the mumbled remnants of some curse words.

"We're wait-ing," Audrey said in a sing-song voice.

Katherine gritted her teeth. "A couple of times," she mumbled, her cheeks heating without her permission.

Audrey shook her head. After "Rick the Prick," Katherine wasn't going to get off the hook so easily. "What was that, Katy?" she asked innocently. "A couple?"

"Fine," Katherine snapped, though it was clear she was more embarrassed than angry. "Three times. There. Three." Somewhat childishly, she crossed her arms over her chest. "I said it. Happy?"

"Three?" Nina mouthed silently, her eyes round. "Wow."

"Very happy," Audrey confirmed smugly, giving up her own battle of the bulge for the day when she saw Nina, Katherine, and Jacie each go for a bar.

Gwen poured herself some coffee and grabbed a package of Sweet & Low from the porcelain dish sitting temptingly close to the dessert. "With all those exes you must at least be getting decent alimony?" She hadn't recalled any additional sources of income for Katherine, but it paid to know every detail.

Katherine rolled her eyes. "Gimme a break. My boyfriends-slash-husbands were all of the 'poor as a church mouse' variety."

Audrey moaned around a bite of nutmeg-laced nuts. "God, these are awesome," she murmured, dusting the crumbs off her slightly sticky fingers and fighting the urge to lick off the gooey droplet of cream cheese frosting that had thus far escaped her lips. "So your new boyfriend is poverty stricken, too?"

"Not really." Katherine's expression turned thoughtful. "I guess he does okay, but I'd love him just the same even if he didn't. He's really different from the other men I've been involved with. Plus it doesn't hurt that I'm crazy about him."

The other women smiled at Katherine's heartfelt declaration.

"Good for you," Gwen announced happily. "Love is the most important thing, but having money does make life's wheels turn a little smoother." She looked directly into Katherine's eyes, hoping to spot a crack in their arctic-blue veneer. "Don't you agree?"

Katherine shrugged. She hoped her face appeared neutral when she said, "I guess. I wouldn't know. But I'll take your word for it." Then she turned to Jacie as though an idea had suddenly come to her. "So, Jacie, what's it like to go down on a woman?"

Coffee shot out of Jacie's mouth, spraying a fine mist all over Audrey. "Jesus Christ, Katy," she sputtered, wiping her chin with the back of her hand and choking a little.

Gwen gasped and Nina's face fell into her hands as her body shook with silent laughter.

"Damn." Katherine let out a throaty chuckle at Jacie's reaction. "That good, huh? No wonder some guys dig it so much."

"Couldn't you have waited till she was finished drinking?" Audrey asked, plucking her napkin from her lap and wiping a dangling drop of coffee off the tip of her nose.

"What?" Katherine complained, taking the napkin from Audrey's hand and wiping her chin as though her cousin were a messy three-year-old. "Like you didn't want to know."

"Well, duh. Of course I wanted to know. But I was going to get her liquored up tonight and hope she'd spill her guts and give us the juicy . . ." she winced at her choice of words. "Errr . . . the interesting details."

Katherine frowned. Why hadn't she thought of that?

Gwen's eyes were a little wide. "Is that really something you consider interesting?"

The cousins looked at each other and exchanged devilish smiles. "Yeah," they said in unison.

"God," Nina chuckled, enjoying the red tint to Jacie's cheeks. "You guys are as warped as ever."

Doing her best Miss Piggy hair toss, Audrey sighed dramatically. "Curious is not the same thing as warped. Besides, couldn't you see that Katy was willing to do anything to get the topic of conversation off her many, many ex-husbands."

Katherine took her last bite of pumpkin bar and unrepentantly licked her fingertips. "Speaking of ex-husbands and lesbians . . . My second husband, Junior, could make you straight, Jacie. I guarantee it."

This time it was Nina who began choking on her coffee.

Audrey slapped her on the back absently as she anxiously waited for Katherine to continue.

Nina gave Katherine an incredulous look. "Where do you get these insane ideas?"

"He could, Nina! Well, maybe he couldn't make her straight. But he sure as hell could make her straight*ish*. At least for one night." Her eyes twinkled. "He was an acrobat who performed on the flying trapeze at Circus Circus in Vegas." Then her voice dropped an octave, "And amazing."

Gwen blinked slowly and allowed her imagination to take hold. "Just how amazing are we talking?"

Jacie's eyes thoughtfully regarded Nina. Her friend was plainly uninterested in Junior's flexibility or talents. When Jacie spoke, her voice was quiet and resolute. "It wouldn't matter how amazing he was. I'm pretty sure your ex wouldn't have had much luck with me, Katy. I know who and what I am, and I'm happy with that." She gave Nina a meaningful look.

"I don't feel very well," Nina suddenly announced, pushing to her feet. Her gaze never strayed from the dark wood tabletop. "I'm sorry. I think I'm going to go up to my room for a little while."

Gwen's words tumbled out in a rush. "Can I get you something? Some medicine? Or a doctor? I could call Malcolm and he could—"

"No." A quick shake of the head and Nina tossed her napkin on the table. "I think I just have a headache." She laid a hand on her belly; her stomach was in knots. "I'm sorry," she mumbled and hurried from the room.

Jacie closed her eyes and rubbed her temples for a few seconds. "I'm going to see how she is."

Gwen jumped to her feet, smoothing her blouse as she stood. "I'll go, too."

"No, thank you, Gwen," Jacie said distractedly, effectively dismissing her host as she walked out of the room.

The remaining women were left in a pool of silence. Finally, Audrey let out a long breath and squirmed a little in her chair. "Boy, that was weird."

Katherine nodded. "Tell me about it. One minute we're talking, and the next Nina is as white as a sheet."

"Maybe it was the topic of conversation?" Audrey ventured.

Gwen's brow furrowed worriedly as she tapped a long, manicured fingertip against the rim of her cup. "Maybe." Then her face cleared and she fought for something normal to say. She hoped she could at least fish something useful from Katherine or Audrey. "So, Katy, if husband number two was so wonderful, why is he an ex?"

Katherine chuckled softly. "It took me a week to figure out that there was no way I was staying in Vegas, that there isn't a big call for men who work on the flying trapeze in St. Louis, and that just being 'amazing' isn't a basis for a marriage." She waved dismissively. "It took me a year to get out of the mess I'd made for myself." She sighed and spared a wistful thought for her younger and far stupider self. "I should have known that something that started out in one of those disgusting, sleazy $29.99 wedding chapels was doomed to bring nothing but pain and misery to both of us."

"Oh, Tina!" Audrey suddenly burst into tears and bolted from the dining room.

Dumbfounded, Katherine and Gwen could only stare after her.

"Dammit!" Katherine slapped the table with an open hand. She looked at Gwen helplessly. "What did I say now?"

"Don't look at me."

"I'd better go see what's the matter." Katherine stood.

Gwen started to rise. "I'll come, too."

"No, thanks," Katherine said, already halfway through the doorway.

Gwen flopped back down in her seat and looked around the empty room.

A moment later, Frances popped her head around the corner, a plastic washtub in her hands. "Oh." Her gaze flicked around the room, finally landing on Gwen. A well-worn apron covered her corduroy pants and thin black turtleneck. "I'm sorry. I thought you'd all left. I can come back."

Gwen sighed and motioned her in. "No, no. Now is fine." She watched the older woman work, feeling the compulsion to offer to help and then quashing it as she'd conditioned herself to do over the years. That wasn't her job.

Frances loaded up the small tub with dishes, careful not to clank the bread plates together. Gwen Langtree was high society, but the other women seemed like most of the guests that Frances encountered. Normal. Or as normal as women who wrestled, tried to spit on, and slapped each other could be. Actually, the more she thought about it, the more it seemed a good idea to lock the door to the servants' quarters tonight.

The white-haired woman performed her task by rote, allowing herself to maintain a curious, sideways glance at Gwen. "How's your gathering going so far?"

Gwen covered her face with her hands. "About like I deserve."

Katherine poked her head into the guest room she was sharing with Audrey. The furnishings were decidedly Victorian with dark delicate wood, a busy rose-patterned wallpaper and mounds of crème-colored bedding and fluffy pillows trimmed in mint green and pale pink. Just seeing it made Katherine want to fling herself out the bedroom window. "Audrey? Don't make me stay in this room looking for you." She poked her head behind a lace screen set up for discreet dressing.

But there was no one in the room. "Sure," Katherine mumbled. "Run off crying and then disappear." She had yet to see the other rooms so she headed down the hall. When she passed Gwen's room she heard Audrey's voice say, "Okay, tell Papa I love him and that I'll call back tonight."

Katherine stepped into Gwen's room just as Audrey was hanging up.

Audrey looked a little embarrassed about being caught in Gwen's room. "There was no phone in our room so I went looking for one," she said by way of explanation.

"Are you okay?" Katherine asked, concerned.

Audrey was a little embarrassed over her outburst. "Your comments about Vegas made me think about what my stupid daughter did."

Katherine's eyebrows jumped. "She ran off to Vegas and got married?"

"Uh-huh."

Katherine winced.

"But I've been dealing with that for weeks." She let out a deep breath as if trying to force away the stress the topic carried.

"They might make it, Audrey."

Audrey sighed. "I sure hope so."

Wanting to move to more pleasant ground, Katherine said, "Would you look at this room?"

"It doesn't look like Martha Stewart threw up in here." The difference between this room and Audrey and Katherine's was startling. This room had a contemporary flair with leather furnishings done in contrasting shades of black and white and the occasional splash of color brought in by throw pillows or a piece of modern art. "It's actually nice."

"Gwen picked the good one. She always did have great taste."

A thought suddenly occurred to Katherine. This was her chance to snoop in Gwen's room. If she were incredibly lucky she would find out whether Gwen was the person who had been investigating her. "Stand guard at the door a minute. I want to snoop."

Audrey's eyes widened. "What?"

"You heard me." Katherine began looking for Gwen's suitcase.

"Jesus Christ, Katy, Gwen is a bitch to be sure, but I'm not going to help you invade her privacy."

"Oh, yes you are." Katherine crossed the room. Then she opened the closet door and spied the suitcase and her eyes took on a determined gleam. "There you are."

Audrey cursed inwardly. Katherine knew she wouldn't let her down, and her cousin was right "What are you looking for?"

"Nothing," Katherine said, kneeling in a surprisingly roomy closet and fumbling to quickly unzip the suitcase.

"Oh, no you don't. Tell me or I'm leaving," Audrey demanded.

Katherine sighed. "Trust me, okay?"

Audrey wrung her hands and glanced nervously at the door. Still torn.

Katherine opened the suitcase and on the top of a pile of clothes was a stack of manila folders. They were unmarked, so she flipped open the first one and spotted her name written on the inside cover. Angrily, she ground her teeth together. "I knew it. That bitch!"

"You can curse at her later. Hurry up, she could come back any minute."

"No." Katherine shook her head. "She offered to come find you and see what was upsetting you, but I said no thanks. I think she'll give me time to figure out what's wrong with you before coming up. You know how Gwen hates messy, emotional scenes."

Audrey licked her lips nervously.

"You go stand at the head of the stairs and act as a lookout." Katherine searched for a light switch in the closet. She could read it if she strained, but it would be faster to get a quick glimpse of the contents. Not finding a switch, she resolved herself to look hard and gather as much information as she could. "Don't let Gwen back in here."

Audrey nodded quickly. "Okay." She had barely turned around when—

"Damn Gwen to hell!"

"Shh!" The brunette ran to the door and looked out. Fleetingly, she wondered where Nina had gone, but her attention was drawn quickly back to Katherine.

"I don't believe it!" Her voice was tinged with anger and something else.

"What?" Audrey ran back to the closet. "What did you find?"

Socks, a navy-blue bra, and a pair of gabardine trousers now lay haphazardly on the floor. She read over a pie chart that detailed her income, assets, and debt. "Nothing you'd be interested in."

Audrey didn't look back in time to see Katherine tuck a few pieces of paper from each folder into her pants and fluff her shirt over the slight bulge.

Audrey blinked at her cousin. "You didn't take anything, did you? That would be stealing."

"No kidding."

Audrey's eyes sparked. "I want to know exactly what's going on. You don't steal."

Katherine chewed her lower lip, trying to decide what to tell her.

She wasn't sure what the folders would contain and somehow it seemed smarter to discover their contents in private. "I—"

Audrey's worried gaze strayed to the door. "Let's go before—Oh, shit!" She heard footsteps coming up the stairs. "Someone's coming."

Katherine's eyes widened. "Who?"

Audrey gave her an impatient look. "Do I look like I have x-ray vision?"

Two sets of eyes stared at the door as they intently listened to the footsteps growing louder and louder. Finally, Katherine cracked under the pressure. "Hide!"

"No friggin' way. We can just tell her we were in here using the phone."

"She won't believe that. Hide!"

"Katy!"

"Shh!" Mashing herself against Audrey, she pulled the closet door closed just as someone entered the bedroom.

It was dark in the closet, but the bottom of the door was a good inch above the ground and allowed in a little light. In fact, Katherine got a good look at the murderous glare Audrey was tossing her way and she put a finger against her lips to remind Audrey to be quiet.

Footsteps moved around the room and then there was the plinking sound of ice being dropped into a heavy glass and the glugging sound of liquid being poured from a bottle.

Then there was a measure of silence and Katherine's eyes narrowed as she imagined several deep swallows of cool liquor burning its way down Gwen's throat. *Oh, great, now I'm thirsty.* Then they heard a muffled sob and despite what they'd found in Gwen's closet, both women felt a stab of guilt over their duplicity and Gwen's distress.

The crying continued for several long minutes, with Katherine shifting uneasily, but silently from one foot to the other the entire time. It was making Audrey insane.

Audrey had almost resigned herself to opening the closet door and facing the music when they heard the melodic tones of a cell phone being dialed.

"Hi, Mal." A long pause. "Yes, things are going . . . Well nobody has tried to strangle me yet. But the weekend is young. I just felt like talking.

Do you have a while? No patients for an hour? That's great. I could really use a friendly ear."

Katherine and Audrey whimpered quietly, seeing their chances of getting out quickly and undetected go up in smoke.

Fall 1982
St. Louis, Missouri

"C'mon, c'mon. Pay up, Katy." Nina, dressed in a University of Missouri-St. Louis sweatshirt and black jeans, tapped her foot impatiently. She'd already asked Katherine three times that day. "I need to bring the rent over to Mr. Gossler before we go to the game tonight." Their landlord lived next door.

Katherine sighed and sat up from her stretched out position on the ratty, burnt-orange-colored sofa that they'd bought at a yard sale for twenty dollars. No matter what they did to it, the couch still smelled a little like wet dog. "Lemme go raid my piggy bank. Hang on." With a groan, she headed to the small bedroom she shared with Gwen and Nina.

The girls of the Mayflower Club were renting a house that was older than any of their grandparents and was located only two miles from the University of Missouri-St. Louis, where they were freshmen. The school had a mediocre academic reputation and underachieving sports teams, but it was cheap, local, and someplace they'd all been accepted—the top three things on all their lists. Only Nina knew that Jacie had been offered a partial academic scholarship to Washington University, though even with the Priest family's meager assistance, she'd been forced to turn it down because tuition and room and board were simply out of her reach.

Nina sat down on the sofa and closed her eyes. She'd have to make up for attending tonight's soccer match by studying all night tomorrow for her first history exam. A small smile appeared. It would be worth it. Jacie did nothing but work or study at the library these days, and if she didn't know better, Nina would have sworn that Jacie was avoiding her. But the more she thought about it, the more ridiculous the idea seemed. Sure, they hadn't gotten to spend as much time together as Nina would have liked, but Jacie was her very best friend, and that would never change.

Her stomach fluttered happily at the thought of an evening together.

Gwen stepped out of their tiny kitchen with a soda can in her hand. She, too, was wearing a sweatshirt in the school colors of red and gold, this one emblazoned with UMSL Rivermen. She sucked in a breath because her tight-fitting Gloria Vanderbilt jeans were cutting off blood to parts of her body she was pretty sure needed blood. Still, she looked fabulous, and as her mother had drilled into her head—beauty wasn't free.

Gwen glanced around. "Where is everyone? We need to go."

Nina looked at the plastic wall clock shaped like an owl, the kind whose demented eyes danced back and forth as the second hand moved. "Katy's in the bedroom rifling the chair cushions for her portion of the rent. Audrey is in the other room and refuses to come out until she's lost twenty pounds and has a date for Homecoming. And Jacie isn't home yet."

"Oh, God." Gwen bared her teeth in a vicious smile. "I could kill that Tommy for making that comment about Audrey's thighs."

Nina's eyes narrowed. "You and me both. There's nothing wrong with her thighs."

"Who could you kill?" Katy asked as she approached the sofa with a thick stack of crinkled one-dollar bills in her hands. The tips she earned waitressing almost made up for her smelling like grease one hundred percent of the time.

Gwen sat down next to Nina. She set her soda on the floor and picked up the earrings she'd left on the coffee table. "Audrey's bastard ex-boyfriend." In one ear she placed a simple, fake diamond stud. In the other ear she slid in a stud with a long chain attached and a longer white feather that dangled at the end of that. Then she adjusted her pink headband. Olivia Newton-John would be jealous. "He really did a number on her self-esteem."

"Is she still in the bedroom?" Katy had assumed since Audrey had been in there so long that perhaps her cousin had ended her self-imposed exile and somehow she'd just missed it.

Nina nodded. "Still in there."

Katy sighed. "I'll go get her."

Gwen looked at the door. "We're going to have to leave Jacie if she doesn't get here soon." She grinned girlishly, her blue eyes dancing with delight. "Malcolm Langtree is going to meet me at the game and I can't be late."

Nina blinked. "The tall boy you've been flirting with since the first week of school? What was his name again?"

Gwen looked aghast. "C'mon, Nina, don't tell me you've haven't heard of the Langtrees!" She gestured wildly. "Are you crazy?"

Nina batted round, innocent eyes. "I'm sure I don't know who you mean."

Gwen stamped both her feet. "Nina!"

Nina couldn't help it; she burst out laughing. "Duh, Gwen." She smacked the taller girl on the arm. "Everyone in St. Louis knows who they are."

Gwen gave her a sheepish look, the color of her cheeks rivaling her headband. "I'm sorry. I'm just—"

"Excited?" Nina gazed at her indulgently. "I noticed."

"He is awfully cute, though," she defended. "And he's taking me out to a late dinner after the game."

"Are those from him?" Nina inclined her head toward a wobbly end table that held a bouquet of fragrant flowers. The flora had been stuffed into an empty coke bottle-turned-bud vase.

"Uh-huh. My first roses!" Gwen's dreamy expression turned wry. "They almost drown out the smell of the sofa."

Both girls began to laugh.

The front door flew open and Jacie, still dressed in the black slacks and black silk blouse she wore every time she tended bar using her fake ID, strode into the living room. "Sorry I'm late, guys, but I need as much overtime as possible this week." An art class she'd taken on a lark was turning out to be her favorite course and the cost of supplies was killing her.

Nina's face lit up when she saw Jacie. She admitted privately that she loved the sight of her in her work clothes.

Jacie stopped near the sofa and looked back at the front door. "Don't be shy, Karen. C'mon in." She motioned to a slender woman who was waiting quietly in the doorway. The woman looked to be in her mid-to-late twenties, and Jacie smiled as she strolled into their living room.

Gwen recalled seeing this woman once before when she'd given Jacie a ride home from work last month. She eyed her red suede jacket enviously. "I saw your coat in the Famous-Barr's store window last week. It's great."

The pretty woman smiled, showing off perfect white teeth. "Thanks. I think so, too."

Nina wanted to gag over Karen's syrupy sweet Southern accent.

"And that's Charlie perfume you're wearing," Gwen continued, looking closer to see if the jacket had the plain gold buttons or the ones with tiny silver flecks in them.

Impressed, the woman nodded. "That's pretty good. I'm barely wearing any."

Gwen blew on her fingers and then buffed them on her sweatshirt. "It's a gift. I'm taking fashion design."

Nina glanced at Jacie, whose gaze was riveted on Karen, and inexplicably felt like growling, the tiny hairs on the back of her neck standing at attention.

"Gwen, Nina, this is my uh . . . my friend Karen-Michelle," Jacie introduced, not able to look Nina in the eye. She and Karen had recently become lovers, and Jacie was drowning in guilt. She had no doubt whatsoever who really owned her heart. And it wasn't Karen. "We met at work." She rocked back on her heels. "And . . . uh . . . she's going to come to the game with us, okay?"

Gwen shrugged. "Sure."

"That's great," Nina said, unable to project a single ounce of enthusiasm into her normally bright voice. Was this who Jacie was spending all of her free time with? She felt the sting of jealousy burning deep in the pit of her stomach and was instantly ashamed. *Stop being an idiot! She's allowed to have other friends.*

Unable to sit still for another second, Gwen popped up off the couch and grabbed her purse from a hook on the wall. "Okay, let's go." She was already moving for the door.

"Katy and Audrey are still in Jacie's room," Nina reminded.

Jacie nodded. "I'll get them and then change my shirt and—Yeow!"

She tripped over a plastic bin of clean laundry that had been carelessly left out by Katy and ended up sprawled out on the carpet like a turtle on her back. "Ugh," she said to the ceiling. "That was graceful."

Both Nina and Karen rushed to her side. "Are you okay?" they asked at the same time. Surprised, they turned and stared at one another with slightly wide eyes. Then each woman stuck out her hand to help Jacie up. "Here," they chorused again. This time the looks they shot each other were filled with annoyance.

Jacie blinked slowly, her eyebrows crawling up her forehead and her gaze flicking from hand to hand.

Forcing herself to act like an adult and not a spoiled girl who now had to share her favorite toy, Nina gritted her teeth and began to withdraw.

Without her permission, Jacie's arm shot out and she clasped Nina's hand, feeling warm, strong fingers wrap around her own. A tiny squeeze was her reward.

Karen's eyes took on a knowing glint.

Confused but smugly satisfied, Nina tugged Jacie to her feet and after a few awkward seconds, reluctantly let go of her hand. She took a step backward, finding something terribly interesting about their avocado-green shag carpet, though she couldn't stop the small smile from appearing.

"Thank you, Nina," Jacie said softly, forgetting for a moment that Karen was even in the room.

Karen rolled her eyes as so many mysteries about Jacie finally came into focus. Now she understood why Jacie, though she'd finally allowed herself to be seduced, had seemed reluctant to move forward with their relationship. She was in love with someone else. The interaction between the two younger women made her wonder why the dishwater-blonde with the intense eyes was so blind.

Finally aware that Karen was watching her, Jacie tore her eyes from Nina and snatched a shirt and pair of jeans from the clothesbasket. The shirt was Katy's but she wouldn't mind, and a quick check at the tag told her the pants belonged to her and not to Gwen, who would mind but would get over it. With a little wave, she headed for the bedroom, giving the clothesbasket a small kick as she went. "One second."

With Jacie gone, the silence in the living room stretched on endlessly.

"So," Gwen began politely, resisting the urge to check her watch again, "what do you do, Karen?"

Karen sighed loudly. "Way too many stupid things." She gave the girls a wry smile. "And I ought to know better."

Not having the faintest idea of how to respond to that, Nina and Gwen just stood there, shifting from one foot to the other and praying that Jacie would come back soon.

Karen turned to Nina. "Will you give Jacie a message for me?"

"Uhh . . ." She pointed to the bedroom in which Jacie had disappeared. "She's just in there. You can tell her your—"

"Why don't you tell her for me?" Karen interrupted, giving Nina a direct look.

Nina's mouth snapped shut. "Well, sure. Okay," she finally muttered.

Karen smiled. "Thanks. Tell her I had a lot of fun and I'll see her around sometime. I suddenly remembered that I have other plans for tonight."

Nina's shoulders slumped. She hadn't exactly been rude, but she hadn't really welcomed Jacie's new friend either. "Look, if you'll just wait—"

Karen waved a dismissive hand. "No thanks. I have a feeling I'll be waiting forever for that one."

"You will?" Nina said, shaking her head a little, clearly befuddled.

Karen's gaze sharpened and she searched the girl's face, trying to decide whether she was being mocked. But a good look into earnest eyes yielded a quick and certain answer and, despite herself, she had to smother a chuckle. If this weren't happening to her, it would have been too cute for words. "I'm sure of it." And with that, Karen saw herself out the front door and out of Jacie's life, allowing the screen to slam behind her.

The door hadn't been closed for three seconds when Jacie showed up, followed by Katy and Audrey. Jacie's gaze bounced around the room. "Where's Karen?"

Nina braced herself for Jacie to be upset. "She . . . um . . . she said to tell you she'd had fun and would see you around."

Jacie's jaw sagged.

"And that she suddenly remembered a prior engagement," Gwen added, quickly losing patience and wondering if it wouldn't be easier to just catch the bus. "Can we go now, please?"

Katy held up her car keys and jangled them. "I'm ready."

"Me too," Audrey said. Having been the recipient of a pep talk by Katy and Jacie, she and her less-than-perfect thighs were once again prepared to face the cruel world.

"I'm sorry about your friend, Jacie," Nina said quietly, really meaning it.

Jacie let out a deep breath, visibly relieved. "I'm not. She sort of invited herself along, anyway."

"Good," Gwen announced. "Now, Jacie, give Nina your portion of the rent. Katy, go warm up the beast. We'll pick Nina and Jacie up next door after Mr. Gossler gets paid." She beamed a smile at Audrey. "And, Audrey, you'll never guess who I'm meeting at the game!"

"Not Malcolm Langtree," she squealed excitedly.

Katy and Audrey were shuffled out the front door with Gwen chatting happily the entire time and literally pushing them along.

Jacie dug into her jeans pocket and pulled out several twenties. She held out the bills. "I figured you'd need this today."

Nina took the money. "Thanks." For some reason, her feet seemed rooted to the floor.

Jacie was equally uninterested in moving from her spot right in front of her friend. Eventually, however, she conceded that they'd better go or Gwen would come back in and have their hides. "I'll get my gloves. I think it's going to be cold tonight." Jacie made a move for the closet but was stopped by a warm hand on her elbow.

Nina audibly swallowed. "You . . . um . . . I mean, if your hands get cold, you could just snuggle close to me." Her heart began to pound and she just kept talking, needing to get this out. "I'm really warm . . . and . . . warm, I guess." Her eyes begged Jacie to understand what she was feeling. "Or you could use one of my gloves and I could use the other or I could rest my hand on yours or I could just be close to you," she babbled. "Or—"

"We could share?" Jacie asked quietly, looking deeply into Nina's eyes, seeing something she hadn't seen before, and letting every bit of love she'd tried so desperately to hide bubble up to the surface and overflow.

The room grew as still as the night, and in those few seconds of electric silence, something profound passed between them. Something that stripped their hearts naked and laid their souls out bare. It was a bone-deep understanding that broke through the questions and doubts and, in that one powerful moment, gave them both more courage than either knew they possessed.

Nina smiled tentatively. It was either that or burst into tears. Her mind was awhirl with scary and wonderful possibilities, and she blew out a long breath as she tried to calm her shaking hands. "I'd like that, Jacie," she whispered, hearing the hoarseness in her own voice and marveling at her own braveness. "I'd like to share. A lot."

As it always did, Jacie's smile reached her eyes, warming them, just a split second before it bowed her lips. And this one was the most beautiful smile that Nina had ever seen. "I'd like that too." Her heart skipped a beat, and she reached out and took Nina's hand, twining their fingers together. "More than anything."

Audrey shook her head miserably. "How long have we been in here?" she whispered as quietly as she could.

"Not even thirty seconds, you big baby. I haven't even put this back yet." She showed Audrey the folder with one hand but continued to very slowly unzip the suitcase with the other. When she was finally finished she laid open the bag.

Next to several other folders and sitting atop a tall pile of clothes Audrey saw something that caught her eye. "She finally got a cashmere sweater. I wonder if it was blue like she always wanted."

Katherine sneered as she replaced the folder. She'd confront Gwen about it if the taller woman didn't come talk to her first. She knew why Gwen was checking her out and guilt assailed her. "Okay, let's go. I can't stand it in here another second," she whispered.

"You just want a cigarette."

Katherine blinked. She hadn't even thought of that until now, and the craving swept over her with such intensity that she swooned at the idea of all that lovely nicotine melting into her bloodstream and infusing her body.

"I'm making a break for it," Katherine announced boldly.

"No!"

Ignoring Audrey, Katherine jumped up and flung open the closet door.

Gwen shrieked and dropped the phone on the bed, clutching a pillow to her chest.

At the sound of a blood-curdling scream, Audrey covered her face with her hands. "Oh, shit." Then she sprung out of the closet on Katherine's heels.

Gwen's eyes were round as saucers as she scrambled off the bed. "Jesus! Katy?" Then she looked at the slightly disheveled woman standing behind her. "Audrey?" Her voice was rising with each word. "What in the—?"

"Surprise," Katherine yelled, pasting on a happy face.

Audrey looked blankly at Katherine, who elbowed her in the boob. "Surprise," she coughed, rubbing her chest.

"Happy birthday to you," Katherine crooned ridiculously. Audrey joined in slightly off key.

Gwen looked at her friends as though they'd lost their minds. "Are you two drunk?

Pretending they hadn't heard her question, Audrey and Katherine soldiered on, continuing to sing "Happy Birthday" to the bitter, off-key end.

Gwen blinked, still in shock. "This is a surprise party?"

Katherine smiled broadly. She was actually going to buy it! "Yes." She nodded once. "Yes, it is."

Gwen picked up her phone and placed it to her ear. "No, you don't have to call the police, Malcolm. I'll have to call you back." A beep sounded as she pressed "off." Then she walked over to the closet and looked inside. Her bags were right were she left them. "If this is my party, then where are Nina and Jacie?"

"Uh . . . ." Audrey looked at Katherine, her mind blank and her face showing it.

"Uh . . ." Katherine looked back at Audrey and began to panic. "Audrey forgot to invite them," she blurted suddenly.

"What?" Audrey screeched, not liking that she'd been made out to be the stupider of *Dumb and Dumber*. "I'm the one who forgot?"

"Yes," Katherine answered confidently. "Yes, you did." She focused on Gwen and made a clucking sound. "God, she can be so dense. Uncle Allan swore she was the milkman's." She stepped away just in time for Audrey's claw-shaped hand to whiz past her.

"Okay," Gwen said with exaggerated slowness, more convinced than ever that the cousins were indeed three sheets to the wind. She looked around the room. "So what do we do now?"

"Gifts!" Katherine shouted. "A party should have gifts." She turned to face Audrey, knowing that Gwen couldn't see her face. "Or did you forget those, too, Audrey?" She stuck her tongue out.

Audrey's face turned a lovely shade of red, and she vowed on the spot that her revenge would be sweet. "Uh . . . . A gift." The actual gift she'd brought was in her bag in her room. But that's something she would have brought to a real party. "Katy has the gift in her pocket." She smiled evilly. "Don't you remember, cuz?"

Katherine paled.

Gwen smiled. If they had a gift, then maybe this was their sad attempt at a party. After all, they hadn't had years to hone their social skills at St. Louis' finest country club. "So, what's my present, Katy?"

Katherine closed her eyes and gave a mental sigh. Then she whirled around and dug into her pocket, hoping that something would be in there. Quickly, she grasped the contents and dropped it into Gwen's out-stretched hands, a little surprised she'd gotten so lucky.

Gwen looked down at her gifts. Her face was totally blank. "Oh, you shouldn't have, Katy."

Katherine blinked. "I shouldn't?"

Both Katherine and Gwen peered with interest at Gwen's upturned palm.

Gwen held up the first item. "A Tic Tac." She lifted an eyebrow and then made a delicate sniffing noise. "Wintergreen. My favorite."

Audrey snorted.

"Ooo . . ." Then Gwen lifted a tiny brown pill and held it up to the light. "A birth control pill from . . ." she squinted and read the expiration date. "1999. How thoughtful."

This time Audrey snorted so hard she began to choke. "Don't you ever do laundry?" she coughed.

A flush worked its way up from Katherine's neck to cover her entire face.

"And finally," Gwen began again, "the *piece d'resistance*. One dollar," she poked through the coins, "and seven cents." She smiled valiantly. "Now I can get that Diet Pepsi I've been saving up for."

"The money part was from me," Audrey inserted, enjoying Katherine's misery.

"Of course it was," Gwen allowed. "Only someone as thoughtful as you could have known that I was secretly saving the state quarters and didn't have Georgia yet."

Wordlessly, Audrey ran around Katherine and pulled Gwen into a solid hug. Then she reached out and grabbed Katherine's hand and yanked her out of the room.

When she was alone, Gwen sat back down on the bed, looking at the items in her hand in bewilderment. What had just happened? She couldn't decide whether to be more or less suspicious of her friends after their bizarre behavior. After lunch, she was leaning toward Jacie as being the blackmailer, but Katy and Audrey were acting too strangely to dismiss either of them. It was all too much to consider. Gwen closed her eyes. "I think I'm going insane. No," she corrected firmly, "I know I'm going insane." She shrugged, "But what the hell," and popped the Tic Tac into her mouth.

Present Day
Rural Missouri

"Nina," Jacie mumbled to herself, "where are you?" She tugged the collar of her jacket higher and stepped over a damp, decaying log. A quick check of the house had yielded nothing. But all the cars were still there, which meant Nina hadn't gone home.

Jacie stood at the edge of the back lawn, where the rock-covered path split in two. She closed her eyes, sucked in a deep breath, and thought of Nina. She homed in on the persistent sensation in the bottom of her stomach, a sensation borne of their kindred spirits and mutual undying love, trusting that feeling to be her guide. Twenty minutes later, cursing, dirty, scratched, and with her jeans wet from the knees down from taking a detour through the woods, she headed back to the fork in the path so she could go the other way. She vowed never to read cheesy lesbian romance novels again.

It wasn't long before she could smell the river, dank and lush. The sun had gone behind thick clouds and the early evening sky was heavy and gray. There, on a knotted wooden bench that overlooked the river's banks sat Nina, tossing stones into its slow-moving depths.

"What took you so long?" Nina said quietly, not bothering to turn around when she heard rocks crunching under sure footsteps. Ker-plunk. A pebble disappeared beneath the murky surface.

Jacie dropped down beside her and picked up a stone from the pile that now sat between them on the bench. "I didn't know where you'd gone," Jacie answered simply, scraping a blade of wet grass from the stone with her thumbnail.

Nina nodded, her eyes still on the water. "When we were kids and would play hide and seek you found me before anyone else. Always." For the first time, she turned and looked at her friend, sucking in a breath at the sight of the painful-looking black-eye she'd given her. Tenderly, she reached up with chilled fingers and traced the swollen flesh. "I thought you were magic."

Jacie quirked a bittersweet grin. "No magic, Nina. You were the only one I ever looked for."

Chapter 7
Fall 1982
St. Louis, Missouri

The throbbing bass of the stereo rattled the dingy windows of the two-story house, and Nina wrinkled her nose at some unidentifiable, raunchy smell that wafted in her direction. The house was being rented by a friend of a friend of a friend of Katy's, and word around campus was that this annual bash was legendary.

The girls had arrived several hours earlier, intent on unwinding and celebrating the momentous occasion of completing their first month of college, but were disappointed to find that most of the guests were strangers. Still, there was beer, although it had grown warm as the evening progressed. And there was a selection of food that consisted of more than just Doritos and pretzels, a rarity at student gatherings. They were quickly encouraged to stay and enjoy the festivities.

A skinny man with a nose so long it resembled a beak more than any human nose, bumped into Nina as he tried to push his way past her.

"Hey." She flicked a dollop of beer suds off the arm of her shirt. "Ugh.

Gross."

Still juggling four dripping plastic cups of brew in his hands, he glanced up at her and smiled, obviously pleased that his unintended victim just so happened to be a pretty co-ed. Unconsciously, he straightened his back and opened his mouth, but before he could say a word, Nina caught sight of Gwen's flaming red hair and began to weave her way through the throng of drunken partygoers. "Gwen," she said loudly, her voice not carrying over the music, laughter, and occasional shriek from an unknown source. Her eyes fluttered closed as the thumping at the base of her skull rivaled the beat of the music. Adding to her misery was the intermingled smell of hops, perfume, cologne, and sweat. That, or the seven chicken wings drenched in an indistinguishable sauce that she'd recently consumed and then washed down with two jumbo lukewarm beers, was making her sick to her stomach.

Nina held up one hand and waved, hoping that her friend would spot her. "Gwen!"

The taller girl paused in her conversation with a small group of students from her French class and glanced around, trying to locate her caller. When she spotted Nina, she motioned her over. "Here!"

"Hey." Nina smiled at strangers as she joined the group. A little green around the gills, she waved off the offer of another beer.

"This is Nina Chilton, one of my roommates," Gwen introduced politely.

"Nina!" the group chorused back in greeting.

Nina chuckled. It was clear that every last one of them was as drunk as a sailor on a three-day pass. She tilted her head up to speak directly into Gwen's ear in an attempt to be heard. "Let's find the others and go."

Gwen frowned. "You want the others to find snow? What will you do with it if you get it?"

Nina rolled her eyes and pointed toward the door. "Go," she mouthed. "I want to go."

Gwen shook her head firmly, the movement nearly causing her to slosh the contents of her drink onto the floor. "Nuh-uh. I'm having too much fun." She'd had several beers already and needed to concentrate to keep Nina's face in focus. She plucked at Nina's wet sleeve. "What happened?"

Nina made a face. "Some jerk spilled beer on me." Then a warm hand settled on her shoulder and she smiled without bothering to turn around, quite certain who it belonged to. While neither Jacie nor Nina had had the courage to take their relationship to the next level, both knew that they shared something more than friendship.

"Hi, Jacie," Gwen said, taking another long sip of the heady brew. "You don't look like you're having much fun."

Jacie plucked Gwen's glass from her hand and polished off the contents in one long sip. "Sure I am." She grinned wildly and licked away her foam mustache.

"Uh-oh. Somebody's going to be sick tomorrow," Nina teased. "And boy am I glad she's not my roomie."

The smile suddenly slid off Jacie's face as she absorbed Nina's words. "Are you really glad?" she asked with surprising seriousness, a tiny pout forming.

Nina's heart clenched and she chided herself for letting Jacie's words affect her so, knowing it was the alcohol that was talking. "Of course not, Jace," she said tenderly, reaching up to clasp the hand that still rested on her shoulder. "I was only teasing."

Jacie's face was suddenly transformed by a lopsided grin. "Don't worry. I won't be sick."

Curious, Gwen watched her friends, seeing them as if it were the very first time.

Nina poked Jacie's belly with mock fierceness. "But if you were sick—"

"You'd be right there." Jacie's grin grew. "Disgusted, but there."

Nina laughed. "Exactly."

Dumbfounded, Gwen continued to silently observe her friends. The rest of the room, she realized, had faded away for them; they only had eyes for each other. She blinked slowly, letting the information penetrate the fog that shrouded her senses. The shared smiles, the position of their bodies, the gentleness in Jacie's normal brash personality, and the openness in Nina's often quiet demeanor, all told her one utterly impossible thing. She grimaced as she felt an irrational stab of envy at their obvious closeness, along with a wave of revulsion.

Jacie's expression gentled and she leaned forward to say something directly into Nina's ear.

Gwen couldn't hear what was being said, but the look on Nina's face said more than words ever could. Suddenly, she felt sick to her stomach. Their relationship wasn't like that! It couldn't be. She'd known them forever, and though it had been a while since either had been on a date, that was just a social slump, not something more catastrophic. *Of course*, she mused silently, *even Audrey goes out more than they do, whereas they only seem contented with each other's company*. On the other hand—Gwen's rust-colored eyebrows contracted—she'd seen them both with boys, seen them kissing boys, in fact.

She scrubbed her face with one hand and then hiccupped loudly. It was all so confusing. Jacie suddenly handed her back the empty plastic cup. Dully, Gwen stared into it, as though the answers to her questions might be written on the bottom.

The front door opened, pushing aside a group of students who were standing in front of it, and Malcolm Langtree strode in, proud and tall. On his heels another small group of rowdy-looking men and women, most of them several years older than the college kids who already filled the house, pushed their way inside and headed straight for one of the kegs of beer.

Instantly, Gwen's thoughts were derailed. Malcolm was so handsome and funny and his smile was so beautiful that she found herself sighing out loud. She glanced back at Nina and Jacie, who were still talking. She looked harder, but this time was unable to see what she'd thought she'd spotted only seconds before. She swayed back a little into the person behind her. "This beer is making me think the craziest things!" she announced good-naturedly, putting her ridiculous thoughts behind her and focusing on something much more pleasurable, like her new boyfriend.

"Whoa." Jacie's and Nina's hands shot out to grab Gwen, who seemed to be tipping over.

"I'm fine." Gwen slapped their hands away.

"You're drunk," Jacie corrected, keeping a light grip on Gwen's elbow.

"So are you," Gwen shot back, irritated at Jacie for pointing out the obvious, and a little ashamed for overindulging. She turned toward Malcolm and waited impatiently for his searching gaze to find hers.

"I sure am," Jacie agreed, suddenly sounding surprisingly sober. "But you don't see me falling into people."

"It's after midnight, you two. We all drank too much and it's time to go home," Nina said, yawning around the words. "Let's go. We've still got to find Audrey in all this mess. She's driving."

Gwen chuckled to herself, recalling Audrey's groaning protest that it wasn't fair that she always ended up as the one who had to stay sober and drive when the drinks were free.

A loud crash caused everyone to jump. And for a long second the room was silent as everyone was too shocked to breathe. Then a wave of laughter rolled over the crowd as a young man opened his eyes, shook his head, and rolled off a pile of wood that formerly had resembled a dining room table. His hysterical buddies helped him to his feet, before he collapsed down upon the pile again.

Jacie shook her head. "We are never having a party at our place. This house is going to be trashed by morning."

Nina's eyes widened as she took in the destruction around her. "You mean it isn't already?"

"Hello, ladies." Malcolm, dressed in a tight-fitting, mint green Polo shirt with the collar turned up, sidled next to them and then focused on the young woman who had captured more than his attention. He smiled boyishly. "Hello, Gwendolyn."

Gwen fought hard not to swoon.

Jacie sniggered. "Gwendolyn?" She'd never heard Gwen go by her full name.

"What is it, Jacie Ann?" Gwen asked in a sugary voice, emphasizing the full name Jacie's family usually used.

Nina covered her mouth to keep from laughing at how quickly that wiped the smug look from Jacie's face.

Malcolm wrapped a long arm around Gwen's shoulder. Clearly smitten, he pulled her close. "There were rumors all the way over at my fraternity that there was a party going on here and, more importantly, that there was a beautiful girl here who was not to be missed." He kissed her cheek. "The rumors were true."

Gwen blushed becomingly, and Jacie and Nina both rolled their eyes, quite sure if there were a rumor like that floating around that Gwen would have been sure to have started it herself.

"We were just leaving," Nina announced, seeing that her friend wasn't going to want to go any time soon. She wrinkled her nose and sighed. "I have to work tomorrow."

Malcolm's eyes went round. "But tomorrow's Saturday!" He protested in horror, clutching Gwen a little tighter as if to ward off the disgusting words.

"No kidding," Jacie said dryly, doing her best not to hold Malcolm's privileged background against him. She had to work the next day and she knew that Gwen did too.

"Let's dance," Gwen said abruptly, before Jacie went and did something stupid and told Malcolm about her own afternoon shift at JC Penny's the next day. She wrapped her hands around his belt and began tugging him in the direction of a corner of the room where the people were, despite the fast tempo of the deafening music, slowly swaying and playing tonsil hockey.

His eyes lit up. In the weeks they'd been dating, she hadn't done more than give him gentle and all-too-brief kisses on the cheek and lips. "Yes, ma'am!" he replied happily, waggling his fingers at Nina as he allowed Gwen to drag him where he most certainly wanted to go.

"Guess she found her ride home," Jacie surmised, happy for Gwen's good fortune with Malcolm. Despite being ignorant of the realities of middle and lower class life, he seemed like a good guy. Maybe Gwen's mother had been right all long. It was just as easy to fall in love with a rich man as a poor one, she'd said. And that appeared to be the truth, at least for Gwen Hopkins.

Nina rubbed the bridge of her nose and whimpered. "Is the music getting louder or is it just that my head is getting ready to explode?"

Jacie gave her a sympathetic look. Her parents were both smokers and the thick cloud that permeated the room was all but unnoticed by her. She knew, however, that it didn't take long to make Nina feel puny. "We're off. We can walk and let Audrey drive Gwen home if Malcolm doesn't."

Nina smiled, relieved. "Deal." They set out to find Audrey and Katy to let them know their plans.

Large, cardboard signs that had been placed all over the house declared the upstairs bedrooms off-limits and so the crowd was sparse there compared to the rest of house. It held only a few brave couples who were using the rooms as hiding places to make-out, and a snaking line of partygoers waiting impatiently to use the house's only working bathroom.

A pair of angry girls were banging on the bathroom door and cursing. "C'mon, your turn's up!"

Jacie's eyes traveled the length of the line. "I don't see them," she said loudly.

Nina looked toward the bathroom, hearing the faint sound of raised voices from behind the bathroom door over the noise in the hallway. "They must be in the bathroom."

Jacie's eyes widened. "Together?"

The word was still hanging in the air when the bathroom door flew open and a red-faced Katy stormed out with Audrey following right behind her.

The line of people all cheered.

"Yeah, yeah," Katy mumbled in acknowledgment, flipping them the bird as she headed for the stairs.

"What's wrong?" Nina asked Audrey.

"She's mad," Audrey said, pushing her way between two rather large men. "Excuse me. Uff . . . Coming through."

"I can see she's mad," Jacie said. "Steam is pouring out of her ears like on the cartoons. But why?"

They made their way down the stairs, with Katy leading a fiery path to the front doorway.

"Because," Audrey continued, setting her near empty cup on a coffee table as they moved. "I told her she couldn't sleep with every guy she thinks is cute. The bathroom was the only place with a little privacy."

Katy whirled around and pointed an angry finger at her cousin, beyond caring that they were now having this discussion in public. "I do not do that, Audrey," she ground out, her eyes flashing.

Audrey lifted her chin along with one eyebrow and Jacie and Nina exchanged worried glances. That meant she wasn't backing down. "And just where did I find you after I spent thirty minutes looking for you?" Imperiously, she tossed a shock of curls over one shoulder as she waited for Katy's answer.

"Where I was is none of your business."

Audrey turned to Jacie. "She was in one of the bedrooms with some guy she met ten minutes earlier."

"Shut up, Audrey," Katy warned darkly, a flush working up her neck. "His name is Frank and I met him a couple of hours ago and all we were doing was kissing." She swallowed, her mouth already feeling cottony after several hours of drinking. "Which we would still be doing if you hadn't so rudely interrupted us!"

Audrey's eyes softened, but she pressed forward because she truly believed what she was saying was for Katy's own good. "Do you really know this guy?"

Katy's cheeks flushed even darker when she was forced to admit that she didn't know much more than she was attracted to him and that the feeling was mutual. "You are walking home!" She jangled a set of keys in front of Audrey's face.

"Why did Audrey give her the car keys?" Nina whispered loudly to Jacie. "Now we'll have to wrestle them away from her."

"Nuh-uh." Jacie could hardly contain her laughter as she pointed to the keys in Katy's hands. Katy was too tipsy to notice they were the keys to Audrey's gym locker.

"The hell I'm walking home," Audrey said, easily waving off Katy's threat. "It might be your car, but I'm the designated driver tonight." She put a hand on one hip. "And just so you know, no guy is going to buy the cow if he gets the milk for free."

"Jesus, you sound just like Granny, or even worse, Gwen!" Katy kicked at the ground petulantly, but her anger was already draining away. Audrey had always been there to watch her back, and she hers; it was comforting as few things in her life were. And yet, sometimes, especially now that they were in college, the closeness was like wearing a tight wool sweater in July.

"This is the 1980s, not the '50s, and I control my own body," Katy said. Her tone was as serious as Jacie and Nina had ever heard it. "It's my milk to give."

"And are you happy with all these boyfriends who don't mean anything?" Audrey asked pointedly, unfazed by the fact that they were having such a private conversation in the middle of a party. "Because if you are, you can make ice cream with your milk for all I care." She crossed her arms over her ample chest. "I want you to be happy, but I don't think you are."

"Audrey!"

"Yeah, yeah." Audrey held up her hands. "I just get worried about you, Katy. It's dangerous to go off alone with a virtual stranger. And what happens when you meet some guy you really love and he finds out you've made out with every other guy on campus?"

"He'll wonder why he wasn't lucky enough to meet me sooner?"

"He'll think you're easy."

"But I—" Katy paused mid-sentence and sighed. It wasn't that Audrey was a prude—she wasn't—it was more that she was a starry-eyed romantic who didn't seem to understand that real life wasn't like the Harlequin Romances her mother bought by the dozen at every yard sale in Hazelton.

Katy nodded a little, reluctantly acknowledging Audrey's genuine concern. When she didn't say more as she turned around and started walking again, her friends knew the argument was over.

An hour-and-a-half passed with the party still going strong, but by two a.m. the crowd had thinned considerably, leaving behind mostly latecomers and those too drunk to travel.

Malcolm was seated at a sticky coffee table with Gwen sitting next to him as he played poker with several Rivermen baseball players.

"You want another beer?" Gwen asked, reaching high above her head and stretching the kinks out of her upper back. She still had a strong buzz going, though things weren't quite as fuzzy as they had been a couple of hours earlier.

Malcolm took the opportunity to drop his cards and tickle her stomach. To his delight, Gwen giggled wildly as he tortured her. "Sure," he chuckled and reached to tickle her underarms where he knew his actions would have their most devastating effect. "But only if you're getting one for yourself."

"Ugh!" She finally wiggled free, then leaned over and gave him a sloppy kiss on the cheek, then lips, feeling more uninhibited than she could remember. A large portion of the smoke had cleared, and although the music was still pounding, the crowd had thinned to the point that she felt like she could breathe again. She also noticed another very strong sensation. "You'll have to wait for your beer now. After all that tickling, I have to use the bathroom." She blushed fiercely when Malcolm lifted his eyebrows.

"Do you want me to walk you up?"

I'm in love with him, she thought giddily. *It's only been a few weeks, but it's true.* Gwen laughed, having more fun than she had in ages. "No, silly." Her gaze drifted to the stairwell. The line to the bathroom was gone. "I saw Phyllis from my Western Civilization class heading up there a few minutes ago, but I haven't seen her since. There must still be a line upstairs." She giggled inwardly. *Or she and that short boy with the glasses are going at it hot 'n heavy in one of the bedrooms.*

Malcolm looked doubtful. "You're sure? I can—"

"Come on, Malcolm!" the other card players moaned. "You're holding up the game, man," the second basemen said. "For Christ's sake, let her go pee on her own. She's not that drunk."

Malcolm began to bristle but was quickly soothed by Gwen standing and affectionately ruffling his hair. "I'll be back after I wait in the never ending line from hell."

He grabbed her hand and gave it a little squeeze before letting go and focusing on his cards. "If you're not back in thirty minutes, I'll look for the puddle," he called after her, his eyes on a pair of aces. The game's other players laughed loudly.

Sure enough, there was a line for the bathroom, but it was blessedly short and consisted of total strangers.

"They fixed the bathroom downstairs," one of the women told the other.

Gwen nodded a little. No wonder the line here had dwindled to nothing. "Lucky us."

Happily, the souls in front of her were quick to do their business, and in only a few minutes she was at the head of the line with no one behind her to talk to.

Two more minutes, and a husky woman with the biggest hair Gwen had ever seen, staggered from the bathroom.

"Careful," Gwen warned the woman as she nearly collided with her.

"Whoops!" Rubber-legged, the woman swerved to miss Gwen, then fell with a mighty thud. "Ouch," she said slowly. She glanced around, clearly confused. "Why am I on the floor?"

Gwen smothered a snort. "You fell. Are you okay?"

"I think so."

Gwen bent unsteadily to help her, making certain the woman had a good hold of the stair railing before her bladder, protesting loudly, forced her to hurry back toward the bathroom door. Gwen's hand had just clasped the cool metal of the doorknob when she felt two warm arms wrap around her and a stubbly cheek nuzzle her neck from behind.

She smiled. Being in love was everything she'd hoped it would be. "Decided you had to go too, huh? God, don't squeeze too hard, Malcolm. I'll have an accident," she chuckled. "I swear." She took a step into the bathroom expecting him to let go. Instead, she was followed inside and she let out a surprised laugh. "You can't come in here with me. That's gross."

Gwen glanced down at the arms that were still wrapped snuggly around her trim waist. A dark sweatshirt covered them. It took only a second for it to register that Malcolm hadn't been wearing long sleeves. Her heart leapt into her throat. "Mal—"

She screamed as she was shoved headfirst all the way inside the small room. The room went black as the harsh florescent lights were flicked off and a strong hand slammed her head against the tank of the porcelain commode.

Her world exploded in pain.

"Shhh," a low voice hissed, the sound dancing at the ragged edges of her awareness.

Stars invaded her vision for several long seconds as fingers dug into her neck and she felt salty sweat from the tank dampen her cheek and trickle downward. She blinked dazedly, her head swimming as she clung to consciousness. Was that blood she tasted? "Puh . . . Uh . . . Ungh."

Gwen tried to bring a shaking hand to her forehead. Then she weakly pushed up from her belly-down position on the toilet. But on her way up, her wrist was instantly grasped and a heavy body molded itself to her back, threatening to send her to her knees. She screamed again as she tried to turn around, but the fingers moved from her wrist to wind themselves in her hair.

She sucked in a breath when her head was savagely yanked back, the skin on her face pulled tight enough to expose her bloody teeth.

"Bitch." The word was spoken harshly, directly into her ear, hot breath raising the hairs on the back of her neck, before it disappeared.

"No!" she cried, panic hitting her full force. But she only had time to gasp before she felt more than heard a low growl. Her face was slammed against the tank lid again. The loud crunch of her mouth and nose against the porcelain caused her stomach to lurch, and this time the dancing stars couldn't be blinked away.

Her breathing came in short pants as she tasted her own blood and smelled urine and beer. One of her arms was twisted high on her back and she squealed in pain, the searing sensation snapping her mind in better focus. "What . . . why are doing this?" She thought she'd said the words out loud, but she couldn't hear them over her thundering heart.

Fingers fumbled over her face until her chin and cheeks were being grasped so tightly that bruises instantly rose to the surface of the soft skin. "Shh!" Then, the fingers gentled and patted her in a comforting motion, much as a parent would a child.

He hiccupped loudly and then clapped his hand over her mouth, his body shaking with silent, drunken laughter.

Her heart was pounding so hard that every beat hurt. The hand quickly left her face and grabbed hold of the waistband of her jeans, jerking her up so that one of her knees came to rest on the fuzzy toilet seat lid. She felt fingers fumbling at the button of her jeans and the realization of what was about to happen slammed home with devastating force, causing bile to rise in her throat. "Stop," she moaned hoarsely, the faint vision of the dark toilet swimming in front of her.

A leg worked its way between hers; at the same time her jeans button finally came free.

"Stop. Stop. Stop!" Her arm was near breaking, and she could feel the tendons tearing as stabbing pains tore through her elbow and shoulder. She drew in an uneven breath and began to sob. "Please, pl-please stop!" she begged, her body fighting to distance itself from her attacker though she had no place to go. *Why is he doing this? Why isn't someone helping me?*

God, I'm screaming!

Her jeans and panties were torn down in a single move, scraping her hips. Then in a panting rush, he struggled with his own pants.

Gwen resigned herself to her arm snapping in two and she opened her mouth to call out, only to have her face pushed hard against the wet toilet tank, blood marring the white surface, his fingers digging into her cheeks.

"Don't you fuckin' move," the man breathed as he positioned himself behind her, his erection brushing the baby-soft skin on her bottom. "Shh!"

Gwen could feel the thrumming beat of the music against her face as the entire house seemed to vibrate with the rhythm of the song. *Oh, God. Oh, God. No one can hear me,* she thought desperately.

He pushed forward, spreading her legs farther apart with a strong thigh, his hand muffling most of her cries.

Then there was a knock on the bathroom door.

The man froze, nearly inside her. And for a second, so did Gwen. But her paralysis only lasted a split second, and she began to thrash around.

He laid all his weight atop her, crushing her against the toilet and covering her head completely. She smelled the pungent odor of sweat mixed with cologne and began to gag, her throat burning. His chest was pounding so hard that she could feel it through his clothes, and she fuzzily realized that his heart was beating every bit as fast as hers.

Seconds passed.

Please open the door. Open it! Open it! Open it! Gwen prayed woozily.

Then there was another knock. "Hurry it up!" an impatient female voice called.

Gwen's entire body jerked when her attacker lifted his head and made a series of booming retching noises. She supposed it was some sort of trick to make the person on the other side of the door go away, because he wasn't really sick and his body shook with silent chuckles between each retch. She waited, her heart slamming against her ribs, just knowing that the door would open any second and the room would be flooded with light and that Malcolm or someone else would save her. Instead, she heard nothing but the music and the man's harsh breathing.

She began to cry again.

Her captor, suddenly angry at being interrupted, pushed off of her roughly. In his haste to get back into position, he grabbed her good arm and wrenched it up her back, placing his other hand in her hair, and holding her face down so hard that her teeth hurt and her own drool pooled in her cheeks.

She whimpered as her injured arm swung down off her back to hang loosely by her side. *I'm gonna be sick.* "Sick . . . I—" *This can't be happening. It can't. I'm gonna throw up.*

A searing pain caused her to lurch forward as he entered her in one violent push, and she cried out against the toilet tank. Her eyes opened wide in the darkness, tears leaking down her cheeks and chin. Her stomach rebelled and she began to vomit, tasting rank beer and soggy chips.

"Oh, yeah," he slurred, oblivious to her retching as he hissed in rapture. He grunted and bucked against her faster and faster. Panting hard, he squeezed his butt cheeks together. It took only a few more savage thrusts for him to come deep inside her, his hands tightening convulsively in her hair and around her wrist.

Gwen spat and sucked in a deep lungful of air as his grip shifted, then loosened.

He groaned, then let go of her completely and staggered back a step.

Gwen fell forward, between the toilet and the wall, dizzy and sick as she continued to throw up. She hurt everywhere and her upper thighs were slick and sticky. She thought she heard his zipper being raised, and leaning unsteadily on one arm, she dared to turn and face him, only to be hit in the face with a wet towel. For a split second, it occurred to her that he might intend to kill her, to choke her with the towel. Her heart stopped beating. *I'm going to die.*

But he just stood there, motionless before her, his features totally unidentifiable in the blackness, even the sound of his breathing swept away by the sounds of the party, now that his lips weren't pressed against her ear.

"Wipe. And thanks," he said, almost cheerfully, causing her to blink and wonder if she'd heard him correctly. In his drunkenness, he had extended a hand to steady himself against the bathroom wall.

Thanks? "You bastard," she seethed, not caring whether he struck her again. But instinctively, she followed his command and wiped at her mouth and chin with the soiled towel.

He opened the bathroom door a crack and slowly poked his head outside. Light poured in, temporarily blinding her, though she could see the vague outline of his body. He wasn't nearly as big as he'd seemed.

She dropped the towel as she cowered between the toilet and the wall, her whole body shaking.

Without a glance back, he opened the door and then closed it again, leaving her alone and crying on the dirty bathroom floor.

"I still don't see why you couldn't come back in the morning. My ears haven't recovered from earlier." Audrey yawned and eased her way out from behind the wheel of Katy's beat-up car. The crowd at the party had grown so sparse that there were no longer any cars parked on the lawn, and they were able to find a spot in front of the next door neighbor's house.

"Because," Katy said, scrubbing her face, "the chances of my purse still being here now are practically zip. There is no way on earth that it would still be here in the morning." She glanced down at her cousin as she walked, and lifted an eyebrow. "I could have driven myself, you know."

They continued to move up the sidewalk, stepping over empty beer cups and other rubbish on their way to the front door.

Audrey's eyebrows jumped. "With as much beer as you've had tonight? I think not. Let's just find it and get out of here." Her tone of voice was suddenly tired. "I need some sleep." Moodily, she shook her head at the loud music that was still pouring through a few half-opened windows.

"I think I left it upstairs . . . next to the bed in the first room on the right," Katy mumbled, casting her eyes downward before they snapped back up. "And don't you start with me!"

Audrey gave her a friendly pat as she opened the front door. "I didn't say a word."

"But you wanted to."

"Well, duh."

Once inside, Katy inhaled a deep breath of smoky air that was tinged with the acrid scent of marijuana. She had found out the hard way that pot made her sick. But seeing all the other happy cigarette smokers made her a little peeved that her roommates had taken a vote and forbade her from indulging inside their house.

Audrey waved her hand in front of her face. "Ugh. Where do we start?"

"God." Katy surveyed the wasteland around her, clucking her tongue. "I don't want to have to touch anything here." Mostly sobered up, she was surprised at how seedy her surroundings now appeared. She stepped aside as a dancing couple nearly collided with her. "What were we thinking coming to this dump?"

"Good question."

Katy sighed. "Let's go upstairs, get my bag, and go home."

Audrey nodded. "I—" she stopped when a small group of young men huddled around a table caught her eye. She lifted a hand and waved and called out, "Hi, Malcolm." She automatically started looking for Gwen, surprised that she wasn't seated next to him.

Malcolm reluctantly tore his eyes from his cards and spotted Audrey and Katy. He glanced at his watch and frowned. Gwen had been gone for more than twenty minutes. His seat squeaked loudly as he stood and motioned the girls over.

"Didn't think you'd still be here," Katy said, moving to his side and plucking the cards from his hand to take a peek. With a dismayed look, she promptly folded on his behalf by tossing his cards into the center of the table.

Disgusted at his latest hand, Malcolm grunted his approval at her actions.

"Where's Gwen?" Audrey spun in a circle as she gazed around the room.

"Bathroom," Malcolm stated succinctly, taking his seat and waiting for the next deal. "What do you women do in there, anyway? She's been gone forever."

Audrey just shrugged, but Katy smoothly answered in a raised voice and with a Scarlet O'Hara accent, "It's because we're trying to make ourselves look pretty for you boys, Malcolm."

He completely missed the sarcastic edge that had entered her voice and nodded. "Will you tell her to hurry up?" His glance darted sideways for a few seconds before it reluctantly met Katy's. He lowered his voice and said, "I miss her."

"Awww . . . ." the other poker players read his lips and began cooing and making kissing noises as Malcolm's cheeks began to heat.

Audrey and Katy gave Malcolm slightly admiring looks. Gwen clearly could have done worse.

"We'll bring her down with us," Katy assured him, impatiently nudging Audrey forward and leaving Malcolm to his game.

The second floor appeared abandoned. The hall lights had been shut off and cups and paper plates littered most of the floor, along with several unidentifiable, but nasty-looking, stains.

Audrey wrapped her arms around herself as a shiver skittered down her back. "It's creepy up here in this light." Only the faint golden glow from the stairwell lit the space, casting long shadows across the walls.

"Hmm. No line at the bathroom either . . . But yeah, it is a little spooky up here." Katy ran her hands along the edge of the wall at the top of the stairs until she found the hall light and flipped it on. They both squinted in reaction.

"Where the hell is Gwen?"

Katy tilted her chin toward the bathroom. "Door's shut. She must be inside. I'll check the room for my purse. You wanna wait for her to come out or look in the room with me?"

Audrey grinned, catching the hopeful note of Katy's question. "And walk in just in time to see some greasy guy's really hairy naked butt?" She blanched. "No thanks. I'll leave that to you. Just make sure that you don't get so interested in what's happening that you decide to join in and leave me here in the hall waiting."

Katy's blue eyes narrowed. "That was cold, Audrey."

"Yeah," Audrey laughed, completely unrepentant. "It really was." She made a shooing motion with her hands. "Go on."

Katy stood outside the door, drawing in deep breaths and fortifying herself before she loudly rapped on the door. "I'm coming in to get my purse." She covered her eyes with one hand. "If you're naked, crawl under the covers, for God's sake!" She grinned. "Unless you're really gorgeous. Then speak up and I won't cover my eyes."

Audrey chuckled as Katy entered the room, her chuckle turning to an outright laugh when she heard Katy bump into something and let out a virulent string of curses. She turned and knocked on the bathroom door. "Gwen? Are you there? You're not sick, are you?"

There was no answer.

Audrey's forehead creased. "Gwen? Hello?" she called again, this time more loudly.

When her second effort was met with silence, she gingerly got down on one knee and looked under the crack beneath the door, seeing only darkness. "Huh. Guess Malcolm was wrong," she muttered under her breath, groaning tiredly as she pushed to her feet.

Audrey took a step to leave but was still curious. Something felt . . . she didn't know what. Wrong, maybe. Malcolm was engrossed in his game, but he didn't seem at all ambivalent about where Gwen was. Giving in to her curiosity, she tried the door handle, praying that it wouldn't be sticky like it was the last time she'd been in that bathroom. In contrast to the stifling heat of the house it felt cool in her hand and a slight turn confirmed that it was unlocked. Tentatively, she opened the door a few inches.

"Gwen?" There was still nothing. Audrey laughed at herself and began to close the door, only to pause when she thought she heard a whimper. When she pushed the door open a little further, what she saw caused the bottom of her stomach to hit her knees.

"Shut the door!" Gwen moaned from her spot on the floor between the toilet and the wall. "Shut it!"

Audrey blinked, momentarily frozen.

"Go away."

The rawness of that familiar voice snapped Audrey out of her momentary paralysis. She reached for the light. "Gwen?"

"Don't turn that on," Gwen begged. "Please."

Audrey's hand dropped from the switch and she rushed inside, her heart in throat. "Are you hurt?" She glanced around quickly, trying to figure out what could have happened. "Gwen, tell me what happened."

The taller girl began to sob, her face pressed tightly against her arms.

Audrey reached for her, only to have Gwen shrink back. Her entire body was shaking.

"Are you hurt?" Audrey asked again, this time more firmly. "Tell me,

Gwen! I need to know if you're hurt."

"I . . . I . . . I—" Gwen buried her face again, nodding wildly.

"Did you fall?" Audrey cursed herself for leaving Gwen at the party after she'd had so much to drink.

Gwen swallowed hard. She opened her mouth to tell Audrey what had happened, but no words came out. Instead, she began to cry harder.

Just then Katy came to the door. "What's up?" Automatically, she flipped on the lights. "I found my—Jesus!" she blurted when she saw Gwen. Her mouth dropped open in horror.

The redhead's hair was disheveled and her face was bloodied from a gash on her forehead. Her cheeks were already sporting bruises in the shape of fingers, and she'd smeared blood down the sleeves of her blouse as she'd cried, leaving a series of startling scarlet imprints on the crisp, white cotton. Her pants were still down around her ankles and she was clutching a dirty towel between her legs. The towel was bloody, too.

"Oh, Gwen," Audrey said softly, closing her eyes.

Teary eyes lifted to meet Katy's, and Katy dropped to her knees next to Gwen.

"Gwen," Audrey said quietly, furious when she realized that her friend couldn't hear her unless she raised her voice. She swallowed around a solid lump that had formed in her throat. "You're hurt. You need to go to the hospital." She reached out to gently graze a purple cheek, her heart hurting when Gwen flinched before she even touched her.

Katy's hands balled into trembling fists. She wanted to murder whoever had done this. "We need to call the police," she ground out briskly.

"No!" Gwen shouted through her tears. Forcefully she tugged at her own hair as her mind raced. "You can't tell anyone. Not the police." Then her eyes grew round and she began to panic. "And especially not Malcolm!"

"Shh . . . C'mere." Audrey pulled her into a gentle hug, heedless of the blood on Gwen.

For a second, Gwen struggled. Then she let go of the towel and sank into Audrey's embrace, clinging to her desperately, her shoulders shaking as she cried silently.

Katy leaned forward and smoothed back a shock of messy red hair to place a gentle kiss on Gwen's head, her own tears dampening the pale skin. "Someone raped you?" From the state Gwen was in and the towel between her legs, she already knew the answer, but she had to be sure. Her chest clenched when Gwen weakly nodded. "Audrey is right. You need a doctor."

"No!" Roughly, Gwen pulled away from Audrey, fitting herself back between the toilet and the wall. She cried out when shooting pains shot through her arm as she lifted it to wipe her cheeks. "No one can know, Katy." Her eyes sparked. "I mean it."

Fearfully, Gwen's face snapped up when she saw a shadowy figure in the hallway.

Katy looked behind her and kicked the door shut with her foot.

"Hey!" an unidentified female voice yelled through the door.

"Go the fuck away," Katy barked.

Gwen jumped and Audrey shot Katy a warning glare.

Instantly contrite, she muttered, "Sorry."

Audrey's insides were quaking with a combination of grief and fury. "Who did this?" She grabbed a wad of toilet paper and tenderly wiped at Gwen's forehead. It was bleeding sluggishly. "I hate to ask this, Gwen. But was it Malcolm?"

"No!" Gwen shrieked, wide-eyed and horrified. "He would never! Never."

"Okay," Katy said in soothing voice. "We believe you."

But Gwen continued as though she hadn't heard her friend. "I couldn't see much. A man pushed me down. He came up behind me. It was dark. It wasn't Malcolm. He was too short." She swallowed and more tears streaked her cheeks. "I didn't do anything! This isn't my fault!"

Katy and Audrey both blinked. "We didn't—"

"I was just coming to use the bathroom," Gwen moaned, slapping the floor with both hands, furious at herself for allowing this to happen.

Audrey took Gwen's hand and rubbed the back of it with her thumb. "Of course you were, Gwen. This wasn't your fault," she insisted gently. "We know that." She turned to her cousin, who was visibly trying not to burst into tears. "Right, Katy?"

"Hell yes, we do. It's the bastard that did this who's to blame."

Audrey nodded.

"We need to call the police," Katy said tightly. "This had to have happened only a few minutes ago. He could still be in the house."

"I won't talk to them," Gwen said stubbornly, lifting her blood-smeared chin. "You can't make me."

Gwen's eyes pleaded with Katy, breaking her heart and filling her with uncertainty.

"I think your forehead needs stitches," Audrey announced, taking the focus off of the police for a moment.

Gwen reached for her forehead wearily. Then let her hand drop. "It'll be fine."

"If you leave it like this, I think it'll scar," Audrey reminded her.

Gwen was silent, but she visibly recoiled at the thought. "You really think so?"

"I really do."

Gwen swallowed and closed her eyes, shaking her head "no." "Don't be mad at me." She began to cry again. "I just can't. Not now." She sniffed a few times. "Maybe tomorrow."

Audrey and Katy exchanged resigned looks, acknowledging that this was as much as Gwen was capable of at the moment.

Gwen wiped her chin with trembling fingers, the taste of blood in her mouth still making her feel like vomiting. "I don't want Malcolm to see me like this. I just want to go home."

Katy's gazed softened. "But Gwen—"

"Are you going to help me or not?" Gwen snapped, desperate, tear-filled eyes glistening in the harsh bathroom light.

Audrey grabbed hold of Katy's arm, but addressed Gwen. "We're going to help you. Can you stand?"

Gwen's body instantly relaxed. "Thank you," she whispered. "I . . . I think I can stand."

Katy nearly bit her tongue through, every cell in her body on the verge of protesting again when she let out a slow breath and hung her head in defeat. "I'll make sure Malcolm is busy while you two go out through the kitchen door. I'll meet you in the car."

"No!" Gwen shrieked. "You can't go alone." Her eyes strayed to the closed door. "It's not safe."

Katy stroked Gwen's hair. "We'll all three stay together until we reach the bottom of the stairs. There are still plenty of people downstairs. I'll be fine there."

"Okay," Gwen conceded reluctantly. "If we stay together."

"Gwen?" Audrey said, causing her friends' heads to turn. Her voice cracked as she spoke. "I'm *so* sorry this happened."

"Me, too," Katy groaned, covering her face with her hands.

Gwen gazed vacantly at the door and nodded slowly. She felt dirty and sick and a big part of her wanted to curl up in the corner and die. She let out a soft sigh, trying not to think about Malcolm and her parents or the man who'd taken more from her than she could fathom. "Me, too."

Late Fall 1982 (Seven Weeks Later)
St. Louis, Missouri

The young women of the Mayflower Club were clustered in their pajamas on Gwen's twin bed, gathered there for a special announcement. A small lamp lit the corner of the room along with a hefty dose of starlight that shown in the bedroom window, closed in deference to the cool breeze. Rain pitter-patted against the window, and a fitful breeze rustled the piles of moist leaves and slapped barren branches against the home's worn siding.

For the first time since the night of the party earlier that autumn, Gwen was smiling.

Nina let out a breath in pure relief. She'd been ready for the worst when Gwen insisted on making her visit to Planned Parenthood alone that afternoon. She'd missed her period after the rape, sending the entire house into a state of anxious worry. But this had to be good news.

Gwen drew in a deep breath, smiling when Jacie took one of her hands and squeezed it affectionately. She squeezed back. "Malcolm has asked me to marry him," she announced.

Three mouths dropped open.

"He . . . he has?" Jacie finally said, filling the awkward silence that had suddenly overtaken the room. She winced when she realized how she sounded. "I mean, he has?" she said more normally.

Beaming, Gwen nodded. She shrugged as her cheeks tinted. "He loves me."

An enormous grin bloomed on Jacie's face while Audrey, Nina, and Katy smothered Gwen in a group bear hug. "He's a great guy," Jacie said honestly, her admiration showing.

"So things went okay at the clinic today?" Audrey asked, just to be sure. The girls were beside themselves all afternoon, regretting that they'd allowed Gwen's stubbornness to win out when she announced she intended on going to the doctor alone.

Gwen's smile faltered, but only for a second. Then she nodded. "Things worked out for the best. I really believe that."

Nina frowned and pulled one of her knees against her chest, her socked foot resting flat on the flowered bedspread. She cocked her head to one side. "That means you're not pregnant, right?"

Gwen licked her lips. "No." She swallowed hard at Audrey's gasp. "I . . . I am pregnant."

"Jesus," Katy muttered while Jacie sat in shocked silence, her tongue refusing to work at all.

"Are . . . ?" Nina didn't really know what to say and a quick glance at her friends revealed that they were all in the same shocked boat. "Are you okay?"

Gwen's chin trembled, and for the first time all day her brave veneer began to crack. Then her expression turned bitter and she snorted. "Mentally or physically?" She raised her eyebrows as she waited for an answer.

"Gwen." Jacie pulled her into a hug and pressed her lips to Gwen's ear. "I'm so sorry." She wished again and again that Gwen had left that god-forsaken party with her and Nina that night. Or that she had stuck with Gwen or done anything different that would have triggered a change in the course of events that had shattered her friend.

Gwen wiped angrily at her eyes, not wanting to cry anymore. She'd done little else for weeks, but now . . . now things were finally getting better. Gently, she disentangled herself from Jacie, feeling several warm pats of encouragement as her other friends moved in to support her. "I'm okay." With effort, she was able to smile again. "I'm going to have a baby and marry someone I love." Cautiously, she searched their faces. "It doesn't get much better than that, right?"

Katy looked away, unwilling to answer that question honestly. Jacie and Audrey suddenly found something very interesting about Gwen's bedspread.

"If you say so, Gwen," Nina said weakly, still not believing what she was hearing.

"Malcolm's a helluva guy," Jacie suddenly inserted, doing her best to be positive in the light of news she couldn't help but view as horrible. "Being willing to bring this baby into his family. I can see why you love him so much."

Most of the color drained from Gwen's face.

Audrey blinked slowly as realization dawned, the weight of it leaving her knees rubbery and her chest heavy. "Oh, my God, Gwen." She turned to look into watery eyes. "You didn't tell him what happened."

Katy sprung off the bed. "Holy shit!" she whispered into her hands. "What have you done?" She shook her head, refusing to look at Gwen when she said, "You suck."

Nina pinned Gwen with an intense stare. "No way, Gwen." She shook her head gravely. This was going too far. "Tell us that Malcolm doesn't think he's the father."

"He loves me!" Gwen defended hotly, refusing to answer Nina's question, and grabbing her pillow and clutching it to her chest.

"No. No. No. This is impossible," Jacie said, her forehead deeply creased, her hands gesturing wildly. "You haven't even slept with Malcolm. You've told us a million times that you were waiting until you married the perfect guy. He can't think the baby is his." She stopped when Gwen's cheeks turned bright red and she buried her face in the pillow.

A lightbulb went on in Audrey's head. Gwen was smart and desperate, a very dangerous combination. "You slept with him after you missed your period so he'd think the baby was his." It wasn't a question.

Gwen nodded miserably, still refusing to look up from her pillow. She couldn't bear the thought of what her friends had to think of her now, but worse than that was the possibility of losing Malcolm. Her stomach twisted. "I had no choice," she said harshly, tears dampening the pillow. "None of you understand." Her fingers clutched convulsively at the soft cotton. "He took me to meet his mother last week."

Nina nodded. They all knew that. "You said it went okay."

"Yeah, it was okay. Except that she barely spoke to me!" Gwen wailed, her face crumpling. "She asked me what my parents did for a living and all about my family."

"So?" Jacie asked, more sharply than she intended. "You don't have anything to hide, Gwen."

The redhead's face snapped up. "So?" Her cheeks turned scarlet. "The Langtrees are one of the richest and most respected families in Missouri."

Jacie rolled her eyes, having heard that statement from Gwen a dozen times in the past couple of months. "That doesn't make them better than any of us."

"They care," Gwen continued, "that my mother is a housewife who didn't graduate from high school and that Daddy sells insurance for a living! They care that I am from Hazelwood and sound like a Missouri hick!" She snarled, "No matter how I tried, I could see the disapproval in her eyes. She thinks I'm nothing but white trash!" She blinked away more tears. "And compared to the Langtrees, I am."

"Bullshit," Jacie said flatly, losing patience quickly with Gwen's class-conscious attitude that had been there since they were little girls. "That's your mother and her delusions of grandeur talking." She pointed at Gwen and then the other girls. "You and all the rest of us come from regular working class families. You are hardly white trash."

"Grow up, Jacie. Do you actually think his family would let him marry me, no matter how much we loved each other, if they knew I was carrying a rapist's child!" Gwen screamed, on the verge of becoming hysterical. "Do you?"

Jacie gritted her teeth. As sickening as it was, she couldn't deny that Gwen was probably right about that. "I—"

"Jacie." Nina placed a calming hand on Jacie's shoulder as Katy made her way back to the bed. "This isn't helping." Her eyes begged her to bring things down a notch, and she smiled softly when Jacie nodded.

Audrey and Katy exchanged helpless glances.

"You don't have to do this," Jacie said to Gwen, intentionally gentling her voice. Then she said what the other girls were feeling, but too chicken to express. "Tricking Malcolm isn't right."

Gwen pulled her hand away as though it had been burned. "What are you talking about?" Her eyes were wide with disbelief. "You still don't understand? This is the best day of my life! Malcolm loves me. This baby could have just as easily have been his. It was only horrible, horrible luck that that bastard did this to me first!"

Nina ran a hand through her hair, shaking her head. "But the baby is not his. You know that for a fact."

Gwen's eyes widened. "Don't say that again."

"Gwen," Jacie repeated, "we'll help you with the baby. You don't have to trick anyone." She glanced around at her friends, who all nodded eagerly. "We discussed it today while you were at the clinic. We'll all help and take turns watching it and help with money, too."

"We can do it," Nina swore to her. "Between us all, including Katy who thinks babies are nothing but poop machines but who offered to help anyway"—this drew a weak smile from Katy—"we can make it work. You don't have to get married or even move back home."

Gwen looked at Nina as though she'd never seen her before. "But I want to marry Malcolm."

Audrey valiantly picked up the ball. "I know you do, honey. But not this way."

"Won't it be hard finishing school if you're married?" Katy tried. "You could just be engaged through college and we could—"

Gwen shook her head. "We're having the wedding during winter break." Unconsciously her hand drifted to her stomach. "Before I'll be showing much. And . . . Malcolm says his mother will likely insist that I drop out of school even before the baby." She took a ragged breath and gazed at the window, not seeing the twinkling stars looking back at her. "At least that's what happened when his cousin got into a similar mess last winter."

"Who gives a shit what his mommy says!" Jacie exploded, seeing Gwen's entire future being shaped by other people. People who didn't care about her. "You want a degree. You can still have that."

Gwen's pale gaze sharpened. "I want Malcolm more," she said firmly, her face hard.

"And this baby," Nina prompted gently, knowing full well that she was treading on intensely sensitive and personal ground, even between the closest of friends. "Do you want it, Gwen? There's nothing that says you have to raise it or even have it." Her expression softened, and she felt tears well up in her eyes. A lump formed in her throat, but she spoke anyway. "Under the circumstances, no one could blame you if—"

"I could never do that, Nina," Gwen admitted quietly. "I've been thinking about it for days . . ." She lifted one hand and let it drop lifelessly. "I just can't."

Nina nodded, quite sure that it was something she could do under the right circumstances, but understanding that this was a personal decision that only Gwen could make for herself.

Katy sighed. "Gwen, maybe you could tell Malcolm the truth but then keep it from his family?"

Audrey, Nina, and Jacie all nodded at once, latching on to Katy's idea with gusto.

Gwen sniffed. "It's too late." She pulled her pillow closer, protecting herself from the world. "I wasn't going to, but it just came out." Her eyes fluttered shut. "I've already lied to him. There's no going back now. He might believe what his mother probably already thinks. That I'm just a gold-digger."

"It's not too late yet," Jacie insisted. "It's like I said before; he's a good guy, Gwen. He won't blame you or the baby for what happened. It wasn't your fault," she emphasized again and received a trembling smile for her words. "He's been worried sick over you these past weeks. He does love you."

Gwen had explained away her injuries by saying she'd been in a car accident. Malcolm had sent flowers, cards, and called twice a day during the days immediately following the rape when Gwen was still in pieces and refusing to see anyone or even leave her room. "Trust him," Jacie urged, shifting closer to Nina, wanting to feel her presence.

"I do trust him." Gwen squared her shoulders. "But right now I have to trust myself more. Please," her last word broke. "Please understand, Jacie. This doesn't have to be a bad thing. Malcolm and I love each other and want to be together. Things are just happening sooner than they would have anyway."

Of all the girls, it was Jacie's understanding Gwen wanted most. In the nights since the party Jacie had tirelessly calmed her when terrifying dreams ripped her cruelly from an already fitful sleep. And though there'd always been a tiny antagonistic edge to their relationship, Jacie's comforting arms would wrap around her each night, making her feel safe and warm until she could find sleep again.

Jacie's lips thinned and once again she felt the loving pressure of Nina's hand, reassuring her. "I do understand, Gwen," she finally said. "I think you're wrong and I wish you'd reconsider leaving school and . . ." Everything was just happening so fast. She swallowed and forced herself forward half-heartedly, knowing her friend needed from her more than logic or reason. She allowed her dark, confident stare to meet Gwen's. "But . . . I do understand."

Gwen let out a sob. "Thank you." She turned her eyes to the other girls, not surprised to see wet cheeks. "You too?" she asked fearfully. "Please?"

Nina tugged a throw blanket up from the foot of the bed and wrapped it around Gwen. Then she surprised her by kissing her on the cheek.

Gwen felt warm breath against her skin.

"We love you forever, Gwen," Nina murmured against the salty, moist cheek. "You know that."

"Forever," Katy and Audrey agreed solemnly.

"I'll never tell another soul about this, and most importantly Malcolm can never know," Gwen reminded them all, hating herself for the lie but not seeing any other way out for herself, Malcolm, and the baby. *This is our chance to be happy. We have to take it.*

"Never," the girls agreed, grasping hands in a gesture that, for them, was as old as time.

Present Day
Rural Missouri

Gwen pulled herself from the past and read over the latest blackmail e-mail that she'd received weeks before. She'd brought it to Charlotte's Web to confront her blackmailer with it. The words sickened her. "Never" had turned out to be twenty-one years.

Tucker isn't Malcolm's son. You lied. You know it, and so do I. And if you don't pay so will your family and friends.

Gwen carefully stowed the note back in her suitcase. Then she lifted her chin and left her room in search of the other women . . . and some answers.

Time was running out.

Chapter 8
Present Day
Rural Missouri

Arm in arm, Jacie and Nina walked along the twisting path that followed the river. The breeze was cool, and Jacie shivered a little as she stuck her hand into her coat pocket. They'd been talking and walking for so long that their noses were red, and the sun, still behind a heavy veil of clouds, was just beginning to sink over the horizon.

Nina turned and looked at Jacie as they walked. "You know," she squeezed the arm wrapped around hers, "when I think of you, you always have that beautiful long hair."

Jacie shrugged, the ends of her hair brushing the bottom of her coat collar. "I haven't worn it long since . . . Well, I cut it right after I left Missouri." She sighed and gazed at the river. "I needed a change."

Nina absorbed that silently and then released a long breath. "I guess I have this picture of you in my mind where you're permanently eighteen."

The corner of Jacie's lips tugged downward. "Are you disappointed in the way I look now?" She'd felt as though she was in the best shape of her life. But that didn't mean Nina would see it that way. "I know it's been a long time. But—"

Nina abruptly stopped, nearly yanking Jacie off her feet with the hasty movement. "Hell, no!" she gasped, steadying Jacie with her other hand. "That's not what I meant."

"I'm sure I don't look like I did in college," Jacie conceded, still scowling. "But God knows I was a skinny, gawky kid then."

Nina rolled her eyes. "Why is it that you've never understood how beautiful you are, Jacie?"

"Yeah," Jacie snorted. "I'm a regular Miss America in blue jeans."

Nina gazed at her fondly, unable to stop herself from feeling a wellspring of emotion. She tucked a blowing strand of hair behind Jacie's ear. When she realized what she was doing, she blushed and pulled her hand away. "Time has been nothing but kind to you, and you know it. You were a pretty girl, but you're a stunning woman. You've improved with age." A tiny smile. "And that's saying something."

A charmed smile lit Jacie's face, which was still stained with dirt from her trek through the woods to find her friend. "Really?"

Nina chuckled and started to walk again. "Yeah, Pig Pen, really."

Leaves and twigs crunched under their feet as they followed the path that ran only a few feet from the river's edge. They were quiet for a long time, enjoying the fresh air and the sounds of the wind in the trees.

"Well," Jacie finally said, trying to recall what they'd been discussing a few moments earlier, "you look just the way I've pictured you in my head."

"Me and the ten pounds I've put on over the years."

They were avoiding the one thing Jacie knew they needed to discuss. Still, she played along with the inane conversation a little longer, gathering her thoughts. She shrugged. "You were always sort of skinny."

Nina smiled. "And I'm starting to find gray in my hair."

Jacie pulled her hand from her pocket and took the opportunity to run her fingers through a few soft strands. "It's only one or two. And besides," she nodded to herself, "it looks good on you."

Nina met Jacie's gaze and struggled not to fall into soft brown eyes. Suddenly, the thought of another moment of small talk was unbearable.

"I want to kiss you or kill you or maybe both," she blurted, licking her lips nervously. "And it's the not knowing which one that's killing me." She studied Jacie's face, desperate to gauge her reaction to the shocking words.

Jacie blinked, astonished at Nina's courage. She stopped walking and cupped Nina's cheek, the chilled skin cooling her palm. "Holy shit, Nina."

She cringed, her bravado fading fast. "I know."

Jacie tried to gather her wits, which were as scattered as the leaves upon the ground. "Well, you've already kissed me and smacked me," she reminded her gently. "But if my opinion matters, the kiss was much nicer."

Nina looked away. "You broke my heart, Jacie," she admitted bitterly, saying out loud what she'd repeated in her head so many times.

Jacie closed her eyes, her resentment building. "Yeah?" She could hear a note of hoarseness in her voice but forced herself to continue, opening her eyes and moving until Nina was forced to meet her gaze. "Well, you broke mine, too." She grabbed Nina's hand and pressed it to her chest as if Nina could somehow feel the damage she'd inflicted.

Nina pulled her hand away. "I know what you think I did."

Jacie's eyes flashed. "Think?"

"Yes, think." Now Nina's gaze was just as fiery as the one boring a hole right through her. "I was afraid and unsure, but I wasn't . . . I mean, I didn't—"

"Stop." Jacie suddenly turned her back on Nina. *Shit. I will not cry.* "You don't need to explain yourself to me. What's done is done, and rehashing it isn't going to help either one of us." But that was a lie and she knew it.

"You were a coward!" Nina snapped, her frustration getting the best of her.

Jacie nodded slowly, her jaw and fists clenching. Nina watched as her back went ramrod straight.

"I guess I was a coward. But I think I've paid for that."

Nina was startled by the ready admission, and it bled some of the steam from her voice. "Don't you see, Jacie? You're not the only one who's paid. And you're wrong," she told her bluntly, grabbing Jacie by the arm and turning her around to face her.

Tears glistened in Jacie's eyes, and Nina blinked away a few of her own. "Even if we're never anything to each other again, I don't want this between us." She swallowed thickly. "We need to talk about what happened. I want to get on with my life. I need to do that."

Jacie's knees felt weak. She didn't want to know the answer, and yet her heart demanded nothing less. "Does getting on with your life mean that there's no place in it for me?"

Nina scrubbed her face, honestly at a loss. "I . . . You've had my heart my whole life. Maybe for me to be happy, I need to take it back."

Jacie's eyebrows rose. "I've had your heart?"

Nina gave her a miserable nod. "Forever, you idiot."

Jacie blinked slowly, feeling as though she might shake apart from within. "Forever?" she croaked.

"Why do you keep repeating me? That's what I said." Nina smiled sadly. "And I should have told you twenty years ago. I fucked up, Jace. And I'm so sorry."

Jacie felt sick. "I . . . I . . . I never knew." Her eyes were wide and glassy. "I mean I knew how I felt. But I didn't think you—"

Nina couldn't maintain even a watery smile. "I know."

"Wow." Jacie rubbed sweaty palms together. "Just wow." Jacie's mind screamed at her to do something. *Do it before it's too late!* "I hate to do this to you, Nina. But I have bad news."

Nina braced herself. At least Jacie hadn't outright laughed at how pathetic she was for harboring feelings all these years and not being able to move beyond them. "Yeah?"

"Yeah," Jacie confirmed, her voice so gentle it was nearly carried away by the breeze. "You can't have your heart back." She shrugged helplessly and gave her the vulnerable look that had always made Nina want to stop whatever she was doing and give her a hug.

Incredulous, Nina just stared this time, her feet rooted in place.

"Sorry." Jacie waited, worrying when seconds ticked by and Nina said nothing. "Are you okay?" she finally asked.

"No!" Nina's body exploded into motion, and she began pacing. "What do you mean, I can't have it back? Don't you see? I haven't been able to think of anything but you these past few weeks. I'm not sleeping.

I'm—"

Jacie stepped forward and took Nina's hands in hers. "You were right. We need to deal with the past. I don't want it to hurt either of us anymore."

This, Nina decided, was what it felt like to have mental whiplash. But, even if it killed her, she resolved to get everything out in the open today. "We don't have anything to lose, huh?" she joked wanly, knowing that wasn't true, at least for her.

"We have everything to lose," Jacie said seriously as she dropped one of Nina's hands and tugged her along with the other, hoping this path along the river was a long one. They were going to be here a while. "We're just doing it anyway."

Late Spring 1983
St. Louis, Missouri

It was just past eleven o'clock when Jacie unlocked the front door and let herself inside the house she shared with her friends. She walked slowly over to the kitchen table and tossed her keys down, her head falling into her hands as she yawned. She heard the faint sounds of the television coming from the living room.

Gwen had moved out two months ago. And while Jacie had been under a financial strain before, now she felt as though she were drowning. Things had gone from bad to worse as each girl worked to pick up the slack left by Gwen's absence. Tempers were unusually short, and during the last few weeks, the house had either been filled with angry raised voices or stony silence.

She and Nina and Audrey had argued bitterly that morning over whose turn it was to clean the shower. Nina had taken Audrey's side against her, and though she'd come to realize they'd been right, it had still hurt to have the person who was always in her corner stand up for someone else.

Nina wandered into the kitchen wearing a T-shirt that fell to mid-thigh and a pair of ratty, fuzzy slippers. Her face was pink from a fresh scrubbing, showing off a spattering of freckles that covered her nose and cheeks. Her sandy hair was wet from a recent shower. "Hey, you." She smiled tiredly. "I thought I heard the door."

Jacie was silent for a moment, then said, "I guess this means you're talking to me?" Both young women had been afraid to give voice to what they'd been feeling for months. And though they'd come close a dozen times, they'd yet to even kiss, their fear of the unknown just enough to hold them back . . . and make them crazy.

Nina winced internally. Things had gotten out of hand that morning, and she'd said a few things for no purpose other than to hurt Jacie. She wasn't proud of that fact, and she moved quickly now to smooth over what she knew was a bad case of hurt feelings.

"I'd like to be talking to you, Jacie." She let her embarrassment show on her face. "I'm so sorry about this morning. I've been . . . Well . . ." *I've been wanting to find out if your lips are as soft as they look and not known how to deal with it, and so I took it out on you?* She mentally rolled her eyes. *Yeah, best friends always love to hear that you're lusting after them.* "I've been sort of stressed lately." She lifted her eyebrows in entreaty. "Forgive me," she said softly. "Please?"

Jacie wanted more of an explanation, but the look on Nina's face was so sad and hopeful that she couldn't hold out for more than a few seconds. "Yeah." She gave her a warm smile. "You know I do." Slapping the table with the palms of her hands, she leaned forward. "I'll even go clean the bathroom right now." She took a step forward only to have Nina reach out and grab her arm.

"I already did it."

"What?" she exploded, her hands shaping frustrated fists. "You weren't supposed to do that!" Now she felt even worse than she had that morning when Audrey had pointed out rather tersely that just because she worked nights didn't mean they had to do her chores. "I'm not a slacker."

"Of course you're not. Relax," Nina urged gently. "I had the time. So no big deal." She tilted her head toward the kitchen table. "Sit and talk with me for a minute? I can't sleep."

Jacie was dead on her feet and quite sure she'd be asleep before her head hit the pillow. "Sure." As she sat, she couldn't help but admire Nina's slender, but curvy form through the thin nightshirt she wore.

Nina took her place across from Jacie at the small Formica table, noting curiously that Jacie's gaze was following her every move. She looked down at her T-shirt, wondering if she'd spilled something on herself. "What are you staring at?" She plucked at the white cotton.

Caught looking, Jacie picked up the keys she'd tossed on the table earlier and twisted them nervously in her hands as she searched for an excuse. Any excuse. Coming up empty, she said, "Umm . . . You look nice is all." She smiled weakly and held her breath, her heartbeat thundering in her ears. Then she let out a relieved chuckle when Nina gave her a somewhat embarrassed smile back.

Nina squirmed a little in her chair, swallowing hard and squeezing her thighs together when she realized that she was pleasantly aroused by Jacie's attention. *God.*

Though their feelings had gone unspoken, things between the two of them had slowly been changing over the past few months. They no longer made excuses to spend time together, simply accepting that being together made them happier than being with anyone else. Frequent, lingering touches skirted the edge of chaste. And sometimes, when Jacie looked into Nina's eyes for too long, she grew tongue-tied or completely forgot what she was saying.

That Nina loved Jacie was not in doubt. She'd come to acknowledge that the girlish crush on her best friend had evolved into something much deeper and much more adult. The heady feelings left her breathless, and the thick blanket of attraction that clung to them at times lent even the most innocent exchanges a hint of sexual tension.

"Are you okay?" Jacie asked, concerned with the deer-in-the-headlights look on Nina's face. She'd seen that look quite a few times lately.

"Fine." Nina nodded quickly, her mouth going dry. "F-fine."

Jacie gave her a doubtful look. "If you say so." Her focus shifted to the swinging door that led to the living room. "Katy home yet?"

Nina snorted softly, glad to have the attention off her for the time being "Does she even live here anymore?"

Jacie shrugged. "Good question. She spends so much time at her new boyfriend's apartment, I figure that any day now, she'll tell us they're moving in together. And I'll be royally screwed."

Nina nodded miserably, well aware that would mean moving out of the house or taking on strangers as roommates, something she was loath to do.

"I wonder if she's even bothering to go to class. I think all they do is make out twenty-four hours a day."

"She told me she wouldn't be home tonight." Nina shrugged. "But she is going to class even if she sleeps through half of it. I—" She glanced up, and got a good look at the dark circles under her friend's eyes. "Jacie," she sighed softly. "Speaking of sleeping, you look beat." Her forehead wrinkled with worry, and she reached out, tracing Jacie's cheekbone, which seemed to have gained more prominence in the past week or so. "Have you eaten yet?"

Jacie leaned back in her chair and laid her hand over her concave belly. "Do six slices of lime and a bowl full of cherries swiped from the bar count?"

"No," Nina said seriously. "They don't." She stood up and moved to the kitchen counter. "What do you want to—"

"I don't have anything here." Jacie frowned, mentally calculating the meager tips she'd earned that night. They were needed for her portion of the electric bill, which was due any day now. "I need to go to the store." The girls bought their own food, sharing only a few staples that it didn't pay to buy individually. Her shelf had been depressingly bare all week long.

Nina peered into Jacie's section of the cupboard, seeing only a can of tomato sauce and a half-empty box of toothpicks. She waved a dismissive hand. "I got paid yesterday and went to the market. I have plenty to share."

"No, thanks."

"It's no problem."

"Yes, it is."

A sigh. "It doesn't have to be."

"Nina."

"Jacie." Said in the same warning tone. "Just let me do this. You're making a big deal out of nothing."

Jacie pushed out of her chair and turned around to face Nina. "I don't want your food," she ground out. The last thing she wanted was charity from Nina. "Not only am I not a slacker, I'm not a mooch, either."

Taken aback by Jacie's anger, Nina felt her own temper rise. This was ridiculous. "I don't care what you want," she shot back. "You need to eat because you look like shit."

Jacie's face turned crimson. "Mind your own business, Nina. I'm not hungry. I had a big breakfast." Just then, her stomach growled, and Jacie closed her eyes. "Great," she murmured disgustedly.

Nina rubbed her temples. "It's nearly midnight; you need something, Jacie. You're on your feet all night. Why are you being so stubborn?" With short, jerky movements, Nina began pulling out cans from her shelf. "Tuna?" She smacked it down on the countertop. "Tomato soup?" Smack! "Or deviled ham?" Smack! She reached inside, grabbing the last of her cans.

Aware that things were spinning out of control, but unable to stop herself, Jacie grabbed the can from Nina's hands and slammed it on the countertop. "I don't want your damned food."

"Deviled ham, it is," Nina snarled, yanking open the drawer and searching for a can opener. When she found it, she set about opening the can at breakneck speed, mumbling all the while. "You don't eat, you don't sleep, all you do is work." She slammed the can opener down. "You're killing yourself."

"Why have you suddenly gone nuts?" Jacie gestured wildly. "I know when I need to eat. Stop babying me."

"Then stop acting like a baby and let me help you."

Jacie sneered, knowing that Nina was partially right but unable to stop herself from egging on the argument. "You're . . . You're going to wake up Audrey." She nodded a little, impressed with her new line of attack. "Yeah, that's what you're going to do."

"A herd of tap dancing elephants marching through your bedroom couldn't wake up Audrey, and you know it."

"If that fuckin' can of ham was all that was between me dying a slow death from hunger or living to a hundred . . . I still wouldn't eat it," Jacie spat, reaching for the can only to have Nina pull it away just in time.

Nina grabbed the can opener again and resumed twisting, having trouble with the second half and cursing under her breath as she worked.

"Oh," she was shaking, "you'll eat the damn ham . . . yes, you will.

Because I'll stuff it down your stupid throat if you don't."

Jacie lunged for Nina's hand and managed to grab the half-opened can. Teeth bared ferally, she lifted her arm to throw it.

Nina's eyes bugged, and she gasped. "Don't you dare!"

Jacie stopped cold, gaping when Nina took the opportunity to snatch the can back.

"Ha!" Nina laughed triumphantly, perspiration making her skin glow.

"Give me back the damned can," Jacie warned, her voice raspy and low as she moved forward a step.

Nina's nostrils flared. She was breathing heavily and knew her voice would be husky before she even spoke. "If you want it so bad, why don't you just take it, Jacie?" she challenged, lifting an eyebrow. She was shocked by her own brazenness but determined not to show it.

The young women glared at each other, panting softly, their faces flushed with anger . . . and something else. Their gazes held, locked for what seemed a lifetime, before something inside Jacie snapped. She surged forward, closing the distance between them in a heartbeat. She grabbed Nina's face in her hands and pulled her forward, crushing their lips together in a searing, desperate kiss.

Nina moaned into the kiss and returned it wholeheartedly, possessively wrapping her arms around Jacie and plastering their bodies together so tightly that she could feel Jacie's heartbeat through her nightshirt.

Tongues clashed and moans were swallowed for what seemed a lifetime before a dazed Jacie pulled back just enough to begin to softly nibble the edges of Nina's lips.

"Jacie," Nina breathed, her eyes still closed as she melted into Jacie's touch. When ardent lips began working their way down her neck, Nina wasn't sure her legs would hold her. "Jac—"

Sensing Nina's dilemma, Jacie gently maneuvered her against the kitchen cabinets. "Better?" she murmured.

"Mmm . . . ." Nina wound her hands in Jacie's thick hair, something she'd wanted to do since they were in junior high school. Then, to her surprise, Jacie deepened the kiss and used one hand to tease the soft skin of her inner thigh. "God," she mumbled a few moments later, her head spinning. "Where did you learn to do that?"

Jacie chuckled softly, delighting in the silken texture of Nina's lips and skin. "Do you really want to know?"

Nina ran her hands down Jacie's arms, her stomach tightening when she noticed that Jacie's nipples were now visible through her black silk blouse. She bit off a groan. "No, I guess I don't," she said absently, her hand drifting up to where her eyes were riveted.

Not to be left out, Jacie reached up and cupped one of Nina's breasts, and this time, Nina couldn't be quiet. She let out a slow, sexy hiss that nearly dropped Jacie to her knees.

"Is this what you want?" Jacie asked quickly, praying that she was right. She hugged her closer. "Us, like this?"

Nina closed her eyes. "Yes," she said, unable to deny the truth. She swallowed hard and did her best to collect herself. She was so aroused that she felt a little out of control. When she opened her eyes, she looked directly into Jacie's brown eyes, her gaze sizzling. "I don't want to stop." Her words set off another blistering bout of kissing and mutual petting that continued as Jacie guided her out of the kitchen and into Nina's bedroom, kissing her senseless along the way.

Nina's bedroom was dark, and the sound of the door latching behind them barely registered over their labored breathing. Jacie knew which of the two twin beds in the room was Nina's, and it was only seconds before Nina was engulfed in soft fabric, Jacie's hot body coming to rest alongside.

Close together, facing each other in the wan light, they smiled nervously at each other. Moonbeams poured through the window, making Jacie's dark eyes appear almost otherworldly and casting Nina in mysterious shadows.

The air between them crackled. Jacie had seen enough movies to know that this was where they were supposed to say something, to declare their true love and swear they'd never let crossing this line hurt their friendship. The words, she felt certain, shouldn't be so hard to say. But her tongue felt heavy in her mouth. To be rejected by Nina now? When she was close to what she'd dreamed of for so long? Her mind violently recoiled at the mere possibility.

"Jacie—"

"Nina—"

They said in unison.

"You first," Nina urged, her hands starting to roam over Jacie's body of their own free will.

Jacie swallowed dryly, her desire ratcheting up with amazing speed. "What are y-you doing?" she said absently, her mind on the fabulous sensations Nina's fingers were teasing from her.

Nina let out a deep breath. "Whatever I want." She unbuttoned one button on Jacie's blouse and slid her shaking hand inside to touch hot skin. "You're so soft." She sighed, easily losing herself in the moment. "I knew you would be." She glanced up from her task and innocently asked, "Am I doing something wrong?"

Jacie would have laughed if there had been enough blood left in her brain to form an appropriate response to the ridiculous question. As it was, every drop she had was headed southward. Furiously, she shook her head no.

Nina bit her bottom lip at the soft sigh Jacie made when her fingertips skimmed the curve of her friend's breast. "I," she had to stop and shake her head, the emotion of the moment stealing her words. "I don't know what to say." A warm hand cupped her cheek.

"You don't have to say anything."

"I—" But Nina's words were lost in another incendiary kiss. And soon Jacie had her aroused nearly beyond reason. In a fuzzy part of her mind, she was glad that Jacie had steered them into the bedroom, because as out of her head as she was at this very moment, she'd have made love to Jacie on the kitchen table.

Frantic hands peeled away Jacie's black slacks and silk blouse, not slowing until they reached a bra and panties. Nina swallowed hard. When she saw all that was in front of her, a moment of uncertainty assailed her. "I don't know what to do." She gave Jacie a worried look.

"It's okay," Jacie said, easing Nina's nightshirt over her head. The sight of her friend naked sent a rush of heated blood to her center, and she started to throb. She smiled devilishly. "I'll help."

Nina's eyes twinkled. "You're generous to a fault, Jacie."

Jacie laughed, glad that the humor seemed to cut through some of the tension. She kissed Nina's chin softly. "Aren't I just?"

Clothes were shed and soon moist heated skin was sliding together.

Smoothly, Jacie's fingers trailed across Nina's stomach, then through soft sandy hair and into her wetness.

Nina gasped, not expecting the intensity of the sensation.

Jacie's hand froze. Terrified, she said, "I'm sorry. I didn't mean—"

"Jace," Nina whispered softly, laying her hand over the one that rested between her legs and giving a tender squeeze. "I was just surprised." She tried to convey with her eyes all the love she felt as she admired how the moonlight danced across Jacie's skin. With her hand, she urged Jacie to continue what she was doing, seeing the glint of white teeth in response to her actions.

Jacie stroked her slowly, using the tips of her fingers and her tongue to bring her as much pleasure as she possibly could. She was by no means an expert at what she was doing, and it took several fumbling but sweet tries to establish a rhythm that seemed to work for them both.

It took Nina a long time to climax. But when she did, she felt as though she might fracture in two, spasms wracking her entire body, and she sought to pull Jacie deeper inside her. "Jesus." With a trembling hand, she clutched the head suckling her breast. She squeezed her eyes tightly shut, her thundering heart nearly drowning out the sounds of the languid moans and soft sighs that caressed her senses every bit as much as Jacie's hands and mouth.

Jacie nuzzled the curve of Nina's breast and grinned. She nipped at the tender skin gently, causing Nina's entire body to jump. "I love you, Nina," she whispered, kissing her way up Nina's salty throat and finding eager lips anxious to greet her.

"You mean everything to me," Nina murmured, tasting herself on Jacie's soft lips. "Everything. And I—"

Jacie plunged her tongue into her mouth and kissed her senseless, grinding her center against Nina's and causing the other woman to writhe beneath her.

"I—"

Jacie slid a hand up between their bodies and pinched one of Nina's hard nipples, causing her back to arch and a throaty growl to explode from her chest. "Yes? You were about to say something," Jacie said innocently, thrilling at Nina's reaction to her touch.

"I . . . I—" Nina's mind went blank amidst the myriad of overpowering sensations. "I forget," she admitted, capturing Jacie's upper lip with her teeth and giving it a playful tug.

Jacie chuckled and promised, "It'll come back to you." She lifted her head slightly so they could see each other's faces. Then she smiled such a hopeful, beautiful smile that Nina fell in love with her, right then in that very moment, all over again. Her heart ached from the sweetness of it.

"I want to touch you the way you touched me," Nina breathed, invigorated by her orgasm, but a little shaken by Jacie's open display of devotion. She ran her fingers down Jacie's cheek, capturing a drop of perspiration on her fingertip and then popping the digit into her mouth.

Jacie's belly clenched, and she bit back a moan. She was teetering on the edge of an orgasm just from tasting Nina, and was beginning to wonder whether watching the other woman would give her a stroke. When Nina lifted her eyebrows meaningfully, Jacie snapped out of her reverie and rolled off her and onto her side, taking a spot next to Nina.

Nina smiled at the change in positions, which placed Jacie squarely in the moonlight and allowed her a full view of her nude body. "You are so beautiful, Jacie." Her eyes landed on a thin scar that ran from the outside of Jacie's elbow and about a third of the way down her forearm. Another failed world record attempt. She traced it lovingly, thinking it didn't detract one bit from Jacie's beauty.

Jacie's gaze followed Nina's. She frowned. "Damn, was I ever a doofus."

"Nuh-uh," Nina corrected as she bent to trace the scar with her tongue. "You kicked ass and took names, Jacie," she said, her faith unwavering. "You still do." She sighed dreamily. "Every inch of my body is still on fire from the way you touched me."

Jacie's nostrils flared, and she sucked in a breath, ready to pounce on Nina, but a firm hand placed flat at the top of her chest stopped her.

"My turn," Nina said simply. She pulled away a little and waited, knowing deep down that not a single one of her wants would be denied. Not when it came to loving Jacie.

For a few seconds a silent battle of wills raged. Jacie felt as though she could devour Nina and never stop. She still hadn't learned all the secret places that she liked to be touched and the tiny things that drove her insane. Well, she had already learned a few of those. But as tempting as it was to persuade Nina to allow herself to be ravished all night, a larger part of her craved Nina's touch. She needed the other woman in an elemental way, like air or water. Then she looked into hungry blue-green eyes and felt Nina's gentle persistence win the war.

Nina sensed it; the second victory was hers and a heady sense of power sang through her veins. With more courage than she knew she had, she boldly stroked and kissed Jacie everywhere she had a mind to, nipping at the tender skin of Jacie's throat with careful teeth. Jacie was moaning with abandon. And when her hand finally found its way between Jacie's legs, the other woman's enthusiastic squirming threatened to topple them from the twin bed.

Suddenly, Jacie's hand covered Nina's and she pushed Nina's fingers inside her. Whimpering, her eyes rolled back in her head. "Yes," she hissed.

"Like this?" Nina increased the speed of her strokes, and Jacie could only nod furiously. Nina didn't have time to be worried that she couldn't satisfy her lover. It only took a few strokes for Jacie to climax, eyes wide open, mouth parted, chest heaving.

The moment was a profound one for Nina, and unexpected tears stung her eyes. She'd never seen, let alone been a part of, something so stunningly beautiful. "Thank you," she whispered, hugging Jacie tightly, possessively, as if daring anyone to take away what she cherished most.

Jacie smiled like a Cheshire cat, contented and satisfied. "I think I should be thanking you."

They laid plastered together for a long time with Jacie tracing idle patterns on Nina's thigh. A tiny part of Jacie's mind was worried that she'd shared too much of herself, opened herself for too much hurt. And yet, with Nina so close, it was impossible to feel anything but confident about the future.

Nina realized how much time had passed when she saw Jacie yawn. She grinned affectionately at Jacie's veiled attempt to fight sleep. While her body felt sluggish and sated, her mind was racing. "Jace?" she started uncertainly.

"Yeah?" Jacie tugged up the tangled comforter and settled it over them both as she closed her eyes and snuggled closer to Nina. She took one of Nina's hands and twined their fingers together.

Nina had never felt so wonderful and so terrified in her entire life. The realization of what they'd shared tonight, what they'd always shared, and the inescapable truth about herself was already beginning to seep into her thoughts. What did this mean for her? Was she a lesbian? How could she not be? That she loved Jacie and wanted to be with her, there was no doubt; but did she want everything that went with loving a woman? Did she have a choice? She didn't even know any lesbians . . . well, except for Jacie. Or was Jacie as confused as she was?

"Mmm . . . Did you say somethin'?" Jacie's voice was slightly slurred.

She swallowed hard and pushed the fear from her mind. Nothing could hurt her while she was in Jacie's arms, the rest she would worry about tomorrow. "Nothing, Jacie." She kissed her on the mouth, lingering there and happily melting into Jacie's warm embrace. "Good night."

Jacie smiled into the darkness, her heart bursting. Life, she knew in her bones, couldn't get any better than this. "Good night."

Jacie fell asleep quickly.

But for Nina, sleep wasn't so easy to find.

The Next Morning . . .

A very pregnant Gwen stood outside the girls' house, the early morning sun warming her skin and easing the chill left by the spring breeze. She lifted her hand to knock and then thought better of it. It was only half past six, and depending on who had to work, one or more of her friends would still be in bed.

She slid the key she'd kept into the lock and carefully opened the door. Gwen tried to scoot inside quickly, but her belly prevented her from sneaking around the partially opened door. She rolled her eyes at herself, grunting a little as she unstuck herself from between the door and the frame and padded inside.

The house was dark and quiet, and she frowned, knowing she'd probably be waiting a while before anyone was up. She hadn't seen Katy's car out front, but that wasn't unusual, and most likely there was someone still tucked in bed that she could talk into treating to a breakfast.

She glanced around the kitchen with a sense of nostalgia that surprised her. While Malcolm was everything she'd hoped for, kind and loving, living in the Langtree family home plainly sucked. It was a beautiful mansion in one of the city's most respected neighborhoods, but sometimes it felt like a prison. Gwen had dropped out of college and was busy memorizing the endless do's and don'ts of what it took to be a member of a prestigious family. She'd already been introduced to the mayor's wife, she was wearing designer clothes, and her new coif, though woefully out of style for her age group, was at least done at the most exclusive beauty parlor in the city. The scent of old money was all around her. But for some reason, it wasn't quite sticking. At least not yet.

The kitchen countertop had several cans haphazardly scattered across it. "Weird." She placed them back in the cupboard, guessing their owner based on the contents and whether they were a generic brand, which Jacie tended to avoid as a matter of taste, but Nina and the cousins embraced. Next, Gwen added grounds and water to the coffee maker on the counter, enjoying the pungent scent of the grounds with unconcealed excitement. While she had continued to speak to the young women of the Mayflower Club on the phone, this was the first time she'd been back to their house in nearly two months. Her face colored with shame when it occurred to her that she hadn't invited any of the girls to her new home.

Pulling the chair out a ridiculous distance from the table, she sat down with a sigh. Malcolm's mother, who Gwen suspected had trained Nazis on discipline in her youth, had done her best to impress on her that she needed to make new friends, the sort that were befitting of someone of her new stature—family people, not single, working-class, college students without connections or clout. Just thinking about it left a sour taste in her mouth. It was the reason she was here so early. She could visit and be home before anyone noticed she was gone. The Langtree estate, except for a few longtime servants, was dead until at least nine a.m., and this way she could avoid the reproachful looks she was sure to receive when asked where she'd been.

Then she thought of the surprise she had in store for Nina that very night, and a broad smile transformed her slightly puffy face. The history major had agreed to meet her and Malcolm for dinner at a posh restaurant downtown. Moreover, the night promised to be one that could change both their lives. Mrs. Langtree would see that there was no reason

Gwen couldn't bring her friends with her into a better life, instead of leaving them by the wayside.

The water stopped draining through the beans and Gwen looked at the pot longingly, willing it to magically fly off the counter and land directly in front of her. As if in answer to her thoughts, the coffee maker belched. "Fine," she groused, getting up.

Then she heard it. A creaking door and whispers.

"Someone's up!" she thrilled, temporarily forgetting about the coffee. She crept to the swinging doors that separated the living room from the kitchen and was surprised to see Jacie standing in Nina's doorway, disheveled and clearly angry. Nina was in her nightshirt and Jacie was wearing her work uniform. Not wanting to interrupt, she peeked over the doors, waiting until whatever argument they were having was over.

"Dammit, Jacie, why are you making this into a fight?" Nina asked, her voice quivering.

Jacie's back stiffened. "It *is* a fight. You kicked me out of your bed!"

Gwen's mouth dropped open.

"Keep your voice down," Nina whispered harshly. "I didn't kick you out of anywhere. Not really. It's just that Audrey could wake up at any time. And she'll wonder where you are. Or Katy could come home. I can't lock her out of her own room."

"Would it be so horrible if they knew about us?" Jacie sighed, suddenly sounding weary. "I'm so tired of hiding this part of myself," she reached out and grazed Nina's cheek with the tips of her fingers, "from my friends." She paused and licked her lips, tension making her head pound. "The only reason I've hidden it at all was because I was worried about how you'd react. The others will learn to live with it."

Wide eyed, Gwen leaned forward a little, riveted on the scene playing out only a few feet from her, even as she felt a twinge of guilt for eavesdropping.

"You make this sound like it isn't that big a deal." Nina sniffed. "But it is a big deal. Really, really big." She couldn't look Jacie in the eye, and she wrapped her arms around herself.

Jacie swallowed so thickly that Gwen heard it. "How can you say I don't think this is a big deal? I told you that I loved you! Do you think that was easy?"

"I don't know what to think!" Nina exploded, doing her best to keep the volume of her voice down, but failing. "I don't know what to feel. I don't think I'm gay. I'm not attracted to anyone but you. Not men or women." She ran a hand through her disorderly hair. "I'm unsure of myself right now. I need a little time to think without your pressuring me is all."

Stung, Jacie said, "You didn't seem very unsure of yourself last night."

"Do we have to do this here?" Worried eyes glanced around the room, and then Nina reached out for Jacie's hand. "I'm sorry if I hurt your feelings this morning, Jacie. I overreacted." She wiggled the fingers of her outstretched hand invitingly. "Come back to bed and let's talk."

"But then somebody might find out about us," Jacie sneered, refusing to take Nina's hand.

Gwen bit her lower lip so hard she tasted blood.

Nina's hands shaped into fists. "You are so stubborn!" She covered her face with her hands, and her voice dropped to a whisper. "I want to be with you, Jacie. But I'm afraid."

The words had a profound effect on Jacie, and she felt a lump grow in her throat. She'd had years to deal with her attraction to women . . . her attraction to Nina. She'd dreamed of having her as a lover. Of making a life with her. This wasn't the way things were supposed to go!

Last night had changed everything, and they were supposed to wake up happily in each other's arms. Nina wasn't supposed to have doubts about her sexuality. She was supposed to profess her undying love, and then they would fight the world and its prejudice together, needing only the other's approval.

They would get their own apartment, finish school, get good jobs, and be a real couple. They would travel, and unlike her own parents, they would share each other's interests and want to spend time together. Hell, maybe they'd even get a dog.

But when faced with eyes dilated from fear, not arousal, Jacie felt more than foolish. Her dream was childish and unrealistic, and she knew it. Still, it was hers.

She schooled herself in patience; fear that Nina might decide she didn't want to continue their relationship was making her queasy. All traces of anger disappeared from Jacie's face. "It'll be okay." She stepped forward to try to pull Nina into her arms. To her dismay, Nina stopped her.

"Not here, Jacie." Her eyes strayed to the front door. "Come back into the room."

Rejected again, Jacie said, "I was going to give you a hug, Nina. I've done it a million times in front of everyone we know. Even lesbians can give hugs that aren't sexual!"

Nina winced inwardly. "I'm sorry." She started to cry. "I don't want to h-hurt you. I lov—"

"Save it," Jacie snapped, her hurt and frustration getting the best of her. "Please," she paused and let out a shaky breath. "We can talk after you've had time to think with me out of your hair. My very presence seems to pressure you. And if I'm not too close then maybe you'll forget how horribly wrong it was for us to sleep together."

Nina lifted her chin. "It wasn't wrong," she insisted, her voice suddenly frantic. "I never said that. I . . . I—" Helplessly, she started to cry again.

Jacie felt her own tears prick the back of her eyes. "You didn't have to." Devastated, she stomped across the small living room and disappeared into her bedroom, her shoes clutched to her chest.

Nina's sobs intensified, and she retreated to her room, locking the door behind her.

Gwen thought she might loose control of her bladder. Numbly, she walked back to the table and sat down with a thump, feeling irrationally betrayed. "How could they do something so stupid? How could Jacie keep that secret from us?" she murmured. "I had a right to know I was living with a lesbian. I should have had a right to choose whether I wanted to do that!"

Suddenly, she looked around the room, realizing that she was talking to herself. How could she have been fooled? Then she closed her eyes as a million shared glances between Nina and Jacie came into focus. "No." She shook her head frantically. A sliver of fear worked its way into her chest. If her mother-in-law ever found out about them, let alone her own parents or even Malcolm, she could never see them again. The Langtrees didn't associate with gay people. They didn't even talk to Democrats!

She could already feel the friendship she'd been fighting to maintain start to slip through her hands. How could Jacie and Nina have done something so reckless? How could they expect to find husbands who would marry them now?

"Okay, slow down," she told herself. "This isn't who they are." They dated boys. They kissed boys. They liked boys. She'd personally seen Greg Parson's tongue halfway down Nina's throat last summer! Even though Jacie hadn't had a boyfriend in the last couple of years, she'd been the first among them to date. They couldn't be gay.

Nina had come out and said she wasn't, hadn't she? Jacie, she was confused is all. Her parents had a horrible, lifeless marriage. Maybe she didn't know a man and a woman could truly be happy together, the way she and Malcolm were. Yes, that had to be it. Jacie's confusion was bleeding over onto Nina. After all, they were best friends. It was bound to affect them both.

Desperately, Gwen's mind latched onto that train of thought. She couldn't lose them as friends, and she wouldn't abandon them when they needed her.

Now the only question was, what could she do?

It was mid-afternoon when Jacie finally emerged from her bedroom to find Katy and Audrey sitting on the couch, eating Lucky Charms dry out of the box and watching *Wheel of Fortune*. Both were barefoot and wearing T-shirts and ratty jeans—their weekend lounging clothes.

Jacie was tired and depressed and flopped down on the couch between Audrey and Katy, who both scooted over a little to make room, their gazes still riveted on the TV screen. In the process, she knocked over the half-eaten box of cereal.

Unconcerned, Katy began eating the cereal directly off the sofa. "George Washington!" she shouted, dry bits of cereal exploding from her mouth as she pointed at the television excitedly.

"Ha. You're such a dweeb," Audrey laughed. The cousins loved game shows, and each tried to outdo the other when it came to answering the questions. "The second word only has six letters."

Katy counted the illuminated tiles. "Oh, yeah. Shit." Her arm shot out again, and she pointed at the screen. "Andrew Jackson!" she yelled, absently reaching between the couch cushions for more cereal. "That has to be it."

Audrey sniggered at her cousin. Then she noticed Jacie's glum expression and suddenly remembered something Nina had asked her to do that morning. "Hey, Jacie," she greeted, reaching over Katy to grab the notepad they always kept by the phone.

"Hey," Jacie answered dully, her eyes straying to Nina's door. *I need to apologize. I freaked out for nothing. All she wanted was a little time to get used to things, and I had to go and be a bitch.*

"I have three messages for you this morning. Nina said you decided to sleep in for once."

"Good for you," Katy murmured, as she watched the show. "You've seemed stressed out lately."

Jacie ignored the comment, knowing it was true but unwilling to admit that she was working too much. The strain of being crazy about Nina but being too chickenshit to do anything about it had taken her to the breaking point. "Nina's not home?" Jacie asked, trying her best to sound casual as she picked at the couch cushion.

"She went to the Laundromat," Katy said, relaxing now that it was a commercial.

Audrey passed over the messages.

The first was in Nina's handwriting and told Jacie that her mother needed a ride to church for the afternoon service. As it often was, her car was in the shop and her mother expected Jacie to find a way to help her. The second message, written in Katy's dark scrawl, was from her boss. Jacie needed to be at work an hour early tonight. "Crap." She didn't want to go to work or go to pick up her mother. She wanted to wait for Nina and beg her forgiveness. She shuffled the papers again and then glanced back up at Audrey. "You said three messages?"

"Yup."

Unexpectedly, Audrey pulled Jacie into a big hug. "Nina said to give you this from her," she squeezed a little harder, "and to tell you everything would be okay."

Stunned, Jacie could only swallow, relief washing over her in great waves.

"That must have been some fight you guys had," Katy commented, her eyes narrowing as a thought struck her. "Nobody ever hugs me."

"Aww." Audrey lunged for her skinny cousin and quickly pinned her in a massive bear hug, squeezing the air out of her lungs. "I'll hug you."

Katy gasped and wiggled frantically to squirm free from Audrey's strong arms, laughing and wheezing the entire time. "Gee." Another gasp. "Thanks."

"Welcome," Audrey said. "Pennsylvania!" She shouted, pointing at a beaming Vanna White, who was rapidly turning over letters.

"Shit!" Katy groused, grabbing the cereal box and stuffing her face for comfort.

Jacie stood up, visibly happier. "Katy, can I borrow your car for a couple of hours?" She hoped she had enough change in her coat pocket for a gallon of gas.

The blonde gestured toward a key rack by the door, her attention once again riveted to the television. "I filled it up last night."

Jacie's face relaxed into a full smile. "Stand up, Audrey."

Audrey's eyebrows jumped. "Huh?"

Jacie tapped her foot impatiently. "Just do it, okay?"

Reluctantly, she did and then let out a surprised whoop when Jacie wrapped her arms around her and hugged her so completely that she lifted her feet from the ground, her curly locks bouncing in all directions. "You give *that* to Nina and tell her I'll be back later."

"Musta been some fight," Katy repeated absently, her fingers finding the toy surprise in the cereal. She examined it from the corner of her eye. "Cool! A glow-in-the-dark four leaf clover ring." She slid it on her pinky and wiggled the digit happily.

Audrey looked down at the ring. "Cool," she agreed. Then her gaze sharpened. "Isn't it my turn for the toy?"

"Fuck, no," Katy said tartly, making a fist to protect her booty.

And then they were grappling for the ring.

Utterly accustomed to the mayhem, Jacie headed for the door, grabbing a sweatshirt from the coat closet along the way. She could feel it bubbling up inside her. Her luck was changing.

◆◆◆

The drive to Hazelwood wasn't a particularly long one, but it wasn't one that Jacie made very often. As she pulled into her parents' driveway, she waved at one of her neighbors who was mowing his lawn. The sight of the freshly cut grass caused a twinge of guilt; she hadn't been home since Christmas.

Her father's car was parked on the other side of the driveway. Jacie shut her car door in disgust. This wouldn't be the first time her dad had refused to drive or to let her mother use his car.

When she opened the front door, she was greeted by the heavy, greasy smell of fried chicken and gravy. Her stomach rumbled in appreciation. "Hi, Mom," she called out, rounding the corner into the living room. "I'm—" she stopped when she saw Gwen sitting in a recliner across from her parents, who were seated stiffly on the sofa. "What are you doing here?" Then the fancy car she'd seen parked across the street made sense. It was Malcolm's.

Gwen drew in a deep breath and laid her hands across her bulging belly, doing her best to calm her raging nerves. "I needed to come by and talk to your parents, Jacie."

Jacie just looked at her. "You did?"

Gwen wrung her hands together. "I—"

Jacie's mother, a tall woman with thick, turquoise eye shadow that perfectly matched the color of the curtains in her kitchen, shot off the coach and glared at her daughter. "Tell me that something so disgusting isn't true," she demanded, her chin quivering dramatically.

Gwen's and Jacie's eyes widened at the exact same second.

Confused, Jacie turned to her father. His square jaw was clenched hard; his dark eyes unreadable as he gazed quietly back at her. "Does anyone want to tell me what's going on?" she said, shifting uneasily from one foot to the other.

Jacie's mother, never one to mince words, got right to the point. "Your friend Gwen tells us that you're a . . ." she paused as her entire body shuddered in revulsion, "homosexual."

Jacie's jaw dropped and she gave Gwen a stunned blink.

"But of course, I told her that couldn't be true," Grace Priest continued nervously, her voice wavering, doubt clouding her eyes. The middle-aged woman fingered the heavy cross she wore around her neck. "I'm waiting, Jacie Ann."

Jacie felt as though she'd been kicked in the chest. A million thoughts roared through her head, each one more confusing and upsetting than the last. How had Gwen known? How could she betray her this way? And worst of all, had Gwen done the same thing with Nina's parents?

"Jacie?" her mother prompted.

The young woman's heart began to race. She had imagined this moment many times, and now that it was here, she took another look at her parents' guarded faces and realized it was going to be worse than she'd even pictured. "I . . . I . . . I—"

"Just great." Jackson Priest bowed his head; Jacie's lack of an instant denial the same as an admission in his eyes. He glanced up at Jacie, his dark green eyes glinting with disappointment and anger. "Girl, what are you thinking? What's wrong with you?"

Jacie's mother gaped at her husband. "Jack, she didn't answer yet." She pointed at him, her hand shaking. "She did not answer! Don't you put words in her mouth!" She made an emphatic gesture toward Jacie. "Tell him. Tell him you're not like that!"

"Ma—" Jacie had to stop and swallow. She covered her face with her hands. This isn't how she wanted things to go. They were already beginning to spin out of control.

Mrs. Priest took a step closer to her daughter. "Answer me, Jacie Ann!"

"Yes!" Jacie blurted loudly, the words hitting her parents like stinging blows. "Okay?" She lowered her voice, her tone defiant. "I am like that. I always have been and I always will be."

Jackson scrubbed his face, his hands rubbing over a heavy layer of stubble that he let accumulate every weekend. "You do realize what you've done, don't you? This isn't something anyone can ever know about. I'm sure your friend Gwen won't say a word."

He pinned Gwen with a lethal look and her head bobbed dutifully.

Jackson nodded. "Have you thought about what decent man would ever want to marry you after this? Or have a family with you?"

"Jesus, Dad, the entire point of being a lesbian is that I don't want a man," Jacie said hotly. "I—"

Smack!

The sound of Grace slapping Jacie hard in the face woke Gwen from her horror-induced stupor. She gasped and jumped to her feet as quickly as her protruding belly would allow. Without regard for herself, she stepped between Jacie and Grace, who were glaring at each other like two prize fighters about to square off. "Mrs. Priest! Stop!" Her gaze flickered to Jacie who was rubbing her face but didn't look half as shocked as she herself felt. In that instant, she knew that Jacie wasn't surprised, and that this had to have happened before. A sliver of doubt about what she was doing wrapped around Gwen's heart and squeezed like an icy fist.

Grace simply spoke around Gwen as though the young woman wasn't even there. "How could you do that to us, Jacie? To yourself? To God?"

Tears formed in Jacie's eyes, but through sheer force of will she refused to let them fall. Her cheek hurt but the pain in her heart was far worse. She suddenly sounded very tired, feeling as though the entire world was ganging up on her. "I'm not doing anything to anyone. I haven't hurt anyone. And I haven't done anything wrong." Jacie began to think she might be the only person in Missouri who truly believed that.

Grace blinked. "You can't know what you're saying. Listen to yourself! You're not only admitting to fornication, but to some bizarre form of unnatural fornication. Your actions reflect on us all. How can you be so selfish as to only think of yourself? What about me and your father?"

Jacie tamped down the urge to roll her eyes. "Everything's not about you, Mom."

Grace's eyebrows rose. "It isn't? Do you really think you can do any sick thing that you please and that people here won't find out about it?" She fanned her face as though warding off a case of the vapors—something she'd never actually gotten, though she acted as if she required smelling salts on a daily basis. "What will Pastor Douglas say? What about the men at your father's office and our friends? He has to work with the people in this town to make a living! Now they'll pity us." Her eyes widened as a terrible thought made her sick. "No, not just pity, blame us for what you've become!"

"Mrs. Priest," Gwen interrupted desperately, her voice an octave higher than normal. "We were talking about counseling for Jacie before she got here. Remember? I told you about the brochures I'd seen for family therapy?"

"*You* were talking about counseling," Grace pointed out crabbily. "Doctors can't fix a person's morals, can they? But maybe prayer and—"

"This has nothing to do with prayer. I don't need to be fixed!" Jacie roared, blood pounding through her veins so hard she felt lightheaded. "Nothing is wrong with me!" She gave her father a pleading look, her eyes begging him to understand and make things better for her instead of worse. "Please, Dad."

A quiet sigh. "Jacie's right, Grace."

Three sets of stunned eyes stared at Jackson Priest in shock.

"Prayer isn't the answer." God, he was tired of his wife's obsession with religion. "Jacie's sick. She needs a doctor."

"Oh, Jesus," Jacie moaned, her hopes disappearing like a wisp of smoke.

"She needs the Lord in her heart," Grace corrected firmly. "She never did listen when I took her to church. You said it didn't matter. But now look!"

"Bullshit," Jack said bluntly, his lips twisting into a snarl. "It isn't my fault that she couldn't stand going to that place anymore than I can."

"I don't want a doctor or a preacher," Jacie broke in, her gaze straying to the door as she longed for escape.

Grace shook her head woefully. "We never should have supported you going to that school. You don't even want to change and God only helps those who help themselves. Somehow that college has put these sinful ideas into your head or maybe you've got some new friends we don't know about."

Jacie shook her head. "There is nobody to blame. So you can stop looking. This is me, and you're going to have to learn to live with it."

The hair on the back of her father's neck lifted as his voice dropped to a menacing growl. "This is my house and I don't have to learn anything. I'm not the one who's doing disgusting things, now am I?"

Jacie's back stiffened. "You didn't even flinch when Mom just hit me in the face." She touched her own red cheek. "That's pretty disgusting from my point of view."

Jackson's face colored, but it was from anger, not embarrassment. "I won't spend a dime of my hard-earned money to support some perverted lifestyle."

"You've never supported me."

Gwen's gaze flew between Jacie and her father. "What does she mean?" she asked finally, the tension in the room so thick she felt like she couldn't breathe.

Jacie almost didn't answer, but things had gone this far and now there was no turning back. "That means he won't continue to give me that entire thirty-five dollars a month he chips in toward my tuition. Even though he knows it'll mean I have to drop out of school." She was speaking to Gwen but looking into her father's eyes the entire time.

From the corner of her eye, Jacie saw Gwen's mouth drop open; she snorted softly at her surprise. "And he only does that because one of his co-workers asked if sending me to college was setting the family back. He was too embarrassed to say nothing."

"I work hard for that money, you ungrateful brat," Jack shot back, a vein in his forehead beginning to show.

"Mom gives five times that to the church every month. And I don't see that fat preacher working two jobs or skipping any meals the way I do."

"Jacie Ann Priest, how dare you!" Grace screeched, trying to step around Gwen to get to her daughter.

Jacie stepped away from Gwen and moved to stand toe-to-toe with her mother. Her voice was low and controlled, rage flickering in her eyes. "Don't think I'm going to let you hit me again."

Gwen began to panic. "What is going on here?" she whispered to herself. Jacie's mother and father were devout people. Devout people wouldn't refuse to help their child when she was in need!

Grace glared at the young woman she couldn't believe she had given birth to. "The church is doing the Lord's work and fighting against the kind of smut you're living, young lady. Be thankful that that's where this family's money goes. It doesn't seem that the money we send you has been doing any good for anybody. We raised you to be normal. Not something else."

Jackson let out a heavy sigh. He hadn't moved from his spot on the sofa during the entire discussion. "Get out of my house, Jacie Ann, and don't come back until you've given up this disgusting notion of yours."

"That will be never," Jacie said bluntly, his words digging deeper than she wanted to show.

Jackson nodded slowly. "Then that's your choice."

Jacie plastered a grim smile onto her face, but Gwen caught the slight quiver of her lower lip. "No problem, Dad." She didn't even look at her mother or Gwen as she stormed from the room.

Gwen ran a trembling hand through her hair. Then she whirled around and looked at Jacie's parents as though they were aliens. "I thought you were going to help her! I only told you so that you could help her!"

"You heard her," Grace answered stiffly. "She doesn't want our help." She turned and gazed out of the window with unseeing eyes. "She's never wanted anything from us at all."

"I can't imagine why," Gwen muttered as she hurried after Jacie, her waddling gate making true speed all but impossible. She made it outside just in time to see Jacie peeling out of the driveway. "Jacie," she called loudly, waving her arms and running toward the car. Not listening, the auburn-haired girl floored the gas pedal without sparing a desperate Gwen the slightest glance.

"Slow down! You're going to kill yourself!" But she was already looking at Katy's car's taillights. In her haste, Gwen fumbled with the car keys, letting out a rare curse when they dropped in her lap as she tried to fit them into the ignition. "Oh, God. Oh, God."

After a lifetime of living nearby, she knew which streets Jacie would take to exit the neighborhood and after getting lucky and making a few stoplights that Jacie missed, Katy's beat up car was finally the one directly in front of her. Gwen laid on her horn, wincing when Jacie merely lifted her hand from the steering wheel and flipped her the bird.

At the next corner, Gwen used the full power of her BMW and shot around Jacie. Gritting her teeth, she swerved into Jacie's lane, cutting her off and forcing Jacie to shoot into the parking lot of a local convenience store to avoid ramming into the back of the Beamer.

Livid, Jacie flew out of her car and stalked over to Gwen, who was trying to pry herself from behind the steering wheel. "Are you insane?" Jacie screeched at the top of her voice. "Have you forgotten that you're pregnant?"

Gwen shot her a tart look as she finally made it out of the car. "Does that even look possible to you?"

"You pious meddling bitch."

Gwen held her tongue, because at that moment, she completely agreed with Jacie. "I'm sorry," she finally whispered, looking away. Then she shut the car door and had to force herself to meet Jacie's searing gaze.

"Do you even know what you've done?" Jacie slammed her hand down on the hood of the car, the sound echoing in the nearly empty parking lot. "I'm going to have to quit school. I can't work any more damn hours. I'm already drowning and one of my best friends threw me a big-ass rock to hold onto!" She slammed her hand down again, this time denting the metal. "Argh! If you weren't pregnant, I would—kick—your—ass!"

Gwen gulped hard. Jacie was deadly serious. "I didn't think that would happen. I . . . I . . . I had no idea. I just wanted to help you. I swear it, Jacie."

"And did you 'help' Nina this way today?" Jacie's gaze sharpened. "Because if you did I—"

"No! Of course I didn't." She looked hurt that Jacie would even think such a thing. "Nina's not gay. I heard her say so. I wouldn't tell her parents because she's not the one who needs help. She was just experimenting or something." Her face took on a sympathetic expression. "It's you that needs help."

"You don't know what you're talking about when it comes to Nina." Jacie's mind flashed to the night before and her heart skipped a beat. She relaxed a little, relieved beyond measure that Gwen hadn't done something so hurtful to Nina at this confusing juncture in her life. Things were scary enough as it was. "What makes you think I need or want your help, Gwen?" She arched one slender eyebrow. "I know what I am and even if I could change, which I can't, I wouldn't want to."

Gwen just stared. "That can't be true."

"It is true. I came to terms with who I was a long time ago."

Gwen crossed her arms over her unusually full chest. "If you weren't ashamed of it, you wouldn't have kept it a secret."

That shut Jacie up for several seconds. She squirmed a little, uncomfortably aware that on some level that was probably true, at least at one time. "I didn't tell you because I was afraid of how you'd react. Afraid it would ruin our friendship." Her face turned to granite. "I guess I shouldn't have worried."

"I'm still your friend."

Jacie was surprised at how much this hurt. "No way, Gwen," she said thickly. "After everything we've been through. After everything this year . . ." She didn't need to mention the hours of comfort and support she'd freely given her friend after her rape.

Gwen's face colored with shame.

A look of pure disgust twisted Jacie's attractive features. "You stabbed me in the back."

Gwen shook her head. "I know you think that now. But someday you'll see. I told your parents for your sake. For all our sakes."

Jacie groaned, already tired of this conversation. Ever fiber of her being told her that she needed to go to Nina, to talk about last night, and to make absolutely certain that they were on solid ground. Not to mention the fact that she craved sinking into her arms and letting Nina sooth away some of this profound hurt. She turned and started to walk away, stopping when Gwen's shaky voice rang out in the parking lot.

"I'm not wrong about Nina. I know you love her, and she loves you. Just not that way." Gwen's stomach was in knots. She knew the carefully chosen words would further wound her already injured friend, but a little hurt now was better than a lifetime of misery, wasn't it?

Jacie turned around, fists clenched, the cool wind sending the pungent odor of diesel fuel back to Gwen and tossing Jacie's thick hair into her face. "She does love me."

Gwen steeled herself, ruthlessly ignoring the little voice in her head that told her to stop and think about what she was about to do. "She's not gay."

"Shut up and leave me alone." She turned toward Katy's car again, not willing to allow Gwen to see the damage her words had done. She needed to see Nina . . . now.

"I can prove it." She gasped when Jacie froze for a split second, then spun around and stalked back to her, putting them face-to-face.

"You don't know what the fuck you're talking about. You're lying!" she spat, her words slurred by anger.

Gwen shook her head, trying to retain control of her badly stressed bladder. "Tonight she's going on a double date with Malcolm and me and his cousin Victor. If she loved you . . . in a romantic way, I mean, would she be willing to date a man?"

Jacie paled. "She's what?"

"A double date. That's why I was at the house this morning and why I heard you two talking." She licked her lips nervously. "I was there to talk about tonight." A partial truth.

"I don't believe you." *No way*, her mind blared. *Nina wouldn't do that. Never.* Even if last night was the first time they'd slept together, things had been slowly intensifying between them for months.

Gwen grabbed the sleeve of Jacie's sweatshirt and dragged her over to a nearby phone booth. "Give me a dime," she demanded, holding out her hand.

Jacie looked at her upturned palm, experiencing whiplash at Gwen's apparent, sudden change of subjects. "Huh?"

"Just do it." She lifted her hand higher.

In confusion, Jacie dug through the pocket of her jeans and produced a handful of change. She handed the entire pile to Gwen. "What are you—?"

"Shh." Gwen put the phone to her ear and began to dial, waiting impatiently for someone to pick up. "Victor Langtree, please."

Jacie's stomach dropped.

"Hi, Victor, this is Gwen." She pulled Jacie closer to the phone. "I called just to make sure everything is set for tonight."

Despite herself, Jacie pressed her head to Gwen's, feeling soft hair brush against her cheek as she listened in on the conversation.

Victor droned on for a moment about how excited he was and how he intended to sweep Nina off her feet before Gwen cut him off mid-sentence. "That's great, Victor. You can come by the house at seven, okay? I'm looking forward to it, too. See you then. Bye."

Jacie moved away slowly, taking a few steps before she began to pace. "That—that doesn't mean a damn thing." But a flicker of doubt shone in her eyes. "You could have gotten Malcolm's cousin to lie." Sweat began to gather at the back of her collar. "Nina never mentioned she was going on a date." *God,* her mind choked, hating the way that sounded more than she could express. "Not once."

"You need to face the truth." Her friend clearly wasn't convinced yet. Gwen bit her bottom lip and went for broke. At worst she could talk her way out of what she was about to do. At best Jacie would be convinced that there was no point in going ahead with her crazy idea of being a homosexual. Nina was clearly a temptation for her and with the temptation removed maybe she'd see how ridiculous she was acting and go back to normal. "Here." Gwen slid another dime into the phone's coin slot, her palm and fingers so moist that she nearly dropped it. Then she said a prayer as she shot well over a line from which she knew there was no return.

Audrey picked up the ringing phone. "Hello?"

"Hi. So, are you all ready for tonight?"

"What?" Audrey took the phone away from her ear and looked at it. "Hi, Gwen. We don't have anything going on tonight, do we?"

Gwen turned to Jacie and looked her right in the eye as she spoke. "Nina, I hope you're going to wear something sexy so that Victor gets a good look at your figure."

Jacie forgot how to breathe as her insides began to shake.

"I am not Nina, you dork." Audrey twisted the phone cord around her little finger as she spoke. "And I can't believe you finally got her to go on that double date with you." She chuckled. Gwen was determined to find them all the men of her dreams. The richer and more handsome the better. Unless, of course, they were richer or more handsome than Malcolm. "Here's Nina." She handed the phone to the young woman as she walked by.

Gwen had to force her hands to stop trembling. She let out a relieved breath and extended her arm to grab Jacie to pull her over to listen. Jacie was standing a few feet away and actually dug in her heels when Gwen tried to pull her closer.

"Hello," Nina answered, perching on the corner of the sofa and reluctantly pulling her nose from a good book.

"So are you ready for our date tonight?" Gwen repeated with Jacie now listening in.

"You bet," Nina answered cheerfully. "I can't wait."

Jacie felt as though a ton of bricks had been dropped on her head. *This can't be happening. Not after last night. Not after everything.* "Ni-nina?"

Gwen's eyes bugged out and she tried to pull the phone away but Jacie's grasp was firm.

"Jacie?" Nina's eyebrows lifted. "Where are you?"

"You're . . . um . . ." Jacie could hardly talk and she thought she might throw up. "You're going out on a date tonight?"

"Well, yeah. It's been planned for a while." She frowned, not liking the tremulous sound of Jacie's normally vibrant voice. "You'll be at work while I'm out, right? But, hey, I really think we should talk before I leave." Her tone went serious. "There's something I need to tell you and it can't wait."

Nina hadn't told Jacie she loved her yet, and the omission had been haunting her since that morning. The happy words wanted to explode from her and she nearly did it right there on the phone, but Audrey was standing only a few feet away and she wanted some privacy when she made it clear to Jacie just how much she meant to her. She'd searched her soul that morning, and while she was still more than a little afraid, she was certain that she and Jacie could work through anything so long as they did it together.

She's going to break up with me? Jacie closed her eyes. "No. No. No!" Violently, she jerked the phone from Gwen's hand, causing Gwen to scream out in surprise as she slammed the phone hard into its cradle, hanging up. "Shit."

Tears welled up in Gwen's eyes at the utterly devastated look on Jacie's face. "Jacie."

"No," she said in voice so low that Gwen barely heard her. She rested her forehead against the phone. Why was her world collapsing on her? Tears streamed freely down her cheeks.

Gwen blinked. "You're," she swallowed, "you're crying?" She shook her head. "But you don't cry. I . . . I've seen you break your arm in three places and not shed a single tear."

Jacie didn't even hear Gwen as her own thoughts raged. *Last night was a lie? Every touch. Every kiss. Every sweet word. All of it. But Nina wouldn't do that!* Her mind recoiled at the mere thought of the person she loved most in the world, the one she trusted above all others, using her. And yet, Nina had admitted as much, hadn't she? *She was keeping a date with some guy.* It was like knives were slicing up her insides and she tasted bile.

Unable to contain the hurt and fury building up inside her, brown eyes flew open and Jacie grabbed the phone's handpiece and began repeatedly slamming it against the phone booth, the pain it caused her palm and fingers not even registering as jagged bits of plastic flew everywhere. "It! Was! Not! A! Lie!"

In a panic, Gwen screamed. Jacie's meltdown was a hundred times worse than she'd expected and it scared her to the core.

When there wasn't enough phone left in her hand to smash, Jacie let it drop and leaned against the phone booth. She wanted to die. Her back to the glass, her knees gave out and she slid down until her bottom hit the dirty floor and she began to openly sob.

Astonished, Gwen didn't know what to say. "You really love her?" She finally asked, her breath coming fast as the true amount of damage she'd just done to Jacie began to hit home. "Not just some crush or friendship? But really love?"

Jacie wrapped her arms around herself in mute comfort. "Always," was all she could get out between sobs.

"Oh, God. The way I love Malcolm?" Gwen couldn't conceive it could be true. Not between two women. "But, Jacie," she gently said with one hundred percent sincerity, "that's not even possible, is it?"

Jacie didn't bother to answer. She was about to throw up, and talking to Gwen was the last thing she wanted. "Get the hell away from me," she growled, her face contorted in pain.

Awkwardly, Gwen got down on one knee, not at all sure that she could get back up from that position. "It'll be okay," the words tumbled out so quickly she could barely understand them herself. "I want to help you. I love you like a sister! You won't have to quit school. I'll—" Her mind raced for a solution. "I'll give you the money that your parents were giving you." Malcolm would understand and if he didn't, she would sell the car he'd just bought her. She reached out for one of Jacie's hands, but Jacie knocked hers away

Bleakly, and with bloodshot eyes, Jacie glanced up at Gwen's desperate face.

For a split second Gwen thought she might tell Jacie everything. That she'd tricked her. That Nina didn't even know that Victor was coming to dinner tonight. However, indecision caused her to hold her tongue.

"Hey, what's going on?" Wearing a dingy green apron, a skinny clerk with a buzz haircut and a cigarette perched between his lips came out of the convenience store. "What are you girls doing?" He glanced at what was left at the phone: a black chunk of hard plastic that swung from the silver cord in the breeze. "My phone!" He began to hurry toward them.

"C'mon, Jacie." Gwen hoisted herself to her feet and reached out for her friend. "We need to go. He might call the police. Hurry!"

Mutely, Jacie allowed Gwen to help her up and guide her over to the BMW. Then when they were a few feet from the car, she bolted for Katy's car, the ignition roaring to life after a few faltering tries.

"Jacie!" Gwen screamed after her, her eyes wide with fear. "Stop! Please!"

Through a haze of tears, Jacie navigated around the BMW and did a speeding U-turn in the parking lot, shooting over the curb and onto a dirt road that ran behind the store. A cloud of dust erupted behind her.

"Jacie!" Gwen tried again.

Falling apart at the seams, and with another surge of gasoline and the stench of burning rubber, Jacie Priest drove out of all their lives.

And never came back.

Chapter 9
Present Day
Rural Missouri

Jacie and Nina had nearly made their way back to the B&B. The autumn sun had almost set, and a blanket of stars was beginning to peek out from behind the thinning clouds. They sat in the forest on a stone bench that was not thirty yards from the resort's large back lawn, taking a break from their walk. The glow from the kitchen window was barely visible through the trees and the smell of the river and wet foliage seemed stronger now, in the waning light, where their eyes were spared the sensory overload of orange, red, and bright yellow leaves.

Jacie's hands were stuffed deeply into her pockets as she stared into space. The haunted expression on her face was starting to scare Nina.

"Hey," Nina began gently. "Are you okay?"

Jacie just stared at her with anguished eyes, not wanting to believe what Nina had said, but knowing it was true simply by the way Nina had said it. "How," she stopped and cleared her dry throat. "How do you know this? About Gwen, about me, about what happened that last day?"

Sympathy shone in Nina's eyes. She hadn't wanted to hurt Jacie, but Jacie deserved to know the truth. "Gwen came by the house after you stormed off in Katy's car. She was beside herself and she pulled me into the bathroom and spilled her guts. I was—" Nina glanced down at her hands. "I was devastated that you thought so little of me that you'd believe I would sleep with you one night and hope to strike up a romance with some strange guy the next."

This time it was Jacie's turn to look away. "But you said—"

"I said I needed time, Jacie. And it didn't take long for me to figure out that you were what I wanted," Nina said in a firm, but gentle voice. "I just never got the chance to tell you."

Jacie closed her eyes. "Jesus Christ," was all she could think to say. The direction of her entire life had changed because of a lie? How do you respond to someone telling you that you threw away happiness with both hands?

Nina could see that Jacie was at a loss for words, but that was all right. She was content to carry the conversation for a while. "When your uncle called Katy the next day and said he had her car, I thought there was a chance." She let out a sigh. "But you'd already gone and he swore he didn't know where. He said he'd come by later that week and box up your stuff."

Jacie covered her face with her hands.

"I never spoke to Gwen again after that day." Nina shook her head a little and sighed. "I . . . I was a mess for a long time. I told Audrey and Katy about Gwen going to your parents, but not what happened between you and me. I think they figured there was more to the story, but I just couldn't talk about it."

Jacie laid a comforting hand over Nina's, and Nina smiled, weaving their fingers together.

"When Katy heard what Gwen had done, that was enough for her. She told Gwen to go to hell and never wanted to hear her name again. I think she was a little lost without you, and even though she wouldn't admit it, she missed Gwen, too. Later that spring she moved in with some guy who lived across the city.

"Audrey was pissed at Gwen for betraying you, and hurt that you didn't feel like you could trust us enough to tell us that you were gay. She hurt for me having lost my best friend and she hurt for Gwen, too, saying that Gwen didn't really understand what she'd done. Audrey tried to get Katy and me to mend our fences with Gwen, but that never got very far and I think that only served to push us all farther apart. Maybe . . . I think she and Gwen stayed in touch for a while, but I'm not sure."

Nina shrugged. "We moved out of the house and for the first time started leading separate lives. That first year after everything happened I ran into Audrey on campus a few times. And we'd stop and say hello. But . . ." She made a face. "I dunno. It wasn't the same. The closeness was still there, but it was buried so deep. Things were awkward. I'd totally lost track of Katy by the time I graduated and then I left Missouri altogether to get my Masters in Museum Studies."

"My leaving split you all apart?" Jacie asked, mortified. Her stomach had already been churning, but this news threatened to make it rebel outright. Especially during those first years on her own, she had enviously pictured the Mayflower Club as steadfast friends, having barbecues at each other's houses, even their children playing together.

"No." Tenderly, Nina squeezed their joined hands. "That wasn't your fault,' she insisted, trying to make Jacie understand. "It's true that things were never the same after you left. But . . ." she searched for the right words. "I couldn't really see this then, but we were all growing apart little by little. It was gradually happening before you left and probably would have continued even if you'd stayed."

"Still," Jacie whispered bleakly. "God, I'm so sorry."

Nina's throat constricted at the emotion in Jacie's voice. "I wanted you to know the truth about what happened." She sniffed. "And now you know. I didn't tell you to make you sad."

It was fully dark now and the air had taken on more of a chill, their breaths sending clouds of vapor from their lips as they spoke.

Nina shivered and Jacie's arms ached from the want of holding her, but she still wasn't totally confident that a hug would be welcomed. "If I'd known that Gwen was lying . . . Things would have been different, Nina. I swear." She gritted her teeth together. "I can't say I'm sorry enough."

Nina shook her head slowly. "That's not true. Yes, you can. I accept your apology, Jacie." She drew in a deep breath, her heart rate picking up a little. "And now I hope that you'll accept mine."

Jacie blinked.

Nina tucked a strand of hair behind her ear, her stomach tightening at what she was about to say. "I figured you'd headed to your uncle's farm that night." She smiled sadly. "We . . . all of us always had so much fun there, swimming and sunning like summer would never end."

"But you didn't know for sure or you could have—"

"I knew."

Jacie's eyes widened.

"I called and spoke to your aunt. She said you'd been sitting in Katy's car in front of the farmhouse for the past four hours. She wasn't sure what to do."

"But if you knew—"

Nina's chilled fingers pressed against her lips stopping her. "If I knew, then why didn't I do something?"

Jacie just nodded.

Nina licked her lips and blew out a long breath. "I don't have a good answer for that question. The truth is that I was hurt and angry that you didn't trust me or trust what I was so sure we had together." Nina squeezed her eyes shut, a tear snaking down her cheek, glistening in the starlight. "I knew you were there suffering, thinking that I was waffling on my sexuality and that I was willing to start dating someone else, and a big part of me thought that's exactly what you deserved."

Jacie didn't say anything, but she snuggled a little closer to Nina, offering her silent support.

"I guess . . . I guess I thought you'd lick your wounds at your uncle's farm and then come back home the next morning and I could explain the whole thing to you. I shouldn't have taken a chance on losing you, Jacie. But I was so angry! I never imagined that you'd actually"—she sighed—"well, that you'd never . . . ." Her voice trailed off.

Jacie looked hard into eyes gone violet in the twilight. She shifted on the bench until she was facing Nina and lifted one hand, gently caressing Nina's cheek with the knuckles. "I didn't think I had anything to stay for. But you've got to believe me," she insisted, her words brimming with conviction. "I'd give my whole life to be able to turn back the clock and change everything about that day. I'd have talked with you the morning after we'd made love instead of allowing my insecurities free rein. I would have believed in us more than anything else. And most importantly, Nina, I wouldn't have let you go. Not for anything."

Nina sniffed, her vision blurring. "I'm sorry I didn't fight for us. I could have stopped you from leaving, but I didn't. I almost didn't come here this weekend. The thought of facing you and admitting what I did . . ."

Jacie shook her head and her voice cracked as she spoke. "You don't have anything to apologize for." Nina gave her a doubtful look, but she repeated firmly, "You don't. But I'm sorry I didn't strangle Gwen when I had the chance."

Nina snorted, glad at the humor, black though it was. "I nearly did. Audrey and Katy heard me yelling at her in the bathroom after she told me what she'd done and how she'd lied to you. They stormed in and barely kept me from doing something crazy. I felt like I'd lost my mind."

"I know the feeling," Jacie murmured wryly. "It's scary as hell."

Nina allowed a small smile to ease across her face. "You're more open than you used to be." She only just stopped herself from turning her head to kiss the warm palm that cupped her cheek. "The Jacie I knew never admitted to being afraid of anything." She thought for a few seconds. "I like the change."

"I finally grew up."

Nina's heart ached for not being there to see that, for not sharing all those glorious and heartbreaking moments between then and now. But she was tired of hurting for the past.

"Jacie—"

"Nina—" they said at the same time.

They both stopped and smiled.

"Me first, okay?" Jacie said.

Nina's stomach fluttered nervously. "Okay."

"Do you . . ." Inexplicably, Jacie found herself blushing. Nina had said she had her heart. But Jacie still wasn't sure there was a possibility for romantic love, after everything that had happened. A love that went beyond the ties of friendship, that while badly tattered, appeared to bind them still. *Oh, God.* "Do you like women?" she asked in a rush, suddenly feeling like an insecure sixteen-year-old who didn't know how to talk to a pretty girl.

Nina looked at her blankly.

"I mean, do you think you could have a romantic relationship with a woman?"

"Nina! Jacie!"

Both women's heads snapped sideways. It was Audrey's voice in the distance.

"Where are you two?" Katherine called out, as she walked alongside her cousin, her eyes scanning the B&B's large back lawn.

"Should we hide?" Nina asked earnestly. Their conversation was just getting to where she'd prayed it would go.

"Are you kidding?" Jacie responded in a hushed voice. "Those two have noses like bloodhounds. They'd find us soon enough."

The women stood up, each shifting from foot to foot, increasing the blood flow to their cold legs and bottoms.

"Did you just ask me if I was a lesbian?" Nina said quickly, hoping she understood the question correctly and that she'd get her answer to the question she asked Jacie before they were interrupted.

"Uh-huh. Sort of. But I need to do something before you answer." Jacie threaded her fingers into Nina's soft hair and quickly pressed their mouths together in a passionate display of affection. Each woman was instantly flooded with warm memories of their first kiss. Hot tongues collided and a low moan tore from Nina's throat as she was literally kissed senseless, the wave of raw want coursing through her veins as powerful as anything she'd ever experienced.

When the sound of footsteps and calling voices got too loud to ignore, Jacie pulled away and looked into Nina's dazed eyes. Then she gave Nina's lips another kiss, this time tender and whisper-soft, just because her mouth was so near and too inviting to resist.

"What . . ." Nina felt dizzy and she thought for a moment that her knees would give out. "What was that for?"

Jacie gave her a flash of white teeth in the moonlight and a hopeful, lopsided grin. "That was just in case you're still deciding about the whether or not you could like women thing." She shrugged sheepishly. "I'm willing to work to convince you." But the fact that Nina hadn't socked her in the nose was a pretty good sign.

Audrey rounded the corner of the wooded path and stopped abruptly when she nearly collided with Jacie, who was intently watching Nina. For her part, Nina's fingers were barely grazing her own lips in wonder.

"There you guys are." Audrey put her hands on her hips. Everyone had been looking for them for hours. "Where have you been?"

"Nina?" Jacie looked at her in question. Her heart felt like it was going to pound right out of her chest. Even her toes were crossed. "You didn't answer."

Her eyebrows lifting, Audrey's gaze traveled back and forth between Nina and Jacie. "What's going on? Jesus, we thought you both had skipped out on us. Gwen's breaking out champagne before dinner and you're going to miss it." She rocked back on her heels. "We've been talking and she's more like I remember her from before school. Not such a . . . well . . ."

"A bitch?" Katherine supplied grimly, still brooding over her discovery in Gwen's closet. She hadn't had any time away from Audrey to review the files yet and was afraid of what she might find.

"Yeah," Audrey agreed. "She seems more like one of us again. More like a lesser bitch."

Only vaguely aware that the cousins were speaking, Nina took a step closer to Jacie. She trailed her fingertips down Jacie's arm. "The answer is yes, Jace." Her voice had an impish, seductive quality that turned Jacie's knees to water. "But feel free to continue convincing me later tonight, if ya want."

Jacie landed back on the bench with a loud thump. She turned her face toward the heavens and let out a soft sigh that signaled a nearly dizzying level of relief. One that Nina instantly echoed.

Then Jacie suddenly shouted a jubilant, "Yes!"

"Wahh!" Katherine stumbled backward until she hit a tree. The action shook the tree and sent a shower of the cold water droplets down on her head. "What the hell was that?" she spluttered, her eyes scanning the woods for a bear or mountain lion or some other fanged creature. She shook her head like a wet dog, her spiky blond hair remaining utterly stiff throughout the vigorous movement.

"I—" Jacie let out a breath that was equal parts pure bliss and disbelief. She looked at Nina and grinned, her smile widening when it was instantly mirrored. "I'm just happy to be here with you guys."

"Aww," Audrey murmured. "We love you, too, Jacie. Now let's go drink Gwen's champagne."

They began slowly walking back toward Charlotte's Web.

Jacie wrapped one arm around Katherine's shoulders and the other around Nina's, the way she'd often done in the fourth grade when they were walking home from school. The motion was so natural she barely realized what had happened before it was done. "What have you been doing this evening?" she asked, her feet lightly splashing along the path.

"Nothing worth talking about." Audrey frowned as she recalled their ridiculous escape from Gwen's closet. Her frown, however, wavered when Nina grasped her hand, connecting them all together in a chain as they walked.

"To the Mayflower Club," Gwen said, lifting her champagne glass. The room was wreathed with nostalgic smiles, and the women drank a toast. Whatever happened later, the seemingly unbreakable bonds of their youth were still worth toasting today.

They'd decided to wait until after dinner to drink their champagne and now their bellies were full and they were lounging on chairs and loveseats in the beautifully furnished parlor. The fireplace crackled peacefully, casting the room in a golden glow and sending the light scent of hickory into the air. And Katherine had out the photo albums that she'd brought.

"Oh my God, Audrey," Nina laughed as she glanced at a photo, "I didn't remember you having big '80s hair."

"Look." Smiling, Gwen pointed at the picture, "You were awesome, Audrey, you had your collar up and a banana clip in your hair! Plastic shoes, too?"

"Pink ones."

"Very boss," Gwen commented sincerely, pouring herself another glass of bubbly. She was starting to feel its effects and she relaxed deeper into her chair, sinking into the soft leather. She was still no closer to catching her blackmailer. Over the course of the evening, she'd changed her mind about the most likely suspect three times, finally settling on Nina.

When Jacie had come back from her endless walk with Nina, Gwen knew that Nina had told her everything by the way Jacie's dark gaze bore a hole through her during dinner. Just thinking about the venom in that look still made her blood run cold. Jacie was clearly the angriest with her, but because of that, she wondered if Jacie wouldn't rather rub her nose in what she was doing rather than remaining anonymous. No, being deliberate and patient was more Nina's style than any of the others.

Audrey primped her curls, her voice pulling Gwen from her thoughts. "I borrowed that banana clip from you, Gwen. But I still rocked."

Katherine snickered. "Yeah, how could we have forgotten how like . . . how like totally tubular you were."

Katherine's Valley Girl accent, one none of them had ever really had as teenagers, caused Gwen and Jacie to burst out laughing.

"Be quiet, Katy," Audrey shot back. "At least I didn't have a tail."

Katherine gasped, her hand unconsciously moving to the back of her head. "That was a low blow, cuz."

"Katy might have had a tail," Jacie grimaced, remembering, "But you had the most bodacious ta tas of us all." She could hardly finish what she was saying before she was laughing, too.

Audrey's face turned crimson.

Jacie bumped shoulders with Audrey, trying hard to control her laughter. "They're to the max, Audrey," she chimed in, surprised at what a good time she was having. Speaking of having a good time, wasn't it time to kiss Nina again?

Audrey turned to Jacie with a wide smile on her face. "I can't wait to tell Ricky that a hot lesbian who used to be my roommate thinks my boobs are bodacious." She looked about ready to burst. "He'll love it!"

Nina and Jacie shared amused smiles. Then Nina cleared her throat. "Guys, I have something I want to tell you."

Jacie raised her eyebrows in question, and Nina answered by giving her a tiny nod. She wanted her friends to know.

Nina drew in a deep breath, a little surprised that she wasn't more nervous. She would love for them to be supportive and happy that she felt comfortable enough to share this part of herself with them. Her lips curled into a genuine smile. But if they weren't cool with it, life would go on. Damn, she was glad she wasn't eighteen anymore. "Jacie isn't the only lesbian in the room."

Katherine and Audrey shot to their feet and, at the same instant, pointed accusing fingers at each other. "I knew it!" they shouted in unison. "It's you!"

"Oh, God." Gwen just shook her head.

Nina rolled her eyes. "It's neither one of you."

But Audrey and Katherine continued giving each other a very skeptical once over, just to be sure.

Nina lifted her chin. "It's—"

"It's Gwen," Jacie inserted smoothly, leaning back in her love seat and raising her glass to toast the tall redhead. She blew her a kiss.

"I knew it!" both Audrey and Katherine shouted again, this time pointing directly at Gwen.

Gwen gasped so violently that she began to choke on her own saliva.

Jacie gave Gwen a slow, seductive wink. "Why don't you pull out your membership card and show Katy and Audrey? I know they'd like to see it."

"There's not really a membership card," Audrey said, trying to gauge Jacie's sincerity. Then she leaned over and whispered to Katherine, "Right?"

"How would I know?"

Once again they traded skeptical looks.

"Jacie!" Nina reprimanded, trying not to smile and sounding very much like the mom that she was. "Not nice."

Jacie grinned unrepentantly and happily ignored Gwen's glare.

"Gwen's not gay," Nina started, then paused and scratched her jaw. "At least I don't think so."

"Of course I'm not," Gwen wailed, throwing her hands in the air. "I'm married, for God's sake."

Both Jacie and Nina just shrugged, making it clear that they considered that a pitiful offering of proof.

"Anyway," Nina swallowed. "I'm the one who's a lesbian. There." She nodded a little and blew out a long breath. "Wow. That felt really good. Why I didn't say it that way to begin with, I'll never know," she said wryly, waggling her fingers at the cold champagne bottle, which Jacie lifted from her swollen cheek and discolored eye and dutifully passed her way.

"You are not!" Katherine blurted, smiling. "No way, I'm not buying that."

Audrey snorted. "What she said, Nina. No way."

Nina couldn't believe her ears. "I am, too!"

"Yeah," Katherine scoffed, rolling her eyes. "Right."

"I'm gay, guys."

Katherine gave Nina a direct look. "Whoa. You said that so seriously you had me going there for a minute. You are not."

"What do you mean, I'm not? I would know if I'm gay. And I'm gay. Way, way gay!" Nina insisted, stamping her foot in frustration.

Audrey and Katherine actually laughed.

Nina's eyes narrowed. Without warning, she sprang to her feet and stepped directly in front of Jacie. "Hi, Jacie."

Baffled as to what Nina was doing, Jacie dutifully replied, "Hi—" But before she could finish Nina gave her a sweet smile and straddled her lap. Everyone in the room heard Jacie's dry swallow. "Wha-What are you doing?"

Nina ignored the question and raised her hands to tenderly run them through Jacie's hair. "So soft," she murmured to herself. Then she smiled warmly at her friend. "May I kiss you?"

Audrey and Katherine's jaws hit the floor while Gwen silently cheered.

Nina's thighs were tightly bracketing Jacie's and Jacie could feel the warmth of Nina's body through the denim that covered their legs. Automatically, she raised her hands and let them rest on Nina's hips. "You . . . um . . . you want to kiss me?" Her voice cracked a little at the end.

"Very much so," Nina said softly. She buried her hands further into Jacie's hair and let her fingers lightly scratch Jacie's scalp, her belly clenching with desire as she looked deeply into her friend's earnest, rapidly darkening eyes.

Jacie licked her lips, her gaze momentarily darting sideways to her friends, who looked like two deer waiting to be smashed by an oncoming truck. "For them?"

Nina thought about the question carefully. She'd started this to prove a point, trusting that Jacie wouldn't mind. But now . . . of its own accord, one hand left Jacie's hair and traveled lightly down the delicate soft skin of her throat, feeling Jacie's thundering heartbeat. Then her fingers moved again, dancing across Jacie's collarbone. She let herself feel the nearness of her friend and the heat of her body, and she moaned softly. She allowed the scent of Jacie's skin and perfume to sink into her blood and overwhelm her senses, willingly losing herself in the loving brown eyes that were riveted on her own. And in the tiny space between that heartbeat and next, the answer became crystal clear. "For me."

Jacie gave her a dazzling grin and leaned forward just a hair. But it was all the invitation that Nina needed. They wrapped their arms tightly around one another and when their lips and tongues came together in an explosion of affection and unconcealed hunger, the glass dropped from Katherine's suddenly limp hand.

With their mouths still hanging open at the sensual display, the cousins looked at each other as if to say "duh!"

Gwen closed her eyes, saying a small prayer to whoever might be listening. As far as she was concerned, second chances were rarer than miracles and more precious than diamonds. And she hoped with her entire heart that these four women would give her one of her own.

By nine-thirty that evening, the effects of the champagne had Audrey's head spinning and Gwen fighting to avoid an all out bout of depression. She'd gone upstairs and made the mistake of checking her e-mail for messages from Malcolm. Instead, she'd found another blackmail demand. Now, she sat alone, facing the fire, running the words over and over in her head.

The newest demand was more urgent and nastier than the others. And for the first time, her blackmailer had given her a firm deadline. Before it was always just soon or something equally vague. And she'd always complied. And now, as if to cap off her failure thus far this weekend, she suddenly had only until Monday to produce the cash or be exposed.

Only twenty years of etiquette learned at the knee of the most demanding mother-in-law on the planet kept her from swilling her drink directly from the bottle.

Katherine and Jacie were playing a rousing game of cards on the coffee table, laughing and arguing over their favorite sports team. Katherine's cell phone rang in the middle of a sentence, and she shot Jacie an apologetic smile. Absently, she dug through her handbag, sitting on the floor at her feet, and answered the phone without bothering to look at who was calling. "Hello."

Katherine felt the blood drain from her face. She winced inwardly, aware that Jacie and even Gwen had noticed her reaction to the call. "Hi," she said tightly, easing out of her seat and excusing herself from the room, very aware of Jacie's concerned eyes on her back.

"What are you doing?" she ground out as soon as she rounded the corner and stepped into the hall. "We agreed that I would call you when I was alone tonight."

Her features softened as she listened to the voice on the other end of the phone. "Yes, of course I missed you." A small smile appeared. "I love you, too." She leaned against the wall, making sure that her voice was low. "This is going to be the first weekend we haven't spent together in months." Her cheeks turned pink at her lover's racy comment. "Ooo . . . I like the sound of that. Okay, well—of course not!" she screeched, clamping her hand over her mouth when she realized what she'd done. "Of course I haven't told her," she repeated, this time more softly. "I promised that I wouldn't. Though I have to tell you, I feel shitty about it." She sighed. "Something is up with her. I think she knows what's going on."

Katherine closed her eyes guiltily, thinking of Gwen as she listened. "Relax, I'll keep my promise," she finally said. "But when I get back we're going to talk about this. I was wrong. I can't keep doing this. Things have gone too far." She rubbed her temples as her boyfriend tried to convince her otherwise. "Bullshit," she broke in angrily. "I shouldn't have agreed to this in the first place. You said that she deserved it and that nobody would get hurt, but being here with her today has shown me that that's not true. Christ, I feel like pond scum!"

Just then, Katherine looked up to see Jacie standing uneasily at the end of the short hallway. She swallowed hard as her friend cocked her head to the side and regarded her with a mixture of curiosity and worry. "Uh . . . are you okay?" Jacie mouthed silently.

Katherine nodded quickly before turning her back on her friend. "Call me later tonight, okay? And I'll tell you about my visit so far." A pause. "I love you, too."

Jacie could hear the smile in her words.

"Bye." Katherine squared her shoulders and turned back, pressing the off button on her cell phone. She tried not to look as ashamed as she felt. For few seconds, she didn't say anything, unsure of what the other woman had heard. "Jacie—"

Reddish-brown eyebrows lifted in question. "Yeah."

Katherine's words came out in a tumble. "Everything is fine. It's just one of those relationship issues." She shrugged. "You know how it is. No big deal."

Jacie looked visibly relieved. Katherine having man troubles was nothing new. "Men are pigs?" she offered gamely, hoping to lighten the awkward moment.

A bubble of laughter erupted from Katherine. Tentatively, she smiled and stepped closer to Jacie. "Normally, I'd agree with you. But this guy's special, so he's worth the trouble." She let out a slightly shaky breath. Jacie hadn't heard enough to know what was going on. *Thank God.*

Katherine scrambled for something neutral to talk about. "So tell me what's up with you and Nina?"

Even though she was filled with hope for the future, things still felt too raw between her and Nina to even consider discussing it. At least this soon. "No."

Katherine took the refusal in stride, expecting nothing less from Jacie than blunt honesty. "So, tell me more about your business then?"

The lame change of subjects was painfully obvious, but Jacie let it pass, deciding that whatever Katherine was dealing with wasn't really any of her business anyway. "Are you sure you want to hear about small business entrepreneurship and the exciting world of tiling?"

Katherine smiled wryly. "Of course not. But since that's the world you live in, I'm willing to give it a try. Just lie to make it more interesting if you have to. I'm not getting any younger, ya know."

Jacie chuckled. "You're on."

Back in the parlor, Nina and Audrey were discussing Nina's recent move back to St. Louis, while Gwen was staring into the fireplace, not even trying to join in the discussion.

Nina leaned closer to Audrey and whispered, "What's wrong with her?"

Audrey shook her head. "I have no idea. She was fine until she went up to her room a little while ago."

"Hm." Nina's brow furrowed, and she dropped her voice even lower. "What happened between you two back in school? There must have been something because you were always trying to get us to patch things up, even after what she did to Jacie. I always figured that you two would be the only ones of us to work things out eventually."

Audrey took a slow sip of her drink, feeling the tingle of alcohol all the way down to her toes. She opened her mouth to tell Nina what happened, but stopped when she again caught sight of Gwen's gloomy profile. For the first time in years, all she felt when she saw or even thought of Gwen was pity and loss. "It was nothing, Nina," she brushed off, not wanting to give Nina another reason to resent their host. "We just lost touch."

"Tell her." Gwen's unexpected voice startled them. She turned in her chair, flung her legs over one arm, said a mental "fuck you" to her mother-in-law and took a swig right from the bottle. "Go on, Audrey. Nina knows my worst. Why not talk about another one of my sins?" She hiccupped. "I have a *heaping* pile of them, you know." Getting Audrey to talk about the past might get her to give herself away as the blackmailer.

Audrey shifted uncomfortably. "Gwen, I don't—"

"Fine," Gwen said easily, brushing off Audrey's reservations with a wave of her hand. "I'll tell her."

Jacie and Katherine entered the room just as Gwen began.

"It was 1985, right?" Gwen glanced at Audrey, who nodded, an unhappy expression on her face. "Right."

"What's going on?" Jacie whispered as she sat down next to Nina.

Craving the physical contact, Nina laid her hand on Jacie's leg and gave it a gentle squeeze. "I think Gwen's a little drunk and she's going to tell us what happened between her and Audrey."

"Gwen screwed with somebody else?"

"I dunno." She squeezed Jacie's leg affectionately. "Shh."

Gwen filled her glass several fingers high and drained it. She lifted her chin and her voice held just a hint of a slur. "There was a new show opening at the Blagbrough Galleries downtown. Malcolm's parents drove us over because anyone who was anyone was going to be there. They wanted to show off Malcolm, who was graduating that year. I remember wishing

I could just stay home and sleep that evening. Tucker had an ear infection and had been awake for two days straight." Despite telling what was obviously going to be an unhappy tale, she smiled a little at the mention of her son's name. "And I was dead tired. But my father-in-law insisted that we attend because he knew the gallery owner." She sneered a little, her resentment showing. "So that was the end of the discussion."

"Malcolm never stood up to his parents?" Katherine asked, keenly interested in what Gwen was saying.

"Oh, he did," Gwen assured her. "We both did. But that would take years and years. In the beginning . . . well, we were both so young and we wanted to show his family that our marriage wasn't a mistake, despite the hurried circumstances." She gazed enviously at her friends. "Neither Malcolm nor I were ever the rebels that you girls were, and more than anything I wanted to fit in." She lowered her gaze. "No matter the cost."

Smelling like dish soap, Frances Artiste entered the room with her apron draped over her shoulder. She breathed a sigh of relief. No one was arguing. "Can I get you ladies anything?"

"Is there more of this in the refrigerator?" Gwen held up an empty bottle of champagne.

Dumbly, Frances nodded and made a mental note to head to the liquor store in the morning.

Mollified, Gwen nodded. "Please, Mrs. Artiste, call it a night. We're all fine here, right?" She glanced questioningly at the other women.

"Fine," Nina agreed. "Have a good night."

"Dinner was great," Jacie chimed in. "Thanks."

The other women murmured their agreement.

"Where was I?" Gwen began, letting one leg fall limply off the chair.

Frances took this chance to flee the room.

"You were nowhere, Gwen." Audrey suddenly stood and faced the fire, the flickering light reflecting off glassy, honey-brown eyes. "Except drunk." She felt a little tipsy herself and was angry that Gwen's story was affecting her so. "Can't we find something better to talk about? The past is dead. Let's leave it buried."

Gwen blinked with exaggerated slowness. "The past always comes home to roost," she said seriously, looking hard at Audrey. "It's not dead at all. It's alive and it's an octopus with slimy, slithering tentacles that go on forever. And one day"—Gwen put her hands around her own throat—"when you're going along happy as can be, one of those putrid tentacles sneaks up on you from behind and wraps around your throat and . . ." She began to squeeze her neck, causing her face to turn bright red.

"Holy shit," Jacie exclaimed, giving Gwen a look that screamed "keep the hell away from me." Shaking her head, she added, "You are one creepy-ass drunk."

But Gwen took the comment in stride. "I'm just heading this off at the pass in case any of you get any bright ideas and try to bleed me dry."

"What are you talking about?" Katherine made a face. "You're making no sense. Bleed you dry?"

"Nuh-huh," Gwen said in a singsong voice. She shook her head wildly and then shook a chastising finger at Katherine. "I'm not telling yet."

Nina and Jacie looked at each other in confusions.

Then Gwen snapped her fingers. "Oh, yes, we were at the Blagbrough Galleries. I'd barely gotten inside when I spotted Audrey. She must have just arrived because she still had her coat thrown over her arm." Gwen recalled the moment their gazes met, the warmth that entered Audrey's eyes upon seeing her and the overwhelming sense of anxiety that she felt when she came face-to-face with her not so distant past. A past she was supposed to have thoroughly outgrown.

Gwen laughed, but there was no humor in the gesture. "It all seems simple now, what I should have done. I was happy to see Audrey. My first reaction was to give her a big hug. But my second reaction, the overpowering one, was to panic. Here was someone who knew all my secrets. Who knew the real me. Not the me I spent my days pretending to be."

She stopped speaking for a moment, seemingly lost in her memories. Just when the other women were about to say something, she started again. "Audrey hurried over to me, all smiles and excitement. And she started asking me how I was doing and all about the baby and if I was taking classes again." With a steadying breath, Gwen lifted her eyes from the bottom of her glass to met Audrey's intent stare. "And then I promptly acted as though I didn't know you at all. I even tried to walk away from you while you were still talking to me."

For a few seconds the room was still, the silence broken only by the sounds of five women breathing and the occasional pop and hiss of the fire.

Audrey looked away, feeling a stab of pain and remembering the bewilderment and anger she'd felt at Gwen's snubbing.

"Jesus, Gwen," Nina moaned, her heart going out to Audrey.

"But Malcolm, who didn't need to earn his place in the family the way I did, remembered Audrey and used her name when saying hello," Gwen continued. "He didn't understand the way I was acting or how I could forget a friend, and so I changed my story on the spot and told my in-laws that Audrey was an acquaintance from school."

Jacie's lips twisted. "An acquaintance?"

"It was the level of contact I thought my mother-in-law would find acceptable, and by this time the gallery owner and the artist himself had all joined us. I felt like I was in a pressure cooker." Gwen rubbed her temples with an irritated hand and forced herself onward. "Audrey was wearing a red vest and black slacks and Malcolm's mother looked down her nose at her and gave her our drink order, thinking she was one of the waitresses." She bit her lip for a second before admitting in a soft voice, "I was horrified, but I didn't have the nerve to correct her."

The women shot Gwen varying degrees of disgusted looks, and Katherine leaned forward in her seat, seething inside over her cousin's humiliation.

Gwen wished she could stop here, but that night things had simply gone from bad to hell with no stops in between. "Then Vice Principal Rodriguez showed up and—"

"For God's sake, Gwen," Audrey snapped. "I wish you all would stop calling him that. We're all adults now. Not to mention that I've been sleeping with the man for nearly twenty years. His name is Enrique."

"Okay, okay," Gwen replied, concerned and a little wide-eyed over Audrey's outburst over something so seemingly benign. "Enrique started making doe eyes at Audrey and I just about wet my pants on the spot. I didn't know they were . . ." She gestured aimlessly. "Together. Then he gave her a little bow and gallantly took her coat." This time even Gwen winced. "And Malcolm's father promptly gathered all our coats and handed them to Enrique," she glanced sideways at Audrey, "along with a five dollar tip."

Nina lifted an eyebrow and sneered. "Let me guess the rest of story. You didn't speak up then either. And you blew off Audrey for the rest of the night to suck up to your in-laws."

Gwen just studied her hands.

"Enrique was angry, but didn't want to cause a scene," Audrey inserted, causing all eyes to shift to her. "We hadn't been dating long and he was there to keep me company while I did a write-up on the show for the school newspaper." She closed her eyes. "As we were walking away, I heard Mrs. Langtree ask Gwen if the Mexican was the same sort of acquaintance that that chubby girl was."

Gwen's head snapped up, and for a second, the room swam. "I didn't know you heard that."

Audrey cursed the tears that were pooling behind tightly shut lids. "I heard. And so did Enrique." Then, to everyone's surprise, she let out a snort of laughter. "He threw all your coats out into the street."

Katy grinned. "Good for Vice Princ—" Audrey's look of warning stopped her dead in her tracks. "Good for him."

"Mm." Gwen quirked a tiny smile. "I always wondered what happened to them. We all froze on the way home."

Audrey moved back to the love seat and Jacie and Nina quickly made a space between them so she could fit in. "Why were you so ashamed of me, Gwen?" she asked, residual hurt still coloring her voice. "I would never have done something to embarrass you. I knew how the Langtrees' opinions mattered to you."

Gwen swallowed hard and pushed her way onto unsteady feet. "You still don't see?" She set down her glass and headed toward the stairway. At the base of the steps she turned back. "I was never ashamed of you. Of any of you. I loved you all then and I always will."

Gwen felt like crying, but the tears wouldn't come. "I was ashamed of me."

The women watched her make her way up the stairs. When she was out of sight, they couldn't help but let out a collective sigh. Gwen was radiating stress and every one of the Mayflower Club felt it as though it were her own.

"Are you okay, Audrey?" Jacie asked quietly.

Audrey smiled weakly. "I wasn't back then, ya know?" She paused. "But twenty years is a big buffer." She gave her head a light shake. "What the hell do you suppose is going on with Gwen? Sometimes she seems okay and other times she's acting so weird. Nobody made her go into all that ancient history." But despite her words, she felt a little better for having aired that old hurt and gotten an explanation, if not quite an apology for it.

Katherine was reminded that she hadn't had the opportunity to take a closer look at the papers she'd stolen from Gwen's bag. She frowned. That needed to change.

Nina's gaze strayed back to the stairs. "I wish I knew."

Jacie leaned over and patted Nina's thigh. "This day has been long enough for me. C'mon." She offered her friend a hand up then did the same for Audrey. Katherine was already walking toward the steps.

"Night, guys," Katherine said absently, already plotting what she had to do next.

"Night," came the murmured replies.

The last woman at the top of steps turned off the light.

"Oh, God." Gwen lay on her back in the dark with one arm thrown over tightly closed eyes. Her stomach was churning with a combination of alcohol and unrelenting stress, and she was giving even odds on whether she'd lose the contents of her stomach or continue to lie there in misery. Hard as she tried to hold them back, the tears that started when she confessed her shabby treatment of Audrey to the other women, continued to fall.

Raw from baring a small part of her soul, she murmured, "What a fool I am! There's one you can't trust. Be careful." She sniffed. "Don't forget." Courting old friends, all the while being suspicious of them, was proving a more difficult task than she'd anticipated. As hard as it made things, she loved each and every one of them. She couldn't help it. And being together again only made that feeling stronger. In all their years apart from the Mayflower Club, she'd never been able to recreate with other women the love and unconditional support that these friends had given her so freely.

She rolled over onto her stomach and swallowed hard. This emotional roller-coaster was an E-ticket ride and it wasn't over yet, and she wondered fleetingly what it was going to cost her to hang on until the end.

Jacie reached out and curled her hand around Nina's. They were lying in their room's only bed, each facing the other, a thin sheet pulled up to waist level. A gentle rain tapped against the window's glass and the occasional flash of lightning briefly lit the room in an ethereal shade of blue.

Nina was wearing an ancient, soft cotton St. Louis Cardinals jersey and a pair of white bikini panties. Jacie had turned her back to allow her friend a moment of privacy while she changed into her pajamas. She was even a little proud of herself for not peeking. But when she turned around and saw Nina, her hair tussled from undressing, smooth legs sticking out from high-cut panties, it took every ounce of Jacie's willpower not to pounce on her and ravage her on the spot. Repeatedly.

Jacie raised herself up onto one elbow and rested her head in her hand. "Do you think Gwen did this on purpose?" Her voice was quiet, and Nina barely heard it above the rain. "The one bed thing?"

Nina fingered the sheets. They were baby-soft and held the fresh, clean scent of detergent. "Maybe. She seems pretty sorry about everything that happened. And I noticed that Audrey and Katy had their own beds. Maybe she's just trying to make up for things." She glanced up at Jacie. "Are you mad about it?"

Jacie grinned. She brushed the back of Nina's hand with her thumb. "Do I seem mad?"

Nina grinned back, her eyes roaming over Jacie's body, which was clad only in a tank top and shorts. "No," she said softly. "What you seem is sexy as hell."

Jacie's smile grew. "Look who's talking?" She flopped onto her back and regarded the ceiling, but didn't let go of Nina's hand. "That kiss tonight, Nina," she let out a breathy sigh and closed her eyes, reliving the moment, "I still haven't recovered!"

Nina fanned herself. "Me neither."

"This is nice." Jacie raised Nina's hand to her lips and gently kissed it. "Just being together."

"It is," Nina agreed wholeheartedly. "I've wanted it for so long and now it's actually happening . . ." She shook her head a little. "It still feels a little like a dream."

"You know how some things aren't as good as you remember them? Or how sometimes over time you build them up in your mind to be better than they were in real life?"

Nina's heart lurched, suddenly fearing that Jacie was going to say that's how she felt about seeing her again. "Yeah?"

"This is nothing like that." The excitement in her voice was obvious. "I can't even explain how wonderful I feel."

Nina laughed softly in relief. "I feel the same way."

Jacie turned her head to look at her friend. She had a million questions, but one had been weighing on her mind even before she saw Nina again. "Tell me about Robbie and . . ." she paused, knowing she was about to poke her nose into something Nina might not want to discuss. "Well, I guess," Nina lifted her eyebrows in question and Jacie promptly chickened out. "Tell me about him."

Nina squeezed their joined hands. "And his father?"

Jacie winced. "It's not my business, I know, but—"

"Shh," Nina soothed. "I want you in my business, Jacie. So it's okay."

Jacie relaxed a little.

"You met Robbie, so you probably saw that he's a handful." She chuckled. "Actually, he reminds me so much of you, Jace. He's brave and a little crazy and an irrepressible dreamer."

Jacie let go of Nina's hand and lifted her arm. She held her breath, hoping Nina would accept the unspoken invitation. *I want to be closer to you.*

She needn't have worried. Nina snuggled tightly to Jacie and curled a possessive arm around her chest, never wanting to let go. She let out a deep breath. "I met Robbie's father in Hawaii about ten years ago."

"Why were you in Hawaii?"

"I had just ended a two-year relationship with Carol, a woman who I worked with at the Detroit Historical Museum. I'd tried so hard to make things work and was sure that this time I'd found someone I could settle down with permanently. But . . ." She hesitated as she mulled over the right words. "But she wasn't a 'permanent' sort of a woman, I guess. One day she told me that she wanted us to see other people. We were living together by then."

"She's a moron."

Nina chuckled softly, her breath warming Jacie's skin. "I held my ground and said no. Monogamy is important to me. And she left me the next morning."

"Make that a moronic bitch."

Nina's chuckle turned into an outright laugh. "Always sticking up for me, eh?"

Jacie let out a soft grunt of agreement. "Through thick and thin, Nina."

"Anyway, I sulked around Detroit for about six months after that, not doing much more than feeling sorry for myself, and one day, while I was walking downtown, I passed a travel agency. In the window was a beautiful photograph of a waterfall not far from Kaneohe Bay on Oahu. I needed . . . something. And so I took some of the vacation I had saved up and flew to Hawaii the next week."

Nina slipped her hand beneath Jacie's tank top, feeling Jacie's ribs expand sharply when she began to gently stroke her belly. "I took a hike to the waterfall I'd seen in the photo, and at the falls I met another hiker named Tim. He was recently divorced and he was in Hawaii trying to make a new start for himself. Just like me."

"And you fell in love with him?" A tiny sting of jealousy accompanied Jacie's words, fading only with the gentle reminder that Nina was in her arms right now.

Nina resituated herself so that she was mostly on top of Jacie and could look her in the eye. The position was so intimate the women were breathing the same air. "No," she whispered seriously. "It wasn't like that at all. We each needed something from the other, and we didn't do anything to put the brakes on the attraction we felt. I was still questioning my sexuality. I found men physically attractive but never really thought of making a life with one. The pull that a woman has on me . . ." She dipped her head quickly and brushed her lips against Jacie's. "Well, nothing about my time with Tim changed that."

"He was interesting and funny and made me feel wanted. And I helped him forget about his ex-wife, if only for a little while. We danced till dawn, drank pina coladas, made love on the beach, and only lived for the moment. And when our vacations were over, we kissed each other on the cheek and said goodbye. Tim went home to Pennsylvania, I think, to try to reconcile with his ex. I went home to Detroit with a tan . . . and pregnant with Robbie."

"Wow." Concern shown in Jacie's eyes. "Were you okay?"

Nina nodded. "I really was. It was a little scary, knowing I'd have to parent all on my own. But I'd always wanted a child, and even though it would have been easier to do with someone I loved, I wouldn't take back what happened even if I could. I love Robbie with everything that I am."

Jacie reached up and played with a lock of Nina's hair, the silken strands falling around her fingers. "Does Tim know about Robbie?"

"We didn't even tell each other our last names, Jacie. We were living some sort of island fantasy and there was no place in that for real life. So no, Tim with the pretty brown eyes, who I hope dearly is happy at home with his wife somewhere tonight, has no idea. I wouldn't know how to find him even if I wanted to."

Jacie leaned up and bussed Nina's chin. "Thank you for sharing that with me."

"Will you tell me about Emily?"

"She's beautiful and smart and nothing like me."

"From your description of her so far, I can see that."

"Ha. Ha." Jacie tickled Nina's ribs, enjoying the feeling of the other woman shaking with laughter. "That's not what I meant. She loves to read and is mature for her age, something I never was. She's a great kid and I can't wait for you to meet her."

Nina felt a thrill as Jacie's words skittered down her spine.

Jacie settled into her pillow as Nina retook her spot on her shoulder. The words were far easier than Jacie thought they'd be. "I met Emily's mother, Alison, about ten years ago. Things were good between us. Then they were bad. Then they were good. A damn yo-yo had fewer ups and downs than our relationship did."

Nina hugged her and Jacie greedily absorbed the warmth and caring, allowing it to act as a buffer between her heart and old wounds. "She wanted children and I didn't. And she was angry with me all the time because of it. Finally, I let her convince me that my hesitancy with regard to starting a family was the real dilemma in our relationship and that if I'd just get over whatever my problem was, things would be wonderful between us."

Inwardly, Nina cringed.

"I was so tired of the fighting and even though I felt like I was jumping off a cliff, I . . . I guess I just wanted to be happy for once. So I gave in. We used a sperm bank and a few tries later Alison got pregnant. I don't know what the hell I was thinking, Nina. Things were always so volatile between us. Having a baby only made our relationship problems worse. The bad times started overwhelming the good. And then the good times pretty much disappeared. But Emily"—her voice held a note of true awe—"she was so tiny and so perfect. It didn't seem to matter to my heart that Alison was the one who actually gave birth to her. I fell in love with her the moment I saw her, and she was my daughter. Thank God, we did a second-parent adoption right after she was born."

The rain intensified and a far-off clap of thunder punctuated Jacie's words.

"I knew you'd be a wonderful mother someday, Jacie."

Jacie gave her a playful pinch. "I used to pull the heads off your Barbies."

"But you always taped them back on," Nina reminded. "You have so much love to give . . . I always thought you'd be great with kids."

Jacie snorted softly. "You were the only one then. I did my best to stay with Alison, but in the end, the fighting got to be too much for me. But true to form, we weren't finished fighting. We ended up in court duking it out over custody." She swallowed thickly. "That bitch Alison told the judge that I never wanted Emily to be born. And my daughter was sitting right next to her when she said it."

Nina closed her eyes. "God, Jacie."

Jacie had to clear her throat to speak. "Yeah. Anyway, we ended up with joint custody, but Alison seems hell bent on making that arrangement as painful as possible. If you want any relationship with me, Nina, you have to know that she's going to make trouble. She hates me and—"

"Honey, you can stop worrying about that right now. Nobody can come between us unless we let them." She tightened her grip on Jacie. "Just let her try," she warned darkly.

Jacie buried her face in Nina's hair. "I've been falling in love with you every five minutes since I saw you again. You know that, right?"

Nina sniffed, her heart near bursting. "I love you, too."

"Nina?"

"Yeah?"

"Why are your feet always so cold?"

Nina burst out laughing, glad when the intensity of their conversation took a sharp turn downward.

Jacie suddenly rolled them over and gently pinned Nina to the bed. She knew there would be time for more heart-to-heart talks later. But for now, she wanted to revel in being so near to someone who could make her heart beat double-time with little more than a smile in her direction. "You should wear socks!"

Nina intentionally rubbed her feet up and down Jacie's calves, causing her to howl. "You should kiss me, woman!"

Jacie stopped all movement and looked down into Nina's eyes. "I should?"

"Oh, yeah," Nina breathed. "All night long."

"But I was going to get up and wash my hair. And do my nails. And . . . um . . . read. Yeah, that's it. Read a good book," Jacie teased, delighting at the evil glint that invaded Nina's eyes.

Nina raised a slender eyebrow. "The offer will only be good for the next fifty years, Jacie Ann."

Jacie's eyes widened. "Forget my nails." She began kissing Nina. "I need to make up for lost time," she muttered against soft lips.

An hour later, after more kissing than any woman should be able to stand, and not spontaneously combust, Jacie and Nina were on their backs, panting softly. A thin sheen of perspiration coated Jacie's skin and Nina had her arm thrown over her eyes. Their emotions had been running high to start, and that only served to add fuel to flames that wanted to burst out of control.

"I can't take it anymore," Nina moaned unevenly. "I'm about to self-destruct from needing you." Then she gathered her courage and spoke her heart's desire. "I want to make love to you. I don't want to wait until we have a bunch of dates. I don't want to wait until we're more secure in our relationship. I want my mouth all over you. Now."

Jacie whimpered. Loudly. "You don't think I'm turned on?" she countered raggedly. "I can't just kiss you all night long and still live."

"Good." Nina rolled half onto Jacie and ran her hands up under Jacie's tank top.

"Nina!" Reluctantly, Jacie captured Nina's hands. "Nina."

"What?" Nina chuckled ruefully at her own lack of control as she hung her head and whimpered.

"I want to do this right. I don't want to screw things up by moving too fast. I've had twenty years to dream about this and I don't want to risk blowing it."

"Since when are you the logical one?"

"Since I had a second shot at the love of my life."

And that caused Nina to collapse right where she was. "But what if I get hit by a bus tomorrow? Life is short. Things happen."

"Don't even joke about dying." Jacie pulled her even closer, trying not to feel Nina's hardened nipples pressing into her own. She bit her lip in a bid for control herself, but couldn't stop her hips from moving forward and seeking firmer contact with Nina's thigh.

Nina's eyes popped wide opened. "Make up your mind!" She scrambled away from Jacie as though she were on fire, then spoke from her side of the bed. "You're trying to drive me insane."

"I can't help it," Jacie complained weakly. Then her voice dropped to its deepest register, the tone and words causing Nina to visibly shiver. "I want you so badly."

"That was just mean." Nina blew out a frustrated breath. "I'm throbbing."

Jacie covered her ears with both hands. "Don't say things like that. I'm so wet I'm about ready to slide off the bed."

Nina's mouth began to water, and she scooted part way back to Jacie. "I could help you with that," she teased seductively.

Jacie's eyes flashed with warning. "I know you could," she gritted out. Then without even realizing what she was doing, her hand slid into her own shorts. And she hissed, her face a picture of both pleasure and exquisite pain when her cool fingers grazed her aching clit.

A flash of lightning illuminated the room and Nina's heart stopped beating. She was shocked that she hadn't simply come on the spot. "What—" She licked her lips. "What are you doing?"

Jacie realized where her hand was and she froze. "Nothing," she lied.

"No, no, no. That's not nothing. You're touching yourself."

Mortally embarrassed, Jacie nodded.

"Right in front of me?"

Another nod.

Nina closed her eyes and swallowed hard. "Sweet Jesus." Lightning flashed and when she opened her eyes again, Jacie could see the fire in them. "Don't stop."

Jacie's hands were trembling. "Really?"

Nina's voice was husky with desire. "Tell me that over the years you haven't thought of what it would be like to see me touching myself."

Jacie's nostrils flared, and the hand in her shorts began to move. "I can't tell you that, Nina," she admitted tightly, a flush working up her chest and neck. "I've thought of it a thousand times."

Nina let out a shaky breath, her arousal close to peaking. Carefully, the way she would approach a spooked colt, she moved closer to Jacie, not stopping until she was lying alongside her, her lips pressed close to Jacie's ear. "And when you thought of me touching myself, what were you doing?"

Jacie could only moan, her free hand clutching the sheets, her other hand working furiously.

"Were you touching yourself, too?"

"Yes," Jacie hissed, drawing out the word as she arched her back.

Nina sucked Jacie's earlobe into her mouth, laving it with a warm tongue.

"Oh, God," Jacie moaned, her eyes slamming shut.

Nina's mouth moved down from Jacie's ear to the tender skin of her throat. She had to nearly sit on her hands to keep from caressing Jacie's breast, but she was powerless to resist the salty skin in her mouth. She sucked hard on Jacie's neck, using her teeth for good measure, her own moisture trickling down her thigh when Jacie bucked one final time and convulsions overtook her.

Unable to stop herself, Nina wrapped an arm around Jacie and murmured things she'd always wanted to say to her in her ear as she climaxed, ending with a heartfelt, "I love you." The way Jacie was panting, she expected her to need a few moments to recover. Instead, she let out a small yelp when Jacie quickly switched their positions and hovered over her with a predatory look in her eyes.

"Nina," she purred. "You are very, very bad." A drop of perspiration snaked down Jacie's cheek and landed on Nina's neck, branding her.

"I'm sorry?" Nina whispered impishly, feeling anything but contrite.

Jacie smiled a beautiful smile. "I'm not." Then her expression went serious. "But don't think we're through here tonight." She took one of Nina's hands and slid two fingers into her own hot mouth, lavishly wetting them, and causing a tortured moan to be torn from Nina's chest. Then she guided the fingers down Nina's belly and in the direction of soft white panties. "Get to work."

It was well after midnight and Audrey was tucked into her bed, the night's champagne causing her to snore like a chain saw. Katherine sat in a rocking chair on the far side of the room, her cell phone clutched tightly in her hand. In her other hand were the papers that she'd taken from Gwen's suitcase. She was afraid to look at them.

Slumping heavily in the comfortable chair, she was nearly asleep when the phone finally began buzzing in her hand. Startled, she jerked upright and fumbled to answer it. Before she could say a word, a soft baritone voice greeted her.

"Hi."

"Hi," she whispered, relieved to hear the familiar voice.

"I can barely hear you. Can't you talk?"

Worriedly, she looked toward Audrey, who had suspiciously turned over in bed and stopped snoring. "I can talk. Just not here. Hang on." Tiptoeing across the room, she eased open the door and slipped silently into the hall. She heard the sound of muted laughter coming from Nina and Jacie's room and, not convinced that she was safe yet, she headed downstairs and out onto the built-in back porch that was located off the kitchen.

The wooden floor was cool against her bare feet and she shivered a little as she walked.

"So," she whispered as she took a seat on a padded lounge chair, "do you miss me?" It was fairly dark, but frequent flashes of lightning illuminated the room enough to see what was contained on the pages.

He let out a low groan. "I feel like I'm dying. I'm counting the minutes until you come home."

She sighed dreamily, well aware of how cheesy his words were but unable to stop herself.

"I'm sorry we argued earlier," he said.

Katherine steeled herself for what she might find, and began sifting through the papers, her cell phone cradled to her ear. "Me too. I hate it when we argue."

A sigh. "Yeah. Luckily it doesn't happen very often."

She squinted and read a chart that detailed her banking activity for the last year. The next page revealed her credit card transactions, her credit rating, and a text summary where she caught the words "poor risk." "Shit," she hissed.

"Honey?"

"Oh, umm . . ." she searched for something to say. "I stubbed my toe."

"Ouch. That hurts. Be careful, okay?"

She smiled despite the fact that what she was reading was pissing her off more with every page. "I will." When she flipped to the next page, she stopped cold. Katherine blinked a few times, and waited for another flash of light to be sure she'd read it right.

"Hey, are you watching television or something?" The voice held a note of impatience.

She winced, realizing she'd been silent for several seconds. "No, no TV. Hey . . ." she considered everything that Gwen had revealed earlier that night as well as what she'd just read. "What you said earlier about my not saying anything about what we've been doing. Well, I think you're right. At least for now."

"It's all for the best, you'll see, sweetheart." His relief was palpable, even over the phone.

Once again, Katherine pushed aside the guilt that was getting harder and harder to ignore. Trying not to picture the other women's faces if they found out, she did her best to focus on their future. "I hope you're right."

"I am," he said confidently. "I'm only doing this for us." There was only a second's pause before he added, "I really love you."

Katherine could hear the smile in his words and her face instantly mirrored the emotion. "I love you, too, Tucker."

Chapter 10
Present Day
Rural Missouri

It was mid-afternoon Saturday and the rain was still falling, a faint staccato against the roof of the bed & breakfast. The morning meal and lunch had come and gone and the women had made a round of phone calls, each eager to check on things on the home front.

Gwen felt as if a monster truck rally was going on between her ears. While she was long accustomed to imbibing, she usually didn't finish an entire bottle of champagne herself and was still feeling the effects of this morning's killer hangover. She came down the stairs and stepped into the parlor, three aspirin tucked into the palm of her hand. It would be nearly impossible to feel worse. Even a short nap hadn't helped. Then she thought about what she had to do today . . . and reconsidered her conclusion.

She looked around for Katherine and Audrey, but they were nowhere to be seen. She glumly wondered if they had packed up and snuck out after lunch.

"Hey." Jacie, who was sipping a cup of coffee and reading the morning paper on a sofa near the window, looked up from her task. Her hair was still a little damp from a long walk Nina had talked her into despite the light rain. "You feel like you're going to die, don't you?"

Gwen's eyes narrowed. "That would be an overly optimistic diagnosis," she answered warily, not really in the mood to be told that she deserved it, even though she knew she did.

"I've got some painkillers in my bag if you need them," Jacie said simply, then refocused on her paper.

Gwen blinked a few times. Was Jacie so calculating as to be blackmailing with one hand while being outwardly kind to her with the other? She didn't think so. Except for the issue of her sexuality, Jacie had been such a straightforward young woman. Then again, she couldn't keep ruling out suspects based on how they related to her twenty years ago. Obviously too much had changed for that. "Uh . . . No, thanks." She held out her hand and showed Jacie her pills, unable to stop her surprise. "But I appreciate the offer."

"No problem."

Jacie's attitude seemed to have thawed considerably since the night before. Between her nap and Jacie and Nina's long walk, this was the first time they'd had a moment to talk all day. *Maybe things went well with her and Nina last night.* Gwen focused on the other woman on the sofa, the one sitting on the opposite end from Jacie, whose socked-feet were thrown across Jacie's lap. Every once in a while, Jacie would absently reach down and tenderly rub Nina's foot as she read. Then Nina's mouth would curl into a love-struck grin and she'd glance up at Jacie, her heart showing plainly in her eyes. *Oh, yeah. Things went* really *well for them last night. Good for you both,* she whispered silently.

Peeking into the room before she entered, Frances Artiste appeared, holding a handful of cloth napkins.

Jacie and Nina exchanged looks of indecision. They'd discussed forgiving Gwen on their walk along the Missouri River but had been unable to come to any real resolution. Gwen's words and actions pingponged between excessively prying into their personal lives and acting so much like the dear, much-loved friend they had known as girls, that they couldn't get a read on her at all. But even so, they'd agreed to this much. Jacie and Nina smiled and stood up as the older woman mysteriously flicked off the lights.

"Mrs. Art—" Gwen began to question, but her mouth clicked shut when Katherine and Audrey wheeled in a small cart holding a white birthday cake. Flaming on its top were what looked like a million candles but were, in reality, exactly forty.

"Don't look so surprised," Katherine said gently, seeing a myriad of emotions flash across Gwen's face. She looked at her intently, uneasiness washing over her. What secrets did Gwen know about? "Isn't this why we're here?"

Frances smiled and quietly excused herself from the room.

For several long seconds Gwen stood motionless. Her eyes filled with tears, then took on the wild look of a panicked animal torn between fight and flight.

Audrey and Nina came forward to lay comforting hands on Gwen's back. "Are you okay?"

"No," Gwen rasped, pulling away and presenting them with her back. She wrapped her arms around herself and shivered. "I'm really not."

Bright yellow candles were melting, dropping golden dots onto the cake's snowy surface. Wordlessly, Jacie began blowing them out as Katherine looked on in shock.

Gwen let out a shuddering breath. *I've got to do this now. If I do it after I tell them about the blackmail, they'll never believe me. They need to believe me.* "We need to talk."

Gwen asked the four women to be seated on the sofa. It was, she mused, a strange feeling: facing a firing squad composed of dear friends and knowing she deserved every bit of their scorn. "This is hard." She chuckled nervously and the noise had an odd, almost hysterical edge to it, the sort of giggle reserved for inopportune occasions like funerals or fiery church sermons.

The other women glanced at each other uncertainly.

"I'm not cracking up," Gwen assured them.

"You're sure?" Jacie asked, remembering Gwen's tentacle comments the night before.

Gwen took a few calming breaths to compose her scattered emotions. "I'm sure. I know we made a pact to get together when we turned forty," she began, well aware that getting started would be the hardest part. "And even though we were just girls, the promises that we made to each other always meant something to us. Always." Her words were greeted with a chorus of nods.

Gwen paced a little as she spoke, the wide legs of her gabardine trousers brushing together with a light swooshing sound as she moved. "But I think we all know that my birthday isn't why we're here."

The women on the couch shifted a little, each acknowledging privately that they'd really come to see their sofa-mates, and that Gwen's presence, at least at first, was mostly incidental to that.

A heavy blanket of guilt wrapped around Katherine. "Gwen, it's not like that. Not exactly. I—"

"Please," Gwen interrupted. She held up a hand to forestall her. "I need to get this out all in one go, or I'm going to chicken out."

Katherine's eyes widened slightly, but she held her tongue as her head bobbed.

Gwen drew in a deep breath and pinned her oldest friends with an intense gaze. "I need to say I'm sorry and I need for you to know that I mean it." She resisted the urge to start begging right off the bat but was unwilling to rule it out for later. "God," she shook her head a little, "I've practiced this so many times over the years, and now when I actually need the words, everything I want to say seems so small and meaningless. But I'm going to say it anyway."

She focused on Katherine. "What I did in college, the way I acted . . . I broke up the Mayflower Club. I guess it's really as simple and as complicated as that. I knew how important all of our friendships were to you and that if I hadn't acted so horribly . . . well, we'll never know what might have happened. I also know that my treating Nina, Jacie, and Audrey so badly didn't just hurt them. It hurt you, too. I never meant for that to happen, Katy. I swear to you."

Katherine blinked a few times, not knowing how to respond.

"I robbed us all of something very precious. I was wrong and I was a fool and I've regretted it my entire adult life." Weakly, Gwen lifted her hands and let them fall. "I'm sorry."

"I forgive you," Katherine heard herself saying. And while the words were hanging there she decided she really meant it. She wanted a future with Tucker, and she wanted her friend back. Even if that meant admitting some things she wasn't proud of.

"You do?" Gwen looked as if a stiff poke with a feather could topple her.

"I've missed you, Gwen. And I didn't get the worst of it like everyone else did. So, yeah, you sucked, and yeah, what you did was wrong and horrible. But I have less to forgive."

A tremulous smile twitched at Gwen's lips. "Thank you," was all she could say.

Katherine smiled back, seeing an echo of her lover in Gwen's puffy eyes. "You're welcome."

"Okay, you next, Audrey." She focused all her attention on the heavy-set woman as she took a seat on the coffee table. "Everything I just said to Katy applies to you, too." She swallowed hard, her stomach clenching nervously. "But of course, there's more. That night at the Blagbrough Galleries, I was unspeakably cruel to you."

"I felt like you'd punched me in the gut," Audrey whispered, having a hard time meeting Gwen's stare. "I was so embarrassed. I didn't understand . . ."

Soft blue eyes conveyed nothing but sadness. "You wouldn't have understood. Even though we were close in a different way than I was with the other girls, you weren't really like me, Audrey. You're fundamentally a kind person. You always thought of the rest of us before yourself. And no matter what was happening, you always wanted to make peace."

Gwen's words were met with a round of nods. "I, on the other hand, didn't really know what it meant to be kind or to think of others before myself. I was at my best when I was with all of you." Her gaze swept the room and she was gratified to see everyone was paying rapt attention to her words. "By the time you and I met again that night, we'd been apart for what seemed like so long, it was like I'd forgotten that I needed to try to work at being a better person. I was scared and stupid and I thought that if I pretended hard enough I could make the Langtrees and all their snooty friends forget that I didn't belong. Problem was, I could never forget. And it showed in everything I did."

Gwen could feel tears welling and she bit them back with little success. "I'm sorry. I . . . I haven't cried this much since I was sixteen and every little thing that happened in life was so vitally important that I nearly died."

Nina and Audrey hummed their agreement, easily recalling that desperate, almost-out-of-control feeling that was part and parcel of growing up.

Gwen closed her eyes. "After I was raped," she paused, slightly startled to realize she'd never said those words out loud before. "After, I felt so bad about myself. I hated myself. I hated my weakness. I hated my poor judgment; after all, if I hadn't been drinking that night it might not have happened." She wiped at her eyes. "I hated my parents for not being there to support me, even though it was my choice not to tell them. And for years, even though I loved him madly, I couldn't help but resent the fact that Malcolm sat downstairs and played poker while some stranger ruined me."

"I wish I'd been there to do something, Gwen," Jacie suddenly seethed, thinking of the stranger who had shattered Gwen's life so completely and started a chain of events that would reach far farther than his intended victim. "I'm so sorry that I wasn't."

"I've wished a million times that I would have gone looking for you sooner," Katherine murmured unexpectedly, with Nina and Audrey chiming in their agreement. "Things should have been different for you."

Gwen sat stunned, her friends' kindness after all she'd done making her feel both small and hopeful. The sentiment touched her in an unexpectedly deep place, but it only served to throw her more off balance. One of these very nice women had been torturing her for months and was threatening to shatter her life. "Thank you," she finally muttered. Then she fixed her gaze on Audrey again. "Audrey?"

Audrey's head snapped up and anguished brown eyes greeted Gwen. "Wh-What?"

"I felt so terrible about myself that I would have done anything to fit in with the people who were now my family. I was so wrong to hurt you. I shouldn't have dismissed you like you didn't matter. You did matter. You were beautiful and good then and you are now, and I'm so sorry that I didn't have the courage to stick up for you and be proud to call you my friend."

Audrey sucked in a quick breath and reached for a Kleenex from a holder on one of the end tables. Instead of using it herself, she leaned forward and wiped the tears off Gwen's cheeks.

The simple action nearly undid Gwen and so Audrey enveloped her in a firm hug, catching Katherine's smile of approval from the corner of her eye. It took a few minutes for Gwen to pull herself together, and when she did, she squeezed Audrey's hand. "Thank you," she whispered brokenly, not believing that things were going so well. She sniffed again and turned her eyes to Jacie and Nina.

Gwen's heart lurched. "Nina," she started, blinking rapidly, "and Jacie. How can I even begin to apologize to you for what I did to you? I . . . I don't know what to say except that I do know that some things in life are unforgivable. And what I did to you both is one of those things."

Nina looked Gwen square in the eye. "That's not true," she said softly.

Gwen's eyes lit up.

"I think that I can forgive you for what you did to me, Gwen." Nina's voice dropped an octave. "But I'll never forgive you for what you did to Jacie. Never."

"Nina." Jacie brows drew together. "You don't have to . . . I mean, I can take care of myself."

"This is not about that. This is about how one of us, one of *us*"—she made a sweeping gesture that encompassed the group—"a person who I trusted as much as my own family, stabbed us in the back," Nina insisted, her emotions bubbling up to the surface in a way she hadn't expected. "And then when Gwen was done outing you to your parents, she twisted the knife by making sure you thought our relationship meant nothing to me. After you left"—she turned back to Gwen, letting her see the pain she'd lived with for so long—"I didn't know what to do with myself, my life. I wanted to die."

Gwen flinched as though she'd been slapped.

Nina was on a roll and she didn't feel like stopping. She pointed an angry finger at Gwen. "You didn't need to be so cruel. We weren't hurting a soul. What you did was petty and hateful!"

Gwen's gaze dropped to her hands, which were shaking like leaves. "You're right, Nina. Every bit of that is true. I was all those things and more."

Nina didn't expect Gwen to be so blunt or truthful and she was a little taken aback. Even when they were all the best of friends, Gwen had had a self-serving streak a mile wide, frequently shifting blame to avoid discomfort or conflict. As Nina regarded her old friend, she saw a measure of sincerity that had been all too rare for Gwen as a young woman. Maybe just growing up had been what Gwen needed all along.

"Why'd you do it?" Jacie asked quietly. "After everything we'd been through. Surely the thought of my being gay couldn't have been so disturbing that you were willing to throw away all our friendships over it. I know you and I were never as close as you were with Audrey or Nina." She struggled for the right words. "But that fall we . . . . I mean . . ."

"That autumn, you more than anyone else kept me from falling apart at the seams," Gwen acknowledged easily, knowing it for the truth.

"So why then?" Jacie repeated.

Jacie's voice held all the bewilderment of a child and it made Gwen's heart hurt. "It's not so complicated, Jacie," she said, hating the sinking feeling that there were some things she would never be able to make up for, no matter how hard she tried. "Getting married to Malcolm so young was such a mistake." Her forehead wrinkled deeply as she considered what she wanted to say. "No, it wasn't exactly a mistake. I just wasn't ready. He tried to be a good husband, but he still spent most of his time on school and sports. I wasn't close to being an adult or even my own person yet. I had no idea how to fill my time if it wasn't with you all. When I found out that you were gay, all I could think about was how you were ruining everything. And how you were making a huge mistake."

Jacie's back straightened. "What?"

Gwen shook her head at her younger self. "I was planning on working my way back into all your lives, but the only way I could see that happening was if you all existed in this perfect little box I'd placed you in. I didn't think that the Langtrees would accept anything less, and my own prejudices made it all the easier to believe that I was absolutely right."

"You were so pretty and smart that I reasoned you could have had any boy you wanted. I thought you were choosing to be different because you were stubborn and you'd confused your friendship with Nina for something more. I thought you were *choosing* to separate yourself from us. Not only did your being a lesbian ruin my plans, but I just knew that you'd end up as miserable and as alone as I was, once you'd realized what you'd done."

Tears streaked Gwen's cheeks and her red-rimmed eyes made her look every day of her age. "I thought I was saving you from a terrible mistake. And I was positive that I was saving myself."

Nobody knew what to say in the face of someone who'd been so entirely deluded. The room went quiet as everyone's thoughts turned inward and it was during that painfully awkward silence that Frances strolled back into the room carrying some maps of local attractions. "Well now, girls," she began in a cheerful, robust voice. "Would anyone like—Uhh . . ." Her eyes shaped twin moons when she took in the room's somber faces. And Gwen, who had been the picture of quiet elegance just the day before, looked like a train wreck. "Never mind," she squeaked and shuffled out of the room so quickly that she nearly ran headlong into the doorframe.

Everyone's gaze followed the older woman out of the room and several nervous smiles appeared until finally Gwen let out a soft snort, which opened the floodgates to everyone's quiet laughter.

"Does that poor woman have more white hair than when we arrived?" Nina chuckled, slipping her hand into Jacie's and feeling strong fingers twine with hers.

"Definitely," Gwen sighed, wishing her painkillers would hurry up and start working. Her head was still throbbing. "I'm going to have to pay her double. She's walked in on a half dozen awkward scenes since yesterday morning. She's earned it."

When the chuckles and murmurs of agreement died down, silence rushed back into the room, filling every crevice. This time, however, Gwen didn't let the silence linger. "So, as I was saying . . ." *What else can I say?* "I was a huge, enormous, gigantic asshole, and I'm desperately sorry, more than you'll ever know."

Audrey smiled gently at her. "You never did do anything halfway, Gwen."

Nina let out a deep exhale, unable to hold on to most of her anger in the face of Gwen's startling remorse. "You might even say you were an overachiever."

Jacie bit her bottom lip in a bid not to laugh even though what Nina said was more true than funny.

"Go ahead," Gwen groaned. "Laugh all you want." She wiped her cheeks. "I deserve it."

Her friends took her up on her offer, anxious to relieve the tension that was making them all uneasy.

Gwen leaned forward and laid one hand on Jacie's thigh, the other on Nina's, feeling the warmth of their skin through their jeans and catching the delicate hint of spice in Nina's perfume. "I know you can't forgive me. But please at least accept my apology and know that I never meant to hurt you. What I did was out of fear and ignorance, never hate."

Everyone looked to Jacie. She had long been the unofficial leader of their group and it seemed that some things would never change.

Jacie laid a hand on Gwen's to take some of the sting from her deadly serious words. "Had this weekend not turned out as well as it has, I think I'd take this opportunity to tell you where you could stick your apology."

"But?" Gwen prompted, crossing her fingers.

"But I have a shot at what I've always wanted." She turned her head and grinned at Nina, her smile broadening when Nina's cheeks turned the most delicious shade of pink. "Not to rain on your big apology scene, Gwen"—she blinked at the taller woman's sudden frown—"but I got over most of my bad feelings about you years and years ago. It wasn't that I forgave you, I just got over feeling shitty about something that mostly wasn't my fault."

She was a little self-conscious about this next part, but it needed saying. "No matter what Gwen did, I shouldn't have just taken off. You all deserved better. It was losing you all, and most especially my best friend, that I was never able to get over." Nina wrapped a comforting arm around her and she smiled in pure reflex. "Now that Nina and I, actually all of us, have a second chance, I'm having trouble feeling anything but wonderful."

Audrey and Katherine elbowed each other, pleased beyond measure at the way things were turning out. They couldn't wait to get back to their room tonight and gossip in private about Jacie and Nina, each cousin now insisting that she knew Jacie and Nina had a "thing" for each other all along.

"I'm not sure that I can completely trust you, Gwen," Jacie said honestly.

"I wouldn't expect you to, Jacie." Gwen felt a rush of hope.

Jacie nodded, glad that Gwen's hopes weren't unrealistic. Surprisingly, she had no urge to rub her nose in everything she'd lost. "It's going to take more than a weekend and birthday cake to mend the damage you've done. And I can't forgive you for what you did to Nina. So the best you can expect on that front is for you to make your own peace with her."

"Understood." Gwen's gaze flicked to Nina and their eyes met. She read encouragement and affection in Nina's expression, and she silently applauded her friend's tender heart, wondering what life would have been like if she, herself, had had one of those from the very start.

Nina mouthed a silent, but sincere, "I'll try," and Gwen was lightheaded with relief. "Thank you," she said unevenly, doing her best not to burst into tears again.

Jacie closed her eyes. "So . . . I'm willing to let the past stay where it belongs and think about the things we can actually do something about."

"Like the future," Nina agreed.

Jacie opened her eyes, and her face relaxed into a beaming smile. "Yeah." Surreptitiously, she looked at her watch again, well aware that it was becoming a habit. Surely it had to be time to kiss Nina again.

Gwen sat there on the coffee table, not sure what should come next. She felt lighter than she had in years and was committed to whatever work it would take to repair their damaged friendships. What she couldn't understand was why no one was talking. This was the time that her blackmailer was supposed to come to the crystalline realization that she wasn't Satan incarnate and she didn't deserve to have her life ruined.

And yet no one said a word.

Gwen eyed her friends carefully, schooling herself in patience. They'd been more generous than she'd had a right to expect, but dammit, shouldn't someone be about to crack? Shouldn't one of them at least look guilty for trying to destroy her family?

Jacie shifted uncomfortably under that same stare that Gwen had been giving everyone all weekend. It was creepy and weird, and she was tired of it. "If you think it would help relieve a little of your guilt for me to punch you in the nose, Gwen, I'll make the sacrifice," she said gamely, a tiny bit of irritation coloring her words.

Nina smiled a little too sweetly, though her eyes didn't convey true malice. "I'll help."

The message was clear. While old grudges might be allowed to wither and die, no one was about to forget anything.

Gwen could live with that. "Gee, thanks," she deadpanned, edging her way off the coffee table in case someone else decided to "help" her. She desperately needed to regroup and was hoping that if she provided a private environment, the blackmailer would seek her out. "I'm going to go back upstairs and relax for a little while."

Katherine stood alongside Gwen, but addressed Jacie. She needed to get everyone but Gwen outside for a private talk. She didn't want to risk Gwen coming downstairs while she was telling Nina, Audrey, and Jacie about the files she'd stolen from Gwen's suitcase. "So, anyone want to see my beautiful car?" She prayed that Gwen was still as disinterested in cars today as she had been in their youth.

Jacie was a little startled by the graceless change in subjects. "No thanks. I already saw that nasty thing."

"Not me," Gwen answered instantly.

"C'mon, Jacie. I know you must be jealous of my Karmann Ghia. Your truck and its big manly tires practically scream 'I have a really small penis!' "

Nina started laughing, eager to join in the banter and be finished with this draining, emotional chat. "So small it's almost non-existent!"

"Jesus Christ, what do you mean almost?" Jacie crowed, bending over to pinch Nina in the thigh before offering her a hand up. "And I need my truck for work." Then she wrapped her arm around Nina's waist and began steering her toward the door.

"Wanna see it up close?" Katherine asked, stretching arms over her head and then quickly following Nina and Jacie.

"You have up-close photos of Jacie's penis?" Audrey enthused, as she pushed off the sofa and eagerly cut in front of Katherine. "Cool! I wanna look first."

Jacie's eyes narrowed at her friends' teasing. "I do not have a"—she shivered hard enough for her teeth to rattle—"penis. You've all seen me naked a hundred times. You know exactly what I've got."

They all hummed their frank appreciation, with Nina letting out a low wolf whistle to boot.

"Very funny, guys," Jacie groused, even as her ego let out a contented purr.

"You can strip down any time you'd like for verification purposes, sweetheart." Nina wrinkled her nose playfully. "I won't complain."

"Aww . . . sweetheart," Katherine taunted as the foursome exited the room. "Ouch, Jacie!" she complained loudly from near the front door. "That's going to bruise!"

Gwen was left standing alone in the parlor with no answers and a birthday cake that looked like someone had tried to write her name in the snow on top of it. She waited a few moments, hoping someone would return to the room to talk to her. But no one did. Then, in growing desperation, she scrubbed her face with both hands. Her head was still pounding from her headache, and she was pretty sure it was only going to get worse.

She vowed, right then, that the sun wouldn't come up again without her knowing the name of her blackmailer. If she was lucky, the three women who weren't loathsome snakes would side with her and help her end this nightmare once and for all. If she was unlucky . . . her train of thought derailed there.

Gwen prepared herself to make her own luck.

Jacie, Audrey, Nina, and Katherine trotted toward the garage to avoid the worst of the light rain.

"Whew," Jacie could see her breath when she pulled open the old carriage house door. "Was it this cold in October when we were kids?" Some well-maintained horse tack from another lifetime had been hung on the walls, partly because it had always been housed in this building, and partly for decoration, a gentle reminder of a slower time. Jacie examined it with interest.

Audrey blew on her chilled fingers. "No. This is unseasonably cold. Looks like we just got lucky like always," she said sarcastically, deciding to stuff her hands into her pockets. "Hey!" She spun in a circle. "Where's

Katy?"

"She ran back inside for her car keys." Nina sucked a breath of cool air, glad to be out of the house. Her mind drifted to Robbie and she hoped that her mother was insisting he wear a warm jacket. Then she laughed a little, realizing that what her son was probably wearing was a permanent scowl because his grandmother had not only insisted on a jacket, but on gloves and one of those goofy hats with a fuzzy ball on the top that only a granny could produce. Still, there were better ways to stay warm. "Hey, Jacie Ann?"

"Hmm," Jacie answered as she poked inquisitively at a sturdy-looking saddle.

"Can I put my hands in your pockets?"

Jacie's eyebrows crawled up her forehead, and she rushed over to Nina so quickly that Audrey burst out laughing.

"Shut up, Audrey," Jacie mumbled.

On the front porch, Katherine slipped on her jacket and began dialing her cell phone. She kept her voice low and her eyes riveted on the front door in case Gwen decided to make a surprise appearance. "Hey, Tuck—" She stopped talking, her shoulders slumping when she realized that it was a new message on Tucker's voice mail she was listening to and not him.

The message she left him was short and to the point. "I'm through doing this to your mom. I'm telling her everything tonight. Show up here by six, Tucker, or I'll do it alone. I'm sorry and I love you, but I . . . I just can't."

She pressed "off" on the phone and stepped out into the air, whispering a quick, "Please don't let me down," before jogging toward the garage.

When Katherine arrived, Jacie reluctantly pulled away from Nina and poked her head outside to make sure that Gwen hadn't decided to join them. Gwen had always detested any talk of cars and Jacie was nearly certain that she'd decide to stay inside while they discussed Katherine's unfortunate choice of vehicles.

Jacie yelped when she felt a pair of hands grasp the back of her jeans and pull her inside.

"You're getting soaked," Nina said, clearly exasperated.

Unable to stop herself, Jacie gave Nina a sexy, lopsided grin.

Much to Nina's annoyance, for the second time in one day she felt her cheeks heat wildly. "Oh, God."

Jacie grinned, finding it impossibly endearing that one minute Nina could be brazenly kissing her senseless in front of their friends and the next minute blushing at some simple innuendo. *I have it so bad.* "Your eyes look more green than blue today," Jacie commented, affectionately plucking at the sea-green fleece that Nina was wearing. She was finding it so easy to get lost in Nina that she was having trouble concentrating on anything else. "Pretty." *So bad.*

Audrey sighed, knowing very well the sweet flood of emotion that came with being in love. But this was too much. "At first this was cute, now I'm just going to throw up."

"Yeah, yeah," Nina grumbled, waving her off. "So why are we out here to look at this ugly car?"

"Hey!" Katherine complained. "It's not ugly!"

"Sure it is." Jacie said.

"We're not here to look at my beautiful car. I have something to tell you guys." Katherine's stomach clenched nervously. "Gwen's been investigating my finances and God knows what else."

Her words were met by utter silence.

"And that's not all," Katherine continued.

"Oh, boy," Audrey groaned. "What did she do now?"

"She's investigating all of you, too."

"What the fuck?" Jacie roared, causing Katherine to jump.

Audrey blinked slowly as she processed what she'd just heard. "Why in the world would she do that?"

Katherine chose her words carefully. "I have no idea why she'd be investigating any of you."

Nina, who usually would work to calm Jacie down when she got into a tizzy, had no compulsion to intervene this time. She was just as angry. "Gwen, Gwen," she muttered, "You've always been your own worst enemy." Nina turned to Katherine. "How do you know all this?"

Katherine bit her lip. "I just happened to be digging around in her suitcase yesterday."

Audrey snorted. "Gwen was always the nosy one. Turns out Katy is our own little Mata Hari."

Undeterred, Katherine admitted, "I found some files. I saw my name on one of them and grabbed a bunch of papers to read once I was alone. There was information about all us in there. Private stuff."

"She doesn't have any reason to check us out!" Jacie spluttered, her anger rising fast.

Audrey slapped her thigh as she paced. "She must think she has a reason. The question is why?"

Nina wrapped her arms loosely around Jacie, her eyebrows narrowing. "So what are we going to do to find out for sure?"

Instinctively, the women gathered in a small circle, crouching down into a huddle as they'd done as children, their hushed voices whisked away by the brisk autumn wind.

Audrey feigned innocence as she sat on the sofa, her feet tucked underneath her. She patted the sofa set to her right. "C'mon, Gwen."

"How was Katy's horrible car?" Gwen joined Audrey on the couch.

Katherine scowled.

"Horrible," Audrey dutifully replied.

Gwen's gaze strayed to the door. "Where are Nina and Jacie?"

"They went to the kitchen to get a snack . . ."

"They went to take a nap," Katy said at the same time.

Audrey glared at her cousin.

Gwen scratched her jaw. Something was up. "They're doing both?"

"Yup," Katherine confirmed, taking the seat on the other side of Gwen. "They sure are. Not at the same time, of course."

Thoughtfully, Gwen nodded. "I think I'll go see if they need any help in the kitchen." She started to get up.

"No," Audrey and Katherine shouted in unison. Audrey put her hand on Gwen's chest and pushed her firmly back onto the sofa.

Gwen's eyes popped wide open. "Why shouldn't I?"

Audrey pulled her hand from Gwen and tried to look innocent.

Katherine licked her lips nervously. "Umm . . . Because—"

"Because Mrs. Artiste is already there to help them," Audrey interrupted, cursing their pathetic attempts at distraction. Even as children they'd always, always, gotten caught while trying to be sneaky.

"No, she isn't," Gwen insisted, looking at Audrey as though she were crazy. "Not five minutes ago she told me she was going to go to her cottage to get some new candles for my birthday cake."

"Oh, well," Audrey dismissed. "Let's sit here and talk. Tell me all about Tucker and Malcolm."

Gwen rubbed tired eyes. Then she reached out and affectionately patted Audrey's arm, pleased that her old friend didn't flinch or move away. "I'd love to tell you both all about them, but my headache is getting worse." Gwen grimaced, fearing she was on the verge of a full-blown migraine. "I think I'm going to go lie down. We'll chat later, okay?"

"You can lie down here," Katy said, getting up and fluffing a throw-pillow for Gwen's head. She patted the sofa invitingly. "It's nice and soft."

Audrey nodded. "Great idea. Here . . ." She picked up a blanket that had been slung over the arm of the sofa and held it up. "You can cover up with this and we can talk while your eyes are closed."

Gwen regarded them warily. "No thank you. The bed upstairs is much more comfortable."

Katherine was at a loss and it showed. Suddenly, she stretched her arms out in front of her and let out a loud yawn. "I'm tired, too. See ya." And with that, she shot a worried look at Audrey and moved quickly for the stairs.

Wide eyes focused on Audrey. "What the hell is going on?" Gwen demanded.

"Absolutely nothing."

Katherine was practically leaping up the stairs now, her spiky blond head bobbing with every lithe step.

Gwen lifted her upper lip and showed a row of straight teeth. "Where are you going, Katy?" She took off after the other woman, dodging Audrey's grabbing hands

"Nowhere!" Katherine called back to her as she disappeared at the top of the steps. She rushed down the hall and tapped rapidly on Gwen's bedroom door. "Get out!" she whispered loudly. She tried the doorknob, but it was locked. A glance down the hall told her she was still alone. "Nina and Jacie! Get out now!"

Nina padded quickly to the bedroom door and Jacie fumbled to gather up the files that she'd taken from Gwen's briefcase and had spread out over the bed for her and Nina's review.

Nina threw open the door. "What? Dammit, Katy, you are supposed to be keeping Gwen busy while we—" Her mouth clicked shut when a lightly panting Gwen appeared directly next to Katherine in the doorway.

A few seconds later they heard Audrey's heavy footsteps pounding down the hall in their direction.

"While you do what, Nina?" Gwen asked, brushing past Katherine and Nina to face Jacie. Two sets of stony-cold eyes met and held. "How dare you invade my privacy!" She glanced at Jacie's hands and recognized the files immediately.

"How dare I?" Angrily, Jacie threw the pile of files at Gwen's feet, scattering pages all over the floor. "How dare you!"

Everyone's gaze was drawn down to the messy piles as Jacie seethed. "You have information on my daughter's school tuition and what I give my ex every month for expenses?" Jacie took a menacing step closer to Gwen. "And my retirement accounts and my truck payments?" Another step. "Where the hell do you get off spying on me?"

"Spying on all of us," Nina corrected gently, inserting herself between Gwen and Jacie before things could escalate out of control. Then Jacie stepped next to her and she caught sight of her swollen shiner and mentally rolled her eyes at herself. This entire weekend had been nothing but a series of out of control moments.

"I had no choice," Gwen shouted, her temper boiling over and her face twisting in rage. "It was you, wasn't it! I drove Jacie away from you and now you want to drive my family away from me." She was looking directly at Nina. "If you wanted to make me pay, then you fucking have. In spades!"

"My God, what are you talking about?" Nina asked, genuinely confused, her eyebrows at their zenith.

Gwen shook her head fiercely. "I don't know who to trust." She covered her ears, not wanting to hear more lies.

"Trust!" Audrey joined the fray, bending to pick up a file with her name written in black ink across the tab. "That's a good one. You spend half the morning apologizing for being an unholy bitch twenty years ago and neglect to mention that all the while you've been spying on us in the here and now and you are wondering who to trust? You need professional help, Gwen."

"Shut up!" Gwen barked, losing any semblance of control. "Shut up!"

Audrey actually backed up a step at the murderous look on Gwen's face.

"I don't need professional help. I need my life back!" Gwen whirled around to face Katherine. "I need to not have to worry every second of every day!" She was gesturing wildly, unaware of the tears streaking her cheeks as she spun back to face Jacie. "I need my husband not to be so confused about the way that I've been acting that he thinks I'm cheating on him!" She began to sob.

The other women stood in stunned silence as Gwen continued to rant at the top of her lungs, tears and sobs making her even more difficult to understand.

"What I need," Gwen spat out finally, "is for the blackmail to stop!" She dropped onto the bed and covered her face with her hands, her shoulders shaking violently as she cried. "Please. Please. Please." She wrapped arms around herself and her voice dropped to a raspy whisper. "Please just stop."

Gwen was falling apart and the sight of it made the other women's stomachs roil. It rendered years of bad feelings meaningless because when it came down to it, when she needed them, they couldn't help themselves; they would be there for her.

Instantly, Nina dropped to her knees in front of Gwen. "I don't understand, Gwen." She reached out and tenderly wiped Gwen's cheeks. She spoke slowly, her voice soothing and clear. "You need to explain things from the very beginning. I'll help you if you'll let me, I really will."

Jacie nodded and placed a comforting hand on Gwen's shoulder. And gave it a little squeeze. "Who is trying to make you pay? And for what?"

"I don't know!" Gwen sniffed. "But it's one of you."

"Oh, my God."

They all turned to look at Audrey, who was crouched down on the floor, scanning an e-mail sent to Gwen. It was from the blackmailer and she read it out loud, scarcely believing what she was seeing.

Pay me now or you'll pay more later. If Malcolm finds out that Tucker isn't his son, you'll lose everything. $10,000.00 is a small price to pay to keep what you love.

Gwen reached out and snatched the paper from Audrey's hand. In a fit of rage, she ripped the e-mail to shreds and threw it in Audrey's face. "I suppose you don't know anything about this either? Well, one of you sure as hell does."

Blinking, Nina sat next to Gwen on the bed. "Someone is blackmailing you over Tucker's paternity?"

Jacie closed her eyes. "Jesus, that's cruel."

"No, really?" Gwen laughed. She was verging on hysterical.

Audrey sifted through several more papers on the floor and found another e-mail. It read basically the same as the first, only the demand went from $10,000.00 to $15,000.00. It was dated last week, sent from someone using a Hot Mail address and calling themselves Truthseeker101. "Is this why you had us investigated?" The letterhead on some of the papers had Gramercy Investigations on it.

"I had no choice. I had to find out who was doing this."

Audrey sighed. "None of us would do this, Gwen."

"Of course not," Nina assured her. "This is sick."

"It has to be one of you," Gwen insisted, her nose leaking down her face. With short, irritated movements, she wiped at it with the back of her hand. "I've never told another living soul my secret. Never! And even the bastard who raped me couldn't know that he got me pregnant. No one knows but the people in this room."

"No one here has more reason to hate you than I do, Gwen," Jacie admitted quietly, her hand dropping from Gwen's shoulder only to be quickly taken by one of Nina's. "But this? No fucking way. I swore to keep your secret. I didn't agree with it then and I still don't, but I'll take it to the grave."

"We all will," Nina promised, remembering the day so long ago that she'd made that vow.

Audrey nodded her agreement, but Gwen wasn't paying any attention to her or Nina or Jacie. She'd stopped crying and was staring a hole through Katherine, who was as white as a ghost.

Jacie sucked in a breath at Katherine's ashen face. "Katy?" she asked incredulously. "You would never tell, right?"

Audrey swallowed hard, feeling as though she'd been punched in the gut. "Katy?"

Katherine's mouth worked for a few seconds before she could manage any sound. And even then it was only a low moan.

"Katy?" Gwen's voice was unnaturally high.

Katherine struggled to clear her throat. "I would n-never blackmail you, Gwen." Her mind was awhirl with thoughts of her young lover. *Sweet Jesus, Tucker, what have you done?*

"Then what's wrong?" Nina asked carefully. Katherine looked as though she was going to lose her lunch any second.

"Tucker," Katherine whispered. She glanced down at Gwen with anguished eyes. "I told him about . . . I told him."

Gwen blinked, all of Katherine's words not registering. "You don't even know him."

"I didn't want to tell you this way, Gwen. Please believe me. I can't believe he would do something so horrible. I . . . I swear Tucker doesn't know the whole story. I swear."

"You don't even know Tucker!" Gwen roared jumping off the bed and nearly giving Katherine a heart attack. "Don't you try to blame him for this! You sent those e-mails, didn't you?"

"No." Katherine shook, her body racked with tension. "I didn't. But I do know Tucker. You did the research yourself, Gwen. Or at least you paid to have it done. It was in my file. I'm the office manager of Webster University's Admissions Office. I met Tucker there last year."

Gwen looked at her blankly. "I don't understand."

Katherine fought the urge to flee from the room. "I met him there and recognized his name. We started talking. I didn't tell him that I knew you. Not at first. But after we went out a few times, I wanted to be honest with him and—"

Gwen's hands balled into fists. All thoughts of blackmail vanished. Her nostrils flared. "What do you mean, 'went out'?"

Nina's mouth was hanging open so wide Katherine could have driven her Karmann Ghia through it. She was too stunned to say a word.

"Please tell me he isn't your boyfriend." Audrey poked her cousin with an irritated finger. "If this is some sort of a joke, it's not close to funny. Tell me you're not dating Gwen's baby."

"That was downright offensive," Katherine snapped, her resentment showing. "Do I look like I'm joking? And, trust me, Tucker Langtree is no baby." Her eyes pleaded with them to understand. "I didn't mean for it to happen. He asked me out every week for two months before I blurted out a yes. I thought it would be a lark and that maybe I'd hear some gossip about his mother. I didn't know that I'd fall in love with him."

"Holy Christ!" Audrey shoved her cousin hard. "You've lost your fucking mind!" She couldn't help but state the painfully obvious. "You're old enough to be his mother!"

Katy covered her eyes with her hands. If she thought about that part too long, things got all yucky in her mind. "I know, but—"

"No. No. No. This can't be true," Gwen rambled, in shock.

"Be reasonable," Katherine begged, close to tears herself. "I love him and he loves me. I wanted to tell you, but he insisted that you wouldn't approve. He thought it would just be easier to keep things quiet."

"Approve?" Gwen looked at Katherine as though she'd never seen her before. "He's so private, all we know is that he's been dating some girl. A girl! As in someone who went to her prom a couple of years ago and still has Hello Kitty wallpaper in her room back home. Not someone who remembers President Nixon and has been having sex since God was a boy! You pervert!" Gwen let out a wild yell and lunged for Katherine, only to have Jacie grab her at the last minute.

Nina watched in amazement as the scene before her played out, irrationally relieved that her son was only in the fourth grade.

"Calm down," Jacie growled, struggling under a surge of surprising strength from Gwen. "You can't kill her. Hey! You can't." Hands made powerful from years of manual labor shook Gwen roughly when it was clear that she was too livid to listen. "Calm down!"

"Let me go, damn you! How would you feel if Katy was sleeping with your daughter? Huh?" Gwen continued to struggle, her eyes flashing. "How would you Goddamn feel about that, Jacie?"

Jacie froze for a split second as she considered Gwen's words. Then she released her grip.

"Jesus, Jacie!" Nina rushed forward, but Jacie held her back from stopping Gwen. This was between her and Katherine.

Audrey gasped as Gwen flew at Katherine like a quarter horse out of the gate.

"Shit!" Katherine ducked a wild haymaker that would have resulted in her not being able to eat solid foods for months. She scrambled backward, holding up her hands to stop Gwen's advance, her eyes wide with fear. "Gwen, stop it! Be reasonable. This isn't that bad."

"You're sleeping with my son and you want me to be reasonable?" Gwen clarified slowly. "You're twenty years too old for him and have been married more times than he's been on dates and you want me to stop?"

Katherine's face flushed red, equal parts embarrassment and anger. "We do more than sleep together. Jesus, I told you we love each other!"

"I'm going to kill you, Katy Schaub." Gwen's voice was so low and wicked sounding that Nina, Audrey, and even Jacie knew they'd have to intervene. The rigid set of her body and guttural quality to her voice left no doubt that she was completely serious.

Nina reached Gwen first and they briefly tussled as Gwen tried to break free from Nina's grasp. They shrieked in surprise when the fabric of Nina's blouse tore and buttons rained down on their feet, exposing to the cool air her pastel green bra and skin lightly spattered with pale freckles.

Before Gwen could draw in another breath, Jacie's vice-like grip took hold of her, cementing her in place and forcing her to release Nina. She muffled a yelp of pain at the long fingers wrapped tightly around her wrists, shockingly reminded of just how strong Jacie was.

Panting, Gwen seethed for a moment, eyeing Katherine with evil intent and cursing Jacie with some virulent word combinations that paid homage to her working class upbringing. But as her pounding heartbeat slowed, and once it was clear that she was locked in an unyielding clasp, she had no choice to but to deal with what Katherine had told her, instead of just reacting. It only took a moment for her fury to began melting into sadness, and finally into a profound sense of betrayal. "How could you, Katy? I know we aren't really friends anymore. But once upon a time we were the best of friends." She gave her a disgusted look. "He's barely grown."

Katherine felt a wave of shame wash over her. Not because she loved Tucker; she knew that her heart had decided that for her. But because she had handled things so badly. She never should have agreed to keep their affair a secret. At least not for so long. And once she began lying and sneaking around, it was almost impossible not to feel guilty about what she was doing.

"We . . . I should have told you from the start," she readily admitted. "But I didn't know where our relationship would lead. At first I thought it was a casual affair with a handsome, younger man. Neither of us were married or attached to someone else, I didn't really care what you might think . . . it seemed harmless enough. But . . ."

An ardent expression flickered across Katherine's face. "He's special. And before I knew it things had gone way past casual. Tucker insisted that you'd never accept us as a couple and that you'd do your best to make trouble for us. After what you did to Jacie, how could I doubt him?"

Katherine's words tore at Gwen's conscience, but this wasn't twenty years ago. "I was a foolish girl when I outed Jacie to her parents. You can't believe that I would ever do anything that would hurt my own son! I love him more than my own life."

"I didn't know what to believe." Katherine looked away for a moment and admitted, "I fell hard and fast, and I wasn't willing to risk losing him." She thought of her earlier conversation with Tucker. "I don't want to lose you as a friend, Gwen. I feel like I've just found you again. But I want Tucker more." Her gaze sharpened and her voice took on added resolve. "If I have to choose between the two of you, as much as it would hurt, there's no contest at all. And I don't think that's a choice you want to give him, either. You might be surprised at the results."

Jacie glanced over at Nina. "We should go," she whispered uncomfortably. "This doesn't involve us."

Nina nodded. This was a little like watching a train wreck where people you loved were the doomed passengers. "You're—"

"Stay." Katherine's voice was weary. "You're going to find out sooner or later. You might as well hear it from me."

A big part of Gwen wanted to strangle Katherine, but an equal part was forced to acknowledge that Tucker had been partially right. She didn't approve of their relationship, and while she would never have actually sabotaged it, she would have done her best to make him see that he had little chance of a future with Katherine.

Gwen blinked rapidly; the sick feeling that was already fermenting in her gut grew exponentially when she suddenly remembered what they were originally talking about. She gently disengaged from Jacie, who was only loosely holding her now, and gave her a little pat to let her know things were all right.

Gwen went back to the bed and sat down, sinking deeply into the fluffy comforter and grabbing a pillow, which she clutched to her chest. Her eyes were so wide they would have been comical under any other circumstances. "When you said you told Tucker about me, you meant that you told him about us being friends once upon a time, right? That's all?"

Katherine squeezed her eyes shut. This was going to be even harder to admit. "I wish it were, Gwen." Reluctantly, she joined Gwen on the bed, leaving the other women clustered at the other end. She spoke gently, knowing the dangerous ground she was about to tread. "Shit," she hissed from between clenched teeth. "I'd give a kidney for a cigarette right now." She held up an unsteady hand. "See? I have the shakes."

"Katy," Nina warned. Gwen looked like she was going to have a stroke before Katherine could spit out whatever it is she was going to say. "C'mon."

Katherine licked dry lips. "Yeah." She blew out a long breath and gave herself a quick pep talk. "Okay. After Malcolm's heart attack—"

"How do you—?" Gwen stopped herself, realizing that Katherine and Tucker had to have been dating for months and months. She made a mental note to raise hell with Ted Gramercy. Gramercy Investigations should have known about this.

"After Malcolm's heart attack," Katherine continued, wishing she had something to do with her hands other than tangle and untangle her fingers. "Tucker was a mess, remember?"

"Here." Jacie moved around the bed and handed Katherine a pillow.

"Thanks," she whispered, taking it and digging her fingers deeply into the cool silk.

Grimly, Gwen nodded, her eyes filling with tears over the recent memory. "We were all a mess." A far-off expression overtook her face as she relived that terrible moment when she had walked into Malcolm's office and found him slumped over his desk. Her own heart had ground to a painful halt for the endless moment it took for her to find a weak pulse. "Malcolm almost died, and it was a nightmare for everyone who loves him. Tucker worships the ground his dad walks on."

Katherine's eyes softened. "I know. He was distraught and confused, I think, and he was determined to quit tennis."

Gwen's gaze snapped back to Katherine. "I didn't know that." A low groan forced its way from her throat. "Christ, was I too big of a mess to even notice?"

She'd spent days glued to a chair in the Intensive Care waiting room, then the hospital chapel, praying that Malcolm would survive. It had taken every ounce of her strength to keep from lying down someplace and never getting up. Tucker had been in nearly as bad a shape, but Gwen was so caught up in what was happening that she didn't really remember much about him during that time.

He was rarely at the hospital, and when he was, he looked so much like a lost little boy that it was physically painful for her to see him. When his visits grew less frequent, she recalled feeling distinctively relieved, along with guilty. It was one less complication when her world was already falling down around her. "I . . . I guess I thought he was dealing with things and trying to keep up with his classes."

"Nuh-huh." Katherine shook his head. "He wasn't dealing at all. He told me that the doctors said his dad's heart attack was the result of a congenital defect and that he was scared to death that the same thing would happen to him. I tried to reason with him and get him to go to the doctor just to ease his mind, but he was talking all crazy about quitting school and hurrying up and living his life instead of reading about people who had already lived theirs. He was freaked. I pointed out that Malcolm was more than twenty years older than he was, but nothing seemed to help."

Gwen's eyes fluttered shut, scattering tears on the pillow she had clutched to her chest. "Oh, God. I didn't know that he was afraid for himself." Bitter self-hatred painted her face. "What kind of mother am I?"

"Gwen," Katherine's tone was gentle. "He didn't tell you what he was feeling because he didn't want you to worry. He said you had enough to deal with."

"I would have done anything I could! He's my son."

Katherine smiled a little. "And he's just as stubborn as you are. One night"—she edited out the "while we were naked and snuggled in bed together" part—"I think it was the day that Malcolm was finally moved out of the ICU, Tucker broke down and started to cry."

Gwen's eyes immediately filled with new tears of her own.

The other women took seats on the bed, tucking their legs beneath them. Their hearts hurt for Tucker, but most especially for Gwen. They'd all lost people they loved; parents, siblings, grandparents, and dear friends, but none of them had experienced the heartrending agony of wondering whether a partner would live or die. Jacie felt a flutter of panic course through her at the mere thought of losing Nina. She snuggled tightly behind the sandy-haired woman, resting her chin on Nina's shoulder and wrapping a possessive arm around her.

Nina leaned back into the warm body that was molded to hers. She gripped Jacie's arm for a few seconds before grasping her hand and bringing it to her mouth, gently kissing her palm.

The simple gesture conveyed more than love; it spoke of a fundamental understanding that they'd shared since the earliest days of their relationship. Jacie pressed her head against Nina's and closed her eyes briefly as she hugged her. She breathed directly into Nina's ear. "I love you."

The sentiment and moist breath sent shivers down Nina's spine. Irresistibly, she turned and gently kissed Jacie on the lips. The touch was whisper soft, but as powerful as anything she'd ever felt. When it was over, she found herself looking into startlingly vulnerable eyes. Not wanting to interrupt Katherine and Gwen, she silently mouthed a heartfelt, "I love you more." Contented despite the turmoil surrounding them, each woman relaxed into the other.

The entire exchange took only a few seconds and went utterly unnoticed by the room's other occupants.

Katherine let out a shuddering breath. "Tucker was about to give up the things that mean everything to him because he was afraid. So I told him." Her heart pounded painfully in her chest. "I never set out to break my promise to you. I swear to God, I didn't. I wasn't going to tell him, but I couldn't stand seeing him so upset. When it came down to helping him or keeping my promise, I chose him." Now she couldn't hold back the tears. "I'm sorry."

Gwen sniffed a few times, torn between wanting to kill Katherine and wanting to thank her for being there for Tucker when he needed her. "I would have told him, too," she finally said. It was the truth. She only wished that she'd been strong enough for Tucker to trust that he could have come to her with his fears. "So now he knows that his father is a rapist." Gwen felt the familiar sting of shame.

"God no!" Katherine blurted, her eyes round. "I didn't tell him that, I swear. I would never! I told him that you were pregnant when you married Malcolm, so he didn't have to worry about Malcolm's congenital heart problems."

Gwen blinked. "That's all he knows?"

Katherine nodded miserably. "I couldn't bring myself to tell him any more than I had to. I thought that once he knew that Malcolm wasn't his dad that he'd talk with you. What you chose to tell him at that point would have been up to you. But after I told him, he never wanted to talk about it again. He was furious at you for a few weeks, but after that he seemed to accept it and settle down. He was more worried about Malcolm's condition than about what I'd said."

A million hurt and sometimes cold looks from her son suddenly made sense. He'd pulled away from her after Malcolm's heart attack, seeming not only to need, but also to want less contact. Gwen had assumed that was his way of coping with the trauma of nearly losing a parent in combination with him becoming more independent and growing up. That's what she told herself, anyway. "How could I have been so clueless?" She felt like screaming.

"Dios mio." Audrey's dark brows knitted. "If no one else truly knows about Tucker's conception then he has to be the one blackmailing you, Gwen." She'd never met Tucker, and after today, she wasn't sure she wanted to. But she knew one thing with a bone-deep certainty. No one in this room was capable of using Gwen's rape against her. "God, I'm sorry."

Tension marred the skin around Gwen's eyes. "I don't want to believe that he's capable of such a thing. God knows he doesn't need the money. He would only be doing this to hurt me." She picked at the bedspread, unwilling to see the truth in Katherine's face. Distraught, she asked, "Does he really hate me that much?"

"No," Katherine said instantly. "He loves you and Malcolm both. That's why it was hard for him to know that you lied to him and that he wasn't related to someone he adores. I don't know what's going on with those fuckin' e-mails." She ran a hand through her short hair, feeling very much at a loss to know how to defend someone who'd done something so despicable. "He's not a bad person, you know that. He wouldn't do something just to be cruel. I have to believe that."

"Could he need money for something else?" Jacie suggested, well aware of how easy it was to lead a hidden life from your parents. "Something you don't know about?"

Nina hesitated, but reluctantly decided to voice what she was wondering. "What about drugs or gambling? A lot of people get into trouble and don't know how to get out, Gwen. He might need help."

"No," Katherine insisted, not giving Gwen time to answer. "And I would know. The answer is absolutely not." The shocked set of her body left no room for doubt. "He doesn't even drink because he thinks it will affect his tennis."

Gwen unconsciously put one hand on her chest. Even breathing hurt. "Then he has to despise me," she choked out. "He thinks I tricked Malcolm into believing that he was his father and that I lied to them both for his entire life."

Katherine didn't want to be cruel, but she wasn't about to ignore reality either. She cocked her head to the side and spoke softly. "That's exactly what you did."

Gwen's opened her mouth to protest but stopped herself. Then she nodded. "Malcolm and Tucker and me, we've been a family from the very beginning. Since before Tucker was even born. Malcolm is Tucker's father in every meaning of the word except one. The fact that they don't share the same blood doesn't mean a damn thing." She paused and forced herself to be completely honest. "But I've been telling the same lie for so long I think that I forgot that it wasn't true." She sighed. "Until those spiteful e-mails reminded me."

The irony of the situation wasn't lost on Gwen. If the worst was true, then someone whom she trusted explicitly and loved deeply had betrayed her in the cruelest of ways. God, she was certain, was surely a woman. Only another woman would appreciate this particular quirk of fate.

Frances approached Gwen's bedroom door warily, half-expecting to find a body on the floor. She'd heard the yelling and what sounded like scuffling from downstairs. For the time being, however, the room's occupants appeared to be talking quietly. She made the sign of the cross in front of her chest and cleared her throat as she showed herself in the doorway. "Excuse me, ladies?"

Five pairs of eyes swung her way.

The white-haired woman shifted uncomfortably from one foot to the other. It was clear by the looks on their faces that she was interrupting something. Again. She almost turned around, but Gwen motioned her forward. "I have the new candles for your birthday cake, which I saw was still left out in the parlor. Did, uh, you want me to put it the refrigerator? It has cream cheese frosting and I'd hate for it to turn and make someone sick."

Frances forced her eyes not to linger on Katherine's and Gwen's tearstained cheeks, Nina's torn blouse, or Jacie's gruesome black eye. She figured that Audrey had remained unscathed only because of the added advantage of having some meat on her bones.

"Thanks, but I'm not really in the mood for cake," Gwen answered, lifting her chin and squaring her shoulders as she gathered what shreds of dignity she had left. "You've been a wonderful hostess, Mrs. Artiste. And under . . . well, unusual circumstances. I'll be sure to recommend Charlotte's Web to my friends and my husband's associates."

A chorus of agreement met Gwen's words.

Frances tried to appear nonchalant as she surveyed the newly decorated guest room for damage, but Jacie easily recognized what she was doing. "I'm sorry for the noise up here. We were . . . um . . ." She struggled to find an uncomplicated explanation for the noise. Somehow it seemed a little awkward to admit that two middle-aged women were about to come to blows over a twenty-year-old college student.

Surprisingly, it was Gwen who distilled things quite nicely. "I lost my mind there for a minute, Mrs. Artiste, and I may do it again." She shot Katherine a frustrated look. "But unless you're sleeping with my son, like *some* people in this room, I think you're pretty safe."

Katherine did her best not to roll her eyes. She was certain that she and Gwen weren't finished discussing Tucker, but for now at least, it looked as though she'd escape the day without a trip to the emergency room. On the other hand, she might have to take Tucker there. After she beat the crap out of him herself. This wasn't the sort of thing the earnest man she knew would do.

Frances's eyes popped wide open at Gwen's words, and she crossed her heart with her fingers shaping something she hoped resembled the Girl Scout promise. "Not counting my late husband, I haven't had a date in fifty-seven years."

Nina smiled kindly at the older woman and gave her a ghost of a wink. "Whew."

"You don't need to fuss over us, Mrs. Artiste." Gwen did her best to smile bravely. "We'll manage on our own."

Frances smiled back. "Heavens, it's no bother. My job is to fuss over guests." Like a magnet, her gaze was drawn back to Jacie's black eye. "It's also my job to disappear when I'm not needed. I'll be in my cottage if anyone needs me. Dinner will be at seven unless someone tells me otherwise." She nodded her good-bye and quietly padded out of the room.

The rest of the women took her exit as their cue to leave.

"Katy?" Gwen said, interrupting her friend's escape. "Would you stay? At least for a little while."

Katherine blinked. "I umm . . ." She shook her head a few times, not believing her ears. "You're sure?"

Chagrined, Gwen chewed on her lower lip. "One of us knows my son. And right now I don't think it's me." She lifted her eyebrows in entreaty. "Please stay so we can talk?"

Katherine eyed her suspiciously. "Are you going to kill me?"

"Doubtful. The knives are all downstairs and I'm too tired to choke the life out of you." A wry, watery grin tugged at her lips. "Though I'll admit that the idea does still hold some appeal."

Katherine blinked at Gwen's honesty. "How about punching me in the nose?"

A red eyebrow twitched. "Maybe."

She shrugged. "Okay. But—" She ducked her head. "I want you to know that I understand what you must think about my being married, well, a few times and about my track record with men generally. It hasn't been good." She glanced up and met Gwen's attentive gaze with a confident one of her own. "But I do know what love is. I really do."

She reached out for Gwen's hand, taking it awkwardly and chafing the unnaturally clammy skin. "It'll be okay." They'd argue like hell over Tucker later, she knew, but somehow they'd work through this. Unless one of them decided to give up on him completely, they had no choice.

Audrey, Jacie, and Nina shared amazed smiles. The day's events were more than they could really digest at the moment, but somehow, like Gwen and Katherine, they'd figure out how to make things work. They'd continue to get reacquainted with their pasts and learn how to forgive each other enough so they could share a joint future.

That's what friends did if they wanted it badly enough. And they did.

Jacie and Nina headed back to their room and Audrey went downstairs for the headphones and CD player she'd left there that morning. They all wanted some time to think.

Once they were left alone, Katherine and Gwen stared at each other awkwardly for a few moments. "I . . ." Gwen began, turning to face Katherine who was sitting at the head of the bed. "I don't know what to do," she said bleakly. "I need to make things right with Tucker and I don't know how."

Katherine gazed at her in sympathy. "Would a hug help?"

Gwen's head bobbed like an eager child's. "Yeah. I think it really would."

Wordlessly, Katherine opened her arms to her friend. "I'll help you with Tucker," she whispered, Gwen's head against her shoulder. "But you have to promise not to sink me with him." She stroked Gwen's back and gentled her voice to take the sting from her words. "As much as you'd appreciate it, I'm not going to stick my neck out just so that you can lop off my head."

She felt the unexpected jolt of Gwen's sad snort.

"I know you don't approve, but you've got to give us a chance to show you that you're wrong. I'll be careful with his heart. I swear."

Gwen went completely still and Katherine was sure that she was about to tell her to go to hell when she let out an uneven breath. "I promise, Katherine."

Over Gwen's shoulder, a slender, broad-shouldered figure appeared in the doorway and Katherine's eyes widened, then thinned angrily at the sight.

Silent and disheveled, Tucker stood there frozen in place, wearing a Nike tracksuit and tennis shoes. His skin was slightly flushed and his hair plastered to his head in a few places where it had been sweaty and then dried without being washed. He'd checked his cell phone messages between his practice sets and dropped everything to race over. No one had answered the front door, so he'd cautiously let himself in through the kitchen entrance, desperate to find Katherine before she could do something crazy.

His thick brows furrowed in confusion as he took in the scene before him. If Katherine had told his mother about their relationship, there was no way they'd be hugging right now. There's no way Katherine would be alive now. They didn't look angry, and yet, both women were clearly upset.

Katherine met Tucker's questioning gaze and her eyes flashed.

His stomach dropped.

"Gwen," Katherine prompted gently, hoping that her friend wouldn't turn around just yet. She kept her eyes locked on Tucker as she spoke. She truly loved him, but if he had done this to spite his mother, she didn't know if she could ever forgive him for it. "How did you feel when you got the first blackmail e-mail . . ." A pause. "From Tucker?"

The blood drained from Tucker's face so quickly that he had to put his hand on the doorframe to keep from keeling over.

Gwen made a face against Katherine's shoulder, but made no move to disengage from the hug. This was the comfort she'd been craving since this whole thing started, and she wasn't about to abandon it so soon. "What the hell kind of stupid question is that? I didn't know it was him then, but even so, I felt like someone was ripping my heart out of my chest."

She moaned as if in pain. "Now that I know it was Tucker, Jesus, I feel ten times worse than that. I love him so much, more than anyone on the planet. And I can't bear the thought that he did this just to watch me suffer." She began to cry again; a little surprised she had any tears left. "He got his wish. It's b-b-een like eating ground glass to think about losing his and Malcolm's love."

His mother's voice was so raw and pain-filled that Tucker's eyes misted over, despite the anger that still burned hot inside him.

Katherine held her friend tighter. "I don't think he hates you. I don't think he knew what he was doing."

"He had to know this was killing me! What other point is there in blackmail!" Gwen's sobs shook her entire body, her stomach twisting. "I think, I think I might be sick," she moaned.

"No," Katherine said firmly. "You're not." *At least I hope not.* "Take a deep breath. Again. Slower," she coaxed kindly. "That's it."

Gwen swallowed hard, letting all the pain, loss, and frustration she felt flow freely. "I can never forgive myself for hurting him. Bu-but I didn't want him to know the truth."

Tucker's jaw worked as he clamped down on his emotions. He forced himself not to say a word, though inwardly he was screaming at the top of his lungs.

"You married Malcolm because you were in love with him and not just because you were pregnant or you thought he was a good catch that you could trick. I know that for a fact." Katherine held her breath for a moment, balancing on a razor's edge before making her decision. She pulled back gently and framed Gwen's face with her hands. "And you didn't want Tucker to know you'd been raped and that that's how you got pregnant."

Tucker's entire body jerked as though he'd been burned.

Gwen nodded miserably, "But I'd rather he think that I cheated on Malcolm than know what really happened. It's better that he hates me than he thinks he was connected to something so brutal and ugly." Her face crumpled. "I know this is all my fault. The lies. Everything. I know that," she said fiercely, her tears pouring over Katherine's hands. "B-but it still hurts."

A tear seared a path down Tucker's cheek.

"I think you and Tucker broke each other's hearts." Though her lower lip was trembling, Katherine managed a tiny encouraging smile. "But, please, please don't let things end there."

Tucker pressed the heels of his hands to his eyes; tears spilling freely down his face. He couldn't stand it another second. He pressed his lips together but had to pause and force the word past the solid lump in this throat. He bent at the waist, feeling sick. "M-Mom?" he rasped.

Slack-jawed, Gwen spun around on the bed, not believing her ears, then eyes. "Tucker?"

Katherine closed her eyes. *Please, God.*

Gwen shook her head wildly, fearing the worst. "What are you . . . Oh, God, what did you hear?" Her heart was beating so hard the words sounded like they were being said by someone else.

Tucker pulled his hands away from his eyes, his handsome face twisted with pain and guilt. "I . . . I heard enough." He rushed to the bedside and dropped on his knees in front of his mother.

There wasn't a second's hesitation, Gwen held out her arms and Tucker wrapped himself around her, crying every bit as hard as she had.

"I didn't mean to hurt you," Gwen whispered into his dark hair, kissing the top of his head over and over.

"I'm sorry," he said at the same time. "I didn't know. I didn't—"

Gwen nodded. "Me, too."

Katherine allowed herself to draw in a breath. She was shaking nearly as badly as Gwen and Tucker. She ran her hands through Tucker's hair and kissed the side of his head. Then she did the same thing to Gwen before going to the bedroom door and closing it quietly, with her still inside.

They had a lot to talk about.

The next day . . .

The members of the Mayflower Club stood in the gray light of morning outside the carriage house, not knowing how to say good-bye. A light breeze that spoke of colder days ahead ruffled their hair and dusted their cheeks with color.

Tucker, Gwen, and Katherine had spent most of Saturday afternoon in Gwen's room. There were neither raised voices nor blood-curdling screams, so Jacie, Audrey, and Nina had minded their own business and spent the time catching up with each other and making new memories.

That night they'd learned, much to Gwen and Katherine's embarrassment, that Tucker had been behind the blackmail. He'd been sure that his mother had cheated on Malcolm and then tricked him into getting married for his money. Filled with anger and stinging from the heinous deception, he'd thought it only fitting that his mother unwittingly finance his search for his biological father. A search made possible by a regular stream of blackmail funds and the services of two private detectives, who had consistently come up empty.

When the truth was finally exposed, Tucker experienced a level of shame and regret that Gwen could intimately relate to.

Their relationship was badly damaged, but not broken. Katherine would see to that.

Gwen was still worried sick over how Malcolm would react to hearing about the rape and Tucker's parentage, but the time for deception was long past. She knew that now and was willing to accept the consequences of her decision to lie so long ago. It was time.

"So?" Audrey poked at her cousin. "We're not going to lose touch again, right?"

"No way," Katherine insisted, wrapping one her arm around her cousin, the other around Nina. "Not after all this. I want the club back."

Jacie smiled. "I want that too. I especially want that with Nina." A beat. "Only I want her to be naked at the time."

They all laughed, but the moment was bittersweet.

"I'll e-mail you all," Gwen promised. She let out a shaky breath, fear still clinging to her like mustiness to an old house. "Just pray you don't see my name in the papers under name changes."

Nina pulled Gwen into a fierce hug. "You're going to be okay, Gwen," she whispered. "I've seen you be stronger than I thought possible. You can do it one more time. Malcolm will understand. He loves you too much not to." She pulled away to look her in the eye. "We're only a phone call away."

Gwen nodded, more than a little choked up at the sentiment. She could see Jacie smiling at her over Nina's shoulder and knew that emotion was echoed by the other half of this newly minted couple. "I don't deserve that."

"I know you don't," Nina answered honestly. "But this is a weekend for second chances for us all." A small smile appeared. "And you're one of us, remember?"

"So you're getting lucky," Jacie added softly.

Sheepishly, Katherine wiped at her eyes. "What about getting together again for a weekend or something? We could do that, sometime, right?"

Gwen felt like a wrung out dishrag, and yet it was the happiest she'd felt in months. "When?" she asked, kicking at a pebble near her feet, a sense of belonging that she hadn't felt in ages, carefully making its home.

The time they'd shared had been great, but Katherine didn't have the overwhelming need for another gathering until she had more to talk about. And a little time needed to pass for that to happen.

They'd never see each other everyday again, or every week, or even every month. But that was okay. They were busy women who had demanding lives to match. "What about this spring?" she finally said. "It's nice before it starts getting humid and I'll get a few days off during spring break."

Audrey frowned. "I can't afford to fly back so soon. And Enrique Junior runs track every weekend in the spring. How about summer instead?"

Jacie shook her head. "That's my busiest season at work and I have Emily full-time once school gets out. I don't want to ship her back to her mom if I don't have to, and we already have a bunch of camping trips planned during the little time I will have off."

"Next fall then?" Nina suggested, tucking her cell phone into her purse. Mentally, she cataloged the exhibitions she knew the museum had scheduled for the coming year. "Maybe around this time?"

Katherine rolled her eyes. "If I still have a job at the university to go back to, it'll be a miracle. October is hard for me because I spend that entire month playing catch-up for September admissions."

The women looked at each other and laughed.

"Why don't we think about it a while?" Jacie suggested, tossing her bag into the back of her truck. "We can still write and call each other, can't we?"

"Write?" Katherine chuckled. "I forgot how to do that. It's all e-mail nowadays, Jacie." She elbowed her friend, who had been sure that computers would never really catch on. "Get with the times."

Jacie's company's inventory, payroll, and billing were all done by computer, and fully a third of her business was derived from an Internet advertising plan she'd come up with herself. Still, she wasn't above playing along with Katherine. She elbowed Katherine right back, only harder. "Freakin' geek!"

"Okay, okay," Audrey broke in, knowing where this was heading. Not that she'd mind seeing Katherine and Jacie wrestling like weasels in heat, but she had a plane to catch. "Maybe we could start one of those Internet lists like my kids are on. Yahoo has something where we can all e-mail each other at once."

"Will you help Jacie with that, Nina?" Katherine asked sassily.

Nina chuckled. She'd spoken to Jacie about Priest Tiling many times over the weekend and knew damn well that Jacie was no technophobe. "Oh, yes," she said seriously. "I'll do my level best to bring Cavewoman into the twenty-first century."

Jacie lifted an eyebrow, but let Nina's comment pass. "We won't lose touch ever again." Her expression went as serious as her friends had ever seen. "Promise?"

Her words were met with beaming smiles. "Promise," came the expected chorus.

And so it was done.

One by one, cars filed out of the carriage house, until Nina and Jacie were left alone, the morning mist infiltrating the large room and dampening their skin.

Jacie leaned against her truck. "Hey, Nina?" she said softly.

Nina stepped forward and wrapped her arms around Jacie's neck, tangling her fingers in thick hair. "Yeah?"

She grinned girlishly. "Can you come out and play?"

Nina laughed. "Depends."

Jacie feigned insult. "On what?"

"Well . . ." Nina tapped her chin with her index finger. "How long do you want to play? I have to plan my schedule, you know."

"Depends," Jacie shot back haughtily. "I have world records to break, you know. I'm a busy woman. How long do you want to play?"

"Forever," Nina answered seriously, tightening her arms around Jacie. "I want you forever. Some things were never meant to change, Jacie Ann."

Jacie could feel a nearly electric current running between them. "Same goes for me. Only for longer if you're free."

"Hmm . . . ." Nina smiled playfully. "Then I'll have to ask my mom." She paused. "And my son."

Jacie leaned forward and brushed her mouth against Nina's, grinning against the smiling lips that met hers. "Lead the way."

"Really?"

Jacie nodded once, the breeze carrying with it a whiff of Nina's shampoo. "Really. I'm yours."

Nina's eyebrows jumped. "In that case . . ." She took Jacie's hand and began leading her back toward the B&B.

"Hey," Jacie glanced back at the carriage house, having to increase her stride just to keep up with Nina. "Where are we going?"

"We're going back inside. I'll find Mrs. Artiste and make sure a room will be available for tonight. Now that I've got you to myself, there's no way I'm giving you up so quickly." Determinedly, she kept on walking. "You got a problem with that?"

Jacie laughed. "No, ma'am. I just thought you were anxious to get home and get ready for your new job."

Nina stopped walking and turned to face Jacie. She laid her palms on Jacie's chest, warm skin heating her hands though soft denim. "Do you really want to know what I'm anxious about?"

Jacie stepped a little closer so that their bodies were touching all along their lengths. "Mm. Of course."

"You're sure?"

Jacie inclined her head and waited.

"Okay, I'm anxious to know when I can see you again and what it will be like and if you'll ever let me get to second base."

Jacie started laughing. "You don't need to worry about that, Nina," she assured her, her voice a sexy purr. "I have dibs on batting first and I intend to make sure that you're too tired to care what happens after that."

Nina's mouth went bone dry, but she did her best to continue. Unfortunately, there wasn't enough blood left in her brain to think straight. "Uh . . . What was I talking about?"

Jacie bit back a smile. God, she loved her. "What you're anxious about?"

"Oh, yeah. I . . . I'm anxious about when I can tell my son, and my mom, and my neighbors, and everyone I meet on the street that you're my girlfriend. I'm thinking of getting a T-shirt made."

Charmed, Jacie let go of her smile. Her friends had always labeled her as the fearless one of the group. *If they only knew.* "What else?" She gave her a little nudge. "C'mon, I wanna hear more."

The smile reached Nina's eyes before the rest of her face. "I'm anxious to hear about what sort of TV programs and music and food you like nowadays and whether you'll invite me to go camping with you and Emily."

"I want to know all those things about you, too."

"Nuh-uh. Wait your turn."

"Were you always this bossy?"

Nina's eyes twinkled. "No, I've really chilled out over the years."

Jacie chuckled. Then she tried to sound aggrieved, but couldn't quite manage it. "Court TV and the Home and Garden Channel, classic rock and sometimes jazz, and absolutely anything . . . . so long as it's pizza."

"Thin crust, extra sauce?"

"Is there another kind?"

Nina sighed. "The perfect woman."

"And you and Robbie are invited to go camping with us and to anything else we're doing." Then she wrinkled her nose. "But I'm not baiting your hook anymore. That's just gross and doing it for myself and Emily is bad enough."

"But you're a master baiter." She fanned herself. "A really great one, in fact."

Jacie couldn't stop her cheeks from heating. "I can't believe you just said that." She looked at her fondly. "No, scratch that. I can *totally* believe you just said that."

Nina threw her head back and laughed. "You don't have to worry about taxing your fishing prowess. Having someone to bait my hook was the entire reason I had a boy child. You're off the hook." She waggled her eyebrows. "So to speak."

Jacie groaned. "You're not going to stop, are you?"

Unrepentantly, Nina shook her head.

Jacie put her hands on her hips. "Is that everything?" She pointed at the B&B. "There's a hot tub we never got to use in there, you know."

"Nuh-uh." Nina peered at her from behind fair lashes. The way Jacie was looking at her filled her with bravery, and so she went for broke. She gently kissed Jacie's chin. "I'm anxious to wake up with you in my bed"—another kiss on the tip of the nose—"and in my arms"—this time the kiss skirted the very edge of full lips—"and to know that it's for keeps." She crossed her fingers and toes, hoping she wasn't pushing farther or faster than Jacie was willing to go.

She needn't have worried.

"Nina?"

Nina gulped. "Yeah?"

"Why don't we shoot for that to happen tomorrow morning? We can go back to your place." Jacie gently tucked a strand of Nina's blowing hair behind her ear.

"I don't have a hot tub."

"Somehow we'll manage." Jacie let herself feel Nina's nearness. It was a heady feeling that she never wanted to end. "I think I'm going to be calling in sick for a few days."

A smile lit blue-green eyes from within, and impossibly, Nina found a way to snuggle even closer. So close, they were sharing the same breath. "You do?"

"Mm . . . . Most definitely."

Nina's heart soared. "So do I." Then she said the first thing that popped into her mind. "Hey, Jacie, isn't it about time we kissed again?"

Jacie grinned. "I thought you'd never ask."

Publications from Spinsters Ink

P.O. Box 242
Midway, Florida 32343
Phone: 800 301-6860
www.spinstersink.com

DISORDERLY ATTACHMENTS by Jennifer L. Jordan. 5th Kristin Ashe Mystery. Kris investigates whether a mansion someone wants to convert into condos is haunted.   ISBN 1-883523-74-5 $14.95

VERA'S STILL POINT by Ruth Perkinson. Vera is reminded of exactly what it is that she has been missing in life.
                                                                              ISBN 1-883523-73-7 $14.95

OUTRAGEOUS by Sheila Ortiz-Taylor. Arden Benbow, a motor-cycle riding, lesbian Latina poet from LA is hired to teach poetry in a small liberal arts college in northwest Florida.
                                                                              ISBN 1-883523-72-9 $14.95

UNBREAKABLE by Blayne Cooper. The bonds of love and friend-ship can be as strong as steel. But are they unbreakable?
                                                                              ISBN 1-883523-76-1 $14.95

ALL BETS OFF by Jaime Clevenger. Bette Lawrence is about to find out how hard life can be for someone of low society standing in the 1900s.   ISBN 1-883523-71-0 $14.95

UNBEARABLE LOSSES by Jennifer L. Jordan. 4th in the Kristin Ashe Mystery series. Two elderly sisters have hired Kris to discover who is pilfering from their award-winning holiday display.
                                                                              ISBN 1-883523-68-0 $14.95